SIX BILLS

M. DIANE VOGT

A WILHELMINA CARSON NOVEL

NEW MILLENNIUM PRESS
Beverly Hills

ISBN: 1-932407-02-2

Library of Congress Cataloging-in-Publication Data Available

Text Design: Kerry DeAngelis, KL Design
Original lyrics by Wendy Cousins-Savage

New Millennium Press
301 North Canon Drive
Suite 214
Beverly Hills, CA 90210

www.NewMillenniumPress.com

10 9 8 7 6 5 4 3 2 1

For Evelyn

Acknowledgments

No book is written by one person alone. My husband, Robert, is a part of everything I do successfully. His support is constant, comprehensive, and unwavering. After thirty years of marriage, he's still the one.

My family has always been there and I can't imagine life without their love and support. Friends and colleagues too numerous to mention have encouraged me on this path.

For help with the authenticity that makes pure fiction believable, I want to thank Hillsborough County Circuit Court judge Katherine G. Essrig, and lawyers and former federal district court judicial clerks Robin Rosenberg, Allison Jennewein, Deborah Jordan, Laura Howard, and Wendy Cousins-Savage. Criminal defense lawyers Kevin J. Napper and Rochelle Reback provided answers to questions only practitioners would know.

The Woodstock Music Festival was a defining moment for a generation in 1969. I thank Dean Allen Foster, Hank Zucker, Jack Ewing, and Janis Clare Galitzer for their eyewitness reports as well as their descriptions of the lasting emotional bonds forged by Woodstock attendees.

Music world advice was provided by musicians Bert Savage, Kevin G. Napper, and Katharine Hill.

Assistance with medical issues came from Lori Dandrea, M.D., and Lori-Ann Rickard. Police procedure questions were patiently answered by Thomas Hill, former director of the Criminal Justice Institute, Hillsborough Community College and sergeant and watch commander, Deerfield, Illinois, Police Department (ret).

Journalism, both print and broadcast media, is a world I'm constantly guided through by Kate Caldwell, Diane Roberts, Amy Sharitt Leobold, and Michelle Bearden.

Tampa in the early 1970s was a very different place than it is today, and Tampa native Larry Thornberry answered questions about old Tampa as well as helping me to keep new Tampa securely anchored in the present.

Thanks are due to the readers of the manuscript for their insights and suggestions: Lise S. Baker, Lisanne P. Davidson, Lynn U. Lewis, Carolyn Cain, and G. Miki Hayden. Lynn U. Lewis and William G.K. Smoak provided research, moral support, and work on the manuscript.

Lucy Zahran sells Herend porcelain in Beverly Hills. The store and the woman are remarkable.

And for the use of her name, thanks to Willetta Heising, Detecting Woman extraordinaire.

Cigar lovers Robert H. Barrow and Ralph Jarmon supplied the smoker's expertise Willa displays.

The folks at New Millennium Entertainment: Michael Viner, who had the necessary faith in the project; Aimee Dow, who did an excellent job of editing the manuscript; Mary Aarons and Suzanne Wickham, who guided me through the morass.

Without Robert Dilenschneider and Robert Stone, this book would not exist in its present form.

Thank you all.

Cast of Primary Characters

The Six Bills
William Harris Steam III (Trey)
 William Steam, Jr. ("Bill")
 Mary Steam
 Prescott Roberts
Willetta Johnson Steam ("Billie Jo")
 William Harris Steam, IV ("Harris")
  Eva Raines Steam
  Willetta Steam ("Billie")
  Wilhelmina Steam ("Willie")
William Walter Westfield III ("Walter")
 Ursula Westfield
Enrique William Gutierrez ("Ricky")
 Janet Gutierrez
William Lincoln ("Linc")
John William Tyson ("Johnny")

Court Personnel
Chief Judge Ozgood Livingston Richardson ("C.J.," "Oz")
Augustus Ralph

Chief of Police Benjamin Hathaway

Wilhelmina Carson's Family
George Carson
Kate Austin Colombo
Leo Colombo
Jason Austin

Tropical Memories©

Turned back home to the city alone, to the cold of winter
You stood by, let me go live my lie,
Let me run from my paradise
Broke my heart, shattered like ice,
Oh,

Tropical memories
The sand inside my shoes
And the ocean's breeze
The deepest greens, the sparklin' blues

As the sun sinks low
In the seas I left behind
You are always on my mind,
You are always on my mind.

I'll return, with the fortunes I earn, then I'll buy us sunsets,
Pay the stars to shower light down from Mars,
If you'll wait, don't drift away,
Latitudes willing, I'll come back to stay.

Tropical memories
The sand inside my shoes
And the ocean's breeze
The deepest greens, the sparklin' blues

As the sun sinks low
In the seas I left behind
You are always on my mind,
You are always on my mind.

Prologue

She wasn't quite sleeping when she heard him arguing with someone outside. He slammed the front door and came into the small rented house on South Packwood Avenue they'd lived in since their child was born. He was drunk. And angry. He stumbled around in the living room and fell a couple of times. She heard him curse under his breath; loud enough to penetrate the old plaster walls. She withdrew into her thin sleep shirt and burrowed down deeper under the covers, as if she were the child instead of her two-year-old son in the next room.

The third time her husband fell down, he knocked an old ceramic lamp off the end table closest to the kitchen. She heard the lamp crash to the floor and shatter. The lightbulb must have been turned on because it gave the little "poof" of an explosion they sometimes make when they break. He let out a stream of curses as he rose to his feet and shuffled loudly into the kitchen. He was swearing at the pain, so he must have hurt himself in that last fall, the one that broke the lamp.

She heard him open the refrigerator and heard the beer bottles clank as he took one out, and then set it down, hard, on the counter. He stumbled again and knocked over one of the chrome kitchen chairs with the red vinyl seats. They'd bought those chairs at a yard sale from one of the neighbors when they'd first moved here from the college dorm where they'd met and fallen in love. She remembered the day vividly because it was one of the earlier, happier times.

When the chair crashed to the floor, he bellowed aloud in fresh outrage, jerking her back to the moment. She shook, involuntarily, with fear. She heard him pick up the chair and set it down heavily, leaning on it, maybe, so that it scooted away from him, scraping along the floor. She could hear his constant stream of angry words, but tried not to listen to them. She prayed he'd be quiet, that he'd stop cursing, pass out or something.

He stayed in the kitchen for a good long time. She heard him get another beer from the refrigerator and her heart sank. She knew what was coming. Soon, he'd stumble his way into the bedroom where she lay shivering in the cool morning air and the darkness. He would reek of booze and pot. He'd want to have sex and she wouldn't be able to keep him off her.

Unless she could get away. Trying to leave while he was in the house would mean she'd have to be quick. If he saw her, he'd never let her go. Absently, she rubbed the fresh bruise on her wrist where he'd grabbed her and held her too tightly before.

She got up from the bed and slipped into the pair of jeans she'd worn for the gig earlier that night. She slid her feet into cheap vinyl thongs, remembering the glass that would be all over the living room floor from the broken lamp. She looked around for a warmer shirt, and could only find one of his lying dirty and crumpled in the corner. Since it was better than nothing against the chill, she slipped the shirt on. Her nose wrinkled in disgust at his permeating smell as the shirt engulfed her in his stifling embrace, squeezing her breath away.

Now she hastened across the narrow hallway, carefully, as silently as she could with the flip-flop noise the thongs made every time she took a step. She crunched up her toes to keep the shoes quiet, and made her way into her son's room. Miraculously, the boy had slept through the noise of the crashing lamp and the sounds coming from the kitchen. She was grateful. She'd seen too many tears in the sensitive little boy's eyes, heard too many of his cries during all the similar evenings that had passed before this one.

She bundled the baby up in a blanket and carried him into the living room. Sneaking past the door to the kitchen, she picked up her car keys but had to leave her purse. The child was heavy and awkward. She couldn't carry anything more.

Opening the door quickly, holding her breath, she made it out to the porch. He hadn't seen her, although she'd had to dash right past the open archway between the kitchen and the small living room. She didn't try to close the door behind her. No time. She hurried out to the driveway and laid her still-sleeping son on the back seat.

She shouldn't have returned to the house for her purse. If she'd just left without her purse, he would never have seen her at all. They wouldn't have struggled with the knife. He wouldn't have fallen. She hadn't thought she'd hurt him. He was so much bigger than she, so much stronger. How could she have hurt him?

But she got out. She quickly returned to the car, started the engine, and sped away, leaving a storm of dust in the dirt driveway.

Hours later, after she'd wrestled free of her fear and mustered her courage, she returned to the house. By then the sun was well up over the horizon. Clear blue sky promised a perfect new day, she hoped.

Maybe he'd still be sleeping. Or awake and hungover, but not so terribly angry. In her daydream, he apologized. Hugged her and held his son. He'd maybe take them out to breakfast, later. The little boy liked to go to the Old Meeting House and eat pancakes with blueberry syrup and whipped cream. He liked the little link sausages and the coffee with cream and sugar that he drank just like his daddy. They'd be the close, loving family she'd always imagined— the family they had been for a while before her husband had become so popular with his fans.

But that never happened. Instead, when she came back to the little house, she found him still lying on the floor where she'd left him hours before. She checked, but he wasn't breathing. Bewildered, without knowing how it happened, she stood over her dead husband, her clothes covered in his blood, her hand holding the knife that killed him. She clutched the old shirt closer around her body, seeking comfort now in the smell of him, as if he still hugged her.

She had only pushed him to get away. Their struggle couldn't have hurt him so badly. There was so much blood. It covered everything. Blood was everywhere in the small house.

Horrified, through her tears, she saw her son run to his father. "Daddy, wake up," he said, laying his small head on his father's bloody chest until he, too, was covered with the gooey mess.

PART ONE

GOOD
INTENTIONS

Chapter One

Where did everything begin to unravel? "Begin at the beginning," my mother used to tell me. But where was that? If I could have found that spot, the point where it all started, maybe I could have changed the outcome. Maybe they would all still be alive. All except Trey. I felt better that there was never anything I could have done for Trey. What I remember as the beginning was Mother's Day. The day I met Trey's son.

I'd like to claim that I walked into the unexpected party with a sense of tragedy that belied Tampa's beautiful spring afternoon, but really I was only feeling slightly out of sorts. I had envisioned a quiet interlude drinking lemonade and eating watercress sandwiches on Kate Colombo's shady garden patio. The reality was quite different.

When I arrived at her home, the driveway was full of cars, and street parking was as scarce as an innocent felon. After circling the block several times, I had finally given up and parked six blocks away in the garage on South Rome in Olde Hyde Park Village.

Sunshine and temperatures in the low eighties, along with the promise of a casual brunch, had convinced me to forego my usual comfortable clothes in favor of a sundress and sandals with high heels for the short drive along the Bayshore and into Hyde Park.

Act in haste, repent at leisure, I chastised myself—at the time only for my wardrobe—as I hiked my way back to Kate's. My feet hurt and I'd begun to glow by the time I had walked from the parking garage in my foolish heels, under sunshine more sweltering with each step. The fashionably big spring hat I'd set on my head before I left home only made me feel hotter, despite my ultra short haircut. Once back at Kate's, I looked around for a place to stash the beastly thing.

The day continued to surprise me. Instead of a quiet afternoon, I'd blundered into an all-out party, consisting mostly of Kate's new husband's fashionable young friends. I saw messy, spiked hair in colors Mother Nature never intended. Tight, black leather miniskirts and belly shirts barely covered lithe bodies standing in every corner. Multiple piercings and tattoos made the guests resemble hip magazine tableaus not found in my social circle. I felt off balance, old and oddly out of place in Kate's home, one of the few spots where I usually felt completely welcome and at ease.

Maybe, thirteen years after I lost my too-young mother to cancer, I should have been able to deal with her loss more effectively. Perhaps I should have developed a personal philosophy about her death that allowed me to go on with my life. I was thirty-nine years old, but I still felt like a gawky and exposed sixteen-year-old on Mother's Day. A calm afternoon with Kate usually helped, but it was not to be.

As I made my way around Kate's crowded house, I was thinking a lot about Mom. The familiar vivid nightmare that reprised the night she died had visited me again in the last hours before dawn that morning. Lingering unease clung to my body like the smell of lilacs that accompanied the dream. I was especially attuned to missing mothers. Or maybe I only think so now, in retrospect, as I try to sort out the events that followed.

"That's Wilhelmina Carson. The flamboyant judge your brother was raving about last week," I heard a short brunette say about me to her companion, as I made my way through the crowd around the punch bowl in the dining room. I stopped for a cup of the fruity liquid and glanced surreptitiously at the speaker. Raving, hmmm? That could be a compliment. I used the hydrangea printed cocktail napkin to wipe my upper lip and dab at my brow. Threading my way through one pretty young thing after another, more males than females, I eventually made it to the back of the house. At the patio door, I looked for Kate and in a minute spotted her.

Kate was standing with her new husband, Leo Colombo, on the backyard patio, which was surrounded by her wild English garden. She wore a royal blue silk dress that matched her twinkling eyes and took years off her age. Kate looked relaxed and happy, as the two of them talked with some of their guests. Leo's boyish chin was outlined by a ridiculous black goatee I hadn't seen before. Dark, sultry eyes and wavy black hair were the stock-in-trade of the successful Italian model he had been years before Kate married him and moved him halfway around the world.

"What a hottie he is! They look so happy together, don't they?" the punch bowl brunette lisped to her friend, around the stud in her tongue. They moved past me at the threshold, and into the backyard. Hottie? Where do these words come from?

"Leo told me that he and Kate are soul mates. How romantic," her spiky-haired chum with the nose ring sighed, causing the butterfly tattoo on her cheek to bat its wings.

I'd seen Kate very little since she had returned home from Italy a few weeks ago and I missed her. We used to talk almost daily before she married Leo. Now, she talked to him instead. But Kate had invited me to her home for brunch on Mother's Day, as usual. I've spent every Mother's Day with Kate since her best friend, my mother, died and Kate became the woman I loved like a mother. A new husband, hottie or not, couldn't change that.

Kate saw me then and waved me over. "Willa, darling," she said, as I bent down to receive her kiss on my cheek and allowed her to take my arm. She paused to introduce me to the other man standing with her and Leo. "This is Leo's great friend, Harris Steam."

I see now—that's where the real trouble started.

Chapter Two

"Really? You're Harris Steam? It's such a pleasure to meet you," I said as I pumped his hand, trying not to sound like an overly enthusiastic admirer, even though I was.

Harris Steam was a local pop star who'd had a few hit songs that made it to the top of the charts. In the fickle way of the music business, he had since faded from the national scene, but that hadn't made a dent in his local popularity. His fans here were rabid and faithful. His relaxed style of music combined a little reggae, a little folk, a little foolishness, and a lot of guitars. Think Jimmy Buffett, but with not as much success, or national fame.

Harris, slightly taller than my five feet eleven inches, was probably in his mid-thirties, a few years younger than me, although his music style appealed to a somewhat older audience. He looked like a *wavehead*, as they say in North Florida—a dim-witted "surfer dude" from the old beach movies that rerun sometimes on late night television. Wraparound silver-framed sunglasses with reflective blue lenses hid his eyes, which were almost level with mine. Harris wore a wrinkled red Hawaiian shirt with the tails hanging outside his unpressed green shorts. His shoes were the popular Teva sandals that resemble a tire tread strapped loosely to the feet. But the smile made his relaxed appearance irrelevant. The display of ivory was a genuine toothpaste commercial, complete with sparkles and it was more infectious than a virus. I felt it spread to my face and stay there.

"I've never met you before, but I owe you a debt of gratitude," I said as I told Harris about the fateful effect he'd had on my decision to become a Tampa resident.

On the day I resolved to leave my Michigan law practice and move to Florida, I was sitting in a blinding snowstorm in the middle of April. I'd been practically parked on the interstate for over three hours, moving toward my office at a snail's pace in the dirty grey snow and snarled traffic. I was lost in thought about the choice to be made because my husband had unexpectedly inherited an historic old home down in Tampa. Should we move? Not?

"Tropical Memories," one of Harris Steam's most popular songs, came on the radio at that exact moment:

> *The sand inside my shoes*
> *And the ocean's breeze*
> *The deepest greens, the sparklin' blues*
> *As the sun sinks low*
> *In the seas I left behind*
> *You are always on my mind,*
> *You are always on my mind.*

The song and its message penetrated my brain in one of those "aha!" moments that make irrational decisions seemingly easy. I remembered there were places in the world where it doesn't snow in April, where the sun shines year round and the blue skies beckon, where I'd never sit in traffic for three hours on the way to work. Like the song that accompanied my first kiss and the one that played when my husband proposed, "Tropical Memories" was forever embedded in my psyche.

"The rest, as they say, is history. We've been living in paradise ever since and never looked back," I finished the tale—to smiles all around the small group.

"If not for 'Tropical Memories,' we'd be having this conversation in Detroit," Kate added, causing Leo to shudder at the very idea. Detroit is a great place for hockey teams and ethnic food, his wrinkled nose conveyed, but not for hottie Italian models.

Harris removed his sunglasses to reveal hazel eyes and an earnest expression and focused on me as if I was the only person on the planet right at that moment. "An artist always hopes his work will bring pleasure to his fans," he said. "If I can really make a difference, improve someone's life in a meaningful way, well, then I've really succeeded. I've heard many stories just like yours and it's good to know that my songs reach people on such a visceral level."

The words themselves resembled a line he might use to pick up women in a bar, but he came off more like a spiritual advisor. He continued to talk about how his music had changed the world and he shared his plans for the future. Although he looked like a punch-drunk *wavehead*, he was a serious man with serious goals. I could easily understand how Kate and Leo could have become so attracted to him. Harris Steam was definitely more than just a pretty face with a pleasant voice. Just meeting him brightened my day and made me want to listen to his music.

Eventually, the four of us walked through the buffet line and moved over to the patio table. During a brief lull in the conversation, I had the chance to ask Kate the question that had popped into my mind when I couldn't find a parking space out front. "Why do you have so many people here today?"

Harris answered for her. "Kate and Leo were kind enough to host a Motherless Day party. For those who have no family to share the day with." The unexpected words hit my stomach with a force like a blow. Motherless. Me, too, and I didn't need to be reminded. "Pretty nice of them, don't you think?" His words were genuine, his tone wistful. I sensed great sadness in his life, but maybe I was projecting a little of my own uneasy feelings.

Knowing my history, Kate explained more gently, "Just about everyone here is alone today. Including Leo. His kids are with their mom in Italy and he was missing them. So we decided to have this party to perk him up."

Another surprise. And not a welcome one. *What kids?* I thought, as I looked over at Leo, who nodded at Kate's words, to show, indeed, he needed cheering up.

"Suits me perfectly," Harris put in, turning to take Kate's hand, the one Leo wasn't holding.

"How so?" I asked, realizing I had to say something and trying to get past the shock of learning that Leo had children of his own, in Italy or anywhere else. I'd been worried for Kate since I first met Leo Colombo and this piece of unwelcome news would only complicate their relationship further. I didn't believe Leo was actually in love with Kate. As dear as she is to me, she was close to twice his age and if the punch bowl brunette was to be believed, Leo was such a hottie that he could have any number of women more suitable for him. I didn't believe Leo and I didn't trust him.

Harris looked down at the ground, a slight red blush creeping up his neck to his cheeks. "My girls are with my ex-wife and my mother is in prison," he replied, quietly, as if he was embarrassed to say so, but had no choice. At the time, I thought it odd that he would share such personal information, but in less than two seconds, Leo cleared that up.

"Yes, Willa," Leo said, jumping right in with his characteristic impetuosity. "Kate and I told Harris you'd be willing to help him get his mother out. Will you do it?"

I was still preoccupied with Leo's children and not paying as close attention to the conversation as I should have been. How could Leo be a parent, I thought. He was childlike himself. "Do what?" I asked absently.

"You do that kind of stuff all the time. Look at all that trouble George was in and you fixed it." I glared at him, to no effect. Leo apparently did not know the meaning of the word tact. He'd orchestrated this scenario so that Harris Steam and I would feel some sort of kinship, I supposed. How like Leo to think that having a loved one wrongly accused of murder would be a bonding experience for two perfect strangers. If I hadn't been so appalled that he would mention George's unfortunate experience in front of Harris Steam, I might have been a little quicker to understand what was being asked of me.

Some time ago, my husband had been arrested for the murder of a United States Supreme Court nominee because of his political connections to the nominee's enemies. No one who knew George would seriously consider him a murderer, but the charges had threatened our marriage and George's misplaced sense of chivalry had nearly destroyed it. George thought he needed to protect me from the scandal and I thought he needed to participate actively in finding the real killer. We'd separated for a time over it. To save my way of life, I had taken matters into my own hands and discovered the identity of the killer. Still, it wasn't the kind of thing I discussed with casual acquaintances at garden parties and Leo shouldn't have brought it up.

After my experience with George, I can hardly go to public events without being barraged with requests for help of all kinds from people who find themselves caught up in the legal system. I get calls and letters all the time, too. Even among my friends and colleagues, there are many who urge me to investigate and solve every murder committed in Tampa.

"You must help Harris get his mother out of prison," Leo repeated, "You have to do it."

Because she knows how I feel about people pushing their problems on me, I was surprised and a little hurt that Kate would allow Leo to do this to me in her home. I tried to hide the growing anger I felt toward both of them for putting me in such an outrageous predicament.

"Harris, I don't think I can help you," I said gently. "I'm a United States District Court judge, which is more than a full-time job. Besides, I'm prohibited from offering legal or financial help in cases now that I'm a judge. I'm supposed to avoid any circumstance that would even appear to influence my judicial conduct or judgment." A federal judge can be criminally prosecuted although even when that happens, it doesn't automatically remove us from office. Still, just because something can be done, doesn't mean it *should* be done. There were ethical rules that judges should live by and I tried to give him the practical and the ethical excuses together, so that he would politely back down. I expected him to say, "Of course, I understand. Please forgive me for asking." Then, I'd let Kate and Leo have the full force of my displeasure another time. And it might have worked, if Leo had kept quiet.

"Oh, you do this sort of thing all the time, Willa. You can free Billie Jo. I know you can," Leo continued to push me.

I wanted to throttle him. But I don't actually keep my nose out of situations where my help is truly needed, and both Kate and Leo knew it. Sometimes, I do accept these challenges, when I see an injustice that I think is appropriate for me to resolve. That's why everyone keeps asking. I figure I'm the best arbiter of what will improperly influence me or my decisions, which is not much.

The truth is that I'm going to get criticized for whatever I do, so I might as well do what I think is right. What good is being appointed for life if you can't follow your own conscience once in a while? So far, no one had tried to have me impeached for improper conduct and I didn't believe I'd done anything to warrant such an action. Indeed, I'd have fewer problems with my colleagues if I allowed them to coerce me.

But this was the first time I'd ever been asked to help free a convicted felon. Freeing criminals is more than a little bit out of my league and it would require much more time than I could reasonably take away from my work. Besides, the chances that Harris's mother was wrongfully convicted were slim. Despite popular fiction, innocent people don't get convicted all that often.

I began to try to extricate myself from the situation as politely as possible. I must have known about his mother's conviction, but until Harris raised it, I had forgotten. "Why is your mother in prison?" I asked, thinking that more facts would provide me with a legitimate way to politely refuse his request, as I do most of the others I receive that are no less deserving.

"She was tried and convicted for killing my father, back in '72," he answered. "But she didn't kill him. She was just a convenient defendant." *Sure*, I thought. *That's what they all say.* I've rarely met a defendant who admitted guilt. The accused's strongest defense is: deny, deny, deny. Even after they're convicted, many inmates continue to protest their innocence and their families try hard to believe them. This was nothing new.

In any case, it's very difficult to prove the police have the wrong suspect after he's arrested. Most police departments do a good and thorough job of investigating homicide. The Tampa Police Department was no different. So long after the murder was committed, it's nearly impossible to demonstrate that the entire judicial system had completely failed. Especially when a convicted murderer has already served three decades. I, for one, find some comfort in the knowledge that we've all done our jobs. Most of the time, those of us charged with administering justice do it right.

I must have looked as skeptical about his mother's innocence as I felt because Harris put down his fork and leaned closer to me across the table. "I know what you're thinking. But you've never met my mom. She wouldn't kill anyone. She certainly couldn't have killed my father. She loved him." His desperation was plainly apparent, but was he right? Or was he just a child who wanted his mother back? That, I could understand only too well. "We've got to get her out of prison before she dies there."

"You mean she's on death row?" I asked. If so, I could appropriately refuse his request. Attempting to free a death row inmate was more than a full-time occupation. I didn't have the expertise to do anything that complicated, or the time to learn how to do the job, even if I had been convinced that I should get involved.

"No," Harris shook his head, "nothing like that. But she's sick. Mom has terminal cancer." Delivered deftly on Mother's Day, when I was already edgy, the words landed another hard blow to my stomach. My visceral reaction only proved to me that no matter how objective I think I am, my emotions are always there to pounce in an unguarded moment.

My pain must have shown clearly on my face. Kate looked

at me with great concern, but Leo took up Harris's cause before she could say anything.

"She's been locked up almost thirty years. Isn't that long enough?" Leo asked petulantly. "The woman was sentenced to life in prison. She's been there a lifetime, hasn't she? Hell, thirty years is almost longer than I've been alive," he needlessly reminded us.

I suppressed a groan, still trying to calm my churning stomach. "Why are you asking me to do this right now?"

"Mom is coming up for parole. She's been up before, but she's been turned down every time. This is her last chance," Harris said. A long series of defeats meant less likelihood of success this time. Kate, the mother of four lawyers, knew this as well as I did. I sent a beseeching glance her way. She had to know what an imposition this request was, how hard it would be to succeed, how much I wouldn't want to become involved. Why was she pushing me?

"This is a good cause, Willa," Kate insisted, rejecting my silent plea to get me out of this. "These days, Billie Jo Steam wouldn't even have been tried, let alone convicted. No justice was done in this case. You might be the only one who can help her after all this time. You need to try."

Leo piped in again, interrupting Kate's explanation. He was as annoying as the kid who always jumps out of his seat in the front row, waving his hand so the teacher will call on him. "She has to get out. And she needs you to help her. That's simple, isn't it? Harris, tell Willa what your mom said about her."

Harris, at least, had the grace to realize he was asking for more than he had a right to request. Only the futility of his mother's struggle seemed to prompt him to continue. "Mom knows you've been through the nightmare of trying to prove your husband was wrongly accused of murder. You feel the injustice of false charges in a way others don't, she said." He gave me his sexy smile—the one I'm sure he'd used to get everything he'd ever wanted since he was old enough to realize its effect on women.

I could no longer resist the three of them, all pressing for a commitment, refusing to let me sidestep the question. More to end the pleading and cajoling than anything else, I considered Harris's request seriously. This was exactly the kind of project that Chief Judge Ozgood Richardson, who thinks he's my boss, would not want me to get involved in. If I helped Harris Steam, I'd have to figure out what to do about the C.J. Maybe that was a reason to take the job right there, I smiled to myself. Thwarting the C.J. was always worth the effort.

But I had another, more emotional reason to look into the matter. Today was Mother's Day. Kate Colombo, who had been everything to me that any real daughter could ask for, was asking for my help. Kate rarely asks me for anything. After all the sacrifices she'd made for me, this was something I could do for Kate, something for which she still needed me. I'd never refused any request she'd ever made of me and now all she was asking was that I help someone else. I wasn't hard-hearted enough to refuse her the courtesy of at least considering the matter.

Of course, C.J. would say this was no affair of Kate's, either. Harris Steam and his problems were far removed from Kate Colombo. Strains of "Tropical Memories" wafted out from the stereo speakers in the house, floating on the scented breeze, reminding me that I owed Harris something, too. His song was at least partly responsible for the happiness I've had living here in Tampa since "Tropical Memories" pushed me over the edge of indecision into paradise.

Not that C.J. would be persuaded by such a frivolous point, but it wasn't frivolous to me and it was just icing on the cake, anyway. An excuse that would seem so silly to him that he would never believe it. But I didn't need C.J.'s permission to do something Kate wanted so badly.

As I listened to the back and forth of my internal argument, I must have nodded involuntarily, because without knowing what was really going on, I felt my arm flailing up and down. Harris had grabbed my hand to pump it the same way I'd been pumping his earlier, his eyes sparkling to match the smile. "Thank you, Judge, thank you so much. I'll send her file over to you by messenger tomorrow. Take a look at it, and then tell me you don't think she should be free." Leo and Kate were beaming, too, as if they'd just won the lotto.

"Harris," I said, trying to extract my hand and stop this roller coaster before it careened out of control. "Listen to me. I don't know if I can help you or not. All I'm willing to do, as a favor to you and to Kate and Leo, is to look at your mother's file. I'm not making any promises."

"I know. But you'll help us. I can tell," he said, refusing to release my hand until I pulled it away by gentle force.

I saw Kate smile her thanks at me and I felt the addictive warm glow of her approval. How far would I go to keep that approval washing over me?

Chapter Three

Monday morning, the situation at my office was normal: all fouled up. I was without an assistant of any kind. Again. Usually, the new one for the week arrived after lunch.

My prior secretary had retired in the spring. Since then, Uncle Sam, through his emissary and my nemesis, the chief judge, has had a series of floaters sitting in her chair on a hit-and-miss schedule. All the temps were seeking a full-time job and were always on their best behavior. Yet none had been worth her weight in good topsoil. I suspected the C.J. was taking particular pleasure in tormenting me with ineptitude, so I hadn't found a replacement yet.

The quality of applicants for the job had been steadily declining and I couldn't hold out this way much longer. My dictation was stacked up and the mail threatened to bury me alive. Messages I was desperately waiting to receive rarely made it to the pink slip stage.

Worse, the C.J., whom I tried to avoid whenever possible, was actually able to reach me because I had no one to properly screen my calls. Not thinking, I picked up the ringing phone.

"Willa," C.J. said in his raspy whine that grated on my last nerve like sucking a sour lemon. "I have better things to do than finding you a replacement secretary. Just pick one."

I held on to my determination to have a good morning, but barely. "I'd be happy to pick one, if you could send someone that had half a brain."

He grunted into the phone. "This is a government job we're talking about. The really good assistants can make a lot more money in the private sector. We don't often get the cream of the crop to choose from, you know." Was he suggesting I wasn't the cream of the crop? The officious jackass.

Excuses. That's what the C.J. always gave me when I made requests of any kind. Usually those excuses were related to lack of money. C.J. played the government game well. He was always spending to the top of his budget because he thought that he'd get more money next time if he could show the current budget was inadequate for our needs.

"Look, C.J.," I tried a little sweetness, "I know money is short and we're near the end of the budget year. But I need someone who has some experience managing a heavy workload. You know how much we have to do over here."

I tried sucking up by appealing to his desire to let everyone know how overburdened the court system for the Middle District of Florida was, and particularly our Tampa division. He wasn't buying it. "You're no busier than anyone else, Willa," he snarled at me. "If you don't take the next one I send you, you'll have to make do without an assistant altogether because I'm totally out of money for temps."

When he slammed down the phone I said something unjudicial and very maturely stuck out my tongue at the telephone receiver. The man was impossible.

Somehow in the midst of the chaos, the Billie Jo Steam file arrived that morning in my office. The file, marked "Urgent," was placed on my chair while I was on the bench. After thirty years in prison, what could still be urgent for Mrs. Steam?

I picked up the heavy green envelope containing the file and put it on top of the stack in my in-box. The heap wobbled, threatening to topple over, but held its "Leaning Tower of Pisa" pose. My assistant's job was to sort the mail and deal with it. Of course, that wasn't getting done, either. I glared at the pile, which unfortunately didn't cause it to shrink any, and turned my attention to other matters.

At twelve o'clock, taking note of the growling tiger in my stomach, I picked up my wallet and let myself out the front door of my chambers in search of a modest lunch. Waiting impatiently for the ancient elevator to reach the third floor of the old federal courthouse where I worked, I paced and fidgeted. My colleagues had long since moved to the new Sam M. Gibbons Federal Courthouse down the street. The much nicer elevators at the new site were only one of the reasons I coveted the other location. But, the C.J. refused to let me move. He claimed he had no money in the budget. *And if you believe that, I've got some swampland to sell you*, I told myself.

Eventually, the elevator arrived and when it opened, there stood Harris Steam.

"Willa! I was just coming to see you! Did you get the file I sent over?" he asked as he stepped out toward me with a hopeful look on his face. Resisting the urge to groan I hesitated a moment in indecision while the heavy, old elevator doors began to close ever so slowly. At the last minute, I stuck my foot inside the frame, allowing the doors to mash it.

When the doors finally registered the obstruction and made their labored opening again, I said, "Harris, walk with me. I need to get a sandwich for lunch and I haven't got much time." As I limped into the elevator, we began our slow descent to the first floor.

"Did you look at it?" Harris asked me a second time, his eyes eager and intent on my face. The loud, creaking noises the elevator made on our trip down were a little scary, but, as usual, I ignored them.

"No, I haven't had time yet. I saw the file on my desk after I came off the bench this morning, but I didn't get a chance to read it."

"But you will," he insisted.

I sighed inwardly in resignation. I'd relaxed at home last night and gotten a good night's sleep. My husband, George, had returned from his annual Mother's Day trek to Grosse Pointe, Michigan, this morning. My world had begun to settle into its normal rhythm and I regretted my impulsive agreement to consider helping Billie Jo Steam. George had told me, "You don't have to save the *entire* world, Willa."

This morning, part of me had begun to hope that Harris had simply been carried away by the day and the moment, just as I had been. What did Harris really expect me to do for his mother?

"A lot of people can help you better than I can, Harris. I could recommend someone for you. Someone who would have the time and the expertise to get your mother out of prison."

I didn't have time to free Billie Jo Steam, even if I had the ability to do so. My caseload is always over eight hundred cases—and growing. I'd spent the morning working on pretrial conferences and I had twenty-five trials set to start next week. Believe me, at least one would begin. And then I'd be tethered to my bench all day, every day, until the trial was over. If Kate hadn't asked me to do this, I'd have rejected the request out of hand. Harris and Billie Jo were the beneficiaries of my desire to be Kate's hero. At least I understood that much.

Harris didn't answer me right away. We walked together, rather swiftly, down Florida Avenue and across Madison to Franklin Street. We passed one of Tampa's oldest and most celebrated power brokers, Prescott Roberts, walking south. Harris raised his hand and said, "Hi, Uncle Prescott," as we approached.

Prescott Roberts nodded in our direction, not stopping his conversation with the mayor to speak to us, but his steely grey eyes met mine for a moment. The look he gave me was piercing, causing me to wonder why. Prescott Roberts was a formidable man, but so far as I knew, our paths had rarely crossed. There would be no reason for him to dislike me.

As we stood in line at the Franklin Street deli, Harris remained silent. Lawyers and judges greeted me, discussing the weather, the Devil Rays, or anything else of no consequence just to have a few seconds of my time. Being a judge in Tampa makes one something of a minor celebrity among lawyers. No one else knows who I am, or cares. Most people are much more interested in my husband, who owns Tampa's only five-star restaurant. He's a real celebrity here.

When I'd ordered my tuna sandwich to go and filled up a styrofoam cup with ice and tea, I stood at the checkout counter with my ten dollar bill ready, having already declined Harris's offer to buy. No one was bending my ear and Harris Steam finally got a chance to talk. "Why don't we sit down here for a minute? I'd like to tell you something about my mother. I want you to know why you're the only one I can count on to help us now."

I followed him to a booth in the back room, away from anyone in a business suit, where we sat across from each other. I opened my sandwich while Harris opened his wallet and pulled out two pictures.

"These are my sweethearts," he said, handing them over. I wiped the mayonnaise off my fingers and took the photos, which were studio pictures, not snapshots. Both pictures showed two young girls, one about a year older than the other. In the first photograph, they were maybe three and four years old. In the second, they were about seven and eight. Both girls were red-heads and blue-eyed. They wore frilly dresses, gloves, and hats. Their hair fell in natural ringlets down below their shoulders. These children looked like elaborately dressed porcelain dolls on display in a showcase. I handed back the glossies, which he continued to look at as he talked.

"The older one is Wilhelmina, just like you," he said, startling me. I'd never met another Wilhelmina in my entire life. I suppose most of the Jims and Jennifers got over this sense of name ownership in preschool, but I'd always been the only Wilhelmina. I thought I was unique, in my little world anyway.

"Actually," Harris went on, looking from the picture to me and back again, "she kind of looks like you, in a way. The red hair, I guess. But her eyes are blue, not green like yours. Anyway, the younger one is Willetta."

"What unusual names you've given them," I observed.

Perhaps a bit old-fashioned, too, for kids these days.

"They're family names, but also sort of superstitious, I guess."

"How so?" I asked, still munching on my sandwich. I had to be back on the bench at two o'clock and I had several things to do before then, including walking back to the courthouse.

"Have you ever heard of the Six Bills?"

I shook my head in response.

"Well, that was the name of the band my parents started when they were in college here at the University of Tampa. Dad was the lead singer. Mom played keyboard. Six Bills had six members, all the guys were named William and Mom is Willetta, which is how the band got its name."

"Really?" I said. "What an odd coincidence."

"Yeah. When some cosmic thing like that happens, you have to take notice, right?" He was giving me that grin again, the one that drives female fans to scream for three hours straight when he's on stage. "I mean, you moved to Tampa because 'Tropical Memories' played at the right moment on the radio."

"It must have been confusing, everyone having the same name," I said. I had visions of mixed-up credit cards, misfiled school records, "wrong number" telephone calls. Once, someone called our house to offer someone named Bess Carson a job as an office manager. Now, my dog Bess is smart, but I think managing a financial services office would probably have been a bit of a stretch for her. Having a household full of Bess Carsons would be even worse.

"Sometimes. Mostly, it's been pretty cool. Haven't you ever heard of the John Smith Society? All the members are named John Smith?"

I shook my head, negative again.

"Anyway, Dad was William Harris Steam the Third. He was called 'Trey.' I'm the Fourth, but they call me 'Harris,' and not 'Quad,' thank God." He smiled again and I had to laugh. "Mom's always been called 'Billie Jo' by everyone. When the girls were born, they had to be 'Bills,' too."

Okay, I guess that made some kind of sense, in an enmeshed way. I'd always enjoyed the special nature of my name. I liked being one of a kind, which was sort of a trademark for me. Given the choice, I'd take solitude and independence over crowds and popularity every time. Which is probably why I would never have become a judge if I'd had to stand for election.

He looked at the pictures one more time, put them back in his wallet and returned the wallet to his jacket pocket. "We call the girls Willie and Billie." He saw me wince. "I guess it takes some getting used to. Now that I'm divorced, I don't see them as often as I'd like. Eva, my ex-wife, doesn't think much of me as a father."

I said nothing about his divorce. Although I don't read fan magazines and I miss out on most of the personal information about celebrities, Harris Steam's divorce had made the local papers read like a late-night soap opera. Infidelity allegations and suggestions of abuse were flung by both sides, mostly in an effort to secure favorable terms for child custody and visitation, since Florida is a no-fault-divorce state. I would have had to live on another planet to miss the gossip.

He dipped his head down again in the charming, shy gesture of an embarrassed young child. "Eva left me because she said I didn't care enough about her and the children. If I can show her that's not true, I think we can get back together again. I still love her, and she knows that."

I swallowed the tuna with a swig of iced tea. "Is Eva right?" I questioned. "Did you give her a reason to think you didn't care very much about your family?" My experience with divorced males is that often they don't see it coming, despite all the obvious signs. If the wife leaves them, it takes a long time before they get over it. Harris seemed like one of those men who never recover from divorce or go on with their lives.

The head dip, followed by the sexy smile, preceded his

answer. "Maybe I wasn't as good at showing my feelings as I could have been. The divorce has made me more serious about getting my mother out of prison, so we can be a family again."

For some reason, he believed getting his mother out of jail would fix his marriage, too. It seemed like a stretch to me, but maybe the two problems were related. I didn't know enough about the situation yet to make an assessment.

"Because she's been in prison, Mom has never been able to spend any real time with me or the girls. All of us need that relationship. Maybe Eva would let us all be together again, too. The girls ask me constantly if that will happen. Families shouldn't be separated by prison walls, should they?"

I didn't answer, but my work has shown me that some families need to be separated by prison walls, given the damage they do to each other, both physically and emotionally. "How do your grandparents feel about it?" I asked him.

William Steam Jr. had been the president of the University of Central Florida here, before he retired. He was still a very influential man in Tampa. His reputation for being rigid and unforgiving was well deserved. He had expelled more seniors just prior to graduation for innocent pranks than any other college president I'd ever heard of. He was active in the most conservative of the local churches, political associations, and private clubs. No, Bill Steam was not a man who would welcome the release of his son's killer.

Nor would he take kindly to me if I got in the way of what he viewed as appropriate justice. Having Bill Steam opposed to her parole would make the task of freeing Billie Jo a great deal closer to impossible than it already was. "Do you think your grandfather will just forgive and forget?"

"It's *my* father she's supposed to have killed. If I can forgive Mom for that, shouldn't Granddad be able to?" The way he said it made me think that his grandparents weren't supporting his efforts to free his mother.

Maybe Bill Steam should forgive, but his heart is hard, I avoided saying in response. If Bill Steam hadn't forgiven Billie Jo after thirty years, it was unlikely he'd do so now. That was a clue to the steely glare Prescott Roberts had cast my way when we passed him on our walk to lunch. Prescott Roberts was Bill Steam's brother-in-law. If they were both opposed to Harris's plan to free his mother, Billie Jo had better get comfortable right where she was.

I swallowed the last of my sandwich with the last of my tea. "It's not that easy, Harris," I said as we prepared to leave. "Your mother was tried, convicted, and sentenced to life in prison. She's been there for thirty years. You told me her parole has been denied before. In this context, 'life in prison,' means exactly that. Unless the parole board decides she can be released, she won't go home. That's how the system works."

Harris's tone instantly became hard and angry. He raised his voice to an uncomfortable level. "But how old will my girls be then? Mom isn't well, Willa. She has cancer. She's been sick for quite a while. She'll be dead soon. My girls will never have a grandfather. They need to have their grandmother, at least for as long as she has left. Surely no one can object to letting Mom die with us."

His anger was seething and I suddenly realized he might be dangerous. What did I know about him, really? There were quite a few people around, I noticed as I picked up the pace; wanting to get closer to the courthouse and all those lovely armed guards we have there.

Harris kept up, walking all the way back to the courthouse with me. By the time we got there, he'd calmed himself down and managed a final plea on the courthouse steps. "Won't you help us?" He sounded like himself again, the man who had spent the lunch hour discussing his children, trying to win me over. He thought there was something he could say to persuade me, but that wasn't true. Harris Steam wouldn't cajole me against my will. If Billie Jo Steam had been the victim of rough and imperfect justice, she needed rescue. That had been Kate's point yesterday. A point with which I agreed, in principle. Kate takes on so many lost causes, it's hard to keep them all straight in my mind. But she rarely asks me to help her with anything. After all she'd done for me I could not refuse her.

More importantly, had the justice system betrayed Billie Jo? Clearly, her son believed so and he was ready to put himself wholeheartedly into the effort to prove he was right, whether the powerful men in his family agreed or not. Much more than that would be required to get his mother released, but Harris's emotional and financial support was a pretty good start. Justice in this country is a lot easier to come by for those with money. Sad, but true. Harris Steam had a decent cash flow, according to the gossip over his divorce. If I helped him, I wouldn't charge him a fee, but we'd have some heavy expenses.

"I'm just not sure I can help you, Harris. Let's do this. I'll study the file you sent me. After that, I'll let you know whether I think you have any chance at all of success. We'll go from there. How does that sound?"

He grabbed my hand and held it between both of his as he looked into my eyes and through to my soul. "I know you'll help us, Willa. You understand what it's like to lose your mother and you're a principled woman. You'll do the right thing. And I thank you for that. Just let me know how I can help."

He reached into his jacket pocket, pulled out a CD and handed it to me. "This is an advance release of my new CD. I've done all of my father's old songs. Some of them have been remastered so that it sounds like we're singing together. Sort of like that Natalie and Nat King Cole CD they did a few years ago. 'Tropical Memories' is on here, too. Listen to this. I think you'll like it. And maybe you'll see why my family is so important to me."

I left him on the steps and quickly went back up to my chambers.

With just a few minutes before I had to return to the courtroom, I carefully pulled the heavy green legal-size envelope labeled *Billie Jo Steam* off the Leaning Tower of Unopened Mail. I used my silver letter opener that had a pair of Labrador retrievers cast into the handle to slit the top edge. Because we own two Labradors, gifts from work friends tend toward every known form of office paraphernalia depicting the dogs. Anyone who'd spent some time in my chambers might think he'd wandered into the American Kennel Club.

I took the contents out of the green envelope: three manila file folders and a long cover letter addressed to me from Billie Jo herself. The letter was my first contact with the woman.

I scanned the cover letter first. It was well written, cogently organized, and straight to the point. Billie Jo Steam clearly had better assistants than I did. Or, if she'd prepared the letter herself, maybe I could hire her.

"My son places great faith in you and I'm praying he's right," the letter began. "Thank you for agreeing to help me overcome my past and leave this place for a better life." As I read her plea for help, I felt the all-too-familiar personal pressure of an insurmountable challenge placed before me. I also felt the pressure to fulfill the hopes of a hopeless woman and reunite a fractured family before another death severed them from each other forever. Bringing Billie Jo Steam home would be like bringing a mother and her family back to life. I'd often wished someone could do that for me.

But would it be a good thing? Should we change the course of the future? A tingle coursed through me from under my scalp to my toes, leaving me vaguely unsettled, as if the choice I made would have tragic, unforeseen consequences. I believe in premonitions. I should have remembered that.

Chapter Four

Billie Jo's letter contained a recitation of the procedural history of her case, probably written for her by a previous lawyer who had tried, and failed, to gain her a new trial. Willetta Johnson Steam had been convicted of the first-degree murder of her husband.

She had been tried in Hillsborough County Circuit Court before a judge who is now deceased. The prosecutor was a man of significant local renown who had committed suicide last year. Her defense attorney was a public defender whose name I didn't recognize. Perhaps he was still around and I could interview him. I noted all the names, along with a reminder to locate and interview Paul Robbins, her public defender.

Her trial took place less than a month after the murder. It had lasted only one day and the jury took less than thirty minutes to find Billie Jo guilty of first-degree murder. She was sentenced the next day to life in prison. In twenty-seven days, Billie Jo's world had gone from young bride and mother to life in prison. Her defense had been simple: She was not guilty. Now, thirty years later, that's what she still said.

Billie Jo had had two unsuccessful hearings before the parole board, seeking her release. Maybe the third time's the charm, I mused, as I put the letter back on top of the three files and placed a large rubber band around the entire stack. I'd take a closer look after my hearings this afternoon.

Somehow, the justice system was intent on punishing Billie Jo Steam to the full extent of the law. That so rarely happens it was worth looking into, just to see why it was happening, I thought as I put on my robe and returned to my courtroom.

Four hours later, my body dragging and my spirit at about the same low level, I came back into my chambers to a cacophony of questions from my law clerks, pink phone message slips stacked three inches high, and the constant "chirp" that my computer uses to tell me I had unanswered e-mail.

Just as I was about to say something completely unjudicial in response to all this, a lanky young black man, dressed in a conservative blue business suit and red tie, walked through the door. "Out! Out! Everyone out! Judge Carson's had a long day. Come back tomorrow!" He ushered the law clerks through the door, followed them out, and closed the door behind him. I had no idea who he was, but at that moment, I might have hugged him.

A few seconds later, this kind stranger returned with iced tea in a tall crystal glass, a cocktail napkin, and a coaster. He put the lifesaving refreshment on my desk and stood there while I drank a long, thirst-quenching gulp. Then, in a lilting voice with a pleasant Jamaican accent, he said, "Good afternoon, Judge Carson. I'm Augustus Ralph. I'll be filling in as your assistant this week. It's a pleasure to meet you. I'm leaving now. I'll be here at eight o'clock in the morning."

He might have told me he was about to change my life forever by taking charge of my office henceforth. I needed a change. The announcement would have been quite welcome. It would have given me some hope that my work life would soon be back in order and I could return to the job Uncle Sam paid me to do.

I would certainly have liked to do my own work, instead of the job my prior assistant performed so well that I'd hardly known she was doing it. Ah, the truth: Assistants are indispensable. If you doubt it, try working without one. As far as I was concerned, Augustus Ralph was already a keeper.

I wanted to follow Augustus out the door, but I thought I should at least take a peek at the pink slips and the list of e-mail messages on my computer. I flipped through both quickly, finding nothing much of interest, except one phone message from my friend, Ursula Westfield, marked "Urgent." Wondering what wouldn't be "urgent" to a television news reporter on a deadline, I picked up the phone and returned her call. The moment that I said my name, the receptionist put me right through to Ursula herself. Maybe I had more clout with the general public than I thought.

"Willa! How good of you to call me back. Can I come over to Minaret this afternoon? I could be there about five-thirty. I need some information for a story. It's five o'clock now." As usual, Ursula's conversation was filled with swift information and inquiry.

I would have tried to stall her, but I've attempted to say "no" to Ursula before. There's no point to it. She doesn't ever hear the word and, in any event, she didn't wait for me to respond. "Ok. See you then," she said, as she hung up.

I picked up the Billie Jo Steam file along with the CD Harris had given me and put them in my briefcase. I made a weary trip down to the car where I saw a note under the windshield-wiper on the driver's side. No one other than courthouse personnel parked in this garage, so I assumed one of my coworkers had left me a quick message. I unfolded the plain white notepaper and read: "Billie Jo Steam belongs in prison. Leave her there."

"What the hell?" I said out loud, to no one in particular. I looked around, but saw no one lurking. Who would have known that I had any involvement with Billie Jo Steam at this point? Especially someone with access to this garage? I stuffed the note in my pocket, more puzzled than concerned, and drove home.

Ten minutes later, I set my briefcase down by the hostess station near the entrance to the restaurant above which I live. Our flat is on the second floor of this nineteenth century home called Minaret. Its name comes from the polished steel onion dome on the top of the mansion. The first floor houses my husband George's restaurant.

Minaret is a grand old building. George's Aunt Minnie married into it and left it to her favorite nephew when she died. We opened a restaurant in the building so that we could afford to keep the place. Inheriting a big, old house is a little like winning prizes on a game show. What they don't tell you is that prizes come with a hefty price tag, because Uncle Sam is right there, assessing taxes on your winnings. In the case of Minaret, we had not only taxes but improvements, and the air conditioning bills alone would support a third world country for a decade. Oh, don't get me wrong. We're not about to start collecting food stamps or anything. Still, we don't work full-time just because we love our jobs.

Minaret was built in the 1890s when Henry Plant, Tampa's equivalent of Donald Trump, decided to build a family home. Plant was then constructing the Tampa Bay Hotel, now the University of Tampa, which he believed would be a mecca for the rich and famous. When his guests came to the hotel, he wanted to show off a fabulous home as well. He wasn't going to be out-done by his rival, Henry Flagler, who had done such a magnificent job in Palm Beach.

Before he could build his house, though, Plant had to build Plant Key itself. Originally, Hillsborough Bay was too shallow for navigation and certainly devoid of any landmass. When the Port of Tampa channels were being dredged to allow passage of freighters, Plant persuaded the Army Corps of Engineers to build up enough solid land for Plant Key at the same time.

He made his island oval shaped, with the narrow ends facing north and south toward Bayshore and out into the gulf. The key is about a mile wide by two miles long and it sits between Davis Islands and Ballast Point in Hillsborough Bay. Plant also built Plant Key Bridge, which connects Plant Key to Bayshore Boulevard just east of Gandy Boulevard. Marine-life ecosystems weren't a big priority then. If you had an island, you had to have a way to get there, didn't you?

Since the dinner crowd had not yet arrived, George's place was nearly empty. I wandered into what was once Aunt Minnie's side porch but is now the Sunset Bar, stopping to get a glass of Perrier from the bartender. Here, too, the tables were all empty, except for one.

Seated with her back to me, enjoying the view of

Hillsborough Bay, was Ursula Westfield. Her tall, slender form reflected the perfect posture she displayed five days a week as anchor of the network's morning news. Her creamy, café au lait skin, ultrashort hair, and luminous brown eyes conveyed the sincerity and competence that millions of Americans trusted to deliver the truth of the latest headline story.

Ursula was more popular nationally than Barbara Walters or Diane Sawyer. Indeed, her ratings put her just slightly below Tom Brokaw with viewers. If she kept moving up, she'd soon be the national news anchor on the evening broadcast. No other woman holds such a position in network television and Ursula was determined to get the job.

Ursula was a local girl made good, and we were all proud of her. She was one of my best friends, but I didn't see her often. Her job and mine too frequently intruded on the time we would have otherwise spent together. Indeed, I rarely saw Ursula at all during the month of May, because May is a television ratings month— one of the time periods when the networks tried to garner as many viewers as possible to assure the highest advertising rates for the coming season. Ursula often spent the entire month at her flat in New York City where she could be closer to her work.

Now, Ursula didn't have a news crew with her. That meant that her professed deadline wasn't as impending as she had made it sound.

After we'd settled in the Sunset Bar and exchanged life updates since we'd last seen each other, Ursula got right to the point, another trademark of the style that had catapulted her near the top of the news game. "I'm doing a story on an innocent woman who's been in the prison system for about thirty years. She's coming up for parole. I want you to be one of my on-air experts," Ursula said.

I asked the question, although I already knew the answer. "What's the woman's name?"

"Willetta Johnson Steam. 'Billie Jo,' they call her. Her son is

Harris Steam, the singer. Do you know the case?"

"Yes," I said, wary.

She laughed. "Don't look so worried. What I'm looking for from you is the legal angle: the reasons why Billie Jo would have been convicted in the first place and how she'd be treated differently today. Stuff like that. I think this will be about a twenty-minute piece on the next *News This Week* episode I'm doing. It's perfect for you."

"Why are you asking me to do this?" I don't believe in coincidence. Ursula's request wasn't serendipity. In my pocket, my fingers clutched the note that had been left on my windshield. If Ursula knew about my potential involvement with Billie Jo Steam, more people were aware of it than I'd suspected. Who would be bold enough to threaten me?

"Harris Steam said you'd agreed to help. I want the inside story. Do you think you can get her out?" Ursula was always focused on her own agenda.

"Did you tell Harris to ask me to help his mother?" I was feeling manipulated here. I just wanted to know who the chess master was.

"He asked me about you. I told him I thought you'd be perfect for it. You could use some positive publicity, Willa, and freeing an innocent woman will give it to you." She was all earnest now. Ursula wanted something from me, but she seemed convinced that this would be a two-way street.

"Federal judges don't need publicity of any kind," I said, more than a little annoyed at her meddling. "I don't know of a single federal judge in any jurisdiction who has ever given a comment on television. It's just not done."

"Well, maybe most of them don't. But you've had quite a bit of negative press in the past few months. Some people think you should be impeached for taking the law into your own hands over that business with George. As your friend, I'm telling you that a little positive publicity isn't going to hurt you any."

Only about a dozen federal judges had ever been impeached in the history of the United States judicial system. Once appointed to the bench, a judge could do just about anything and still keep her job. Still, there was the public trust and confidence in the judicial system and the rule of law to consider. I'd taken an oath to uphold the law and I intended to keep it.

Ursula shifted in her seat, checking the diamond encrusted gold Rolex on her wrist in the manner of a person with a plane to catch. Seeing I wasn't convinced, she added, quietly, "It's a lot easier to do nothing, but that's not your style. You didn't take the job to toil safely in obscurity, while hoping to make it up the judicial ladder. When you accepted your appointment, you said you'd follow your own conscience and make your own choices. Now's your chance."

Again, I didn't immediately consent, although her words had pricked my conscience, just as Ursula intended. The president had nominated me, late in his last term, to fill an empty seat on the federal bench. Because I was young, I'd had no judicial experience, and these seats were sought after by candidates much more qualified than me, there were people who weren't satisfied with his choice.

At the time I had been astonished and thrilled, in almost equal measure. Viewing my appointment as a sign from the universe, I took the job, vowing to use my position to help people. Ursula was right that, so far, I hadn't been as bold as I could have been in pursuit of my self-defined goals.

Ursula sounded exasperated with me now. "You've got some powerful enemies, Willa. They're looking for an excuse to bring you down."

I don't like to think of myself as a woman with enemies, so my tone was harsher than I intended. "Don't you think getting myself publicly involved in a parole hearing where the attempt is to free a convicted felon will just give these enemies you say I have more ammunition?"

"This woman is innocent. People would love to see her freed. If the public is on your side, then your opponents will have a harder time getting rid of you," Ursula replied.

"Look. I'm not interested in what my enemies think. If I help Harris and Billie Jo Steam, it'll be because I think it's the right thing to do. Not for any other reason." Maybe I spoke a little too hotly. I was tired, overworked, inconvenienced, and not interested in being on television.

Nor was I willing to be bullied by "they." I am used to making my own decisions. My friends call me principled, independent, and passionate. I think they mean it as a compliment. When George is angry with me, he calls me "stubborn and pigheaded," which is probably closer to the truth. Regardless, I make my own choices and I take full responsibility for them.

Realizing she wasn't making progress, Ursula tried to find a more winning tack. "Okay, then think about Billie Jo Steam. The woman trusts you. Everyone who has tried to help her has failed. Do you want to leave her to someone else? Someone who won't care whether she spends the rest of her life in prison?"

I already felt the pressure to perform a miracle. What if I failed? Did I need such a public failure? One televised to multi-millions, worldwide? Sure, winning would help my public image. But, what if I didn't win? Putting the case under a spotlight could easily backfire on not only me, but also Billie Jo herself. "Maybe that's where she belongs, Ursula. Did that ever occur to you?" I said, softly voicing my own doubts. "Billie Jo was tried and convicted in one day. Does that sound like a complicated case?"

"It sounds like a railroad job to me, that's what it sounds like," Ursula said with the conviction of the righteous, as she set her drink down with a thud for emphasis.

Trouble was, that's what it sounded like to me, too. After Ursula left, I pulled the threatening note out of my pocket, crumpled it up, and dropped it in a trash can. I wouldn't be bullied. And certainly not by someone too cowardly to sign their name.

Chapter Five

I came wide awake with a jolt at four o'clock in the morning. My heart pounded wildly as I tried to catch my breath. The nightmare seemed so real, that I didn't realize I was home, in my own bed, my husband sleeping beside me.

In the dream, I'd seen Billie Jo Steam on a stretcher, a white sheet covering her dead face as the paramedics carried her out of her prison cell. For some reason that I couldn't dredge up from my subconscious, Billie Jo's dream death was my fault and the guilt was overwhelming. Her image was embedded in my eyelids and reappeared every time I closed my eyes. I couldn't shake it. Sleep was impossible.

I left George and the dogs in our bed, oblivious to my distress, and padded out to the kitchen to make a cup of my Cuban coffee. There's not much to do at "deep-dark-thirty" in the morning, alone in a quiet house. It was too early for the newspapers, and early morning television doesn't interest me.

I took my mug into the den, where my gaze fell on my briefcase. Maybe I could erase the dead woman in my dream if I got started on the job of reviewing Billie Jo Steam's file. I pulled out the file materials and closed the door. Then I settled into one of Aunt Minnie's armchairs, put my feet up on the ottoman and began to read.

Two hours later, the file completely finished, I stood to stretch my aching back and refill my "I hate mornings" coffee mug. When I opened the door to my study, I nearly tripped over our Labradors, Harry and Bess, who were lying as close to the threshold as they could get and still be in the hallway. As soon as I righted myself, they both begged for attention. I quickly changed into the well-worn running clothes I wash and wear every day, opened the back door, and we all bounded down the stairs like caged birds allowed to fly.

The day was glorious, the water blue and flat, the sun low in the morning sky, and the temperature just perfect. May begins to get hot early in the month. By month's end, midmorning temperatures would be well above eighty degrees. Today, though, a cold front must have been pressing down on us. It was only about seventy-two degrees and the slight breeze wafted the heavy sweet smell of jasmine my way. All of my senses were alert and I was thrilled to be alive and outside and not cooped up in a Florida state prison.

My thoughts returned to Billie Jo Steam, as I threw sticks into the water for Harry and Bess to retrieve. "Fetch the stick" was the one game they loved above all others. They would play it long after my pitching arm tired and I fell to the sand. Such simple pleasures: the sunshine on my face, the jasmine-perfumed air, enjoying my pets. All of these delights had been denied to Billie Jo Steam for thirty years. What would such sensory depravation do to a person? How could one survive emotionally? Why not just give up the struggle and let prison kill you?

Yet, survive she had. Her file and her letters to prior lawyers, those who helped her and those who couldn't or wouldn't, had broken my heart. Billie Jo described her tragic life with a voice of quiet dignity that probably hadn't existed in the twenty-one-year-old girl who was tried and convicted of her husband's murder.

The girl was the one who tugged at my heartstrings. The young Billie Jo Steam. Not much older than I had been when my mother died, young Billie Jo lost her husband to murder and her son to less-than-loving in-laws. She had been unable to hold her child to comfort his nightmares or celebrate his victories. That girl vanished as she served her time at one Florida state prison after another. The Billie Jo Steam of 1972 was nowhere to be found in the materials I'd been reading in the wee hours of the morning.

Except in pictures. Her pictures revealed a charming but haunted girl with waist-length brown hair at different stages: curly and unruly outside her home the night she was arrested; tamed by a ribbon at the nape of her neck at the courthouse on the day of her trial; and shorn short for easy care in the prison photographs ever since. The most current pictures showed a middle-aged woman, still tall, a little heavier.

But she signed her letter, *Billie Jo*, with a little circle to dot the 'i,' and a long curly loop under her name. The signature told me that some essence of the young girl in those early pictures continued to exist. Even if I couldn't see that essence in her prison photos, I wanted to meet her. I wanted to know how she'd managed to survive. I wanted to help her.

I knew C.J. wouldn't like it, and he wouldn't be alone in his displeasure. But Kate had been right all along. I did need to try.

When Harry and Bess finally looked as if they might be willing to give up the stick game, I sat down on the sand and played with them a while longer. I shuddered to think what would happen to me if I'd gone, like Billie Jo Steam, into prison.

Bess nudged my leg, waiting for me to throw the stick again. I threw it one more time before I called the dogs over to the outdoor shower, rinsed them off, and put them in their kennel to dry.

As I climbed the stairs, I acknowledged that no one was threatening me before I got involved in the Billie Jo Steam project. Although there were the usual nuts out there who didn't like one thing or another that I'd done as a judge, this anonymous note was the most blatant attempt to scare me. Somebody wanted me to leave the case alone. And they wanted me to get the message that I was easy to find and I'd be at risk if I helped Billie Jo.

Billie Jo Steam was a woman with powerful enemies. And now her enemies were mine, too. Their sheer existence convinced me I was on the right track.

Once upstairs, I walked into the shower stall and got ready for work. On my way out the door, I stopped by the telephone and dialed. "Ursula, it's Willa," I said into the answering machine, after the beep. "I've looked at the Billie Jo Steam file and I'm ready to talk. Give me a call." I placed the receiver down with a solid thump, feeling the weight of my decision settle on my shoulders like stocks on the accused in a colonial town square.

Chapter Six

I found Augustus Ralph straightening up my in-box when I arrived at my chambers. He was dressed better than I was, as usual, in a grey conservative suit and a yellow tie. His shoes were highly polished cap-toes and he wore a small yellow rose in his lapel. The rose was so tiny, one needed to step up close to identify it as a living flower. The miniature rosebush from which he clipped this bud was on the corner of his desk, alive and well.

Augustus was clean shaven, with his hair cropped short. His nails were neatly trimmed and highly buffed, but not polished. In short, if I had a daughter, I'd approve of her dating such a fine-looking young man. So far, Augustus Ralph was perfect, which the C.J. couldn't have known or he wouldn't have sent Augustus to me. I hoped I could keep him.

"I've made fresh coffee, Judge. Let me get it for you." He had a large pile of mail in his hand to take back to his desk. The pile remaining in my in-box was now a manageable size, barely peeking over the edge. He returned in a moment with perfectly creamed, aromatic coffee in a china cup and saucer, handing it to me as he said, "The finest Jamaican Blue Mountain coffee. I order it from home."

I tasted the coffee, believing I'd landed in the middle of heaven, for sure. "Augustus, sit for a moment," I requested as we took the two ugly green client chairs on the visitors' side of my desk. He crossed his legs, being careful to preserve the crease in his trousers, and folded his hands over his knee. "Tell me. Where did you come from and why are you here? And how long can you stay?"

"I am an American citizen," he said, in his rhythmic Jamaican accent, so pleasurable to my ear. "I was born here to a Jamaican mother and an American father, and then my parents became Jamaican missionaries. They sent me back here to school. I'm now in graduate school at night, working during the day. I can stay as long as you need me, Judge Carson," he said. And that was all I needed to hear.

At the noon recess, I returned to my chambers to find my conference table set for lunch, complete with my tuna sandwich on a china plate, and iced tea, with lemon, in a crystal glass. Augustus had set out a cloth napkin and silverware. The contrast from yesterday's lunch was marked. I gave quick but heartfelt thanks to the man who had sent this marvel to me, and vowed to be sure Augustus stayed forever. I sat down at the conference table with the newspaper and then remembered the quick phone call I needed to return.

"What made you decide to help, if you don't mind my asking?" Ursula said, when, once again, she took my call immediately.

"Have you looked at the file Harris sent me?" I asked.

"Of course."

"The whole of it just doesn't pass the smell test. Trey Steam's wounds were too extensive for the small struggle Billie Jo described that night. She was rushed through trial and into prison. Since then, the system, with its desire to cross cases off the list, has kept her inside." I didn't have time to discuss the matter further at that point and I wouldn't tell her about the note. Not yet, anyway. "So, what's the first step?" I asked.

She sped through her plan like a pace car out in front of the race, not caring whether the rest of us were following, not giving me a chance to interrupt. "I'll tell my producer that you'll be working with us. She'll be in touch. I won't be involved in the details, but I suspect she'll begin by putting the story in news teasers, making it known that you're involved. Just your involvement will make a difference and will get people noticing."

"But—" I started to say.

She bullied her way right through my protest. She simplified the internal processes of the network to keep our conversation short. "Someone may call the network's local stations and request a ten-second interview to lead their six and eleven o'clock news programs. A reporter and a photographer will come over to your office at some point to get some footage. Then, they'll begin to promote the *News This Week* piece, which has been scheduled to air the day of the parole hearing," she told me cheerfully. That would give the show the immediacy of the story, although none of us would know the outcome of the case that early on.

"Then, we'll do follow-ups after the hearing until we get the result. With any luck, we can do a couple of victory pieces afterward." She had settled the matter before we had even started the process.

I squirmed a little. I remained uncomfortable with the way I'd resolved the ethical issues. The C.J. wouldn't like how I'd managed it, and he might even be right. Theoretically, Billie Jo might appear in my courtroom someday, and if that were to happen, I'd have compromised my objectivity by getting involved in her parole hearing now. I'm supposed to avoid even the appearance of impropriety, so such a theoretical possibility should be accepted as probable and I should not get involved in her parole hearing in any way. That was the textbook answer.

And like most textbook answers, it ignored a very real rule of legal construction: hard facts make bad law. Billie Jo was in real trouble and she needed real help.

If there was any chance that she might actually appear in my courtroom, I would have found another way to solve Billie Jo's dilemma. But that would never happen. If nothing else, she'd be dead by the time such a request could be made. She only had me, now.

There was no valid, real-world reason for me not to help Billie Jo and there were a thousand reasons why I should. Reassuring myself that I'd made the only possible decision under the circumstances, I still said, "No. I don't want my participation in this publicly known until I absolutely have to make an appearance somewhere. And I hope that will never happen."

I saw no reason to make a public spectacle out of myself. Or more accurately, a bigger target than I already was. Nor was I in a big hurry to give the C.J. and my other enemies the opportunity to skewer me over my decision. I have the courage of my convictions, but I'm not deliberately foolish.

"I'm willing to work behind the scenes. I can't publicly comment on your story, and I won't be used as a story myself. Nor will I improperly influence the process for Billie Jo Steam's advantage," I told her. "That's where I draw the line."

She thought about it for a few minutes, trying to reshape her vision. "Okay. I can accept that," Ursula finally agreed, not because she wanted to concede, but because I gave her no choice.

I didn't ask her what she would do in place of her original plan. "I need to talk to Billie Jo first, before we do anything else. I have quite a few things I'll need to know directly from her."

Ursula hesitated only slightly. "Okay. I'm sure she'll see you any time. I'll fax over the telephone number and the contact at the prison. Or you could ask Harris to bring you to meet his mother," she suggested, her attention already on the next item on her personal agenda.

I considered how I wanted my first physical contact with Billie Jo to go. I've seen many, many criminal defendants in my courtroom over the years. Some were defeated, some defiant. The defiant ones had a better chance of surviving our justice system.

"No," I said slowly, "I think I'd rather see Billie Jo alone the first time I meet her. I need my own impressions. I need to get a sense of her in my own context."

"When will you go? We'll start working on the promos right after you talk to her," Ursula said.

"Soon," I promised her. "I'll go soon."

I wasn't exactly looking forward to visiting Billie Jo in prison. Just reading her files had been hard enough. The memory of her death in my nightmare continued to haunt me. After a couple of days of avoidance, I screwed up my courage and prepared myself to enter the physical reality of confinement. I scheduled the appointment in the late afternoon, after court, before I could chicken out.

I didn't have any real difficulty getting an interview with Billie Jo Steam. She'd been expecting me. Being a judge, I had no trouble passing through security or getting admitted to the Marianna Women's Prison, a relatively new minimum-security facility not far from Tampa.

Inside the prison, though, I felt a palpable desire to leave at once. Even though the prison resembled a college dorm, I was instantly claustrophobic. Billie Jo must have felt this way every day of her life.

I waited for her in a small conference room, a private place where prisoners meet with their lawyers. Billie Jo's file materials proved she was no stranger to such encounters.

When she had arrived in prison in 1972, she was that rare inmate—a college graduate. She'd gone to work in the prison law library for a number of years, toiling to free herself, as well as to assist other inmates with their clemency and parole proceedings. Sometimes she worked twelve hours a day, seven days a week, to help others, while serving a life sentence for her husband's murder.

Billie Jo had seen more than one woman freed, in part due to her own heroic efforts. Indeed, she'd been one of the few women honored while in prison for her work with battered spouses.

But in the case of Billie Jo herself, she didn't begin to ask for a new trial for the first few years of her confinement. Later, judges had denied her requests for a new trial eight times, even in the face of brand new evidence.

One of her lawyers argued that Trey Steam had defensive wounds on his hands and arms, and that he'd bled to death from one of the wounds to his lungs. All of this suggested he'd put up a prolonged fight with his attacker. How could the court reasonably assume that Billie Jo herself could have escaped injury in such a fight?

Yet, neither photographs nor the jailhouse physician who examined her found any such laceration or bruising on her body at the time. And she wasn't gone long enough for Trey to have bled to death from whatever injury she might have caused him.

Nor was anything of that magnitude mentioned in her testimony. She admitted that she and Trey had argued and struggled with the knife and he fell, but Billie Jo denied that she had been hurt in the struggle and also denied that she'd injured Trey. She said he was fine when she left the house with their son.

The appellate court said all of that evidence had been available when Billie Jo was arrested, and disregarded it, denying her motion for a new trial. Lawyer after lawyer had tried to help Billie Jo, but all had failed. Now, here I was, retreading old tires.

Thirty years later, looking at the government-issue metal table and chairs within the institutional-green, windowless walls, I felt Billie Jo's cause was hopeless. How was I ever going to pull this one off?

Chapter Seven

Billie Jo was escorted into the room by an armed female guard. During the small talk between the guard and me, Billie Jo stood quietly to one side, hands folded in front of her, head slightly bowed so that I couldn't see her eyes. When the guard left, Billie Jo looked at me straight on for the first time, with piercing blue eyes. She smiled that tentative smile I'd seen in the young Billie Jo's photos.

"Hello, Judge Carson," she said in a soft voice that hadn't been hardened by cigarettes, another rare thing for a prison inmate. What do they have to do, after all, but smoke? The threat that smoking might shorten their lives must seem like a promise of a shorter sentence to lifers like Billie Jo.

I stuck out my hand and felt the small, soft fingers give mine a light pressure in return. "Hello, Mrs. Steam. It's nice to meet you. I've heard such wonderful things about you from your son," I told her, gesturing toward the chairs I'd arranged across the table from one another.

"Billie Jo," she said, as she sat down and folded her hands on the table in front of her. She looked like a small child who had been called into the principal's office and didn't quite know what to do about it. "I'm grateful you're here, ma'am. Thank you for trying to help me."

"Please, call me Willa. Your son does." I smiled at her, trying to relax her somewhat. This was the moment to be brutally honest and to give her the disclaimer. I wanted to start right out with that so we would have no misunderstandings.

"I hope I'll be able to help you, Billie Jo. You need to know that I'm not an expert. I've never tried to win a prisoner's release before. In fact, I'm usually the one who sentences convicted felons to spend time in prison." I told her that for starters, then I said that I thought she'd be better off with someone else.

"This is your life and your choice," I added quickly. "Just let me know, and I'll help you find someone who has half a chance of success."

Before I had the words out, she was already shaking her head, no. "Billie Jo, there are excellent reasons why I've never been a criminal lawyer. For one thing, I'm not good at it. I got my worst grade in law school in criminal law classes and the few pro bono cases I worked on in school were dismal failures."

What I didn't tell her was that I've never wanted the responsibility of holding someone else's life in my hands. So far, I hadn't been asked to preside over a criminal bench trial, and I hoped that would never happen. As a judge, I apply the law to those the system has already found guilty. Their lives didn't depend on my competence as a lawyer. No. Not for me. I'd chosen to leave life and death to God, where that decision belonged, in my view.

Billie Jo continued to shake her head in the negative. She had made up her mind. I felt keenly the heavy obligation I was now assuming. There would be no turning back.

"I've had the experts, Judge. I've lost eight bids for a new trial and countless requests for clemency, all handled by experts. I don't need an expert. I need someone with some compassion. A large dose of personal integrity would help me a lot. And I need someone with clout. That's what Harris said you and Ursula have. Clout. That's what I need."

She reported this without any hesitation or shyness. She'd obviously thought it out thoroughly and had no shame in asking me to use whatever influence she believed I had. I was quickly learning how special Billie Jo really was. Life had not been kind to her, yet she had kept her balance and her purpose. She was determined to free herself from this prison not of her making. I had to admire that kind of resolve.

"The law has rules about these matters, Billie Jo. I've taken an oath to uphold the law. I can't bend the rules for you or anyone else." I probably sounded as sanctimonious as I felt. She had to know, though, that I would make my own decisions along the way. I wouldn't do anything for her that I considered unethical, even if it meant that she lost her bid for parole.

Although the C.J. would say I was already bending the rules, I disagreed. Billie Jo's case wasn't before me in my courtroom, and would never be there. She had exhausted all of her appeals. Her habeas corpus claims had all been denied. She'd been in prison so long that the likelihood of another habeas corpus petition, one that just might be randomly assigned to me, was slim to none. Besides that, no one was going to make a legal objection.

I was slicing the salami pretty thin here, and I knew it. But the law is decided in thin shavings. Sort of like the old *Price Is Right* television game, the goal of the law is to get as close as possible without stepping over the line.

Billie Jo was misty-eyed now, conviction in every word she uttered. "I know all about the law. I didn't kill my husband, but the law doesn't care about that." She focused away from me, then was suddenly intent on me. "If anyone were applying the law, I'd never have been convicted in the first place. Or I'd have been let out years ago. I didn't understand that then, but I know it now. Someone has been pulling strings to keep me in here all along. You've got to help me, Judge. This is my last chance. I'm sick. If I don't get out of here now, I'll die here. I know I will."

"Harris told me you think you have cancer. Do you have documentation in your medical records to support that, Billie Jo? It could help us to get you released early if you really do have a terminal illness."

She snorted. "Oh, I've got a terminal illness, Judge. I've got colon cancer. Do you know what that is? It's going to kill me soon. Right now, I don't have many symptoms. But the symptoms I do have are getting worse. My mother died of it, and so did my only sister. It runs in my family and I know I've got it. Dying of cancer in prison is not 'death with dignity,' believe me."

"I didn't see that in your medical chart," I said slowly. "If you have cancer, why doesn't it show up in your records?"

"Why should I tell them anything?" she asked, looking out the small window toward the guard who had treated her curtly when bringing her in to see me. "Give 'em the satisfaction? They wanted me to spend my life in hell and it looks like I will. That should be enough." She sounded tougher now, and I was glad. The defiant survive.

"So you haven't been going to the prison doctors for treatment? They might be able to do something for you. Colon cancer is treatable. And you could have something other than terminal cancer, you know." Billie Jo didn't seem like a hypochondriac to me, but I didn't know her well. She could be imagining this illness, or subconsciously creating it for convenience sake. Surely she realized that the parole board wouldn't release her just because she said she was dying.

"You think not having terminal cancer would be a good thing for me? Why? So I could live another thirty years in this place? I'm going to die here, Willa. They've made certain of that. It's just a matter of when I'll die. Sooner is better than later if I have to stay in prison." Her words brought back my nightmare when I saw her dead body carried from the prison on a stretcher. I shuddered.

I didn't think to ask her which "they" she was referring to. I assumed she meant all of society. "You'll need to see a doctor, Billie Jo. Get formally diagnosed. If you're right about your condition and you want to play with your grandchildren before you die, you'd better get the examination quickly. I'll arrange it."

I stayed a while longer, talking with Billie Jo, getting to know her. She discussed her son, and her grandchildren. We stayed away from controversial subjects until I asked about her in-laws. "What about Bill and Mary Steam? Do they believe you killed their son?" I questioned her.

Billie Jo lowered her head. Then, she took a deep breath and raised her eyes to mine, unwavering. "Do you get along with your mother-in-law?" she asked bluntly. She could tell from my reaction that I wasn't my mother-in-law's favorite person. She smiled, then turned serious again. "I haven't talked to Bill and Mary since I was arrested. After they took my son, they kept him from me until he was eighteen."

Her eyes filled with tears and she stopped to gain some composure. "Bill and Mary Steam believe I'm not good enough. Mary hates me. She always has. She thinks I trapped Trey into marrying me, even though Harris wasn't born for over a year after we married. Bill Steam is a very stubborn, hard man. He and Trey never got along." She added that Bill and Mary had fooled themselves into thinking that Harris loved them more than he loved his mother. She saw them as believing they could be the parents to Harris that they had never been to his father.

I should have used our time to ask her about the facts of her case, how her husband died, and who had killed him. But I'd already read most of that in her files and she clearly wanted to talk with me about other things. I thought we'd have plenty of time to deal with those issues later. Before I knew it, the guard signaled that our time was up and I had to leave.

"Bill and Mary think my grandchildren are their personal property. They won't give that up without a fight," Billie Jo told me. She squared her shoulders. "Nor will I."

I watched as the guard escorted Billie Jo back to her cell and then gathered my papers and headed to the parking lot. Before I reached Greta, my beautiful Mercedes CLK convertible, I could see something was wrong. She was leaning to one side. As I got closer, I could see that both right tires had been slashed and my beloved car was resting on her rims.

Outraged, I pulled out my cell phone and called for Mercedes twenty-four hour road service. I opened the glove box and removed the disposable camera I kept there. I took a few pictures of the car and the tires that I thought would never show anything worthwhile, but made me feel useful.

While I waited for the tow to arrive, I called our police chief, Ben Hathaway. I told him about the note, cursing myself for throwing it away. I also told him about the tires.

"Do you have any idea who's behind this?" he asked me. Really. Sometimes cops drive me crazy.

"No, Ben, I don't. But I don't like it."

"Well, then, maybe you should try sticking to your day job."

"Like that's any safer," I snapped at him before I hung up the phone. I believed that my anonymous vandal was trying to scare me away from Billie Jo's case. I wasn't going to be deterred by threats from someone too cowardly to show his face. The jerk.

Chapter Eight

I was somewhat surprised to find myself sitting at the Tampa Club, waiting to have lunch with Ursula's husband, W. Walter Westfield. I had no idea why he'd summoned me. I thought for a moment that he might be the one behind the threats I'd been receiving, but the notion strained my imagination. Walter was usually more than willing to assert himself in person.

I arrived a few minutes early and was seated at a small table by the window overlooking the University of Tampa. I had a view of our home, Minaret, sitting serenely on Plant Key, its own private island. From this distance, I couldn't see much, but knowing my sanctuary was there was comforting.

I'd dressed in the most casual attire appropriate for a judge to dine at the Tampa Club. I was wearing a raw silk, oatmeal pant suit, with a chocolate silk blouse and low-heeled, brown pumps. This outfit contrasted sharply with my usual khaki slacks, polo shirt, and deck shoes. I generally dress in the most comfortable clothes possible. Under my robe, and seated at the bench, who can tell? Here, though, there was a dress code.

The view from forty-two stories atop the Bank of America building was spectacular. From here, one could see how Hillsborough Bay caressed the Bayshore—Tampa's ribbon of road along the water—with a perfectly calm blue blanket that glimmered in the sunlight.

This was not the Franklin Street deli, where patrons felt free to approach me at their whim. In one of my devil-be-damned moods, I'd ordered a glass of chardonnay. Because I'm a federal court judge, some people think I should live more quietly than a cloistered nun. That would include never drinking at lunch, particularly in public. As if drinking a glass of wine at lunch was worse than drinking a bottle of bourbon every night after work in the privacy of one's home. Most judges accept the custom-made straight-jacket of propriety as one of the necessary evils of a job that requires public trust at the same time it promises power and a lifetime appointment. Public piety seems more like a life sentence without parole to me. Playing it safe is not in my nature.

I sipped my wine, realizing I could have waited for Walter forever, enjoying the view, the solitude, and the quiet respect all guests get here once you've passed the gauntlet of other diners and made it to your table. I couldn't have been farther from Marianna Women's Prison if I'd flown to Mars.

As I waited, my thoughts returned to Kate and Leo. Kate would make a good mother to Leo's small boys. Kate's children are grown and on their own—four lawyers, if you include me, all doing well. Although Kate isn't my mother, I consider myself a part of her family. Beyond that, Kate has three grandchildren. Her second son, Mark, was as big a family man as his brother Jason was a power broker. One thing Kate didn't need at her age and station in life was more children.

Leo had become something of a project for Kate. She had discovered him in Italy, brought him here on a visa, found him a job, and catered to him as if he were something truly special. To be fair, I hadn't spent any time trying to befriend Leo or figure out what, exactly, Kate saw in him. She couldn't realize the situation she'd gotten herself into with Leo.

Kate was such a sweet soul. She'd never knowingly allow Leo to use her friends or family, although Kate would put *herself* at Leo's disposal if she felt she could help him in any way. Leo was a matter I needed to address soon. I put him on my mental "to do" list, later to be transferred to my Palm handheld organizer, another of the technology demons George detests and I can't live without.

A gentle stirring among the gentlewomen and gentlemen discussing business over Tampa Club Chowder interrupted my reverie. I looked toward the slight noise to see Walter Westfield, threading his way over to my table, stopping to shake hands and politick with everyone he passed on the way. He'd recently announced that he was planning to run for senator against the Republican incumbent my husband supports and Kate's son Jason works for.

Walter's wiry body was as well toned as that of a man firmly ensconced in middle age could be. About six feet tall and one hundred and seventy pounds, Walter appeared sincere in his three-thousand-dollar blue suit and conservative tie. His once dark hair was now touched with grey at the temples, which made him look more mature and conservative. His public persona was of someone trustworthy, experienced, and in glowing health. He portrayed everything the voting public would want on its side in Washington.

As Walter made his way slowly toward me, I looked around at the other diners and was startled to see Leo Colombo, as if my earlier thoughts had conjured Kate's husband out of thin air. Leo was lunching with my new assistant, Augustus Ralph, at a table to my left and slightly behind me. They were too far away for me to hear their conversation, but both were engaged in a discussion that seemed particularly earnest. Neither was smiling.

How could Leo and Augustus possibly know each other? And what use did Leo have for Augustus, came my uncharitable next thought. Because, at least subconsciously, I had decided that Leo was a user. He was using all of us, whether Kate realized it or not. And Augustus would just be the next patsy on his list.

Neither Leo nor Augustus looked up from their table or met my eye. *Could Leo be the mastermind behind the car vandalism and threatening note?* I dismissed that idea as quickly as it flitted through my head. Leo wanted me involved with Billie Jo. He wouldn't try to warn me off the case.

A waiter, winding between tables toward Walter, carrying a heavy tray laden with several plates of hot food, grabbed my attention. When Walter turned abruptly, losing his balance, he and the waiter nearly collided. I caught my breath. The waiter's strong arms and adroit footwork had barely managed to evade a potentially harmful and noisy collision. As our collective breathing returned to normal in the dining room, I realized that if I'd only seen the last of the encounter, I'd have thought Walter was drunk, he seemed so unsteady on his feet.

Both Walter and the waiter recovered quickly and Walter continued to make his way toward me, bobbing and weaving like a boxer, still stopping at every table. He took a good ten minutes to make the thirty-foot trip. Walter was clearly well known and popular here on his home turf. Perhaps the senatorial incumbent was in for a bigger challenge than we all had anticipated.

Finally, twenty minutes after our arranged meeting time, Walter arrived at our table. I had the impression that all eyes were now focused on Walter Westfield's luncheon companion, a judge whose husband is a highly placed member of the opposition. George would be supporting the Republican incumbent with every ounce of his considerable influence. Walter wouldn't be foolish enough to think otherwise.

Walter leaned over and patted my arm a little harder than necessary. Then, when he straightened up, he knocked over the saltshaker with his jacket sleeve. Setting the shaker right, Walter took a pinch of spilled salt, threw it over his left shoulder in the age-old plea for good luck, and sat down.

The elaborate show of Walter's arrival left me to wonder whether he'd staged our lunch to try to suggest a political rift between my family and me as to the best candidate for senator. I'd known Walter a long time. I wouldn't put it past him.

To say that Walter Westfield is manipulative is like saying Machiavelli was somewhat controlling. Walter had learned manipulation at the knee of the master, Prescott Roberts. One learns, over time, not to try to thwart Walter. Or to even think about it.

Now that I'm on the bench with a lifetime appointment, I don't have to worry about Walter anymore. I find him an interesting specimen. But I still didn't like being used to serve Walter's purposes. And I wondered whether Walter was one of the powerful enemies Ursula had referred to. He was certainly powerful. If Walter could serve his own ends by discrediting George or me, he would. Perhaps, if I failed at getting Billie Jo Steam out of prison, I'd be handing Walter a weapon he could use politically at the same time.

"Quite an entrance, Walter," I said. My mouth was dry, but not from the exquisite chardonnay.

"It's like that everywhere I go now. I'm always campaigning," he said, smiling his campaign grin once more, for the benefit of any spectators who might be watching.

"How do your partners feel about that?"

For the past ten years, Walter had been the managing partner of "Florida's Best Law Firm," according to their advertisements. Not the largest firm, but the most influential, well-respected firm. Once known as Jameson, Dew, Alton, Roberts and Westfield, the firm had recently shortened its name to Jameson, to create that all-important "brand" the law-firm marketers were selling this season. Walter's was the law firm with the reputation for excellence and the one with which other law firms tried to compete.

Walter had been the handpicked successor for the firm's top position by his mentor, Prescott Roberts, the firm's prior managing partner. Like his mentor, Walter had been president of the American Bar Association, the Florida Bar, the Hillsborough County Bar Association, and the Chamber of Commerce. Now, Prescott Roberts had assembled a powerful political machine dedicated to putting Walter Westfield in the Senate.

Walter shrugged with apathy. "Doesn't matter. I'm ready to move on. I knew when I threw my hat into the ring that, win or lose, I'd have to leave Jameson. It's time for me to do something else with my life."

This was a surprise. Walter leave Jameson? He'd practically

become synonymous with the place. Walter's leaving was the kind of gossip I should have heard. Nothing is a secret in Tampa for long, and certainly not such big news as Walter Westfield leaving Jameson. He'd practiced there more than twenty years and had run the place with an iron hand for ten.

The only small burp in Walter's career was his marriage to Ursula while he was still in law school. She told me once that he'd taken a big chance when he married her because she was black and Walter's family was not only white, but as Old South conservative Democrat as they come. But, it was the seventies, the era of liberalism, and they'd fallen in love. Besides, back then, they were young and neither of them expected to become the public force they were today. Walter's family connections to Prescott Roberts got him a job at Jameson right out of law school. Otherwise, being married to a black woman would have kept him from employment at any of the prestigious firms back then.

As Walter moved up in the ranks of his firm and the bar, people came to know Ursula and accept her as his wife until a bigger obstacle arose—Ursula's job as a young copywriter developed into an on-air television spot. Having a wife who was a member of the media set Walter's progress back a couple of notches because in those days, the one thing a successful conservative lawyer couldn't do was to bring unwanted attention to his clients by being too much in the public eye.

But after a few short years, Ursula's accomplishments eliminated even that small issue because her success made Walter very visible, in the most positive way possible, bringing unexpected clients and revenue to Jameson.

On-air television reporters often use stage names. But Ursula Westfield used her own name and Walter was only too happy to consent to her doing so. They traveled in some fairly elite national circles because of Ursula's celebrity. Now, Walter and Ursula Westfield were Tampa's highest profile couple.

Ursula hadn't said anything at all to me about Walter leaving Jameson. But, maybe she had. She'd told me she expected to be transferred to Washington or New York soon. Perhaps that was what Walter now planned. A failed run for senator didn't rule out a move for some other reason. As I said, Walter is manipulative. To him, it's all a game, and both he and his wife have friends in high places. They had lots of options.

"Why did you want to see me?" I asked, after we'd ordered our lunch. Mine was grilled tuna with asparagus. Here, though, I had to dress up to eat it and the tuna wouldn't emerge from a can.

"Ursula told me about Billie Jo Steam. She said you were working with her to get Billie Jo out of prison. I want to ask you to stop." Walter lifted his glass to his lips.

I couldn't have been more surprised if he'd asked me to endorse his run for the Senate. Walter and Ursula always discussed everything with each other. They were joined at the hip, strategically speaking. I hadn't asked her, and not that I cared, but I'd assumed she'd cleared the Billie Jo Steam project with Walter before she'd taken it on. Walter had been helping Ursula map her own career for almost as long as she'd been helping to map out his. The idea that they were not in complete agreement was a new one to me. I narrowed my eyes and watched him more carefully.

"You don't know everything about the Trey Steam murder, Willa," Walter continued, as the waitress arrived with our food. "You didn't live here then."

"I think I've learned quite a bit about it lately. What does where I lived in 1972 matter?" I asked him, not following his logic.

"You've read newspaper accounts and talked to the family. You've looked at the story from Billie Jo and her son's perspective. That's all. You didn't know Trey Steam. I did. Believe me, Billie Jo killed him and she's better off in prison." His tone was calm, matter-of-fact, as if Walter and I were discussing a legal case reported in one of the books in my office.

"How did you know Trey Steam?"

He looked at me with some chagrin and a crooked smile, the

one I remembered from my law practice days. That smile said, "I was wrong," although those words would never come out of Walter's mouth. Like many powerful men, Walter had trouble admitting his mistakes. What he tried to do was to forget them and hope you would, too. Sometimes that worked. When it didn't, he'd give you that grin and count on the southerner's polite refusal to encourage unpleasantness to allow him to avoid further discord. In Tampa, it was a good strategy. Such dodging wouldn't work in Washington.

What he said, with the smile in place, was a revelation. "I was a young man when this all happened. But Trey Steam and I were in college together, here at the University of Tampa. Ours was a small class. I knew him fairly well."

He took another sip of his iced tea. For him, it wouldn't do to be seen drinking anything stronger in the middle of the business day, in full view of half the movers and shakers in Tampa, when he was campaigning for public office. Walter was now a slave to public opinion. I took another sip of my wine.

Walter said, "I was a member of the Six Bills. The 'W' in my name stands for 'William,' although I've never used the name except for that brief time when I was a Bill." He smiled in fond reverie, recalling a younger, more innocent era. "I was away from home for the first time, excited to be in college and to have a solid group of friends like the Bills. We'd see each other on campus and we'd point our finger at each other and say, 'Hey, Bill,' at the same time. It was a great game. We were a group, you know?"

We shared a smile over the small joys of college life. Walter is several years older than I am, but we'd both been to college and enjoyed the experience.

"I loved the guitar," he continued. "I still play. My singing voice isn't half bad, either, if I do say so myself. In another time, I might have been a rock singer, too. Look out James Taylor."

Walter grinned at me, expecting appreciation. I smiled back. Why not? Walter was a personable man. He couldn't have gotten this far in the world otherwise.

Now, his countenance abruptly changed. Horizontal frown lines deepened on his forehead as his carefully trimmed eyebrows came together over a tanned complexion and troubled grey eyes. He leaned a little closer to me over the table and lowered his voice.

"Trey was stabbed to death with a knife. The blood in that apartment covered everything within twenty feet of where he lay. Trey Steam was a father. He had parents, family. His mother is Prescott Roberts' sister. Prescott would never have allowed his nephew's killer to go free." His tone brooked no argument. "And Prescott was convinced Billie Jo killed Trey. That's all anyone needs to know."

What I thought was, poor Billie Jo. After being accused of killing not only Bill Steam's son, but Prescott Roberts' nephew, the young girl of the photographs never had a chance of acquittal. "So you didn't believe she was innocent? Even for a moment?"

"No. Johnny Tyson was there when she claimed to have found the body. He told me how she reacted. She just stood there, looking at Trey, while his son ran over to the body screaming 'Daddy, Daddy, Daddy' over and over again, kneeling down to hug his dad, covered in blood. She didn't try to comfort her son and she didn't seem at all surprised." He ran his hand though his well-styled hair. "Hell, Johnny was throwing up out in the yard, while Billie Jo just stood there. And she's never shown one ounce of remorse. Not once. Because she doesn't feel any." Walter spoke with fresh anger, as if Trey Steam had been murdered yesterday.

I have this ability to "see" things in my head, like a movie. As he described Trey Steam's body, the little boy covered in his father's blood, I could visualize the scene, the horror of it.

"Exactly," Walter said, when he saw me give an involuntary shiver. "Trey Steam was a jerk, Willa. A class-A jerk. He treated Billie Jo like a piece of dirt and he treated all the rest of us that way, too. He was definitely a spoiled little rich kid." He shook his head slowly from side to side. "But, to answer your question, no. I've always had faith in the fact that she killed him."

Walter told me then that Prescott Roberts himself had examined the facts of the case against Billie Jo and believed her guilty. To Walter, that was the same as saying God himself had made the judgment. Walter had advanced quite far in the world on Prescott Roberts' influential coattails by taking just such a position on every decision Roberts made.

"Prescott is as honest as the day is long. If Prescott said Billie Jo was guilty, then she was." He leaned forward, invading my personal space. "You don't want to be on the wrong side of Prescott Roberts, Willa. Neither do I. Trust me."

I straightened up a little, my appetite for the tuna now completely gone. I took a sip of water to give me time to consider Walter's horrible story. Billie Jo Steam was the one who had powerful enemies. If I helped her, they could become my enemies, too. That's what Walter Westfield was telling me.

To change the subject, I asked, "Who is Johnny Tyson?" It was odd that I hadn't seen a statement from him in Billie Jo's files, if he'd been a witness at the time of the murder.

Walter looked a little surprised at the question. "Johnny?"

"You said Johnny Tyson was there with Billie Jo and Little Trey when they found the body," I said, using the nickname the Bills had given Harris as a child. "Who is Johnny?"

Walter fidgeted a bit now in his seat. Pushing back his chair and crossing his legs, he put his napkin over his knee and gestured to the waitress for some coffee. He didn't answer my question until after she'd cleared the plates, poured the coffee, and left the table. That pause had given him the opportunity to compose his answer precisely and I wondered why he felt the need to do so.

"John William Tyson. He was another of the Six Bills in those days. He played the drums in our band. We called him 'Johnny' then."

"And he was with Billie Jo when she found the body?" I asked. "Where is he these days?"

"I don't honestly know, Willa. I haven't seen him or the other Bills in years. Not since Billie Jo was convicted." Walter went on to tell me how, after the trial, the group had broken up. They had all gone their separate ways.

"I think we didn't want to be together any more after Trey was murdered. At least, that was the reason for me. I didn't want to be reminded. I had nightmares for months afterward, where I'd see Trey covered in all that blood, Little Trey playing in it. Hell, I didn't even play my guitar again for years." He shook his head as if to clear it of the unwelcome images, then he reached across the table and covered my hand with his. "Willa, we've known each other a long time. You're one of my wife's closest friends. For your sake, and for mine, don't dredge this all up again. Prescott won't like it."

I drew away my hand. "Because it wouldn't be good for your campaign, Walter, to remind the public that you were once involved in a murder? Even tangentially?"

"Do you really think so little of me? Trey Steam was a jerk, but he didn't deserve to die for it." Walter seemed completely sincere. "Billie Jo didn't have to kill him. Even back in 1972, one could get a divorce fairly easily in this town. Let her serve her time. Trey's parents have had enough heartache, don't you think?"

He stared at me, full in the face, and said with deep sincerity. "You, of all people, should know that criminals don't stay in our overcrowded prisons unless there's a good reason to keep them locked up. Do us all a favor. Let Billie Jo stay where she is."

As we walked out of the restaurant, I realized I had one more thing to cover. "It's clear that you don't want me to help Billie Jo, Walter." I said. "How far are you willing to go to keep me off her case?"

"I thought I'd just done it. I explained everything. What more do you need?"

I judged his puzzled tone to be sincere, but I didn't trust him. "Someone's been threatening me. First I got an anonymous note. When I came out after my visit to Billie Jo, the tires on my car were slashed. You didn't do that, did you?"

He was angry now. "Oh, come on, Willa. You watch too much television."

"So you didn't threaten me, then," I said, watching his eyes closely.

A shocked look came over his face that seemed sincere, but Walter had a good grip on himself. "Someone's threatening you? Have you reported that? You're a federal judge, Willa. There are a lot of nuts out there who might want to do you some harm. You'd better take that seriously."

No kidding, I thought. But if someone had wanted to harm me, they could have done so. I believed this was an attempt at intimidation and I'd just spent an entire lunch hour allowing Walter to demonstrate that he was fully capable of that much. Then again, so were a number of other people I'd been spending time with lately.

Chapter Nine

"I noticed your lunch companion," I said to Augustus at the end of the day, when we were both wrapping up and preparing for the *Madison v. Cardio Medical Corporation* trial set to start the next day.

"And I, yours," he replied, with his characteristic calm. "Mr. Westfield is not the kind of man a person of your stature should be lunching with, Judge Carson." His comeback surprised me.

"How's that?"

"I've been knowing Mr. Westfield for many years, ma'am. He's got a ferocious temper, that one. I worked over there at Jameson for a time. I have friends there. Best to avoid him, for sure. He can't be trusted." Augustus was picking up stray file folders, mail, and cups and saucers. He busied himself in my chambers, moving back and forth to his desk in the reception area as he spoke.

"Why did you work at the Jameson firm?"

"Oh, my uncle helped me get a job there a while ago," he said. "The stories I could tell you, if you're interested sometime." I should have asked him who his uncle was and what kind of stories he was talking about, but I was focused on other things.

"I'd rather talk about Leo Colombo," I said, a bit more sternly than I meant to do. Tales of Walter Westfield's reputation among the staff at Jameson had reached my ears before. I hear everything, but I don't encourage my staff to repeat gossip. "What were you doing having lunch with Leo?"

Augustus stopped momentarily, startled by my question. "Why, ma'am, I can't tell you that. That's Augustus's own business, isn't it? Besides, you'll spoil the surprise."

"What surprise?"

"That's all I'm going to say. If you want to know more, you

should talk to Leo yourself."

He turned, letting himself out, closing the door behind him and leaving me with the unsettled feeling that Leo Colombo had invaded every sphere of my life.

I should have spent the evening preparing for the *Madison* trial, but tomorrow's schedule only called for the last of the settlement conferences on the case and any remaining pretrial motions. I'd heard and denied dispositive motions last week, so I had a good working knowledge of the facts and the issues. This case wouldn't settle, anyway.

Madison was the type of case all lawyers and judges detest: very thin proof of liability and high exposure to a sophisticated corporate defendant. Making a corporate defendant settle a case by writing a multimillion-dollar check is hard to do under the worst of circumstances. Usually, the defendant's point of view is "let the jury decide," by which they mean, "The jury will never give you that kind of money."

Of course, these are the same defendants who, when the jury awards multimillions, are the first to decry the jury system. In the next session of the legislature, they introduce further tort reform laws. The cycle is as predictable as tomorrow's sunrise.

No, the *Madison* case wouldn't settle and I was looking at a three-week trial. I'd have plenty of time to learn the case once we got started.

This is part of a judge's life most people don't give a thought to: all the time it takes to get ready for trials and motions. Anyone who thinks a judge's job is nine to five doesn't understand the process. Oh, sure, we have judges who work hard and those who don't. But even judges who don't work hard aren't nine-to-fivers. This is a government job, with all the pitfalls and few of the benefits. Judges don't take these jobs for money or an easy life. At least, I didn't.

I had taken the appointment for the same reason I'd committed to help Billie Jo Steam: I believe in our justice system. With all of its problems and susceptibility to manipulation, it's still the best system of justice in the world. I can do a good job of making sure justice happens, when I'm allowed to try. At least, on good days, I get to do justice. The rest of the time, I try to focus on the good days.

Billie Jo Steam's case was the kind of situation that gave our justice system a black eye. I could fix that, one case at a time. On the other hand, I didn't have a lot of time. I repaired to my den, with coffee for a clear head, and opened Billie Jo's life once more. The three manila folders she had sent me were filled with summaries of her case at its various stages: trial, posttrial motions, and requests for parole and clemency. I opened the last two folders, looking for the arguments and evidence that had been presented, and had failed, before.

I combed the pages with an experienced eye, looking for fine distinctions and minutiae previously missed. I saw little to give me any hope of finding the necessary new evidence sufficient to get Billie Jo another trial. All the arguments, good and bad, had already been made. Turning to the trial folder, I reviewed the list of evidence, witnesses, and summaries of testimony.

The folders did not contain the actual evidence admitted at trial, which would have been somewhere in the court files at one time. For instance, there were no crime scene photographs. I found nothing but the underlying support for the information I reviewed. Even back then, they did blood-typing on the blood found at the scene. The reports didn't suggest that the murderer had left any blood behind, but I wasn't sure how thorough the investigators had been. They had a suspect, red-handed, as it were, standing over the body holding the murder weapon. How much further did they really need to look?

At the end of three more hours of reading, I came away with only two new pieces of information that might help us: No DNA tests had ever been done on any of the evidence collected at the scene of Trey Steam's murder; and Billie Jo's cancer, if it existed, was a new and additional fact that might support her request for an early release. Otherwise, everything had all been argued before. As Billie Jo had said to me when I visited her in prison, the system wants to keep a closed case closed. In Billie Jo's situation, that meant she would die in prison, if the system had its way.

But was that justice? Ursula's opinion that Billie Jo's trial had been less than fair could easily be supported by the bare facts. The police had apparently considered, arrested, and charged only one suspect. Only two prosecution witnesses were presented at the trial: the medical examiner and the investigating officer. Billie Jo was the only defense witness. She was forced to admit that she'd been in a tempestuous relationship with Trey Steam for years, that they'd fought that night, and since he died after she left the house, that she had no alibi for the time of the murder. No evidence had been offered to suggest any reasonable doubt as to her guilt. Billie Jo's word that she hadn't killed her husband wasn't convincing to the jury.

Except for the prominence of the victim, the state's judicial system tries cases exactly like this every day. Sometimes the trials last a little longer—maybe three days—but just as often they don't. A one-day trial didn't necessarily mean the trial was unfair.

Billie Jo might have been the victim of rough justice. That's what it felt like. But more likely, the murder of the son of an influential Tampa family commanded a speedy trial and certain conviction of a defendant where motive, means, and opportunity combined with no reasonable doubt of guilt.

I reviewed my notes and reconsidered Billie Jo's options. DNA testing didn't exist in 1972, which, in Billie Jo's case, might have been a good thing. The police found her at the scene with blood all over her clothes. Billie Jo's fingerprints were on the knife determined to be the murder weapon. Successful DNA analysis usually shows evidence transferred from the perpetrator to the victim during the crime. Evidence that the victim might have left on the perpetrator is usually lost because the perpetrator has destroyed it.

In this case, however, Trey Steam's blood was surely all over Billie Jo. She was covered in blood when the police found her standing over the body, as was her son. Trey's blood on her clothes would have supported her conviction, not her defense, even if DNA testing had been possible back then.

After an exhaustive review of the file, I felt I could offer no help to Billie Jo in continuing to challenge her conviction on the facts. The effort had repeatedly proven to be a sure loser.

A terminal cancer diagnosis, if it existed, would be more likely to get Billie Jo paroled. The prison system isn't well designed to care for terminally ill inmates. Nor is such long-term health care well funded. The aging prison population promised to be a significant challenge to the system in the next few years because more inmates would need long-term health care. This was a fact of prison life that might help Billie Jo now.

Billie Jo had been in prison for more than thirty years of a life sentence. If she did have terminal cancer, she'd need expensive end-of-life care for several months. We might have a chance at success by seeking to appeal to the fiscal as well as the humanitarian side of the parole board. Surely, since she'd paid a large chunk of her debt to society, they would want to let her family pay for her last illness. It was a much more promising tack than anything else I'd seen in the file, even if a clemency parole wouldn't provide the vindication Billie Jo and Harris wanted.

But maybe the DNA could help, too, if we could still find the evidence and get it tested before the parole hearing. The likelihood that DNA evidence existed on such an old crime was, to put it politely, slim. Beyond that, we'd have to get over the state's objections that the time limits for Billie Jo to request DNA analysis had long since expired. The cost of doing DNA testing at this late date would also be significant. But Harris Steam told me he had an unlimited supply of money, so I didn't worry about who would pay for the testing.

I had been taking copious notes and listing the potential

avenues of pursuit since opening the files hours ago. Now I stood and stretched my weary muscles, refilled my coffee, and dictated my plan of action into an e-mail I sent to myself. Tomorrow, I'd put my plan in motion. Time was running out for Billie Jo Steam. Literally.

Chapter Ten

I wanted to get started on Billie Jo's case right away, but my other work came first. I stuffed my impatience behind my judicial countenance and looked across my conference table at the plaintiff in the first of ten settlement conferences I'd scheduled today.

My courtroom deputy called the first case. *The Estate of Stanley Madison v. Cardio Medical Corporation et al.* would never settle. I only held the final settlement conference because the court rules required me to do so. The hearing was a waste of everyone's time and we all planned to make it short.

In this country, our policy of open access to the courts means that anyone can file a lawsuit, whether or not the case has any legal merit. The *Madison* case presented a very flimsy claim of product liability for the death of an artificial-heart patient that I would have preferred to dismiss. Unfortunately, when a jury trial has been requested, my hands are tied. I must let the process run its course, whether I feel the plaintiff's claims are meritorious or not.

After taking care of a few paperwork issues and preliminary matters, I told the participants to report to my courtroom tomorrow morning at nine o'clock, sharp, to begin jury selection. All of us were relieved when the formal conference was over; we'd recited our lines, and now they could get on with the main bout.

The remaining lawyers and their clients with legitimate matters on my trial calendar, in line behind the *Madison* entourage, were ushered in for more fruitful attempts to settle their cases. A few actually did get resolved. The others were returned, re-ordered to the trial calendar, and told they were on twenty-four hour call. When they learned the names of the lawyers that were ahead of them, the attorneys told their clients to go home and relax. No one else would be going to trial at all this month.

Surprisingly few of them were outraged at this misuse of resources that caused the justice system to grind that much more slowly.

Augustus had opened and printed my e-mail file before I arrived in the office, putting the printed pages into a green file folder on my desk, awaiting my attention. I'd had no opportunity to look at the e-mail before now, but I took it over to my conference table to leaf through during my midday appointment with Charlie Tuna. Most of the e-mails were of no importance, but I scribbled some replies on them that Augustus would send after lunch. One of the e-mail messages jumped out at me.

"Billie Jo Steam is a killer. Watch yourself," it said. I looked at the printed message, which had none of the computer mumbo jumbo on the bottom that reflected the path it had taken through the maze of the Internet. The return address was Concerned@messenger.com, one of hundreds of free e-mail programs available to anyone with the ability to dial a phone number.

Augustus had gone out, so I couldn't ask him where this e-mail came from. I went over to my computer and searched for the offending note in my e-mail program. It wasn't there. I checked for recently deleted messages. It wasn't there, either.

Where did this note come from and how did it get into my green folder? I couldn't figure that out. My office wasn't open to the public. If the message came to me through my computer, it should still be there, but it wasn't. If it came into my folder in some other way, then one of the members of the staff or a lawyer or litigant or juror or someone who worked in the building would have to have put it there. I didn't like the idea that someone had breached my inner office and this note made me feel more vulnerable than any of the other incidents so far.

I put the page into another folder and stuck it into my desk drawer, intending to give it to Chief Hathaway at the earliest available opportunity. I probably should have called someone else, a federal officer, but I didn't want to draw the C.J.'s attention to the situation if I could avoid doing so. I didn't seriously consider that Trey Steam's killer might be behind the attempts to get me off Billie Jo's case. It seemed too far-fetched.

When I'd done all I could think to do about the note for the moment, I turned my attention to the two-pronged plan I'd made last night for Billie Jo Steam's parole hearing.

Reviewing my summary and plan again, with the benefit of a good night's sleep and proper nourishment, I could see no other avenues to pursue. Having taken on this project because I believed in it, I was now determined to win Billie Jo's release. My competitive spirit had kicked into high gear. The harder it seemed to free Billie Jo, the more I wanted to prove I could do it. I had to make a decision on tactics and stick with it, knowing I could be wrong and accepting the consequences of that choice. It was hard to accept the consequences of either choice when I knew those consequences could hurt Billie Jo and her family, but this was no time for timidity.

Going over the possible strategies again, I decided to pursue what had to be the one sure winner: her illness, and disregard the other issues that would only confuse the parole board and weaken our strongest argument. If only I knew what the one sure winner was, if I could just see the future. But predicting the future was one skill I'd never developed.

I reconsidered whether to further investigate the Trey Steam murder itself. Whether or not Billie Jo had killed Trey Steam had been so thoroughly explored in prior proceedings that such a focus would result in certain defeat, once again. Our only hope lay in completely ignoring the facts of the murder and focusing on Billie Jo's medical condition. We needed to make a case for humanitarian clemency.

Ursula Westfield and Billie Jo Steam wanted to tell the story of the innocent woman wrongly convicted and held until near death in prison. But a more tactical approach was the only one I believed would win the day. Lawyers hope for the best and plan for the worst. So that's what I did. I reconfirmed my decision to follow the compromise I'd reached with myself last night. I'd pursue the weaker issue of potential DNA evidence only to appease Billie Jo and Ursula.

If DNA cleared Billie Jo, great. If not, I'd also prepare the stronger, more likely to succeed, humanitarian angle. That way, we would have a solid argument to present to the parole board regardless of how the DNA issue played out. Time was running short and I did have a full-time job to do.

Doing one more task that wasn't in my job description, I picked up the telephone and began making the necessary calls to schedule Billie Jo's medical examination. It took only a brief conversation to hit the very brick wall we were up against.

After half a dozen more calls, and pulling in a few favors, I found a colon specialist who would agree to do the test. Next, I had to figure out how to get Billie Jo to the doctor.

The prison system wouldn't pay for Billie Jo's exam, which wasn't a big problem, since Harris would. A bigger problem was that they wouldn't agree to let Billie Jo out of prison to go to a local hospital for the necessary colonoscopy to confirm the diagnosis.

I didn't realize how difficult it would be to get a prisoner to an independent medical facility because prison doctors were already paid by the state to do whatever medical work the state deemed necessary. Eventually, after more telephone calls than I could count, I managed to get the Florida Department of Corrections to agree to the procedure only after a United States district court judge promised that Billie Jo Steam would be uneventfully returned to prison immediately afterward.

After all the permissions were obtained and the test was scheduled, I turned my attention to the second, less probable, item on my list.

DNA evidence. It's frightening, really. DNA can sometimes prove guilt beyond a reasonable doubt, such as proving the identity of a rapist. Somewhat more easily, DNA can prove innocence by excluding a particular suspect because the DNA doesn't match. Sometimes. When Billie Jo Steam was convicted, no DNA technology had been available. She was convicted without DNA, the way many defendants are convicted, based on circumstantial evidence. When O.J. Simpson was found not guilty, which is another thing entirely from innocent, a mountain of DNA evidence was not enough to convict him. Go figure.

In Billie Jo's case, though, I thought she might have finally caught a break since her last appeal. The State of Florida had recently agreed to consider DNA evidence in the case of every death row inmate where such evidence was available. The larger, philosophical point of the decision was to free the innocent and stop the slaughter of the wrongly convicted. Over 130 cases so far, across the country. Sadly, in some cases where DNA evidence remained available, it did prove innocent people had been convicted. This was enough to shake everyone's faith in our judicial system and for us to continue to bend over backwards to fix its flaws. Even on behalf of those who literally get away with murder.

The smaller point of the new law was to stop the endless appeals by those who claimed to be innocent, but truly were guilty of the crimes for which they had been charged. Either way, making DNA testing available for evidence that remained in existence could have been a gift for Billie Jo, but a lot of "ifs" had to be resolved first.

When I reviewed her file, I learned that the knife with which Trey Steam had been stabbed was, of course, taken into custody. It was admitted as physical evidence at the trial. This long after trial, all evidence actually admitted would normally have been destroyed. While the knife was a potential source of DNA evidence, it was probably not still in existence.

At the time of the investigation, the police had collected Trey Steam's bloody clothes. They had taken blood samples from the body and compared the blood types to Billie Jo's.

The records revealed that Trey Steam had been an organ donor, too. Given the nature of the stab wounds to the middle of his body where his major organs were located, and how long the body went undiscovered, the only things left to donate must have been the eyes. For some reason, none of that evidence had been admitted at trial, although the medical examiner had testified to his findings.

In one of the quirks of Florida procedure, physical evidence not admitted at the trial might still exist. I made a note to check to see if the evidence existed, was currently in storage, and, if so, to get it tested.

The last item on my e-mail to myself was controversial and I'd wrestled with it since it first occurred to me. The reason I'd been chosen was because Ursula, Billie Jo, and Harris Steam felt I had influence that could be used toward a positive purpose.

Initially, I felt the law should run its course and set Billie Jo free as a matter of justice. But after the thorough file review I'd done, I now believed that expediency and influence had put Billie Jo behind bars in 1972 and kept her there. The length of her unsuccessful appeal and clemency history told me that legal maneuvering would not get her released.

Under these circumstances, was it wrong to level the playing field? Should I use what influence I had to help Billie Jo? That was the question I'd asked myself, over and over.

Billie Jo Steam should be released from prison if she was truly dying of cancer. It was the humane result. Even if she did kill her husband? Did she kill him, or not? Although I'd read the file carefully, several times now, I still wasn't sure. But I felt that it was no longer in the interest of justice to keep her incarcerated.

The courts that had considered her appeals and motions over the years had used the law as a shield to keep Billie Jo from reopening a closed case. No appellate court had ever said that Billie Jo was guilty. To be fair, neither had a court ever indicated any doubt about her guilt. But the cases read like a text book on the finality of judgments, not like a well-reasoned analysis of the facts and the evidence in an effort to do justice.

Looking under the rock of influence, I'd found some creepy crawly things. Billie Jo's trial was short, the witnesses' testimony dry, and the evidence presented pointed only to the defendant. But what was the other evidence? What other suspects had been investigated? Then, as now, Bill Steam and his brother-in-law Prescott Roberts wielded significant clout in Tampa. They could get the state attorney elected or defeated. Judges, too, for that matter. If Steam and Roberts believed Billie Jo killed Trey and they had enhanced the evidence pointing to her guilt, could we be sure that Billie Jo had gotten a fair trial?

And yet, a new trial wouldn't do Billie Jo any good now. If she was truly dying, she didn't have time for a new trial, either. Beyond that, without new evidence, the result would be the same. Even assuming we could find DNA evidence, it was unlikely to conclusively establish her innocence.

None of these things justified bending the law. But who you know and who you are makes a difference. If Billie Jo had been the daughter of an influential man, would she have even been charged with murder, let alone convicted? Maybe not. Or, at least she would have had a more even contest.

Arguing with myself was getting me nowhere. I simply didn't know what to do. I put the files aside, hoping tomorrow would bring inspiration.

Working long hours and then toiling over Billie Jo Steam's predicament was affecting me in unexpected ways. Always before, when faced with my unending workload, I would have put my nose to the grindstone, shoulder to the wheel, burned the midnight oil, and all those other clichés, to dig myself out of whatever hole I'd gotten into.

Since my visit to the prison, though, and my exposure to Billie Jo's restricted life, I found myself taking every possible chance to be outside, spend time with my husband and my dogs, be with nature whenever possible.

I managed to leave the office by six-thirty and made it home about half an hour later. Normally my commute is a ten-minute drive, during which I try, usually unsuccessfully, to leave my cares at the office in the rush home. More often, I do the drive on autopilot and arrive in front of my house with no awareness of how I got there.

Today, I sauntered to Greta, new tires in place, parked saucily across two spaces in the garage attached to the courthouse. I walked all the way around the car and assured myself that she was fine. People tell me that Greta's much too flashy for a judge to drive. But, how could I give her up for a mere job? I put Greta's top down, and she and I spent a while driving the length of the Bayshore, thrice, enjoying the wind in my hair, the sunshine baking my skin, and taking in the fabulous view of my hometown.

I drive the length of the Bayshore every day, but I never see it. I pay attention to the cars, of course. But what I mean is, until this afternoon, I hadn't noticed the new building that's gone up at the corner of Bay-to-Bay and Bayshore. The bank for wealthy customers they'd put there looked prosperous. I hadn't noticed the new metal sculptures in the median or that someone had finally moved into that giant home that looked like a Mediterranean hotel at the corner of Albany and Bayshore. When had this all happened? It could have been years ago for all I knew. The realization startled me.

I drove from downtown west to Gandy and then back east to Franklin Street, under the convention center, and then west again on Brorien. All the while, I looked at everything. Noticed the joggers, the cyclists, and roller bladers. Watched dads push jogging strollers, seniors chat in pairs, and twenty-somethings flirt with each other. I drank it all in. Smelled it. Savored the view.

On the fourth circle, I was about to turn onto the bridge from Gandy Boulevard to Plant Key when I changed my mind and headed back toward Hyde Park, the area of south Tampa that was a little run-down when the Six Bills were in college at UT and is now an upscale historic district. I turned north onto Rome Avenue and headed toward Old Hyde Park Village, but at West Morrison, I turned left.

I passed the renovated Kate Jackson Park and turned right onto South Packwood Avenue, one of the residential streets that has remained mostly undisturbed by the gentrification of the area.

I have a quirky memory for numbers. For some reason, they stick in my head as if they'd been burned to my internal hard drive. I remembered the address. South Packwood consisted of a short three blocks from Morrison to Swann. In the 700 block, on the east side of the street, the dreary little white clapboard house where Trey Steam died still stood. I parked Greta near the curb and walked over to the sidewalk.

The house was white with green shutters and a small screened porch on the front. Three cement steps, bordered on each side by a cement block wall painted green, led from the side-walk to the front door.

It needed a good coat of paint and the yard was mostly dirt. In this area where home improvement had run amok, the house looked old-fashioned and worn down.

At first I didn't see the elderly woman sitting in the shadows on the screen porch. I probably wouldn't have noticed her at all, except that she called out to me. "Hey," she said, in the quintessential southern greeting. She was tiny and frail and she had probably been talking to passersby from this porch for most of her life. She'd consider herself rude to ignore me, since I was unwittingly staring right at her.

"Hello," I called back, friendly. "I'm Willa Carson and I live nearby," I told her.

"Nice to meet you, Miz Carson," she said. "Would you like to come up and set a spell?" She reached over with a gnarled hand and picked up a small baby food jar, removed its lid, and spit a dark stream into it. She wiped her mouth with a lace handkerchief and returned the jar to the table.

"Thank you, I will." I opened the creaky screen door and entered the porch. She waved me to another rocker next to hers.

"I'm Turah Masters," she told me. "Folks call me Big Turry." She was no bigger than a twelve-year-old child. The years had bent her spine into what must have been a painful "S"-curve and she had trouble looking up. Thick glasses too big for her small face magnified her bright eyes. I smiled at her and sat down so that we'd be closer to eye level to one another.

"How long have you lived here, Mrs. Masters?"

"Long time, I guess. My mama owned this house when I was a girl. She used to rent it to college students, but after my husband died, I moved back here. My daughter will be along in a few minutes to bring my supper. I'd offer you some iced tea if you'd go get it out of the refrigerator." Turah Masters was the kind of old woman I didn't run into very often. She was probably ninety years old and she'd lived in Tampa all her life. In her day, neighbors dropped by unexpectedly and stayed to visit. A hostess was expected to offer her home and share her food unrestrictedly.

"I'd be glad to," I said, taking the opportunity to go inside the house.

There was a time when Big Turry would have known everyone who happened to walk by. Still, I thought I'd suggest to her daughter that she keep the old woman from inviting perfect strangers into her house. Tampa has a small-town feel, but it's a big city. Bad things can happen to old ladies who invite strangers into their homes here, the same as everywhere else, I would warn her.

Inside, the living room was small and dark and looked as if it hadn't been redecorated since 1972 when Trey Steam died here. A built-in bookcase was the only separation between the living room and the old-fashioned kitchen. The kitchen sink had a window above it that offered a view to the tiny backyard. The pine cabinets were unpainted and the kitchen was nearly as dark as the living room. The refrigerator was on the left. If Trey had his head in it or was looking out the kitchen window, Billie Jo could have walked from the hallway through the living room and out the front door without him seeing her, just as she testified at her trial.

I wanted to walk down the hallway and look in the bedrooms, but I thought that would be inappropriate, so I just craned my neck in that direction as I carried the glass of iced tea to Mrs. Masters. She accepted it gratefully and took a big gulp of the sweetened liquid. I thought then that she might have had trouble doing the small task for herself, which was why she asked me to come inside.

"I saw you looking at my house from the street," she said to me when she'd swallowed the tea. "It's not for sale, you know. Not 'til I die, anyway." She spit again into the baby food jar. I saw the can of snuff sitting next to the jar and figured out she was dipping. How she managed to dip snuff and drink iced tea simultaneously was a mystery. "All these houses along here used to belong to my friends. They're all dead now."

"Actually, I was interested in the house because of something that happened here a long time ago," I told her.

"The murder, you mean."

"Yes, ma'am."

"That was sure a tragedy, all right. I felt sorry for that little boy. That's why I'm living in this house now. We couldn't rent it after that. Nobody wanted to live in a house where a murder happened. Couldn't get the blood stains out of the floor, either." She gave me a pretty sharp glance then. She was frail, but she seemed to have full possession of her mental faculties. "Why are you so interested?"

So I told her I was trying to help Billie Jo Steam, the woman accused of the murder and I'd just wanted to get a look at the house. "Go on in and look around, then," she offered.

This time, I walked down the short, narrow hallway and looked into the two bedrooms. They were right next to each other, their doorways on opposite ends of the hallway and the bathroom across. I walked into the larger of the two rooms and listened to see if there was anything I could hear.

The walls were pretty thin, and the street noises were audible. I heard two men talking as they walked by on the sidewalk outside. Billie Jo could have heard Trey arguing with someone out in the driveway, as she'd testified.

I walked quickly from the master bedroom to the even smaller bedroom next to it, which would have been the child's room. Billie Jo could have gathered him up quickly and then turned to make her way out the front door. Once she worked up the courage to take the chance, it wouldn't have taken her long to make the dash.

I walked the distance from the master bedroom to Harris's room and out to the front door in less than thirty seconds, but I was taller than Billie Jo, so it probably took her a few seconds longer. Big Turry showed no interest in me when I walked out to the screen porch and returned to the living room.

Trey, if he'd turned from the kitchen window, would have had a clear view of Billie Jo when she came back for her purse. Even intoxicated, he could have managed the few steps he'd taken to reach her, easily. She was nimble, and he was drunk, but he might have made the connection anyway. Why he had the knife in his hand and why they'd struggled over it, I couldn't discern. But I could see how he might have fallen, given his intoxication and her desire to be gone quickly.

An oval, braided area rug covered the center of the living room. I rolled it up to look at the bloodstains that remained on the old pine floor Mrs. Masters had mentioned.

A large dark area covered much of the floor, but without moving the furniture, I couldn't get a clear picture of whether the blood had been splattered or just pooled in one place. I'd never seen any crime scene photographs, so I had to simply use my imagination based on the testimony. This was another one of those instances where a picture would have been worth a thousand words.

Billie Jo's testimony was that she found Trey in the same location as she'd left him when she ran away. The knife was on the floor beside him. Would she have looked to see exactly how and where he landed when he first fell? I thought not. She'd been afraid, she had already put her child out in the car. No. She'd have left quickly after he fell and she couldn't have known how and where he landed or if he'd gotten up again.

The kitchen floor was covered with old-fashioned linoleum that had been cleaned many times in the past three decades. Worn spots on the floor in front of the sink, the stove, and the refrigerator reflected its age. There was no way to tell now whether Trey Steam had moved around or lost blood in the kitchen. I looked at the floors in the bedrooms, but they were covered with wall-to-wall carpet now.

The other thing I noticed was how dark it was inside the house. There were few windows and the walls in all of the rooms were covered in dark paneling. There was no overhead lighting.

Billie Jo said the room's only lamp broke when Trey bumped into it before she tried to leave that night. She wouldn't have been able to see him clearly in the dim light that reached the living room from the kitchen.

Even now, the house gave me a creepy feeling. I could understand why no one had wanted to rent it after the murder.

When I heard Big Turry talking to someone else out on the porch, I thought I had probably learned all that I could for now. It helped to get the feel of the place, even though much had changed. I returned to the porch and met the daughter. I said goodbye to Big Turry and thanked her for the view of her house.

"Come back anytime," she said as I left her. "I don't get very many visitors." *No*, I thought. *People who still have elderly rela-*

tives are too busy to visit them these days.

When I arrived home at Minaret, cars in the parking lot reflected the dinner hour in full swing. I wanted to freshen up, as they say in old movies, so I took the back stairs two at a time, letting myself in the back door. I called downstairs and asked the hostess to let George know that I had arrived home and would join him for dinner at eight o'clock.

When we remodeled Aunt Minnie's house, we replaced the plumbing, doubling the size of the old master bathroom, but kept her wonderful, old claw-footed tub. I turned on the water, and filled the tub with an aromatic bubble bath Kate had assured me would restore peace and tranquility. I put my favorite Bob James CD in the player and lit several candles. An inflated bath pillow, a glass of sturdy cabernet, and a quiet soak to wash away the aura of death from my skin.

An hour later, when I joined George downstairs, I looked and felt like a new woman. I had chosen a long, slim, emerald silk dress that could be worn without panty hose, which I am convinced were the invention of Ivan the Terrible, the misogynist. On my feet, I wore flat, strappy sandals. Simple silver jewelry completed the outfit. I felt almost human again.

I waited in the dining room for George to join me. My evening had reminded me of a lesson I'd learned when my mother died: Life is short. Some people learn this lesson long after the age of sixteen. But learning early is a gift, too.

If Billie Jo Steam did indeed have terminal cancer, she should be released from prison. It was as simple as that. For her last days on earth, she should be able to do the things I had done this evening. I'd decided not to tell George about the notes, or the tires. For now. He'd only drive me crazy with overprotectiveness and insist that I give up Billie Jo's case. That, I would not do, so why even argue about it? Besides that, I needed to butter him up. My final deed for the day was to get my politically well-connected husband to do me a big favor.

George is an active and influential Republican. He is very close to the chairman of the Republican Party here in Florida, the fourth largest state in the union. George doesn't hold any office in the party, but only because he doesn't want to. Which is to say George is a very highly placed Republican, even if most voters have never heard of him. And that meant I might be able to manage a visit to the governor's office. I would attempt to persuade the governor that Billie Jo Steam should be granted clemency. Or at least, I might get George to invite him to our home for dinner, where I could present the issue for discussion.

Chapter Eleven

When I took the morning recess the next day and Augustus handed me the pink telephone message slips, I was shocked to see the one right on the top. "When did he call?" I asked.

"About an hour ago." Augustus repeated to me what he'd already written on the message slip. "He said he'd be here at the recess. He's waiting now."

I closed the door to my office so that I could look at myself in the small mirror I kept posted there. I'd taken the time this morning to put on lipstick, which was now all chewed off, but I hadn't done much else to make myself presentable. Comfort was one thing, but the grunge look is not the image I try to project nor the armor I needed now. I rummaged around in my desk drawer for the small cosmetics case I kept there and hurriedly put on my face. I fluffed up my short auburn hair with my hands as best I could and added a quick swipe of lipstick again. There wasn't much I could do about my clothes and I rejected the idea of putting my robe back on to cover up my habitual casual attire.

This was the best I could do on five minutes' notice. I then pushed the intercom button and told Augustus to show Prescott Roberts into my chambers.

Prescott Roberts had never, ever been to my courtroom before. He had no legitimate reason to be here now. Prescott had been a transactional lawyer, back in the days when he actually practiced law. He was a deal maker, not a litigator. Prescott Roberts thought judges and trial lawyers were bit players in the real world of business. And not very impressive bit players, at that. To Prescott Roberts, and men like him, we judges were mere public servants. Which was why he hadn't interfered with my appointment to the bench. He thought it was a position from which I could do no significant harm.

Augustus ushered in a tall man, albeit bent with advancing age. Prescott Roberts must have been physically imposing in his youth. Now, he was imposing in more dangerous ways. He was the kind of man who could get things done. For the first time, I wondered if he had been behind the attempts to scare me off this case. Since those attempts hadn't worked, was that why he was here now?

Prescott was born to an influential family and had had decades to accumulate more power. He came from money, married money, and made money. He was not a man to cross. We exchanged pleasantries and then I waited for Prescott to make the first move.

Prescott examined my dreary chambers in this second-class building and me, the judge who presided here, as if we were mildly amusing curiosities. Eventually, he spoke directly to the point. "Walter tells me that you have decided to ignore your ethical responsibilities to get Billie Jo Steam out of prison. Unethical conduct isn't the kind of good behavior the constitution protects."

He referred to Article III of the U.S. Constitution, which gave me a lifetime appointment only during good behavior. In the absence of an opponent with significant political clout, that would mean that I could do just about anything and still keep my job. But a man like Prescott Roberts, who had put more than half of the elected officials in Florida where they are today, had the political pull to get rid of me faster than a bull gator devours a small child.

"I've decided to work with a group that's trying to help her," I told him, holding my hands clasped in front of me on the desk. "I don't think there's a breach of ethics in my doing so."

"Perhaps," he said, as if I'd just made the most blatantly stupid statement of my life. Prescott Roberts's view was that he was the arbiter of good behavior and if he said my conduct didn't suffice, he'd have no trouble convincing the right people that he was right and I was wrong. "I'd like you to stop working on this project."

The literal words might have been a request, but spoken, they were most definitely an order from a man used to being obeyed. He wasn't threatening me. He didn't have to. He had the clout to convince the Justice Department to follow through on his complaints. Visions of an embarrassing televised impeachment hearing and subsequent trial forced their way into my head. Even if he was unsuccessful, the entire process would ruin my reputation. I'd be forced to resign to avoid the disgrace.

Perhaps I should have been brushing up my résumé, but he'd gotten my back up with his condescending attitude. "Why?" I asked, knowing that no one had dared question Prescott Roberts in more years than I'd been alive. I'd already made up my mind. I wouldn't back down now. Billie Jo and Harris were depending on me. Besides, Prescott's mere presence here in my chambers convinced me that I was onto something. Just exactly what I was onto, I didn't know.

Prescott looked quizzical, as if the answer was obvious. He'd made the request, his look seemed to say. What more reason could I possibly need? "You're aware that the woman killed my nephew," he said, by way of steely response.

"She says she's innocent." I held my voice steady. Unlike the C.J., if Prescott Roberts wanted me fired and run out of town on a rail, he'd have no trouble making that happen. He'd been consulted and had agreed to allow my appointment to this position. He had the wherewithal to get rid of me. He knew it, and so did I.

Loathe to explain himself to me, he said, "She's far from innocent. Billie Jo Steam was properly convicted and she belongs in jail. Leave her there." This time, both of us absolutely understood that he was ordering me to cease and desist my efforts to free Billie Jo. And I considered it. Seriously. While I might not want to be a federal judge forever, I preferred to choose my own departure date. But the specter of Billie Jo dying in prison that had haunted me in my dream was still too real. I couldn't let that happen.

"What about Harris? He's the one who asked me to help his

mother. Do you want me to just ignore his request?" I thought he might have some affection for his grandnephew that would keep him from squashing me and my career like a tiny bug.

"We've been looking after Harris since he was a child." He said "we" as if he were the king of England. "Harris doesn't know what's best for him. Or best for his children. Nor does he need you to help him with anything." And Prescott Roberts not only knew what was best for all of us, he could take care of whatever needed to be done as well, was the unspoken message.

Prescott rose from the ugly green client chair and now towered over me at my desk. To even the playing field, I rose to see him out. At the door, he turned to me and said, "I'll take it personally if you refuse my request, Judge Carson."

Fortunately, before I could respond, he turned and walked out, closing the door softly behind him. Neither one of us was confused by his meaning. If I hadn't had powerful enemies before, I was certainly in a position to acquire one now. What had I gotten myself into?

I returned to the bench and finished out the trial day, replaying Prescott Roberts's visit in my mind until I had memorized the dialogue. I struggled with myself for a while over whether I should bow out of Billie Jo's life. Until the visceral memory of his hulking presence faded.

Who did he think he was, anyway? Washed-up old has-been threatening a United States district court judge? The man was wrong. That's all. He didn't know the truth. He couldn't threaten me and get away with it, I told myself with bravado. The plans I'd made for Billie Jo's hearing would march forward. I had been given the chance to change the catastrophic outcome of Billie Jo's death shown to me in what I now thought of as a vision more than a nightmare. It was a path I had to take.

I had set all of the necessary wheels in motion and now events had to play themselves out while I turned my attention to my own work and tried to push uneasy thoughts about Prescott Roberts and his agenda to the back of my mind.

Days stretched into weeks, during which I presided over the *Madison v. Cardio Medical* case and attended to the other aspects of my life, everything that normally overflowed the boundaries of the twenty-four hours I'd been allotted each day without the added work of trying to help Billie Jo.

Augustus was working out better than I had ever hoped. In the few short weeks since he'd been with me, he'd become indispensable. I liked him immensely, and I tried not to worry about his relationship with Leo and his inside knowledge of Walter Westfield's temper, or how he'd come to me when the C.J. had been trying to sabotage my selection for so long. I couldn't really imagine Augustus as sinister, so I tried to expect the best.

I thought about the upcoming parole hearing frequently and checked on the progress of the work I'd delegated, but things were moving slowly. Although I tried, every day, there was little I could do to speed them along.

Several snafus had occurred in getting Billie Jo's medical tests performed. I'd tried to smooth over the problems and work around the red tape, to no avail. Billie Jo had never mentioned any medical problems of any kind to the prison system's doctors, so the administration was skeptical of her claimed symptoms now. They'd seen inmates try every possible ploy to evade serving prison time, and they refused to cooperate with our requests at every juncture. Working around their objections took too much time, and I sensed the hand of Prescott Roberts working against me. But maybe I was just being paranoid.

Even using my contacts and Harris's money, we weren't coming any closer to what I believed would be the key to opening Billie Jo's prison cell: a positive terminal-cancer diagnosis. Because of the system's opposition, I couldn't get her examined to confirm it. The irony of hoping Billie Jo had a terminal illness so I could save the rest of her life wasn't lost on me.

The search for DNA evidence from Trey Steam's murder was moving slower than a visit to the endodontist. Harris had talked with his grandparents, who told him that none of Trey's personal effects had been returned to them at the time of the original investigation or after Billie Jo's trial.

Theoretically, that meant the evidence should be in the evidence room of the Tampa Police Department. But thirty years is a long time to hold on to old, blood-soaked clothes. And TPD had moved, more than once, in the meantime.

In addition, searching for questionably relevant thirty-year-old evidence wasn't a high priority, with all the TPD had to do every day. The short of it was that if any evidence that could be tested for DNA still existed, no one had been able to find it and our time was running out.

Less than a week before the parole hearing, I found myself at square one with Billie Jo's case. George hadn't been able to arrange a talk with the governor; Billie Jo's medical exam hadn't been done because I couldn't get around the prison system's red tape; and no DNA evidence had been found, let alone tested. I suspected Prescott Roberts was working to thwart me at every turn, but I hadn't seen or heard from him since his visit to my chambers weeks before. Chief Hathaway had not been able to find a suspect to attach to the threats I'd received. Nor had I received any more. It was almost as if the perpetrator had resigned himself to my activities. Which made me wonder what he knew that I didn't.

Yet, Ursula Westfield had done her part. Due to her involvement, the station had been airing teasers on the nightly news about Billie Jo's impending release and the Billie Jo Steam story. I had made a couple of "the system works"-type sound bites, meant to represent the "experienced judge" angle, without publicly revealing my personal commitment to Billie Jo or involvement in her parole efforts.

After the first one aired, the C.J. came down like a ton of

bricks on my voice mail. I erased his tirade while crossing my fingers and giving thanks that I hadn't answered the telephone.

Every day, as I sat at my desk and looked at my month-at-a-glance calendar, I was reminded of the clock ticking and moving us closer to the date set for Billie Jo's hearing. And every day, I was more aware that I had absolutely nothing to offer to free Billie Jo that hadn't been tried, and failed, before.

Too soon, I realized I had just four days left, and my anger at my own impotence kicked in. Nothing ever got done unless I did it, I fumed to myself. Flush with fear of failure and public humiliation, and tired of butting my head up against the bureaucratic wall, I turned purposefully to my telephone and started with the man over whom I have the most influence.

"George, when is the governor coming to dinner?" I challenged abruptly when my husband answered the phone.

George said the only thing that would get him off the hook. "Tomorrow night. Shall we have squab?" He named one of my favorite fowl in a further attempt to butter me up.

I said, "Great," and hung up, moving on to the next uncooperative male on my list.

I usually avoid calling Tampa Police chief Ben Hathaway on business, particularly when I'm sticking my nose into his. Ben is an uneasy friend of ours, depending on whether I'm involved in his departmental affairs or not. When I'm trying to get him to do his job my way, he gets more than a little bit miffed. Ben is a very professional cop, and his department generally does excellent work. But nobody's perfect. Ben could use a fresh eye once in a while. Naturally, he doesn't always see my help that way.

Now, I had no choice but to cajole Ben to action. The new statutes and court rules that governed Billie Jo's case said that DNA evidence from old crimes had to be analyzed by current police procedures. Once again, we were running short on time and long on the need for what were essentially favors. The list of Florida inmates waiting for DNA analysis was longer than the list of Fernandezes in the Tampa phone book. Sometimes, the wait takes months. Billie Jo didn't have months. We had four days. Ben could push the search for physical evidence and rush the DNA analysis. I went to see him personally.

The distance from my courtroom to the Sun Trust Building, or what is colloquially known as the Cop Shop, was a few short blocks. Ben Hathaway's office had been relocated there from the old police station on Tampa Street, a longer walk in the other direction. The former location had about as much aesthetic appeal as an abandoned warehouse. TPD's new building had been a bank at one time, so it had marginally more style, except that the bright blue facade was startling. I took advantage of the brief cold front that kept our temperatures around seventy-five in the morning hours, and walked.

Once or twice, I had the creepy feeling that someone was following me. But when I looked back, I could see nothing unusual. My imagination was working overtime.

Chapter Twelve

The quick ride up to Chief Hathaway's office in the express elevator left my stomach behind somewhere about the third floor. I was a little woozy when I stepped off into the lobby of the Tampa Police Department's executive offices. The receptionist seemed surprised and skeptical when I told her my name and whom I'd come to visit. But she would have considered it impolite to challenge me. Impolite doesn't suit in Tampa. I haven't looked, but "being impolite" might actually be a felony here.

In a few minutes, Ben Hathaway himself came out to the lobby, his shirtsleeves rolled up, and with a big smile on his round jowls. He stuck out his beefy right paw to swallow mine, then bellowed his greeting to let everyone within hearing distance realize he was making nice with federal judge Carson. This bonhomie lasted about three seconds after we went into his office. Then he closed the door and moved his considerable bulk to his desk chair, which groaned in protest while he lowered his seventh of a ton into it. He kept the smile, because we could be seen through the glass walls that surrounded his desk. But, his tone was wary.

"What can I do for you, Willa?" he asked, coming right to the point, holding his clasped paws in front of him on the blotter.

"Why do you sound so hostile, Ben?" I chided him.

"You don't make social calls on the likes of me, Judge Carson. You come here when you want something for one of your pet projects that you have no right to ask. If you had a right to it, you'd just call me on the phone. When it's a favor you're after, you count on your considerable charm to get you what you want." I didn't bother to deny the obvious.

"Okay. So we understand each other then." I smiled, all the same. "Hey, I'm a taxpayer. I'm entitled to public service, too."

He nodded. "I take it you want something for your favorite project of the moment, Billie Jo Steam. Don't look so surprised. Ursula Westfield's already called me. Greased the way for you. Said we'd all be heroes when an innocent woman gets set free. I'm gonna help, so you don't have to sweet-talk me. You coulda just called. I'm on it."

"On what?"

"The DNA, what else?" He tried to convince me that he was still grumpy about the imposition. "Found Trey Steam's clothes and the murder weapon, too. No small job, let me tell you, with all the evidence we keep track of around here. No missing evidence in my department. No chance." His countenance dared me to contradict him.

"I'm thrilled to hear it, Ben. Maybe you could give our FBI some tips, hmmm? They lose things all the time." I smiled, trying to coax him into a better mood. After all, I was asking for a favor and he'd already told me he'd do it. I had no need to be discourteous.

"Ordered the DNA analysis last week and called about it again today. I hate to say it, but you were right. Here. I got this today." He handed me a slim piece of paper with lab results that even I could decipher. Trey Steam's bloody clothes had been analyzed. His shirt and jeans were soaked with a good deal of his own blood, but also the blood of someone else. Not Billie Jo.

The DNA analysis done on the murder weapon, too, showed Trey's own blood, of course, but also the blood of the same unknown person on the knife handle and blade. Again, not Billie Jo's blood. The DNA proved the blood belonged to a man.

Trey Steam's defensive wounds aside, he must have had possession of the knife at some time during the fight. From the evidence showing the amount of blood that wasn't his, Trey had done considerable damage to his killer.

The file I had reviewed included the investigating officer's notes. Billie Jo had had no cuts on her body anywhere when she was arrested.

"Where'd you get the samples to confirm that any of this blood actually belonged to Trey Steam?" I knew enough about DNA evidence to understand that comparisons were made to identified samples. Billie Jo had, of course, donated her blood for the test. Having a sample of bodily fluids from the long-since dead Trey Steam, himself, would have also been necessary to reach a definitive conclusion like this.

Ben smiled his canary-eating grin at me, the one he reserves for times when he knows he is absolutely in the catbird seat. "Trey Steam was an organ donor. When you donate, the organ banks take blood samples and freeze them. They keep the samples forever. We got a court order for a bit of Trey's frozen serum." He looked as if he were expecting a Nobel Prize for this piece of information. If I were on the committee, I'd have given it to him.

The only possible conclusion, to my way of thinking, was that this DNA analysis proved Billie Jo Steam had not murdered her husband. Some people would have thought she was justified in killing Trey Steam, from everything I'd heard and read. But she'd spent thirty years in prison for a crime she'd never committed at all. I smiled at Ben Hathaway. He came around his desk and shook my hand warmly this time, giving me a genuine grin of pleasure.

"How does it feel to be on the right side, Ben?" I asked him, smiling wide enough to show my ecstasy and resisting the urge to hug him. I didn't tell Ben that I had actually been wrong. I never believed DNA would prove Billie Jo's innocence. I'd had no faith in the effort. I was glad to be wrong, though it would remain my private joy. I wasn't going to humble myself to Ben Hathaway. I'd never hear the end of it.

"We're doing a good thing here," I told him. "This whole case has been a travesty. Thankfully, they didn't put her on death row all those years ago. Otherwise, she'd be dead now."

"True. But the evidence against her was strong at the time,

Willa," he said as he walked me out to the lobby. "Very strong."

"Too strong," I said, knowing that to a cop evidence was never too strong.

His reply was short and startling: "Give my regards to the governor." News travels fast in Tampa.

Although the city itself is lovely, dinner in Tallahassee isn't anything compared to George's. Which probably explains why the governor was more than willing to come down on his way to Miami later in the evening to a dinner catered by George's award-winning chefs. This was the first time in years we'd had dinner in our dining room upstairs. George had had the restaurant's cleaning people in all day, dusting, polishing, and washing the china. One of the waiters was coming up to put the food on the table. In many ways, I was looking forward to a quiet and private meal in our home. And I knew it would be edible, since I wasn't cooking it.

George's Aunt Minnie had been a kind soul with a more-than-colorful past. Minaret had been her home until she died and left it to us in her will, completely furnished. Although we loved living with her beautiful things, most of her furniture was as old and uncomfortable as the heating and plumbing had been. The only things we still used, and not regularly, were her table settings.

Tonight, the dining room's Waterford glass chandelier sparkled as it had not done in many months. Antique Irish lace linens and several full vases of flowers decorated the room. I was on cloud nine. I felt close to victory for Billie Jo Steam, and I was simply thrilled. All that was left were the details.

The governor arrived alone, fashionably late, and dressed in a business suit. I'd understood that he was on vacation, so his attire was somewhat surprising. George and I were underdressed.

But the governor is a kind man, more than a little attractive, who excelled at putting people at ease. In a few short moments, he made us feel comfortable as we stood on the veranda with our cocktails, discussing the weather and the Devil Rays. His height is something I'm not used to. Not many men tower over me. When we finally sat down to dinner, I could look him in the eye.

"Well, Willa, George tells me you have a special request to make," he said, enjoying the squab in lemon caper sauce.

"I appreciate your willingness to hear about this, Governor. I'm not used to requesting favors from anyone, let alone a highly placed politician." I looked over at George, who was staying out of the conversation, although he found nothing unusual in having a discussion with the governor.

"You're one of my constituents, Willa. If I can do anything for you, that's what you put me in office for. I hear these kinds of requests every day. I just don't usually hear them over fabulous food in wonderful surroundings." He smiled and the glint in his eyes was the one displayed on television. He was bright, charismatic, and as smooth as, well, a successful politician.

"Thank you, Governor," I began.

"Call me Jake," he interjected.

"Okay, Jake. My request isn't for me," I started again.

"I didn't think it would be. What could you possibly want that I would have the ability to give you? I assumed your request was being made on behalf of someone else." He was trying to make this easy for me, but I'm just not good at asking for favors. I've always taken care of myself, and everyone around me as well. People come to me for help, not the other way around.

I put down my fork, placed my hands in my lap, and began again. "I want you to release Billie Jo Steam, a woman serving a life sentence in prison for murdering her husband. She's up for parole, but she should be pardoned. The DNA evidence proves she didn't murder her husband. She was wrongly convicted in the first place. She's spent thirty years in prison for a crime she didn't commit and it's time to release her." This was the first time I'd actually said the phrases out loud, and I had put my case forth inarticulately. I'd need to practice.

He'd also set down his fork and he looked more troubled the longer I spoke. "Past time, I'd say, if all you tell me is true. How sure are you of your facts?"

"Very sure. It's my job to evaluate evidence and reach conclusions. If the evidence used to convict Billie Jo Steam had come before me in my courtroom, I would have dismissed any indictment brought against her and instructed the federal prosecutors to find the real killer," I told him, demonstrating, even to me, just how much conviction I had over Billie Jo's cause.

"What evidence do you have besides the DNA?" he surprised me by asking next.

"What evidence do you need besides the DNA?" I responded, a little hotly. "It's the best evidence that she didn't commit the crime. Why is anything else necessary?"

He continued his easy, conversational argument. He wasn't emotionally involved with this decision. "I've looked at this case a little bit, Willa," he grinned. "We get the news up in Tallahassee, too, you know. Nobody is interested in keeping innocent people in jail. The state attorney might consent to a motion to dismiss based on this evidence if you asked him," he suggested.

Not if Prescott Roberts got wind of it, I knew. Prescott's visit to my chambers and all the trouble I'd had getting her medical exam told me that his influence was one of the things that had kept Billie Jo's prior attempts at freedom from succeeding. "I know he might, but if the parole board will just do the right thing, it'll be faster and easier to get Billie Jo released," I told him. "Her hearing is in three days. I couldn't get the state's attorney on board that quickly."

Again, he looked thoughtful. "Even if she didn't stab her husband to death herself, she could have been involved. She admitted that she and Trey struggled and he fell while holding the knife. That kind of admission muddies the water, doesn't it? She could have hired a killer, or maybe a quarrel between two men over her, where she was the instigator. In other words, she could have been the killer, or an accomplice, even though she didn't stab the man to death. Are you sure she's innocent? That's all I'm asking." The question was a reasonable one.

"I'm sure she wasn't charged and convicted as a conspirator. The theory that sent her to prison was her hand on the murder weapon. We know that wasn't true. Whether she might have been guilty of some other crime was never proved. But if she wasn't the actual killer, she'd have been given a lighter sentence, which she has surely served by now." My conclusion was equally as reasonable as his.

And that would be enough to get her released at her upcoming parole hearing. I'm not sure it's enough for a pardon, though." He looked over at George, and then continued to eat his dinner, as he changed the subject, or seemed to. "You both know I'm going to have a reelection fight on my hands soon. I need to watch the decisions I make more closely than ever in the next few months. What I'd like to propose to you, Willa, if it's acceptable, is a compromise."

He looked to George to intercede, but George remained wisely silent. The governor would be leaving after dinner but George would stay to sleep in my bed. George is a very practical man sometimes.

"What compromise did you have in mind?" I asked.

"What if we let the parole hearing proceed as it normally would," he suggested, looking at me again with all the sincerity that kept him employed. "You'll present your newly discovered evidence and I suspect Billie Jo Steam will be released. Especially if you can get the deceased's parents to publicly agree to the parole at the hearing. The victim's family is persuasive in these matters, you know. The process can be served; the public will feel that everyone gets the same fair shake; and Billie Jo Steam will be out of jail in thirty days or less." He wrapped it up like a present with a bow on top.

"And if they don't let her go? It won't help anyone if Billie Jo

Steam becomes another Elvin Edwards," I said, naming a Florida death row inmate who died of cancer in prison, just days before DNA evidence definitively proved his innocence. The prosecutors had blocked Edwards's attempts to obtain DNA evidence that would exonerate him. This governor had refused to release him. When the DNA had conclusively proved Edwards was innocent of rape and murder, he was already dead. The entire Florida justice system was still reeling from the black eye the case had given us. No one, most of all the governor, wanted a repeat of the experience.

"Then you have my word that I'll step in and take care of it," he said, looking at George with meaning in his glance. I knew the governor was doing me a favor that was being traded for other favors. And these favors weren't my primary consideration. My problem was that I had become certain that Billie Jo Steam had unjustly spent the last thirty years of her life in a place where I couldn't spend thirty hours. It was time for everyone to do the right thing. Whatever George had to give the governor in return was an insignificant price to pay.

Chapter Thirteen

The time passed in a blur of activity as we rushed toward Billie Jo Steam's parole hearing three days hence. I adjourned the *Madison v. Cardio Medical* trial for a week. Since the case had started, the jurors had been entertained while the lawyers, who perceived themselves as gladiators, skewered one another in the ring, but no real progress was being made. I'd originally estimated a three-week trial, thinking the case would be finished before Billie Jo's hearing. Now, I feared this trial would last much longer. A week off would do everyone some good, I rationalized. No one objected to the idea.

Now, with new DNA evidence, I felt we needed a lawyer to appear at the parole hearing on Billie Jo's behalf. The case was a sure winner, the lawyer would have free publicity, and Harris would pay him well. I suggested that Harris hire Paul Robbins, the public defender who had represented Billie Jo at the original trial. Robbins had been there when Billie Jo was convicted and it appealed to my sense of justice that he should have his victory, albeit thirty years later.

I was mindful of the governor's caution that the DNA evidence didn't conclusively assure victory, but I put aside my attempts to get Billie Jo's medical tests done. I simply had no time to follow up with that project or get it completed now. I put all effort into the DNA argument.

I planned to attend the hearing, but to sit in the gallery with the other spectators. We scripted the arguments over long sessions in my chambers, assigning parts to Harris, Ben Hathaway, the new lawyer, and to Billie Jo herself. I would have no speaking part, until after the hearing.

I considered meeting with Bill and Mary Steam, but Harris said to leave that problem in his hands. He felt he could convince his grandparents not to come to the hearing and not to object to Billie Jo's parole, although they had done both at her two prior parole board hearings. My limited knowledge of Bill Steam had left me with the view that he was a flinty old bastard who would not likely change his mind. Since Mary Steam was Prescott Roberts's sister, I figured I could pretty well predict where Trey Steam's parents would come out on the question of Billie Jo's parole. But I had to rely on Harris for this important piece of Billie Jo's defense.

Ursula participated in our meetings, although she wasn't substantively helpful. She was putting the finishing touches on her story, so that she could air it the night of the parole hearing. She offered suggestions that were more related to the back-story of Trey Steam's murder, reciting aspects of Billie Jo's trial, conviction, and earlier attempts at release.

But Ursula was a master at crafting words into catchy sound bites and phrases that would ring with confidence and stay in the minds of listeners for days or weeks to come. We used every ounce of that expertise.

Augustus supplied refreshments, kept the phone and the e-mail quiet, and surprised us a few times with solid suggestions on strategy. He was quickly becoming indispensable to the effective operation of my office, and I gave appropriate thanks for him on a daily basis, while keeping my fingers crossed that my appreciation wasn't shortsighted.

George stayed in the background, running his restaurant and offering moral support. He had never fully embraced this project, but that was because his first concern is always for me. Especially because of Prescott Roberts's involvement, George felt I was putting my career and myself in jeopardy this time, for unnecessary reasons. Because he was right on all counts, I couldn't argue with him and I never told him about the threats. In my defense, the only thing I could offer was that saving those who are in over their heads is a compulsion I didn't really want to control, even if I could.

I'm a night owl, but when my alarm woke me at five-thirty that Friday morning, I was instantly awake and ready to go. I'd slept little for the past three days, but my lack of sleep didn't seem to matter. I wasn't the least bit tired and I felt more energized than I had in a very long time.

No federal judge I know had ever appeared at a parole hearing for any reason. This trip had the aura of the forbidden, an illicit quality that elevated my excitement. Whatever I did, there was bound to be someone who wouldn't approve. No matter. I'd given up trying to please all the people all the time long before. Sometimes, I just had to comply with my conscience and let the chips fall where they may. This was one of those times.

I selected a conservative, charcoal grey suit and daffodil silk blouse, the likes of which I hadn't worn since I was sworn in. Low-heeled pumps and pearls completed the outfit. A quick blast of the blow-dryer, five minutes with my makeup, and I was downstairs waiting in the still-dark morning, under the almost-full moon.

The limousine Harris sent to take me to Peter O'Knight Airport on Davis Islands arrived right after I'd finished my short prayer for success. The driver took me to join the rest of the party in the private jet Harris had chartered for the trip, while I focused on containing my anxiety.

Harris had ordered another limousine to meet us at our destination. We arrived about a half hour early for the ten o'clock hearing. An armed guard at the front door and police cruisers with lights flashing held back the gaggle of media. So many people rushed our car that the driver had to fight to get the doors open at the building entrance.

The airing of Ursula's news teasers over the past few weeks had worked the press into a frenzy. Billie Jo's saga had everything: celebrity; murder; and a beautiful, innocent woman. The story was too good to resist. Apparently, the reporters didn't know or didn't care that Ursula was using them to feed the material she mined from the past. Ursula called it "investigative reporting." Some would say Ursula had impermissibly created the story, orchestrating it like a Bach concerto.

Thankfully, Ben Hathaway and Harris Steam were with Billie Jo's former public defender, Paul Robbins and me in the car. All three of them were as formally dressed as I was. We looked quite a respectable bunch, in stark contrast to our bedraggled and worn appearance during our crunch-time preparation sessions.

Both Ben and Harris had called ahead and arranged security. Four armed bodyguards surrounded us as we ascended from the street, up the stairs, and into the boxy, uninspired government building that housed the parole board. I had had no experience dealing with suffocating crowds, since a federal judge doesn't usually generate much interest. I didn't count on the effect of being seen with a celebrity like Harris Steam or the frenzy Ursula had created. I was grateful for Ben Hathaway, our personal police escort. For the first time, I understood how a crowd of people could crush someone to death.

By the time we made it to the policemen at the door, Ben had his badge out. The posted officers held back the reporters and waved us forward into the building. We placed our briefcases on the X-ray conveyor and walked through the metal detectors empty handed while Ben allowed the security officers to check his handgun. Once we were in the lobby, we made our way to the tenth floor and into the hearing room.

Honestly, if you've been in one government building, you've been in them all. I sometimes wonder if the local, state, and federal governments conspire to buy this cheap metal furniture by the gross just to make us all feel either satisfied with their thrift or relaxed in the familiar presence of nondescript squalor. No wonder government buildings are defaced almost as soon as they are completed. They look low-rent from the outset.

The hearing room itself resembled every administrative

hearing room I'd ever been in. The basic setup was a table at the north end of the room and a second table facing the first one. Three metal folding-chairs waited behind the front table and two metal folding-chairs sat behind the facing table. Then, two rows of folding-chairs on either side of a small aisle were set up, theater fashion, for spectators in the gallery. Judging from the ten or so chairs for the audience, few people generally attended a parole hearing. Today, all of the spectator chairs were full. I found a seat in the back only after a gentleman rose to offer me his.

News media cameras were allowed inside the hearing room, although the room was small and not many people would fit. I noticed two or three photographers in the back. I didn't see Ursula or any reporter I recognized, but several of the other spectators had notepads.

Across the aisle from me sat a nondescript, middle-aged man. He would have been completely unremarkable, except that he was almost the only person in the gallery without a notepad. He made me nervous. The one thing we couldn't control was who acted as spectators. Interested parties could raise objections to Billie Jo's release. I fretted over who the man was and why he was here, until I noticed a bigger problem.

In the front row, on the right side of the aisle, sat Trey's parents, Bill and Mary Steam. They sat tall and straight, eyes facing forward, his arm around her shoulders. My heart sank. They could only be here to oppose Billie Jo's parole, as they had done at every previous parole hearing she'd had. Harris had promised to manage his grandparents. To keep them away. Obviously, he hadn't. Concern gnawed at my nerves. I half expected Prescott Roberts to walk in any minute.

Harris, the consummate performer, went over to his grandparents, hugged them, and thanked them for coming. The press eavesdropped shamelessly and wrote down what they heard. Billie Jo's lawyer approached the Steams and greeted them, too, smiling for the reporters. I mentally kicked myself for failing to anticipate and resolve this problem. If Bill Steam opposed Billie Jo's parole after the governor had told me to gain the family's support, we were sunk.

Delegating never works, although I didn't know what I could have said to keep Bill and Mary Steam at home. But I should have at least tried. As it was, I felt I'd let Billie Jo down on what might turn out to be the most important issue today.

Ben Hathaway went over to a uniformed bailiff who was standing in the corner and flashed his badge again. The bailiff soon returned with two more chairs for our team at the prisoner's table.

After a while, Billie Jo Steam was escorted into the room and led to her seat. Her hair was curly wild. She was dressed in her prison garb and wore no makeup. She looked old, tired, and sick, an appearance Ursula had orchestrated without my knowledge. I fumed. This entire matter was rapidly escalating out of my control and the uneasy sensation in my stomach spread.

Billie Jo and Harris hugged quickly, as if to avoid making a bigger spectacle of themselves than they already were. Billie Jo shook hands with her lawyer and then shook hands with Chief Hathaway, whom she was meeting for the first time. In a moment, she turned to look at Bill and Mary Steam. She didn't smile. Billie Jo had told me earlier that she was resigned to their hostility and opposition, but hoped for the best.

Billie Jo's eyes found me in the crowd and gave me a tentative smile that pierced my heart. Her smile said I had let her down, right at the time she needed me most. Trouble was, I agreed with her. By this time, I was convinced that Bill Steam would make sure Billie Jo died in prison. There was nothing more I could do.

Billie Jo's gaze slid past me and continued to scan the gallery, until it froze on the man seated across the aisle. When she found him, her face lit up like those of the Apostles in paintings of the Last Supper. The man returned her gaze with such hope and love that I was again shaken out of my complacency.

I'd spent a great deal of time with these people, put my professional reputation on the line, and compromised my safety to help. Yet, someone was here about whom I knew absolutely nothing at all. Who was this man? And how was he related to Billie Jo? I realized he was important—I just didn't know why. I had so much of myself at stake now that this vacuum of knowledge sucked out the last of my confidence. I'd gone from feelings of euphoria to the depths of anxiety and the hearing hadn't even started yet.

The three members of the parole board eventually entered and sat at the head table, facing us. A court reporter came in next with her steno machine, sat unobtrusively at the right-hand side of the head table, and prepared to take down every word that was said in the room.

The man chairing the parole board read the name of the case, which was *State of Florida v. Willetta Johnson Steam*, into the record and the reason for the hearing. He introduced the members of the board and then asked Billie Jo's lawyer to present his team. Of course, my name wasn't mentioned. Then, he asked Billie Jo's lawyer, Robbins, to report "any matters this board should take into consideration at this time, prior to making its decision on the prisoner's request for parole."

Paul Robbins only took about fifteen minutes to recite the argument we had agreed upon. I had asked him to read from a prepared statement, but he'd practiced it so many times, he knew it by heart. He made an impassioned plea, doing a good job of demonstrating his conviction and commitment to his cause.

He explained the newly discovered DNA evidence. He described the facts from the court files that corroborated the proof of Billie Jo's innocence. He disclosed Billie Jo's health status, even though we had never received any medical support for a diagnosis and, as he said, we'd been prevented from getting the medical evidence by the state's failure to cooperate. This was no time to hide whatever we had to offer.

Finally, Paul told the board, "Harris Steam, Billie Jo's son and the only living child of the deceased, wants his mother released from prison to spend what is left of her short life with him and the rest of her family."

Harris rose to give the prepared statement we'd worked out for him, stressing the wishes of the victim's family. "I am Trey Steam's son. I request that my mother be released and my two children, who are Trey Steam's only grandchildren, are waiting for their granny to come home."

I had a prepared text for Ben Hathaway and one for Billie Jo, too. They delivered their statements beautifully. Ben said he'd discovered the lost physical evidence and had it tested. Tearfully, Billie Jo expressed her innocence and desire to be released. I felt like a playwright. I'd written the words but I couldn't open my mouth, even once. I had to watch the actors in my drama and trust them to play their parts to perfection.

I was just beginning to breathe again, thinking we'd made it through our planned presentation without a major problem, when the board chair asked for comments from the spectators. I prayed that no one would want to make a comment. Bill Steam stood.

"Yes, sir?" the chairman asked. Bill and Mary Steam could undo everything we'd put before the board. Although I had the governor's word that he would issue a pardon if parole was denied, we couldn't rely on that promise should Trey Steam's parents oppose parole. Ursula's story would backfire. Billie Jo would stay in prison until her death if public opinion turned against us. The governor did, as he told me, have to stand for election soon. He needed public opinion, and the votes it represented, on his side. I held my breath as I waited for Bill Steam to deliver the killing blow to all of our hopes.

"I'm Trey Steam's father, Bill Steam. This is my wife, Mary," he said. He put his hand on Mary's shoulder. She bowed her head, hiding her face in a lace-embroidered handkerchief.

"For many years, I've been convinced that Billie Jo killed my boy. Now, I just don't know. I think my boy's killer might still be out there. But my wife and I want to say we're no longer against letting Billie Jo out of prison, if that's what Harris and you all think is right."

The reporters were writing furiously. I almost fainted with relief. My faith in Harris was restored. He'd done his job.

"Thank you, sir," the board chair said, as Bill Steam retook his seat. "Would anyone else like to speak?"

I looked at the man across the aisle, but he said nothing. I still had no idea who he was.

"If no other matters are to be brought to our attention, this hearing is concluded. The board will consider Willetta Johnson Steam's request for parole and render a decision within seven days. Thank you all for coming. This hearing is adjourned." The three members of the board left the room, followed by the court reporter, and then Billie Jo and her jailers.

That was it. Something I'd been working on for weeks was now, for all practical purposes, over, just like that. Paul Robbins, Harris, and Chief Hathaway turned around to weave through the gauntlet of media and join me at the back of the room for our retreat to the limousine.

As planned, we stopped at the top of the steps and took a few questions. Harris passed out copies of the prepared statements. Robbins repeated the sound bite we had all crafted, "Justice will be served when Billie Jo Steam is released and Trey Steam's real killer is arrested."

We fought our way to the waiting car, returned to the airport, and flew home. Everyone in the plane was quiet, spending time with his own thoughts. For my part, I focused on everything that had gone wrong, and hoped for the best.

Altogether, the entire event had taken the better part of the day. I was home in time for dinner and was able to watch the seven o'clock evening news. I settled into my den with my Sapphire and tonic, a fresh Partagas, both dogs, and George. If anything negative was going to be said about the day, or me, I had armed myself with all the support I could muster on short notice.

"This just in. The parole board today granted Willetta Johnson Steam's parole request after deliberating for only two hours. New evidence presented at today's hearing 'was persuasive and compelling' the board's written opinion stated."

In a state of shock, a quick and hearty "Yes!" tumbled out of my mouth followed by the release of laughter. I saw my face on the screen being interviewed after the hearing, giving my prepared sound bites. "I feel confident that the parole board will render a swift and just decision. Based on the evidence presented inside, Billie Jo Steam should be spending time with her grandchildren by this time next week." When I said that this afternoon, I'd been full of false bravado, hoping for the best and that a "swift decision" would come in about seven days. That they'd made the announcement today was astounding and very welcome news.

I tipped a toast to the newscaster and took another sip. George gave me a high five and the dogs, realizing something fabulous had just occurred, began to frolic around on the floor.

After my statement, the news show played quick statements from Paul Robbins, Harris, and Ben Hathaway. The advertisement for Ursula's *News This Week* report was replayed, along with a few of the teasers she'd been running for the past few weeks.

George's quick flip through the channels revealed the same story on all four of the major networks, and the same news was the lead on the cable stations. Shortly after that, the telephone began to ring.

PART TWO

THE ROAD TO HELL

Chapter Fourteen

The promise of new beginnings filled everyone with hope. Weeks ago Harris had rented George's restaurant for the big victory celebration. He told me then that he was visualizing success in our effort to free Billie Jo. Now, the day had arrived.

Guards were posted at the Bayshore side of the bridge to Plant Key, allowing people to enter only if their names were printed on the approved guest list. Based on the number of guests, I concluded that Harris had invited all of Tampa. People were everywhere. Wending my way through the crowds was nearly impossible. If Trey Steam's parents were present, I didn't see them.

Nor was Trey's powerful uncle, Prescott Roberts, anywhere to be found. *Thank God for small favors*, I thought. After Billie Jo was released from prison, I waited for Prescott's revenge to surface like waiting for the other shoe to drop. Whatever form his revenge would take, I had no doubt he'd follow through. I thought the anticipation was killing me, but maybe it was the weather.

The heat that had been slow to arrive in early May now enveloped us like a shroud. The flowers were wilted, and the party-goers didn't look a whole lot better. I felt my makeup sliding off my face like grease off a nonstick skillet, but I was helpless to stop it. I had no other option than to keep a frozen margarita constantly in my hand, and a good grip on my sense of humor. *This, too, shall pass*, my tranquil side soothed. *By October*, my snide self replied.

George had set up several bars inside Minaret's downstairs dining rooms and outside on the grounds of Plant Key. Buffets with food of all kinds were placed in the various rooms of the restaurant. Wandering waiters passed bite-sized pieces of everything from artichokes to zesty baked cheese paté on pita points.

113

The guests were dressed from grunge to haute couture, and much in-between. I noticed several rock musicians, a few lawyers and judges, and others involved in Billie Jo's release. Also there as guests were hundreds of people I had never seen before, and, with any luck, would likely never see again. A person shy of crowds, like Billie Jo, might have felt a high level of panic, turned and run. Even I felt a little edgy. The person who'd been threatening me was probably here, and I braced myself for unpleasantness.

Harris and George had arranged everything about this party. I wasn't consulted, and, from the way she looked, Billie Jo hadn't been either.

Harris and Billie Jo Steam were making the rounds like the bride and groom at a wedding reception. She held onto her son's hand with both of hers and shrank back behind him every time he approached a new conversation group with her in tow. After a short time, Billie Jo would manage to avoid peeking around her son's back, as if she was the same age as her granddaughters. Then, Harris moved to the next group and the pantomime began again.

Regardless of how she felt, Billie Jo looked marvelous. She wore a simple dress, long and flowing. Someone must have selected it for her because it suited her perfectly. She'd been locked up for so long, Billie Jo could have no fashion sense. One more thing she'd had no chance to do in life was to develop her own style.
A sophisticated cutter had conquered her short, fuzzy hair. Gone was the practical prison look. Her hair lay in perfect waves that complemented her wraithlike features. The streaks of grey hair now seemed to highlight her lovely face rather than age it. The right makeup had been artfully applied to enhance her incredible eyes and delicate features.

Billie Jo was a beautiful woman still, despite the years of hardship she'd endured. I tried to ignore the months of heartache that would come if she truly had terminal cancer. As far as I knew, she still hadn't been tested or formally diagnosed, although she was free to do so these days. Now that she was out of prison, she was much less interested in claiming an illness that would ravage her body and end her life.

I turned my head to a passing waiter and traded my now-melted virgin margarita for a fresh, cold one. I wasn't drinking them. I was using them to cool my hot face. George came by to give me a quick hug. Ursula and Walter Westfield soon joined us, followed closely by Ursula's news crew. They were shooting footage that would later be edited down for a follow-up to the *News This Week* story. More television attention was the last thing I needed.

"Willa, are you out of your mind?" the C.J. had screamed at me when he'd learned after the fact about my part in Billie Jo's parole. Our angry confrontation had kept the courthouse staff in gossip for days.

Augustus had been the only one with enough nerve to say anything directly to me about my shouting match with C.J. "Didn't I tell you, now?" was his comment, followed by, "It's not smart to cross Prescott Roberts and Walter Westfield." If I'd had a prayer of ever getting another replacement, about that time I'd have fired his butt.

Today, Ursula was the only media person on Harris's guest list. Harris had given her exclusive rights to the party, which she deserved. Ursula had orchestrated the entire successful Billie Jo Steam epic and was now in a position to make the most of it. Multiple Emmys were on the horizon.

Ursula put a microphone in my face, while Walter and George waited out of camera range. Knowing I'd just have to get it over with or she'd never leave me alone, I lowered the margarita to put it, too, out of sight. "Judge Carson, how do you feel being a part of such a huge victory? It must be rare that you have a chance to help set an innocent woman free."

"I'm always interested in justice, Ursula. Here, justice has finally been done." I'd learned the lesson of twenty-first century television. Nothing more than seven seconds would make it past the cutting room floor. Short and sweet is how American viewers prefer their TV news. Ursula must have liked the sound bite because she put the microphone down and waved the crew away. They left us, continuing to pan the crowd to pick up comments for later editing.

"Thanks, Willa. That was a good line. Did you practice? You could have a great career as a television commentator," she laughed.

"Maybe in another life," I said, noticing the look of concern on Walter's face. "What's wrong, Walter? Isn't this good publicity for your campaign? I would think you'd be happy to be on this bandwagon. Look at all these voters." I wasn't kidding when I said it, either. This was exactly the crowd that Walter would have to persuade to vote against the incumbent. Otherwise, he'd never prevail in the senatorial election.

That the governor hadn't acted overtly to free Billie Jo Steam could be spun to Walter's advantage. They were on opposing sides. Anything the opposition did wrong could be used to further Walter's goals. I'm not a political strategist, but genius wasn't required to figure out that one.

Walter was dressed in a trendy, sage, long-sleeved linen shirt and long, well-pressed, linen trousers a shade or two darker. Brown accessories, including his Tods, completed this season's GQ version of the well-dressed urban male. Good looks had replaced comfort, though. The day was much too hot to be wearing long pants. Walter lifted his glass. The hand that held the glass trembled slightly on its way to his mouth. The last thing I needed was for him to have heatstroke here on my property.

"It's a long time since I've been in this particular crowd," Walter said. "It's nice to see Billie Jo Steam free, but sad how much older she looks. How much she's lost of her life. I keep wondering if I could have changed that somehow."

Ursula rolled her eyes as I said, "Oh, good grief, Walter." Obviously, since our lunch, he'd been practicing the spin he wanted to put on Billie Jo's release. How many focus groups had Walter tried this version out on before deciding to run with it? Getting on the bandwagon long after a successful conclusion to a controversial problem didn't make him senatorial material in my book. But then, most people wouldn't know that he'd had a change of heart. Made me wonder what I didn't know about Walter Westfield.

However, this was a party, not a campaign debate, so I put on my social mask and asked him, "Why would you think that? What could you have done?"

Walter adopted just the right concerned but puzzled countenance. If he were a pipe smoker, he would have put the pipe in his mouth and puffed a few times, for contemplative emphasis. As it was, he rubbed his free hand over the side of his thigh, trying to look pained. What a ham. "I don't know, really. I didn't even know Trey had died until months after the fact."

And then, in case we'd all gotten just a little too complacent, George said, "But, if Billie Jo didn't kill Trey Steam, who did? Have you thought about that?"

In truth, I'd thought about very little else since Ben shared the DNA evidence that had freed Billie Jo. I'd thought about the fact that I'd made Prescott Roberts look like a fool in front of those who knew he'd used his influence to get Billie Jo convicted in the first place as well as to keep her in prison all these years. He wouldn't be thinking kind thoughts about me right now, either. "Who, indeed? And another question is, why?"

"The killing could have been random, I suppose," Walter offered.

George countered that idea. "But things were different around here back in 1972. Tampa was still a fairly small town. Everybody knew each other. You didn't have random psychopaths stalking citizens like that guy who killed one of the local doctors a few months back. No, whoever killed Trey Steam must have known him. Which means you must have known the killer, too," George said, looking in Ursula and Walter's direction.

"It's an unsettling thought," Walter responded. At this, he did his best to look unsettled, practicing his lines. We'd hear a version of this delivered on Ursula's follow-up show, and in campaign speeches ad nauseam. Now that Walter had adopted Billie Jo's cause as his own, he'd play it for all it was worth. I wondered what Prescott Roberts would say about that.

"It's more than unsettling, Walter," I told him with very little patience. "A friend of yours was murdered. Don't you want that person brought to justice?"

"Well, the killer could be dead, himself," Walter said. "It's been a long time since 1972." That much was true. But it still bothered me that we didn't know for sure.

Later, both Kate and Leo appeared at the buffet table, as if by magic. Leo was the one who had introduced me to Harris Steam, so of course he would be invited to this gig. Seeing Leo with Kate, possessively guiding her with a hand at the small of her back, bending over to laugh at something she whispered in his ear, was as alien to me now as it had been since Kate first brought Leo home. Would I never get over this? *I would,* I said to myself, mentally squaring my shoulders and setting my determination.

Fortified by a fresh, icy cold margarita and still flush with Billie Jo's victory, I walked toward the corner where Kate and Leo were now holding their plates and eating peacefully. As I wound my way through the mingling crowd, not paying attention to my path, two little girls ran past me, chasing each other. I had to stop short to avoid being run down. I recognized them from the back by their flowing red curls. "Billie and Willie, no doubt," I said to the tall young woman who followed them, swiftly, but not as recklessly.

She smiled. "I'm sorry. They're just excited." She held out her hand to shake mine. "I'm Eva Raines Steam."

"Willa Carson," I replied.

"I know. The girls thank you for helping their grandmother. They haven't stopped talking about Billie Jo. It's 'Grandma' this and 'Grandma' that, every available minute. You'd think they did-n't already have a grandmother living right in their own home, they've been so excited." The words were positive, but Eva's tone wasn't. She didn't sound thrilled to have her daughters so focused on Billie Jo Steam. I'd have described her tone as jealous, if Eva being jealous of Billie Jo wasn't such an absurd idea.

Eva had on a sleeveless Sunday church dress that left her well-toned, muscular arms bare. The dress was buttercup yellow, trimmed in white. Despite the heat, she had on panty hose and high-heeled shoes. Her makeup looked as if it had been done by Bobbi Brown herself. Her own long, red, curly hair was held up with a gold barrette. Eva's daughters were miniature versions of her.

"Excuse me, please. I need to attend to my children," Eva said. "It was nice to meet you." She followed the small wake of space the girls left in their rush forward through the crowd. Eva and Harris, along with the two girls, made quite a good-looking family. They were caring parents. What had gone wrong? You never know a marriage until you live in it, but what had really caused their divorce? It seemed a shame to break up such a potentially sweet family. Maybe Harris was right. Maybe they would all get back together now.

I continued on my way toward Kate and Leo. He was as stun-ningly attractive as ever. He and Kate wore a couple of outfits that made them look like extras in a country music video. Despite the oppressive heat, both of them were dressed in royal blue and white western wear, complete with blue ten-gallon hats and royal blue western boots. I'd never seen Kate in such ridiculous garb. Still holding on to my margarita courage, I leaned over and kissed

Kate on the cheek. Leo kissed me on the mouth and I didn't grimace. Progress. "Hi, Willa, darling. Lovely, lovely party," Kate said.

"Just perfect," Leo added. "George certainly does have a knack for this sort of thing, doesn't he?" A knack? Calling George's ability to build, manage, and maintain a five-star restaurant at Minaret a "knack," was like calling a whale a fish. George's chefs have won the Golden Spoon Award five times and *Florida Trend* magazine has called his restaurant the best in Florida more than once. Knack, indeed.

With difficulty, I kept up my cordiality. Which is to say, I didn't hit him. "Yes, Leo," I said sweetly, instead. "George is quite accomplished. Thank you for noticing." While Leo might have observed George's "knack," he hadn't realized my distaste for him. But Kate had. She gave me the look. The one all mothers give their children when we're being rude. The look that says, "That's enough, young lady."

"Aren't you glad now that you decided to help Harris out with his mom?" Leo asked me. "Isn't this great?"

"Yes, Leo, it's great. But don't volunteer me for this kind of thing again. You could have gotten me into a lot of trouble."

"But I didn't. What I got you was a great opportunity to do something really wonderful for some very nice people. What's wrong with that?" Leo said, reasonably. I didn't bother to try to explain.

Chapter Fifteen

"Who is that man holding hands now with Billie Jo?" Kate asked us both, changing the subject before the conversation could take a negative turn again. I looked where she pointed with her chin and noticed the man I'd seen in the back of the room at Billie Jo's parole hearing.

"Why, that's Johnny. Johnny Tyson. Haven't you met him before?" Leo answered. As I shook my head, he continued, "Looks like you'll get your chance then. He and Billie Jo are headed this way."

Today, Johnny Tyson was dressed much like Harris was—comfortably, casually, and expensively. But as I noticed on the day of Billie Jo's hearing, he was average in every way: average height, ordinary build, plain brown hair, and unremarkable brown eyes.

The only thing extraordinary about Johnny Tyson was the adoration Billie Jo showered on him for the entire world to see. The luminosity of their faces when they looked at each other was so bright that it seemed unnatural. If Leo and Kate looked like a happy country music video, Billie Jo and Johnny seemed like an advertisement for a honeymoon getaway. The obvious love they shared made them both extraordinary in a way their features alone could not.

Billie Jo let go of Johnny Tyson's hand to give me a long, hard hug. Then she stepped back and took Johnny's hand again, as if letting go of him for more than a few seconds would make her lose him for another thirty years.

"Thank you, Willa. I know I have you to thank for this. I am so grateful. You simply cannot imagine what it means to me to be out of that place. I've been with Harris and my grandkids for a whole week now. I just love them so much. I can be with Johnny now, too. My life is looking up. I just know it." She beamed like a small child with a helium balloon, holding happiness in her hand. Basking in the glow of it made me want to find my true love and float away, too.

"Johnny, it's nice to meet you," Kate and I both said, as we shook hands with this shy man. He looked at me briefly and then looked away. "How do you know Billie Jo?" My curiosity just wouldn't wait any longer.

Billie Jo herself answered my question. "Why Johnny was one of the Six Bills. Johnny was our drummer. A great one, too. I thought everybody knew that."

Johnny Tyson was the one who had found Trey Steam dead along with Billie Jo. I guess Walter had mentioned that to me several weeks before. But I'd forgotten. When I made the decision not to investigate Trey Steam's murder, I had partitioned out everything related to his life, too. Working under the tight time pressures we had, I saw no reason to learn about the Six Bills. Johnny was, so far, the third member of the group I'd met, after Walter Westfield and Billie Jo. Besides Trey Steam, I wondered, who were the others? "What have you been doing with yourself since 1972?" I asked Johnny.

He raised his gaze for a few brief seconds as he answered. "This and that. I've been teaching at a local high school and visiting Billie Jo whenever I could. Now that she's out, we plan to get married." Billie Jo looked at him with a loving expression and he returned the look with longing. If Ursula Westfield herself had orchestrated the ending to this story, she couldn't have come up with anything better. A long, lost love. A post-release wedding. What next? I was beginning to feel like a character in a fairy tale.

"That is so romantic," Kate said. "You two have been seeing each other all these years? And you're still in love. How wonderful." She held on to Leo's arm now, too, unconsciously mirroring Billie Jo's possessive pose with Johnny.

"Johnny's visited me every Saturday for thirty years. And

brought me flowers. He wanted to marry me while I was in prison, but I didn't think that was fair. I thought he might find a free woman someday." Billie Jo beamed, showing off an old-fashioned wrist corsage of pink sweetheart roses like the one she might have worn to her college graduation.

"I've got me a free woman now, and I plan to keep her," Johnny replied, patting her hand, which lay now on his forearm. He reached over and kissed her cheek, while she continued to bask in the light of his obvious love.

I noticed the long, jagged scar on his right forearm as he brushed away the hair from her face, letting his hand linger there, just to touch her. I spent a short second or two after they wandered away wondering what had caused that scar and I made a mental note to find out.

Harris Steam had brought his band to play for the crowd. He and his musicians started up on the front parking lot. After they played the first song, Harris spoke into the microphone. "Welcome, everybody!" The crowd cheered and yelled back, just as his audience of fans responded at every concert he performed. "Today is a very special day for me, as all of you know." He waited a few beats for the crowd to cheer and clap. "My mother is here with me, to see me perform for the first time ever," he went on, and the crowd went wild. "This entire concert is for her. I love you, Mom." The band began to play a quiet love song and Harris crooned out the lyrics like we'd never heard him sing before, from his heart, every word.

"This next one is for a very special friend of mine. She knows who she is," Harris said, as the band went ahead and played "Tropical Memories," the song that had made me change my life that fateful snowy April, so long ago. Harris's eyes met mine and we smiled over the heads of the crowd.

The band played a few more pieces, making too much noise for anyone to have a conversation. Leo and Kate seemed to enjoy the music as much as I did. George joined us for the rest of the concert, taking some time from his "knack" to spend a triumphant moment with his wife. This was truly a special time, for all of us, and we reveled in it, reveled in our success.

Too soon, Harris stood before the microphone and thanked the members of his group. "I have a treat for you all, now," He said, as the band members disconnected their instruments and left the stage. Sensing the concert wasn't over, the crowd perked up again. "I have asked a special bunch of people to help me with your entertainment today."

Billie Jo, Johnny Tyson, and Walter Westfield walked to the front, along with two others I couldn't see. Walter and the two men picked up the guitars that had been left on the stage, as Johnny took a seat behind the drums and Billie Jo stood behind the keyboards.

"Ladies and gentlemen, I give you the remaining members of Tampa's best band of 1971, the original Six Bills!" The crowd went wild again. The hooting, applause, cheers, and screaming were loud enough to wake the dead. Ursula's crew filmed every minute of the concert, while Ursula walked closer to the stage to get her own microphone nearer to Harris.

"With your permission," Harris continued, "I will sing." The crowd drowned him out until his next words could not be heard. Six Bills began to play songs I often hear on the oldies stations: Bob Seger, Mitch Ryder, Janis Joplin, the Rolling Stones. Even a little Jimmy Hendricks. And then, a song that I'd never heard before: "As I watch you out of sight, enveloped by the darkness of the night," Harris crooned.

I turned to Leo, who was singing along with every word. "Do you know this one?"

"It's a tune his daddy wrote," Leo explained. "It's called 'Billie Jo.'" A chill ran down my spine again as the mournful love song continued. George held me closer while we listened to Harris's husky voice singing Trey Steam's poetry.

After the third Trey Steam song, Harris concluded his concert, and told the crowd to enjoy the rest of the party. I saw Billie Jo and Johnny join hands again and leave the stage together. Well, good, I thought. It was time for some happiness in Billie Jo's life. And in Johnny Tyson's, too. Harris had gotten his wish. His mother would be home, near his children, and live out the remainder of her days as a happily married woman. I love happy endings.

Chapter Sixteen

Spending time with my journal the next morning, I wandered through the mind-field of my work on the Billie Jo Steam matter. Thoughts and feelings came out on the fine linen paper while I wrote the experience away, preserving it for later appreciation. The longer I live, the less I recall about my life. Now, I record as much as possible of the essence of it all. I'd been journaling and keeping better track of my experiences for the past few months. I find it comforting to sit and have conversations with my inner guidance, as Kate calls it.

I had filled several spiral-bound notebooks by now, a new one for each calendar quarter. When I'd first started journaling, I did it for a specific reason. I was in a spot of trouble. I couldn't quite figure my way out of it without writing everything down and looking at the nuances. Now, the habit was as much a part of my day as my morning run and my evening cigar. I found deep relaxation in pen, paper, and solitude.

As I sat there, still bathing in the glow of success and yesterday's victory party, my pleasure flowed easily from my pen. I wrote about Harris, Billie Jo, Johnny, Ursula, Walter, and the rest. I found myself smiling and congratulating myself on a job well done. As much as I bristle at George's teasing over what he calls my Mighty Mouse routine, sometimes I have the ability to do what others can't do for themselves. Billie Jo's case was one of those instances.

At first, page after page of self-congratulation flowed forth, describing my hard work, clever investigation, and perceptive analysis. In hubris, I wrote in detail of my persuasive powers with Ben Hathaway, the governor, and the parole board. I was still uncomfortable with the public appearance piece of this project that Ursula had brought to my plate since I've never been a natural public speaker.

But without Ursula, I wouldn't have had the entire experience. She gave me a chance to help Billie Jo, to do what I was born to do. Ursula was thus entitled to her self-interested bit of the result, too. And I had performed well in front of an audience of millions, I wrote, in halting praise.

Which brought me to George's observation about Trey Steam's real killer never having been brought to justice. I'd never told him about what I'd come to regard as the intimidation tactics employed against me. Once, I'd considered whether they were actions taken by Trey Steam's real killer. Could that be true?

As my pen flew over the lines, writing my thoughts, I became more and more troubled. Who had killed Trey Steam, after all was said and done? Would he be a threat to me and others now?

When we'd first found the new DNA evidence, I asked Ben Hathaway to run a check in the state's computer database to see if the DNA on Trey Steam's clothes and the murder weapon matched any known felons. But, it didn't. Ben ran the fingerprints found at the scene, too, with the same negative result.

As far as the state was concerned, the police had no suspects and no leads. The crime was old and no longer a top priority. Most of the evidence was long since contaminated, lost, or destroyed. Ben said it was unlikely that Trey Steam's killer would ever be arrested and tried.

Something about the situation wasn't settling well with me, or at least with my psyche. The smug self-congratulation I'd been engaged in just a few minutes earlier felt tarnished now. "How could this be over, with Trey Steam's real killer unexposed?" I wrote.

When I finally took a sip of my coffee, it was stone cold. I looked up at the clock in my study and saw that it was past noon. Trey Steam's murder had been unsolved for more than thirty years. I foolishly thought the solution could wait. I closed the journal, determined to return to my earlier euphoria and enjoy the gift of a quiet Sunday. At least for today. I was going to have some R and R. I stood and stretched the kinks out of my body.

The dogs and I took our time running around Plant Key. It was already over eighty-five degrees out, and humid enough to curl even my short hair. Only one lap today. I wouldn't make it around twice. I jogged slowly, the dogs way ahead of me. I watched them run in and out of the water to cool off as we made our way around the island.

When we arrived back at the house, all three of us splashed into Hillsborough Bay and frolicked a while. I don't frolic very often. Relaxing and enjoying the exercise and the company of my dogs, I felt nearly blissful. I was grateful for a beautiful day, the water, George, Harry and Bess, our home, and a successful conclusion to a job well done. Without conscious volition, a sigh of contentment escaped my mouth.

Physically exhausted, I left the dogs to dry in their kennel and trudged upstairs for a shower and a nap.

It was after five o'clock when I woke up. I found a note from George propped on my pillow, along with a single red rose. The note was written on his personal ivory note card, with his name engraved in navy ink on the top. George's strong and distinctive script flowed across the page in blue fountain ink. "Please allow me the pleasure of your company this evening. I invite you to dine with me at eight o'clock. Cocktails at seven. All my love, George."

I smiled, held the card to my nose, smelled George's Old Spice aftershave, and kissed the paper. How many women, after seventeen years of marriage, got handwritten invitations to dine with their husbands? I was blessed, indeed.

I glanced over at the clock. I had more than enough time to prepare for dinner in the way such an engagement required. I drew a hot bath in Aunt Minnie's claw-footed tub, lit the candles, put on my music, and poured a glass of chardonnay. I luxuriated there for an hour with a moisturizing masque on my face and joy in my heart.

I dressed leisurely, choosing a simple ivory silk dress that George had bought me on our last trip to Palm Beach. I slipped sexy ivory sandals onto my bare feet. I couldn't do much with my short auburn hair, which falls into the same style every day, no matter what.

My makeup, too, was minimalist. I added a deep purple-red lipstick for drama, then fastened Aunt Minnie's diamond and amber choker, set in platinum, around my neck, and clipped the matching earrings onto my earlobes. I rarely wear Aunt Minnie's jewelry because most of it doesn't go well with T-shirts. But whenever I put on one of her pieces I am reminded that she must have been a flamboyant woman, one who ignored public opinion. As far as I knew, Aunt Minnie was never married. Where all of her baubles came from was a mystery I planned to solve someday.

Last, I spritzed my signature scent on my wrists, the one I have been wearing for years on very special occasions: Cartier. I turned around to view myself in the full-length mirror. My eyes widened involuntarily at the person reflected there. She was someone I hadn't seen in a very long time. She looked relaxed and happy, like a woman who had a date with a handsome man at a posh restaurant.

The phone rang and I was tempted to ignore it. Instead, I walked over to the instrument and saw the flashing light on the answering machine. I compromised. I picked up the phone, but not the messages.

"Hi, Willa, darling," Kate said. "I just wanted to call and congratulate you and George on an excellent party yesterday."

I felt again the warm glow of Kate's approval surround me. "I love you," I told her.

She laughed. "I love you, too," she said.

"I've got a hot date tonight. Can I call you tomorrow?"

"Sure. It's nothing important. Just wanted to gossip about Billie Jo and Harris. It can wait."

I signed off, returned the phone to its cradle, and resisted the urge to light a Partagas. I admired Aunt Minnie's Herrend zoo while I waited for George. Aunt Minnie had been unconventionally wonderful. I think she'd had a Hungarian admirer at one time. He gave her the whimsical Herrend porcelain figurines painted in the technically difficult fishnet pattern. Judging from how many she had, the relationship must have lasted for a while. Aunt Minnie gave all the animals names, which she itemized in the inventory we received when George inherited the house.

To the extent that Aunt Minnie's ghost or spirit still lives with us, she must be pleased that I admire her zoo and that George is adding to her collection. Whenever a particularly special opportunity arises, he orders an unusual piece from Lucy Zahran, in Beverly Hills. Lucy is quite remarkable, herself. She and Aunt Minnie would have been great friends.

I picked up the pair of blue bunnies that were joined together, sharing a quiet moment. These two were "Willa" and "George," according to Aunt Minnie's inventory. "Forever bonded, quietly a pair," she had said. I considered renaming them Johnny and Billie Jo for the same reason.

The music continued to play softly in the background, and I amused myself with my thoughts for the short twenty minutes before George rang the bell. When I went to the door, I saw my knight in shining armor standing there, dressed in his tuxedo, ready for our big date. "Won't you come in," I said, formally, with a smile, inviting him to enter his own home.

George resisted spoiling the mood he had created with his formal invitation by my pillow. "My dear, you are beautiful," he said as he kissed me. "Would you care to dance?" We danced around the living room for a little while, feeling like characters in a romance movie.

Then we went downstairs to a spectacular dinner in one of his private dining rooms and returned to our flat to make love. Very late or very early, depending on your point of view, we decided to have a nightcap on the balcony. George poured two small aperitifs and I put Harris Steam's CD on to play. When we got settled in with the dogs at our feet, I lit a cigar.

We talked of inconsequential things: the restaurant, a vacation we were planning in the winter to Pleasant Harbor, Michigan. It was late and the night was quiet. Downtown Tampa's skyline lit up beautifully in the distance.

Then, sirens abruptly pierced the quiet. We heard an ambulance leave Tampa General Hospital, across the bay from where we sat looking toward Davis Islands. Another ambulance and two police cars soon followed. The rescue helicopter started up, its rotary blades further blasting the quiet night air. All five vehicles headed in our direction and continued on past Plant Key toward Ballast Point. The noise was loud enough to wake the dead.

"Looks like another fatality," I said. The helicopter is usually a sign of a serious injury, and death sometimes occurs before the helicopter arrives.

"Maybe not. They get there in time fairly often," George reminded me, unwilling to spoil our happy mood. We could see the helicopter lighting up the sky not too far away.

The sirens and the noise from the helicopter blades continued in the distance. More sirens followed, but they entered the Bayshore from another direction and we couldn't tell whether they were police vehicles or fire trucks. Maybe it was a fire or a different type of catastrophe.

The helicopter returned a short while later and landed. We couldn't see anyone rushing out to the pad to collect patients, but we weren't sitting at the right angle for a clear view.

George asked me, "Should I turn the television on to see if there's any news?"

I didn't want to spoil the mood with voyeurism. I was afraid I'd see bodies on stretchers and I didn't want to risk a return of my Billie Jo nightmare by the suggestion. I shook my head. "No. Let's wait until tomorrow. They won't know much tonight, anyway." We finished our nightcap and went to bed.

We fell asleep without once mentioning Billie Jo Steam or Johnny Tyson, although their obvious love for each other at the victory party yesterday had joyfully influenced us both.

My sleep was the peaceful passing of restful time, unencumbered by any knowledge of the future.

Chapter Seventeen

As it inevitably does, the Monday morning sun followed Sunday's moonlight, ending my idyllic respite. *Someday*, I thought, as my alarm's ocean sounds began roaring at six o'clock, *I'm going to go to sleep when I'm tired and wake up when I'm ready.* Someday. But not today.

I pushed the "off" button on my alarm, got my running clothes out of the dryer, and met Harry and Bess in the kitchen. They ate their breakfast and then we all went down the backstairs for our morning run. Before the sun came up, the temperature was just bearable. They started with a splash in the bay as I began my slow warm-up jog east. In less than two minutes, they caught up with me and ran so far ahead I could barely see them in the gloaming.

Once I picked up the pace and made my way around the first curve, I could see the downtown Tampa skyline. The early sunrise reflected off the copper First Union building, coloring the morning sky a pink lemonade hue. One foot in front of the other, slogging it out, my body protested the rich food and wine I'd consumed last night just as my mind returned, with pleasure, to the same event.

George and I so rarely spent time together alone. The evening had been wonderful. We'd promised each other more such evenings. We'd agreed, once again, to a regular Sunday night date. Both of us tactfully refrained from mentioning that we'd made this vow and broken it several times before. But our marriage had, of course, recently ridden over a few bumps when George was wrongly accused of murder. Not many couples have to face a challenge like that, and it hadn't been easy for us, either. Both of us had been making extra efforts to get back on track as quickly as possible.

And speaking of marriages, my good angel said loudly over my pained and ragged attempts to breathe, *didn't Kate and Leo look like young lovers at the party?* As soon as the thought crept into my head, I tried to banish it. I didn't have enough oxygen going to my brain to think about Kate and Leo while I ran this eight-mile trek. But I'd need to consider them soon and give myself a strong lecture. Kate had found happiness. She deserved great joy. I needed to get out of the way. Not that she was letting me obstruct her, in any event.

I worried about Leo, though. I knew nothing about him. What I *did* know, I didn't like. My reaction was visceral. He'd done nothing but behave well around me and make Kate sparkle like a sixteen-year-old in the throes of first lust. I put Leo on my mental checklist as a person to bring up in my journal tonight.

Unable to keep my thoughts on success, love, and pleasant evenings, my oxygen-starved mind turned of its own will back to the *Madison v. Cardio Medical* case. Trial would resume at nine-thirty this morning. We hadn't gotten very far into the plaintiff's case over the past month and they wanted another three weeks to finish up their proofs. I saw no reason for the case to continue so long, except that the gladiators couldn't resist fighting over every square inch of turf. Although I'd tried, my efforts to tactfully limit the scope of their shenanigans had met with little success.

Today would be different, I promised myself. I'd get this trial going again and get it over with. Maybe these lawyers lived for the battle, but I don't. My job is to resolve legitimate disputes and get cases crossed off my docket, making room for more legitimate claims. Two months with a single case that was frivolous at best and downright ridiculous at worst would put me seriously behind.

Once home, the dogs were rinsed off and I was breathing semi-normally again. I made coffee and headed toward the shower. I put on my wedding band and small gold knot earrings, and left the bathroom less than twenty minutes later. George says I'm fast, for a girl.

Greta and I drove over our bridge off Plant Key, away from Minaret, and turned right onto Bayshore, heading downtown. I reveled in the view. Thoughts of last night's sirens didn't enter my head. Hillsborough Bay, particularly along the Bayshore, is truly beautiful. The drive down Bayshore, over the Platt Street Bridge, toward the convention center, is one of my daily pleasures. I savored my last moment of solitude until the end of a very long and extremely contentious trial day.

Downtown Tampa, once almost a ghost town, is now bustling and busy. The downtown consists primarily of new construction, giving Tampa a young, vibrant feel. Our newest hotel is the Marriott Waterside, across the street from the Lightning's new hockey arena. Hard to believe you'd find hockey fans in Florida, but true. Garrison Seaport's shopping, theater, and dining district, called Channelside, had recently nestled along the waterfront between the arena and the Florida Aquarium. And farther into the city's center, buildings were being demolished and replaced. Today's Tampa would be unrecognizable to Trey Steam, if he were suddenly resurrected.

My building, though, the old federal courthouse, is circa 1920. In 1920, the middle district of Florida was a much smaller place than it is now. The building is old, decrepit, and much too small for the district's current needs. The C.J. hasn't seen fit to move me to the new federal building yet. I've been hounding him to let me move over with the other judges, but after our recent fight, I doubted he'd be thinking kindly of me for a while. I was probably stuck here until the next millennium.

As the most junior judge on the bench in terms of seniority, age, and the C.J.'s affection, I have the least desirable location. It's the Rank Has Its Privileges Rule: I have no rank and no privileges. My courtroom and chambers are on the third floor, in the back. Getting there from the parking garage helps me keep my schoolgirl figure.

I pulled into my reserved spot in the near-empty garage, and parked Greta across two parking places. I've always parked like this, and building security has given up attempting to change my ways. There's really plenty of room since everyone but my staff and me moved to the new building months ago. If I could move to the new building, I'd have a better parking spot, too. With difficulty, I managed to keep the wistfulness out of my thinking. I had only about an hour to prepare before the *Madison* trial resumed.

I picked up my briefcase and walked quickly from the garage to the building's entrance. Skipping the creaky old elevator, I bounced up the three flights of stairs to my office. I was pleasantly surprised to see Augustus at his desk, a few minutes before eight o'clock.

"Good morning, Augustus," I said cheerfully, as I barreled on through the reception room. He tried to say something to stop me, but I was moving quickly and didn't pay attention. When I pushed open the door to my hideously decorated chambers, I realized what Augustus had said: "Ursula Westfield is here to see you."

Ursula had her back to the door, waiting for me. She'd taken a seat in one of the ugly green client chairs that faced my desk. She sat quietly, not reading or checking her Palm Pilot, or doing any of the other fidgety things she normally did whenever she had to wait. Ursula wasn't used to waiting and patience was not her strong suit. Now, she was silently and calmly just sitting there. I was startled to see her, but I greeted her cheerfully.

"You haven't heard, then," was the first thing out of her mouth, before I could set down my briefcase or turn around to look at her. I did so now.

"Heard what?" I sat in the other ugly green client chair, next to her, on her right. The little Napoleon who had reigned in this office before me had elevated the desk on a platform. I never sat there when I had a welcome visitor. At five feet, eleven inches tall, I didn't need the extra height to tower over most people.

Ursula clasped her hands together tightly and brought them up to her bowed head. She was trying to gain her composure, blinking furiously to keep the tears from spilling over the bottom lids of her already red and swollen, almond-shaped eyes. She got up and made her way to the television in my office. She tuned in to the local all-news channel.

At first, I saw pictures of a house with several police and other emergency vehicles out front, obviously taken during the night. The next few shots were too graphic. A full body bag being hauled out on a gurney appeared on the screen giving me a sense of flashback. Ursula had muted the sound. I knew what was in the body bag before Ursula said, "Billie Jo Steam's been murdered."

"What?" Oh, my God. I had put the woman back on the street. She'd lived peacefully in prison for more than thirty years. She'd been out for less than two weeks and she was dead. "How could I have been so stupid?"

I should have seen this coming, I chastised myself inwardly. I knew the real killer was out there. At least I could have called Billie Jo. Warned her. I sat there writing in my stupid journal, getting all caught up in my life, while someone had killed Billie Jo, too. How could I have let this happen?

"It gets worse," Ursula continued, barely suppressing a sob. "How could it be worse?" I finally worked up the courage to ask, but I didn't really want to know. I most emphatically didn't want to know.

She moved away from the television set so that I could see the rest of the picture. A man was seated in the back of a police car. Then, the camera replayed an earlier scene. A man in handcuffs, head down, was walked out to the police car and guided into the backseat. A man I recognized.

"Harris has been arrested and charged with killing her," Ursula finished in a near whisper, and now the tears did spill over and run down her smooth, brown cheeks. Her lovely face with the high cheekbones and beautiful complexion was contorted with grief. Tears streaked her makeup, but she made no effort to wipe them away.

"This is my fault, Willa," she hiccuped. "I should never have done this. Walter warned me, but I wouldn't listen. If it wasn't for me, Billie Jo would still be safe in prison. Harris would be with his girls. This is just not right. It's not right. It's not right," she repeated, over and over.

I stared at the picture on the television set. I grabbed the remote and turned on the sound. The voice-over was repeating the information Ursula had just given me. I had no idea what to say.

I didn't feel any better that Ursula was blaming herself for what was clearly my fault. I couldn't see the irony in both of us taking full responsibility for the deliberately ruthless act of another. Nor did I dwell on the obvious: that Billie Jo should never have been in prison in the first place and that it was a minor miracle she hadn't been killed there.

None of it mattered, anyway. Billie Jo was dead. Harris in jail. All the smug satisfaction I'd felt at serving justice by getting Billie Jo released evaporated like ether.

I remembered something Ben Hathaway said to me once. "Beware of success and happiness," he'd said. "You let your guard down when you're successful and happy. You feel calm, serene. Then, the bullet slams into your heart and pierces you, letting your life leak out with your blood. The bullet is both a blessing and a curse. The blessing is that your last minutes, hours, days were happy ones. The curse is that you're still dead."

I shook my head to clear the thoughts. "Why did they arrest Harris? That's got to be a mistake. He loved Billie Jo. He'd never have killed her." I paused. My mind was reeling. "What's the explanation for that?" I finally asked, when I had gained sufficient composure to speak again. I couldn't drag my gaze from the pictures on the set. I might as well have been right there last night when it all happened.

Ursula was shaking her head back and forth before I finished. "That's the worst part, Willa. The very worst part. It's not a mistake."

"It has to be a mistake. There's just no way Harris killed Billie Jo. I know people. I know him. I'm sure," I insisted.

Ursula kept shaking her head. "I thought so, too. But it's true. He confessed."

At first, I couldn't process what she said. Harris confessed? To what? To loving his mother? To spending most of his adult life devoted to getting her out of prison? To investing large amounts of money in her appeals and her clemency hearings? To singing love songs to her in front of half the population of Tampa? Hell, just the cost of the victory party had been staggering. Why would he bring that much attention to himself and to her, only to kill her once she was free? It made no sense.

"I don't believe it. No. Not possible." I tried not to think about the notes someone had left me. *"Billie Jo belongs in prison. Leave her there,"* the first one had said. Why hadn't I listened?

"I didn't want to believe it, either," Ursula responded, "but it's true. They called me from the newsroom. They heard the news on the police scanner. A reporter from the network is over at the police station now. It's all true."

Ursula continued to cry, while I sat there, stunned. I listened to the news story as it ran again, repeating everything Ursula had said. But it had to be a mistake. It couldn't be true.

Before I knew it, I'd made up my mind. Harris Steam did not kill his mother. I did not get Billie Jo Steam out of prison at her son's request just so he could kill her. I wouldn't believe it. Ever. I would find Trey Steam's killer. Whoever he was, he must have killed Billie Jo, too. It had to be the same killer. Otherwise, none of it made any sense. Harris did not kill his mother and I would prove it. Otherwise, I might go crazy.

Chapter Eighteen

After Ursula left, I picked up the phone and called Ben Hathaway. His secretary said he wasn't available. I left my name and number. I had a courtroom full of litigants and jurors waiting. I could do nothing but return to work. Life goes on, even when we think the earth can't possibly continue to rotate on its axis because of the gravest devastation.

Marilyn Madison sat in my courtroom with her lawyer-gladiators in search of vengeance, not truth or justice. She had filed a criminal complaint over her husband's death, but the prosecutor had refused to pursue it. Now, she was looking to the civil courts to extract her pound of flesh. Unfortunately, anyone with the filing fee and a typewriter can sue almost anyone else in this country.

During the pretrial proceedings, my clerks had been calling Madison's lawyers Frick and Frack because we never saw one without the other. Their real identities were much more intimidating. Lead counsel was Sidney Lehman. Lehman's co-counsel was David Royal.

Regardless of what you called them, their firm was at the apex of the handful of lawyers in Florida who represented survivors in egregious wrongful death cases. These suits were ones where the stakes were highest, verdicts reached multiple millions of dollars, and trials turned into public spectacles. The kind of cases that made me squirm when other lawyers filed them back when I was in private practice. Now, such cases make me angry because they needlessly consume so much of our judicial time and energy that legitimate litigants get far less of our resources than they deserve.

Phillip Sloat on the other hand, represented Cardio Medical Corporation and the corporate officers, sued individually. Phillip Sloat believed that all plaintiffs were frauds seeking a way to milk the system. Surely somewhere between the two extreme positions of these ego-driven lawyers there should be room to compromise, I once thought. After years of exposure to this type of conflict, I now realize there is nothing for a hardworking judge to do but bear it.

All three lawyers were colleagues at the bar, but all were warriors. With the three of them sitting in my courtroom, there was so much testosterone in the air that I was afraid to breathe. I patted my head to be sure my hairline wasn't receding.

Marilyn Madison, for her part, was a nice-looking woman, about sixty years old. Her husband of thirty-five years had died six days after surgery to implant an artificial heart. Cardio Medical argued that the death was caused by the doctor's negligence, poor patient selection, and several other excuses. In short, the company raised anything and everything as a defense except placing blame on a problem with the device itself.

Unfortunately for Cardio Medical, the doctor was small potatoes in the suit. His insurance company had already paid a million dollars to settle the case against him. Lehman and Royal argued that the artificial heart was defectively designed and rushed to market. They said that with a better design Mr. Madison would be alive today. The lawyers wanted Cardio Medical and its officers to pay multiple millions of dollars in damages. Marilyn Madison said Cardio Medical had killed her husband. Intentionally. She wanted revenge.

Truly, this was a run-of-the-mill death case, if the death of a human being can ever be considered thus. The case would not have involved any of these lawyers, meaning I could have settled it for the one million dollars already paid and marked it off my docket, but for one thing. The deceased, Stanley Madison, was the creator of the cartoon comic strip *Corgi*. The strip featured an intelligent, bright green Welsh corgi with an active fantasy life.

Corgi's creator, Stanley Madison, had been a very, very wealthy man with the ability to create even more wealth in the future. As far as Lehman and Royal were concerned, wealthy men don't die due to physician error during emergency surgery on vacation in the Florida sunshine. No matter what, they intended to prove that someone must be at fault, preferably, a large corporate defendant with a very deep pocket.

Whenever she'd had a chance to speak, Marilyn Madison had shown me she was a whiny, "poor me" type. Her motives were no doubt complex and her solution lay in intense psychotherapy. This trial would never satisfy her, I was sure, no matter what the outcome.

"Madison v. Cardio Medical Corporation." My courtroom deputy called the case as I walked in covered with the black judicial robe from crew neck to loafers. I looked out over my domain to see all the litigants in place. Sid Lehman and David Royal were at the plaintiff's table, the table closest to the jury box, with Marilyn Madison seated between them.

Phillip Sloat and his bevy of female assistants sat at the defense table with Cardio Medical's corporate officer defendants. The company's insurance adjuster sat behind the bar in the gallery, from whence he pulled the strings on his marionettes, like a master puppeteer. Unless you knew what to look for, you couldn't see him working the cords.

"Ladies and Gentlemen, we have been at this trial for three weeks. I have only two more weeks that I can allot to your case. Other litigants are waiting for their day in court." I ignored the collective gasps from all concerned. "We are going to have to shorten this trial. Mr. Lehman, how many more witnesses do you have to put up?"

Sid stood, adjusted himself, and folded his hands, holding them low in front. "Judge, I must protest," he began somberly.

"Save it, Mr. Lehman. You have been wasting your time and the court's. I've been more than lenient with you. How many more witnesses do you have, and who are they?" I barely curbed the sharpness I was wont to deliver. They had been taking too long with their case, but much of my discomfort had nothing to do with the way the lawyers had conducted themselves. I chafed under the heavy collar of responsibility for Billie Jo's death and Harris Steam's arrest, not the yoke of the trial.

Before Lehman could answer my question, Sloat piped in. "Judge, I appreciate the court's interest in getting the plaintiff to finish her proofs. But we have a lengthy defense to offer ourselves. We can't possibly put our defense case on in two weeks, let alone finish the entire trial in that time."

How did I know he was going to say that? These lawyers and their clients would stay in this courtroom forever, if I allowed them to do so. The sparring was what they all lived for. And it didn't hurt that they were speaking at the request of their clients and got paid for it, too.

"All of you know that even after the trial, this case will never be over. Appeals will follow for years..." Now that I'd started my lecture, I couldn't seem to stop myself from continuing. "You lawyers and your clients are more interested in fighting with each other than you are in resolving your disputes. No matter how the jury decides, a verdict will not bring Mr. Madison back to life." I had started to wind down, but I took one more deep breath and finished. "The legal fees paid in this case will not only send the lawyers' children to college, they will pay for their early retirement. And Mr. Madison will still be deceased."

All of them had the grace to look chagrined, except the adjuster. He looked horrified. Of course, he was footing the bill for Cardio Medical's legal fees and costs. Like many adjusters before him, he probably hoped to save some money off his duty to pay a judgment and costs of defense. He must have just realized that the widow's claim would melt through layers and layers of money. Until now, he'd probably thought the one million dollars already paid by the surgeon would be enough, as far as the jury was concerned. He wasn't the first adjuster who hadn't properly calculated Lehman and Royal's tenacity.

David Royal took a turn now. "Judge, Mrs. Madison is truly bereft. She and Stanley were married for over thirty-five years. It is completely untrue that she is just here for the argument. What Mrs. Madison is entitled to is a judgment against this defendant for killing her husband." His tone was just as piously sanctimonious as that of a crooked preacher at a revival meeting.

This was more than Cardio Medical's officers could accept. "That's outrageous!" the president blurted out. "Our product didn't kill Mr. Madison. Artificial hearts don't kill people. We save lives!" The adjuster nodded in firm agreement, as all the others began to talk at once, raising their voices, ever louder, in an attempt to drown out the opposition. An onlooker would be hard-pressed to tell the difference between my courtroom and a bad cable television talk show.

I held up my hand in the "stop" position and pounded my gavel. No one saw, listened, or heard. When I couldn't get them to pipe down, I just got up from the bench and left the room. I could still hear them shouting when I reached my chambers.

"Augustus, please bring me some of your fabulous coffee and the calendar. We need to make some progress." I spoke into the intercom as I returned to sit at my desk. Augustus brought the coffee, along with a sheaf of pink telephone message slips, a stack of yellow printed e-mail messages, and the calendar.

"Chief Judge Richardson has called four times," Augustus told me, as if I hadn't seen the message slips for myself. I tossed all but the last one in the trash. Most of the other telephone calls were from various members of the local media, which I threw away also. They were looking for comments about Billie Jo and Harris Steam, no doubt, and I hadn't any wisdom to offer them. I found no message slip from Ben Hathaway.

I picked up the phone and placed another call to his office. The secretary again told me Ben was unavailable. I left a second message, realizing that he probably treated his pink message slips the same way I did. I wasn't a priority for Ben Hathaway right now. He'd call me back when he could.

"I really think he'll come over here to see you, if you don't call him back," Augustus said.

"Who?"

"Judge Richardson. He sounded quite upset the fourth time he called." Great. The C.J. was the last thing I needed. Really, he has no power over my life, but he doesn't believe that. He thinks that his title "Chief Judge" means he's the boss. This is his fantasy, one in which my colleagues and I refuse to indulge him. I am a United States District Court judge; no one can tell me what to do.

Chief Judge Ozgood Livingston Richardson—"Oz," to his friends (who don't include me)—is sixty-five years old, going on ninety-five. Actually, I think the C.J. was born old. If he ever laughs, it's politely. He's well connected and fairly well preserved, but he is one major pain in the backside. C.J. and I play this little game. He calls me. I ignore him. Augustus was simply too new to know the rules.

After we went over the calendar, I thought I might be safe in returning to my courtroom. At least, I couldn't hear any more shouting on the other side of the door. I buzzed my deputy and requested that she join me in my chambers.

"What's the climate in there?" I asked her.

"They're all seated again. Contemplating the universe, I guess." She smiled at me. I looked down at my watch. I'd been in my chambers for an hour. I nodded, sending her back to the courtroom. I picked up the phone and called Ben Hathaway again. Same result.

Chapter Nineteen

I slipped on my robe, pushed the buzzer to let the court security officer know I was on my way in, and heard him say, "All rise. The United States District Court for the Middle District of Florida, Tampa Division, is now in session. The Honorable Wilhelmina Carson presiding."

Once we were all seated, I said, "Let's try this again. We are going to finish this trial in two more weeks. That's two weeks longer than we reserved on my calendar based on what you told me you'd need when we set this case for trial. Mr. Lehman, how many witnesses do you have left?"

A subdued Sid Lehman stood and said, quite respectfully, "I believe we can conclude our proofs with two witnesses, Your Honor."

"Good. Mr. Sloat, that will give you eight days to put on your case. We'll have closings and instruct the jury on day ten. Please bring the jury in." The jury filed in slowly. They'd been waiting, listening to the lawyers shouting for the last hour. I ignored their inquisitive looks. "Mr. Lehman, you may call your next witness."

"Plaintiff calls Marilyn Madison, Your Honor."

The bereaved widow was sworn in and took the stand. At the noon recess, the lawyers informed me that after the plaintiff's last witness—a criminal psychology expert—both the plaintiff and the defendants would be presenting motions for directed verdict.

This is a formal motion that asks the judge to grant judgment in favor of one of the parties on the basis of the evidence already submitted. Such motions are rarely granted and the few times I'd granted one, I had to hold my breath until the Eleventh Circuit Court of Appeals gave me its seal of approval. Usually, granting a motion for directed verdict is a sure way to get reversed and boomerang a case right back into my courtroom for trial all over again, a result that drives C.J. crazy because he has to fit the cost of another trial into the budget.

While my calendar would have been quickly cleared if I simply granted one of the motions, I didn't want the appellate court sending this case back to me, or any other judge, again. It was bad enough that the case had consumed the court's time in the first instance.

Augustus had laid out my noon repast. Pecan tuna salad with dried cherries and a fruit cup. He obviously felt I needed a change. Before I sat down to eat and read the day's mail, I picked up the phone and called Ben Hathaway yet again.

"I'm sorry, Chief Hathaway's not available," his secretary told me one more time. Thinking I might get lucky twice in a row, I dialed the C.J.'s extension. Unfortunately, he was eating lunch in his chambers, too.

"Good afternoon, C.J. What can I do for you?" I asked him, knowing his earlier calls were not social.

"You can start thinking before you jump into a mess that you can't get yourself out of, that's what you can do for all of us," he said, snapping it out as if he had the right to give me orders. Allowing me no opportunity to retort, he continued to censure me. "A blind man could have seen this Billie Jo Steam situation was going to be a nightmare before you got into it. What's wrong with you, Willa? You're a judge, for God's sake! When are you going to start acting like one?"

"You know, Oz, you're the chief judge. You're not God. And you don't seem to mind my meddling so much when I'm helping you out," I snapped right back at him.

One can only hold on to judicial temperament for so long. Then, something's gotta blow. From the time Ursula had delivered her message, through the outrageous behavior of the lawyers in my courtroom, the pressure had been building. Now wasn't the time for the C.J. to mess with me.

We both took a couple of seconds to breathe and consider. I didn't need the Justice Department slamming down my neck. He didn't need me as an enemy. Nor would it help him out if I made a fool of myself. This was still his division to manage, and I was still part of it. Whether he liked it or not.

C.J. was the first to break the silence. "All right, Willa. I hope you've learned your lesson. With any luck, we've heard the end of this. But Prescott Roberts called me this morning. He's blaming you for what's happening to Harris Steam. Don't be surprised if the Justice Department takes an unhealthy interest in you. Leave the detecting to the detectives, and get back to your own job. You've got a big bottleneck in your courtroom right now. Turn your attention to that." Before I could formulate and deliver a suitable retort, he'd hung up on me again.

By the end of the noon recess, I was bone weary and depressed. I had to return to the *Madison* trial, but I was completely uninterested in the case before me. "I'd rather listen to a Senate filibuster than go back in there, Augustus."

"I've heard some of those senators, Judge. Believe me, the "Sid, David, and Phil Show" is much better. More fireworks." He grinned and I felt a little cheered. And this wasn't the first time he had mentioned some experience I wouldn't have expected the son of Jamaican missionaries to have.

"Augustus, how did you come to work for me?" I'd never asked him how he'd appeared in my chambers, afraid the answer might have been that he'd be leaving soon. Augustus was a true gift to my office life and I wanted him to work here forever, although I understood that he was much too talented for that.

"Leo told me about the job," he replied, unconcerned.

"Leo Colombo?"

"Yes. He said you needed a good assistant and he knew I was looking for something worthwhile to do until I finished my degree."

Now, I was sorry I had asked. If there was one thing I didn't want, it was a Leo Colombo spy in my office. Nor did I want to be either indebted or grateful to Leo Colombo. "How long do you think that will take? To finish your degree?" I asked, with trepidation. Should I get rid of Augustus now, before I became even more attached to him?

"Forever, at the rate I'm going. I have to earn money to finish school. Unless you want to adopt me."

"Why would I do that?" I was thinking that being a child was a problem, but being a parent had to be worse.

"Not all families are as messed up as Harris and Billie Jo Steam, you know."

"What?"

"That family has been a mess for years. It's no secret that Harris was a handful. His grandparents struggled with him for a long time," he told me.

"How do you know about that?" I felt a little like I'd fallen through Alice's looking glass and landed in a totally different world.

"It's no secret. Everybody knows."

"Knows what?"

"Didn't Prescott Roberts tell you when he was here? That man Trey Steam was a wild one, and his son is a chip off the old block. This isn't the first time Harris has been in jail, you know." At that, he smiled on his way out to answer the door to our chambers.

Before I went back into the courtroom, I tried Ben Hathaway again. This time, I got lucky. Ben was finally in his office and the secretary put me straight through. Ben sounded tired and despondent when he picked up the phone. "Hello, Willa. No doubt you've heard." He had been avoiding me. Ben hates to gloat over me almost as much as he hates my doing his job. Even when he's telling me to keep out of his business, he secretly hopes I'm right.

"Yes," I concurred, solemnly. "What happened?"

"Not much I can tell you that wasn't in the news all day. That damn Tampa News Twelve gets to the scene almost as fast as we do, and the other stations are not far behind. I'd ban police scanners if I could. I've already had three calls from Ursula Westfield today, too." His tone snapped like a rubber band.

"I've talked to Ursula, but I'd like to find out the facts from you," I told him.

I could hear his smile over the telephone. "What? You think the media maybe slants things, just a little?"

I said nothing. I had heard Ben and his colleagues enjoy many a conversation about the commercial nature of the media and the way they report the news. Ben's view is that the media must sell their stories, and they make the details as salacious as possible in order to do that.

What I've noticed about these conversations is that people who think "ethical journalist" is an oxymoron haven't met very many "honest lawyers," either. They often tell me that doctors are just out to make money, all cops are crooks, and stockbrokers do nothing but churn accounts for fees. That is, some folks just distrust everyone, for reasons that have more to do with the opinion holder than any real misdeeds of the actors. Arguing the point at the moment wouldn't get me the information I required, however.

Another sigh, then Ben relented. "We were called by a neighbor very late last night. The neighbor could hear Harris Steam screaming inside his house. At first, they didn't think much of it. When he and Eva were still married, Harris's screaming was a regular thing. Since the divorce, I guess he's had no one to scream at." He stopped for a few seconds. "Anyway, this time, the screaming kept on for quite a while. The neighbor went over to the house and found Harris holding Billie Jo on his lap, keening. By the time we got there, Billie Jo was long past dead." His voice was resigned and sad.

Ben was as upset by Billie Jo's death and Harris's arrest for her murder as I was. He had gone out on a limb for them both, too. He had told the parole board Billie Jo should be released. Enough guilt existed to go around on this one, although Ben would never admit those feelings to me.

"How did she die?" I asked.

"She had two bullet holes in her head. Death was probably close to instantaneous," he answered me. "She didn't suffer."

I shuddered, thinking of Billie Jo lying there on the floor, dead, being held by Harris as he cried in grief. "Why did you arrest Harris?"

"The gun was right next to him on the floor. It was his gun. The gunshot residue tests on his hands were positive. He'd fired the gun, no question about that." Ben paused for a moment in the telling, as if to decide whether or not to continue. "He's got a history of violence, you know. And he did confess, Willa. He was crying when we got there, saying over and over, 'I'm sorry, Mom. I'm sorry, Mom.'"

"That's hardly a confession, is it?" I was still holding to some hope that this was all a horrible mistake.

"And then he said, 'I didn't mean to. I loved her. I didn't mean to do it.'"

I dropped my head and closed my eyes. Hearing the facts from Ben Hathaway was devastating. I realized I'd been hoping that the media was exaggerating the story just for its commercial appeal. But Harris truly had confessed to killing his mother. *Why had this happened?*

"Why?" Ben responded, making me realize I must have spoken my thought aloud again. "Hell, Willa, I don't know why anything happens. Harris has a lawyer, so I haven't been able to ask him." Ben's tone was pure disgust.

We both knew that people confessed to crimes they didn't commit with alarming frequency. Their reasons were varied and complex. Some confessed to lesser crimes because they were afraid a jury would find them guilty of more serious offenses. In the past, confessions were coerced more than Ben Hathaway would admit. But none of that made any sense in Harris's case.

"What possible reason could Harris have to kill his mother?" Ben continued, in the same state of bewilderment as I resided. "He worked so hard to get Billie Jo out of prison. And he knew she was dying of cancer, anyway. Why kill her? Why ruin his life?" He stopped again, sighed, and then finished his thought, "Some people just live out a Greek tragedy over and over and over. I can't explain it. You see that type of thing every day, just like I do. Can you explain it?"

Of course I couldn't. Honestly, I didn't expect Harris to provide any reasonable justification, either. The whole thing made absolutely no sense.

My own involvement in the matter still weighed heavily on my mind. In no small way, I had helped to make this possible. Billie Jo would have died a natural death in prison, but not for a while yet. And, if she had died there, at least her son would have been able to continue the rest of his life in peace.

Now, Billie Jo was dead and Harris's world was shattered. The ripple effect to his children, his grandparents, and everyone affected would be catastrophic. Not to mention how Prescott Roberts viewed the situation. Maybe he'd wanted Billie Jo left behind bars to keep her alive. Maybe I really should be polishing up my résumé.

Ben and I commiserated a while longer over human frailties and the multitude of things people can do to mess up their lives before we hung up and I put my head down on my desk.

Chapter Twenty

Sid Lehman called his last witness, an expert in criminal psychology. What the man could possibly offer in this civil trial was a puzzle, even to me. After the psychologist had testified to his qualifications, however, Sid got right to the point.

"Doctor, tell me, how many violent criminals have you treated in your practice?" Sloat didn't object to relevance, which told me that he knew what was coming, even if I didn't.

"I've interviewed or treated over fifteen hundred different murderers, serial killers, and other violent criminals over my thirty years as a forensic psychologist," the expert answered. "I've written several books and numerous articles on the subject."

Sid straightened his tie and fastened his coat. He walked away from the podium and approached the witness. I allow the lawyers to leave the podium, although most federal judges require them to stay put. "The defendants in this case include two corporate officers. Have you ever examined corporate officers accused of actions that included criminal intent to harm consumers?"

"Yes, sir." Still nothing from Sloat. Curious.

"Have you interviewed these two Cardio Medical executives at the table on my right?" was Sid's next question.

"No, sir, I wasn't allowed to do so. But I have read their depositions and reviewed the documents they've written in connection with Mr. Madison's death." What followed was a recitation of all of the documents the expert had reviewed prior to coming to testify. A couple of the jurors were nodding off during the dry testimony the law requires as foundation before opinions can be offered. Unlike cable television courtrooms, real courtrooms require some demonstrated expertise before witnesses spout off.

Next, Sid asked the important question, the one he'd been

building up to: "Based on your education, training, and experience, and based on the information that's been provided to you, what, if any, opinions have you reached about these men, sir?"

I looked over at Sloat, but still he did not object. Perhaps he was just asleep at the switch. Or maybe, he'd made the tactical decision not to underline this witness's testimony by objecting. Sometimes, the jury was just bored and not paying any attention at all. Given that plaintiff's quasi-criminal claims of willful, wanton, and gross negligence had survived Sloat's earlier efforts to get them stricken, perhaps he was hoping the jury would doze through this expert's testimony.

The strategy was already successful with two of the jurors. I dropped a heavy book on the floor to jerk them awake and Sloat flashed me an annoyed glance.

The witness cleared his throat. "Well, as I mentioned earlier, my research has conclusively shown that two of three factors are always present in killers: mental illness, neurological damage, and some kind of childhood abuse. In each of these two corporate officers, all three elements are present."

"And what does that mean?"

"What this means is that humans who have two of these three factors present in their background can't control their violent impulses as well as they should. They express violence under stress or at times of jealousy or anger. Such as here," he finished.

This seemed pretty far-fetched to me. So a person with a head injury was, in effect, a loose cannon, firing at will in all directions when under stress? Surely Sloat wouldn't let that pass, I thought. But he did.

"Would people who lived or worked around such a person have any warning that violence might be coming later?" Sid asked.

"Maybe," the expert said. "The person might have tried to manipulate events to serve their purposes. Sometimes they will exhibit smaller violent acts that their friends or family believe are just incidents of bad temper. But when a bigger stress event happens, the violence can escalate without warning."

Sid looked over at the jury when he asked the next question. "What you're saying is that based on the evidence you reviewed, you came to the conclusion that these two corporate officers deliberately made decisions that they knew would kill patients like Stanley Madison?"

Now, finally, Sloat jumped to his feet. "Objection, your honor. Move for an immediate mistrial."

I dismissed the jury and took arguments on Sloat's motion. The idea that criminal charges could be brought against corporate officers was not new. Presidents and CEOs have gone to jail in Florida and in other states around the country, either for direct acts they have committed or for failure to properly supervise their subordinates.

Nor was it unique for plaintiffs to claim that corporate officers were guilty of conduct amounting to manslaughter, giving rise to claims for punitive damages. Sloat had to have known that argument was coming in this trial. The only thing unique in this expert's testimony was how Lehman and Royal were attempting to prove that the actions of the defendants approached criminal conduct.

Behavioral psychology generally isn't admissible in civil trials to prove behavior consistent with certain character traits. In this argument, though, Sid Lehman wanted the expert to base his opinion on the scientific studies coupled with acts and omissions that had already been admitted by these two officers. The idea was clever. I hadn't faced it before, and very few things remain that I haven't seen tried in my courtroom.

Arguments on the motion continued for the next thirty minutes. As much as a mistrial might be the best solution to this dilemma, I certainly didn't want to start this trial over. We were almost finished, I wailed internally. I decided to strike the witness's testimony and instructed the jury to disregard it. Sid demanded an opportunity to make an offer of proof by putting on the rest of the testimony outside the presence of the jury. I allowed him to do so, which meant I had to listen to the expert testify about his work with serial killers.

The expert retook the stand and testified to administering neuropsychological tests of cortical function and motor and sensory function on known serial killers. Such tests had not been performed on these defendants, so I felt a little better about my ruling.

The other point was more troubling to me. The expert said that since morality and ethics are also expressed through the brain, if something is wrong with the brain, there could very well be a correlating fault in the person's expression of morality and ethics. This was, of course, the backbone of his opinion that the two Cardio Medical officers acted criminally in failing to prevent Stanley Madison's death.

The implications were staggering. This expert was saying that science had proved a connection between immoral or unethical behavior and brain injury. He wanted us to believe that where a brain injury has occurred, stress could trigger criminal conduct. There are so many brain injuries in this country every year that almost anyone could be a walking time bomb using this analysis. For example, football players often get several concussions every season. Anything that caused the brain to move around inside the skull could cause a brain injury that might, in effect, create a murderer.

By the time he was done with this mumbo jumbo, I had a headache. A recess was called for. I, for one, needed a break.

When we reconvened, David Royal took up the argument for a directed verdict in favor of his client, Marilyn Madison. He opened with the standard language requesting judgment based on the evidence so far presented. Then, he warmed up to his cause.

I thought Lehman and Royal would have come up with a better argument. In short, they argued that people were not necessary to the operation of sophisticated machinery, and should not be depended upon. That machines were better than people. It was a tough sell. Most people who worked for a living, such as our jurors, would find little comfort in that position, even if such statements were supported by the evidence. Which, so far, they had not been.

"Thank you, Mr. Royal," I said. "I'll take your motion under advisement. Mr. Sloat, would you please present your motion now."

Sloat took the podium. He, too, began with the required language requesting judgment in his client's favor.

Sloat's argument let me down, too, and would be equally unpopular with a jury of hardworking people. Sloat was essentially saying that well-trained, experienced people, even in jobs where the stakes were high, were not infallible. While there is no question that humans make mistakes, most potential patients, such as our jury, would not want to believe that doctors who worked in our local hospitals made fatal errors. All patients want to believe that doctors are perfect and every surgical result exceeds expectations.

I hadn't had an opportunity to review the legal memoranda that had been submitted on both sides of these motions. As much as I'd have liked to end this case here and now, I wanted to make the right decision, too. Not only because my job was to decide matters like this in accord with the law, but also because I wanted this case to be off my calendar forever, once it was over. I felt that the jury would be dissatisfied with both positions. How they would decide the case remained a mystery.

"Mr. Sloat, I'll take your client's motion under advisement as well. Let's bring the jury back in. Plaintiff can rest her case formally, and you can present your first witness." After that, the trial droned on until the end of the day.

I stopped at Publix on Brorien and Platt to pick up all the late editions of the local newspapers on my way home. We don't have afternoon papers in Tampa, but some of the morning editions are printed later than others. My media friends tell me that the newspapers print yesterday's news. If you want current information, they insist, you need to watch television, where everything is "breaking" and "up to the minute," depending on which news teasers you watch.

I prefer to get my news from the papers. The stories are longer and they contain more information, names are usually spelled right, and I can keep the pages if I want to. Even the online versions of the newspapers are more helpful to me than television news is. I guess I don't feel the need to be up to the minute. What I'd rather have is complete information in a hard copy.

When I got home, I went up the backstairs and let the dogs out. Then I took the papers onto the veranda, joined by a pair of scissors and a Bombay Sapphire and tonic with a twist of lemon. I lit up my Partagas, the first of the day. I had started smoking cigars long before it was fashionable to do so. But I had no interest in seeing my picture with a stogie in my mouth and I assumed most of my friends and colleagues didn't either. I smoke only in the privacy of my home and I'm going to stop smoking, altogether, someday. Today was not the day.

Billie Jo's murder and Harris's arrest had made the late editions of both the St. Pete *Times* and *The Tampa Tribune*. Most of the information I'd gotten from Ben Hathaway was repeated, so there were no secrets at this point between the police and the press. In a high-profile murder like this one, the police rarely keep information from the public. While keeping information back might give the police some useful element of "surprise," doing so would inevitably result in suggestions of a cover-up that they simply didn't want to incur. In this situation, they had no need for surprises. The case was closed the second they opened it.

Still, I did get the name of the neighbor who had discovered Billie Jo and Harris together in their last embrace on the living room floor of Harris's home. I'd seen the woman on television clips earlier in the day. I didn't recognize her name and didn't know her.

I also got the timing details from the papers. Of course, the readers were given the inevitable rehash of the entire Billie Jo Steam story, or as much of it as the paper could dig out of archives on such short notice.

I clipped all of the relevant articles from both papers. Mostly, they reprinted the news of Billie Jo's parole hearing and the new DNA evidence that had freed her. Trey Steam's murder was given very little coverage, but would likely fill the papers for the next several days. Until a new story came along to bounce it off the front page.

Interviews with Harris's other neighbors were printed, but, again, these were short and few and mostly irrelevant. These people knew nothing about Harris and even less about Billie Jo. The interviews were printed in order to fill space. Nothing more. I looked at them just to get as clear a picture as possible of the murder and arrest scene.

At length, I placed all the articles in a file envelope and set them on my desk near my journal. Then, I returned to the bar for a refill on my Sapphire and picked up another cigar.

When I got back to the living room, the telephone began to ring. I let the machine pick up the call. "Willa, dear, please call me when you get home. I know you're upset and blaming yourself. Let's talk about it." It was Kate.

I was in no mood to hear her tell me Billie Jo's death was not my fault. The fact was: Billie Jo would be alive today if it weren't for me. I wasn't happy about that, but I wouldn't deny it either, to Kate or to myself. As had been said in my courtroom today, since I'd had control over getting Billie Jo out of prison and putting her in harm's way, I should take responsibility for her death. If I hadn't bent the rules, she'd still be alive.

Standing over the machine, I noticed I had several other messages. I pushed the play button and listened to them. Ursula, other reporters, the message I'd just heard from Kate. And one more I'd never have expected. "Willa, Leo Colombo here. I'd like to come by and see you. I need to talk to you. It's about five o'clock now. I'll be at the Sunset Bar at seven."

I made a note on my calendar of the date, time and location of Billie Jo's funeral, which Ursula had left on my answering machine. Then I looked at my watch. It was 7:15 now. Leo was probably downstairs waiting for me. It was the first time he'd ever called me or tried to see me without Kate. It would be unacceptably rude not to go meet him.

Reluctantly, I put down the cigar and poured the gin in the sink. I walked slowly down the stairs, watching the guests, looking again at Aunt Minnie's tastefully decorated nineteenth century foyer. When Aunt Minnie lived here, these were her secretaries, breakfronts, and sideboards. Even the small butler's table, between the upholstered camelback sofas in the center, were Aunt Minnie's pieces. The soft blue fleur de lis wallpaper had been restored to match its former gilded excellence. Would Aunt Minnie be pleased to have her beautiful things returned to usefulness, or horrified that strangers came into her home for lunch and dinner seven days a week?

I walked through the lobby and into the Sunset Bar. It took me about a nanosecond to find Leo Colombo waiting in my favorite booth. He was staring straight at the door and saw me immediately. I stopped by the bar to order the second Bombay Sapphire I hadn't drunk upstairs.

Leo got up when I arrived at his table, greeting me with the thousand-watt smile that, if possible, made his face even more blindingly handsome than it was at rest. Leo kissed me full on the lips before I could turn my head. I restrained myself from slapping him, but just barely.

The bartender brought my drink, and another Perrier with lime for Leo, whom I'd never seen consume alcohol. This was Leo's appointment. I let him start. He began by putting his hand over mine on the table. I pulled away, resting both my hands in my lap to avoid any repeat attempts to touch me.

"I know you don't like me. No," he said, holding up his hand in the same gesture I'd used in court this morning to stop my polite protest. "Don't bother to deny it. I can tell. What I don't know is why you don't like me. I've been kind to you. I've done nothing to make you dislike me. What's wrong?"

His approach had the desired effect of catching me off guard. We don't talk honestly with people in Tampa. People here never tell you what they're thinking. At least, not what they're thinking about you. We do a lot of talking about everyone else. Apparently, things were different in Italy.

I took advantage of his directness. "It's not that I don't like you, Leo. I don't know you well enough not to like you. What I don't like is that you've married Kate." At least, that was part of what I wasn't happy about. He was thirty-five years old, without a job, had no money, and now I'd found out he had two small children in Italy whom he wants Kate to raise.

Leo was barely raised himself. I resented, too, that he was asking Kate's son Jason to help him bring his children here. To say nothing of whatever his relationship was with Augustus, about which I was still uneasy. Nor did I like him pawing me as if he was a special friend, when nothing could be further from the truth.

And all of that was before we got to the fact that I had him to thank for the mess I was in with Billie Jo and Harris Steam. If Leo hadn't pressured Kate to get me involved in this, she'd never have done so. I took full responsibility for the choice I'd made, but I hate it when someone so effectively pushes my buttons.

"But, why? I love Kate and she loves me. We're soul mates. We're good for each other," he pleaded.

Well, I thought uncharitably, at least Kate has been good for you. Without Kate, you'd be living in Italy, working as a model, under who knows what conditions. I said none of that.

"Don't you think Kate is happier since we married? She doesn't live alone anymore. She has fun. Doesn't that count?" He had leaned toward me with both hands under the table, giving me his most earnest expression.

The gin, the day, Billie Jo, Harris, life, everything just came to a head at that point. Leo was in the perfect spot to take the brunt of my emotions. What the hell? "Yea, Leo, it counts. Kate's happiness is the only thing that counts. As long as she stays happy, that's enough for me. But the moment that changes because of you, you'd better be long gone from here."

Leo jumped back as if I'd slapped him in the face. He replaced his earnest expression with shock and then surprise. "Why would you think I'd make Kate unhappy? That will never happen!"

"See that it doesn't," I said, and got up to leave.

He grabbed my wrist, forcing me to turn back to him. Now, his handsome face was red with anger. "Don't threaten me, Willa. No woman threatens me. You mind your business and I'll mind mine. We'll see who makes Kate happy. At the moment, you're not doing so well in that department yourself."

I pulled my arm free, turned, and stalked out.

Chapter Twenty-One

My encounter with Leo had the advantage of getting my adrenaline running full speed. Maybe I couldn't shield Kate from certain heartbreak at the hands of Leo Colombo, but I could help Harris Steam by finding out who had killed his father and his mother. As quickly as possible.

I put on a pot of Cuban coffee for a clear head, returned to my den, and closed the door. I spent three hours with my journal, the newspaper clippings, and what I knew about Billie Jo's murder and Harris Steam's confession. Was it just yesterday that I'd decided to find out who had killed Trey Steam?

As a place to start, and maybe because Billie Jo never tried to find the real killer, I assumed that Trey Steam's murder was related, somehow, to Six Bills. I hadn't talked to the band members during the work I'd done for Billie Jo, partly because I hadn't had the time. But also because I hadn't needed to investigate Trey Steam's murder to complete the job I was doing for Billie Jo. If the two murders were related, I needed to know about the group and what between them could have motivated someone to kill.

I pulled out the CD Harris had given me and located the complete names I needed listed on the back. I wrote all five of their names, one on each page of journal paper:

WILLETTA JOHNSON ("BILLIE JO") STEAM
JOHN ("JOHNNY") WILLIAM TYSON
WILLIAM WALTER (WALTER) WESTFIELD III
WILLIAM LINCOLN ("LINC")
ENRIQUE WILLIAM ("RICKY") GUTIERREZ.

Then, as an afterthought, I added the sixth one:
WILLIAM HARRIS STEAM III ("TREY").

Looking at the list, I added one more:
WILLIAM HARRIS STEAM IV.

Harris had been there, also. He might have been too young to remember anything, of course, but at this stage I didn't have enough information to reach any conclusions or to rule anyone out.

I spent another hour with my journal, listing everything I knew about each member of the Six Bills. For some of them, the list was short. Like Ricky Gutierrez. I'd never met him, although he must have been at Billie Jo's victory party and was one of the most prominent men in Tampa. His family had owned and operated a cigar manufacturing business here for over one hundred years. George might know Ricky, though, and I made a note to ask.

I also didn't know much about Johnny Tyson. I'd seen his obvious love for Billie Jo. Love could be a powerful motivator for murder. And it also might explain the guilt that kept him faithful all those years that Billie Jo was in prison. Hard to believe Johnny would have let Billie Jo remain in prison, when all the time he'd had the key to her release—if he had in fact killed her husband. But he did have that scar on his arm, which could have been a defensive wound. It would have accounted for a lot of blood on Trey's clothes and the murder weapon, too.

Nor had I met William Lincoln, the one they called Linc. I had no idea whether he was living in Tampa anymore, or what had happened to him. I would find him if I had to.

I went through each name, listing my knowledge, my intuition, my questions, and my action plan. Again, I assured myself that the plan was sound. I simply needed to execute it. I spent the rest of the evening figuring out how to do just that. I didn't realize when my head fell to my chin. I went to sleep in the chair with troubled thoughts about life and death spinning in my head.

The slow screech of the French doors that led out to Mom's beloved garden nudged me in my half-sleep. I felt a small, soft breeze on my cheek as the old door fell open slightly. The sweet, unmistakable fragrance of mature lilacs wandered into the room, overpowering the sickroom smells I'd become immune to. The perfume was early, the lilacs already in full bloom, as if knowing Mom wouldn't be there if they waited another couple of weeks. Even the lilacs had accepted what I, at sixteen, was unable to accept.

The cool breeze and the whiff of lilacs roused me more fully awake. I had dozed off a few hours before with my head bent to my chin. Now, sitting upright in the chair, I moved my head back and forth, seeking relief from the crick in my neck. The quiet, rattling breaths coming from my mother on the bed across the room continued to reassure me. I lifted my hand to the back of my neck to massage the minor pain as I got up, checked on Mom, and felt her shallow breathing.

Her green eyes, the ones she had passed on to me, were closed and easy, as they had been for several days now. Gentle snoring around the oxygen tube in her nose, barely audible over the other sickroom noises, was the only sound she made. I cherished each one because it meant she was still here.

Mom had been on morphine for several days before we brought her home from the hospital. She asked to come home to die and Dad honored her request. She hadn't spoken a coherent word since we placed her in the large, four-poster bed she slept in alone, and she'd never said good-bye.

Despite Dad's urging and the assurance that the nurse would sit by Mother's side, unmoving, until I returned, I refused to leave her room for anything other than to go to the bathroom. I feared I wouldn't be here if she woke up. Or worse, that she'd leave me when I wasn't with her. The life-robbing malignancy had, out of fear or denial, or both, been left to grow too long before she let the doctors find it. Whatever could be said between us had been said the past few months. Still, I wanted to be with her as long as possible.

"I love you, Mom," I said, brushing her golden hair back from her lovely forehead, allowing my hand to linger while she slept her morphine sleep. I was sure she could hear me, although she made no reply. She looked at peace. Reassured that Mom was resting as easily as she could, I walked back to the old door. I reached for the knob to close out the chill and leave the lilacs alone in the too cool night air.

Just as I pushed the door toward its threshold, another small whoosh of breeze gently caressed my face, like the cool reassuring hand my mother placed on my feverish child's brow, repeating the gesture I'd just made for her.

I closed the door firmly and turned the lock to keep out the darkness. When I moved back to the bed, Mom was gone, ending her slow dance with death from breast cancer. She'd waited until my back was turned to leave me. In death, as in life, she thought only of my comfort, that it would be easier for me if I didn't see her go.

Tears began to stream down my sixteen-year-old cheeks. I finally realized I would never share so many things with my mother that daughters want to share. My high school graduation, my wedding, perhaps the birth of my own children. The lilac's fragrance was cloying now as hope died in my chest. Grace Harper would never be a grandmother or smell the flowers in her garden again. I began to cry in earnest then. Great gulping sobs.

Now, the dream sobs jerked me awake from my dream world, with tears in my adult eyes and a heavy, knowing heart. I rubbed the ache in my neck, trudged to bed. I spent a restless night thinking about Harris and his tragic family. About a mother's life cut short and how that hurt never goes away.

Harris had hired Paul Robbins as his lawyer, again. When I asked Paul for permission to visit his client, he said, "I hope you can get more sense out of him than I have so far." Paul told me they were holding Harris at the new jail on Orient Road.

Hillsborough County had once used the jail on Morgan

Street, but the federal government now leased that facility. It didn't take me long to get over to Orient Road early the next morning, but finding a place to park was a problem. Parking illegally was always an option, say in front of a fire hydrant or a driveway, but not a smart thing to do right by the jail.

Actually, Tampa cops rarely write out traffic tickets. I once asked Ben Hathaway why. He said, "They tell me they don't have time to write tickets because they're too busy filling out accident reports." The irony of it wasn't lost on Ben. Still, testing my luck by parking illegally right in front of the Sheriff's Office seemed foolhardy.

After I'd circled the block three times, I was able to wait for a spot while another car pulled out. I had spent ten minutes driving to the station and twenty minutes parking the car.

Before I had gotten involved in the Billie Jo Steam case, the number of times I'd visited a jail could be counted on one hand with fingers left over. Jails were unfamiliar territory to me. I tried to forget them. My nose remembered and began to clog itself up before I entered, anticipating the pungent odor of unwashed bodies and urine, masked only slightly by disinfectant.

Inside the almost pristinely clean building, pine scented sprays misted the air at regular intervals from deodorizers that must have been replaced every two or three hours. The jail was clean, but it was a jail, nonetheless. I didn't have any desire to live here.

I waited for Harris in a room that was almost identical to the one where I'd first met his mother, Billie Jo. The duplicate government issue metal table sat starkly inside the same four government green walls.

The Harris Steam who entered the room and sat down across the table from me was barely recognizable. He was a distant cousin of the man I'd first met at Kate's house on Mother's Day, let alone the happier Harris I'd seen at Billie Jo's victory party.

A three-day growth of beard covered his face, the grey in it plainly visible. His hair was matted and dirty and his breath smelled like a feral animal had died in his mouth. The rest of his body odor made me grateful for the pervasive pine scent that kept me from gagging. Barely.

Harris hung his head and wouldn't meet my eyes. Gone was the carefree singer, sexy man, heroic son, and loving father. This guy looked like the men accused of crimes you'd see in news footage any given night of the week.

Before I saw him, I'd been sympathetic to his situation. Now, the sadness of the outcome threatened to crush me. I didn't believe Harris had murdered his mother. I couldn't believe it. Because that would mean I had killed her. I got her out of prison. I put her in that house the night she died. I couldn't live with that. Which was why I was here. Harris was innocent. He had to be.

I had permission from Harris's lawyer to meet with him. Harris planned to plead guilty, which he had an absolute right to do. The lawyer was trying to talk Harris out of that foolish course of action. He hoped I'd make more progress in persuading Harris than he had.

I got out my tape recorder. I didn't want to take notes, but I wanted an accurate record of what we said to each other. For later. When I proved he was innocent. Or, more cynically, when someone accused me of improper conduct.

"Harris!" I had to shout at him to make him hear me. He had traveled to a distant place in his mind, not caring what went on around him. "Talk to me!" Harris raised his head slightly and looked at me a couple of seconds before he lowered his head again.

"Why?" he said. "What's there to say? I killed my mother. Why would you want to talk to me? Why would anyone want to talk to me? Just leave me here, until they execute me." His resignation to his crime and his own death was total. And totally devastating to me. Besides that, he was starting to piss me off.

"Why did you kill her, Harris? Why'd you do it?" I challenged, trying without success to get some emotion out of him. Any emotion.

"I don't know," he said, without inflection in his voice.

Another tack was called for if I was going to get any information from him at all. I started again. "Tell me about the night your mother died, Harris. Where were you?"

"We were at home. At my place." He answered me like a robot, just giving me the information. No feeling. No life.

"Who else was there?"

"Everybody."

"Everybody, who? Tell me." He said nothing. "Was Billie Jo there?"

"Yes."

"Johnny?"

"Yes."

"Who else?" Nothing. I thought about my list of the Six Bills, the only real starting place I had to name Harris and Billie Jo's friends. "Linc?"

"Yeah."

"Ricky?" He hesitated a few seconds.

"I think so."

"Who else?"

"I don't know."

"Were other people there, too? Come on, Harris. I'll just ask them all. I'll find out. Tell me who was at your house Sunday night." I was cajoling him now, realizing part of what he was resisting was my angry tone.

"Ricky's wife was with him. Walter and Ursula." I hid my surprise at that one. Why hadn't Ursula told me she'd been at Harris's house the night Billie Jo was killed? Something to check out.

"Who else was there?"

"I don't know. A whole crowd of people. It was a party, you know?"

"What kind of a party was it?"

"Celebration."

"Celebrating what?"

"Billie Jo and Johnny got married."

"Got married? When?" I was astonished, although I shouldn't have been. Billie Jo had said they planned to marry.

"That day. They were celebrating." A faint memory seemed to enter his mind.

"Was Eva there? Your girls?" If this was a wedding celebration, the family was probably all together, I figured.

A vein began to throb in his forehead, while his face suffused the color of an overripe tomato. He slammed his hands down on the table and leaned toward me, making me feel threatened in a way I'd never have believed possible. "You leave Eva out of this! Leave her alone!" he said, hissing the words with enough force to more than get his point across.

"Okay, sure," I said, trying to calm him down. He glared at me a while longer, and then resumed both his seat and his distracted, disinterested pose. It was as if two men lived in his body, the defeated one and the defiant one. I remembered thinking the same thing about his mother. I changed the subject. "How long did the party last?"

"A while. Well into the night. We drank a lot. I smoked a little." He meant he had smoked marijuana.

What I figured was he'd done more than smoked a little. I made a mental note to find out if they'd given him a drug test when they brought him in. Maybe we could do something with diminished capacity.

"Then what happened?" I asked him, my old deposition techniques resurfacing. When questioning someone about an event of which you have absolutely no knowledge, the best thing a lawyer can do is to ask open-ended questions until the picture emerges.

He shrugged. "I dunno. We partied. People came and went. After a while, I passed out."

"And then what?"

He started to cry. Not just to cry, but to keen and to rock back and forth in his chair. "I woke up," he said, between sobs. "I woke up and Mommy was dead. I killed her. My mommy is dead." He wailed this last part, like the frightened two-year-old he was when he had found his father dead. Harris was reliving that nightmare, a nightmare he probably didn't consciously remember.

He was making so much noise that the guard came back in to check on us. Harris wouldn't be able to tell me anything else now. I took my tape recorder and put it in my pocket, said some soothing words to Harris and let the guard return him to his cell. I had work to do. Which was a hell of a lot better than feeling helpless and guilty.

Chapter Twenty-Two

I made it back to my courtroom just in time to take the bench at nine o'clock. The *Madison v. Cardio Medical* team was all assembled and I instructed the court security officer to bring in the jury. Phillip Sloat put on his case for the remainder of the morning session, until our break at eleven o'clock. The testimony was moving toward introducing evidence to support the motion for directed verdict that Sloat presented to me yesterday, which the jury had not yet heard. Sloat put three witnesses up in two hours, so he had taken seriously my admonition to move the case along.

For their part, Lehman, Royal, and Marilyn Madison were alternately bored, outraged, and devastated. The three put on quite an entertaining performance. Unfortunately for the little Greek chorus, no Academy Award is given for trials.

By eleven-thirty, I was ready for a break from these jokers. From the looks on their faces, and the comments the court personnel overheard while the jurors were filing back and forth from the jury room, the jurors all felt the same way. The trial had gone on way too long. The jurors understood both sides and they wanted to return to their own lives. The novelty of sitting as a juror on the Stanley Madison trial, regardless of how famous Stanley and *Corgi* were, had worn thin.

Augustus and I went over the day's activities. Then I gave him the list of names of the Six Bills from my journal. "Please look up telephone numbers and addresses for these folks before the lunch break. Just make your notes right on that sheet. I don't want that information in the computer. And then call over to the Hillsborough County Clerk's office and order the court file from the Trey Steam murder trial."

Augustus looked at the list, and then back to me. A troubled expression clouded his face. "These folks should all be listed in the phone book. It won't take me long to find them."

I nodded at him, over my china cup and saucer with the Jamaican Blue Mountain coffee that had quickly become my second favorite. "Great," I said, turning my attention back to mail requiring a response. When I looked up again, he was still standing there. "What?"

Augustus's troubled frown deepened. "Why are you getting more involved in this thing, Judge? I know these people. They're members of that old band, the one Harris Steam's father was the lead singer for. And you've got Eva Steam on here, and her parents. What are you planning to do?"

Resisting the urge to tell him to mind his own business, I said, "I know you're concerned for me."

"Concerned isn't a strong enough word. Two people involved with that band are dead. The son is in jail, accused of killing his own mother. These are bad people, Judge Carson. You should stay away from them all." Augustus's Jamaican lilt was more pronounced when he was upset. His words were stern, but his voice was melodic, almost like a song. The effect was incongruous, light and dark at the same time. Like Augustus, himself.

"Please. Just do as I ask. I promise you, I won't put myself in any kind of danger." He continued to look at me in mild rebellion. "If you won't do this for me, I'll just do it myself." Augustus sighed then and took the list with him out to his desk, giving up on making me see it his way for the time being.

By now I'd learned Augustus's manner of operating. He did what he wanted to do, and perpetuated the fiction that I was the boss when that fiction suited his own purposes. But we had bonded quickly. I felt, rather than knew, that he totally supported me and had my best interests at heart. "Trust your instincts," Kate always tells me. With Augustus, I was.

The rest of the morning trial session continued as the earlier portion had. At lunchtime, I returned to my chambers. Today, we had tuna with pasta, a hard roll, and half a pineapple. Augustus was determined to change my life in as many ways as possible.

Next to my plate was the daily green folder containing matters that required my attention before I resumed the afternoon trial session. A couple of telephone message slips that required a response were on top now, followed by a few judicial orders for me to sign, invitations to professional meetings, and, under the pile, the list of names, addresses and telephone numbers I'd requested. Scribbled on the bottom in Augustus's nearly indecipherable scrawl, was the notation: "Steam file in storage, ordered."

I took a bite of the tuna salad. The small deviation from my normal routine was refreshing, I thought, as I wrote a number by each of the names and circled it. I would interview each of these people, in an order that made sense to me. Starting after the trial day, I would speak to the one I knew absolutely nothing about.

"We was known as the Six Bills," Linc told me, in a strong drawl with bad grammar that belied his college education. He used them both as a badge of heritage, I supposed. Or out of laziness. We'd gotten settled outside on the white plastic chairs in the postage-stamp-sized lot on which his trailer sat. The trailer had seen better days. It looked older than the man himself.

I figured him to be about the same age as Walter Westfield, fifty-two. His name was William Lincoln, but he'd always been called Linc, even before he became a member of Six Bills, he told me. Once, he'd have been good looking in the craggy, unkempt way that was popular back then.

His brown hair was wavy, a little too long, a little too streaked with grey. He reminded me of the movie actor, Sam Elliott. They could have been brothers. Linc still sported the 1970s big moustache. He had a pair of fierce eyebrows that might never have been trimmed. His eyes were a nondescript hazel, the skin around them a network of deep lines, likely caused by smoking and squinting around it. His face was weathered brown, like a man who'd spent years on the ocean exposed to unrelenting sunlight.

The best thing about him was his voice. Linc's voice was raspy and deep, the kind of voice you'd listen to late at night and feel like you'd found a friend. A voice that went well with wine and candle light.

"We met in 1968 at UT, then all six of us graduated in the spring of 1972. We played around here, recorded a couple a singles that never went nowhere. Naturally we'd want to go to Woodstock. We were rock musicians. It was sort of like a business convention for us." He grinned.

I'd heard a lot about the music festival held in Woodstock, New York, in 1969. I was much too young to have gone, even if such a thing had crossed my mind, which it hadn't. Up until now, I thought I'd never met anyone who had been to Woodstock. At least, if I knew any of the participants, they'd developed the discretion later in life not to discuss it.

What was that old joke? "If you remember Woodstock, it's because you weren't there"? The stories of drug use, free sex, and constant music in the rain and mud were legendary—and maybe more-than-a-little exaggerated, I'd always believed.

"Even before the trip, we was an uneasy club," Linc continued, talking around his cigarette as he tuned a string on the acoustic guitar he held on his knee. "Billie Jo was the keyboard player, married to Trey Steam. Trey had a bad temper and a heavy hand. But the voice. Man, he had a pack-a-day Rod Stewart voice long before Stewart, you know? Trey was Six Bills' lead singer. Groupies followed him everywhere."

"Free love?" I asked.

Linc chuckled, caught some of the smoke in his throat, and coughed. "Well, that was more a figment of media imagination in 1968. We was pretty clean-cut college kids. UT wasn't Berkeley. But, Trey had his share of girlfriends."

"What about Billie Jo?"

"None of us knew why Billie Jo married him. Maybe it had somethin' to do with how good lookin' he was or how he could sing so it made you cry. But she married him in early sixty-nine, not that he acted married. He sure expected her to though." Linc continued to fiddle with the guitar strings, tightening this one, changing that one, then playing a chord or so as he talked, picking out a little melody and then stopping. He kept the cigarette perpetually perched in the corner of his mouth, ignoring the ashes that fell onto his denim shirt.

"What about Johnny?"

Linc shook his head. "I'm not sure when that started. Johnny was a quiet one. He was shy and alone. Kind. He'd listen to Billie Jo cry over Trey; hold her hand, you know? Offered her a sympathetic shoulder, I guess. The rest of us just wanted to stay clear of Trey's temper. We'd all had more 'n one run-in with him. None of us was tryin' to repeat the experience."

"At some point, Johnny must have fallen in love with her?" I commented, lifting my voice at the end of the sentence to make a question.

He nodded. "It wasn't hard to do. We were all a little in love with Billie Jo." He grinned at me, mashing the cigarette out in the sand under his dirty, bare foot, without flinching. Linc was telling the story now, so I kept quiet and let him tell it in his own way.

"By the time we got into the van to go to Woodstock, we all figgered Johnny and Billie Jo were lovers, 'tho Johnny would never say so. Trey musta known, too. He acted like he didn't care about Billie Jo, anyhow. He'd kiss other girls all the time, with all of us, including Billie Jo, right there. Even then, I didn't like it. Johnny didn't either."

Linc got up and went inside. He brought back two long-necked bottles of Rolling Rock and screwed the tops off, handing me one. Then he sat down and picked up the guitar again. He lit another cigarette. Unfiltered, but he took them out of a package, so I hoped he was smoking tobacco.

"We had us a good time at Woodstock, boy. It made us even closer, somehow. We were inspired. When we came home, we practiced more, played more. Spent even more time together. That's when we had a couple, three hit records. Local folks knew us, even if the national audience hadn't noticed yet. Best days I ever spent, them times. Man, I loved making music with them guys." Smiling, he shook his head, as if to clear the memories, then swigged the beer.

"What about Harris? Where was he then?" I asked Linc.

"Oh, this was before Little Trey was born. Billie Jo and Johnny were together a lot. When Billie Jo turned up pregnant, there was some speculatin'. Billie Jo said the baby was Trey's. We believed her. Hell, I don't think anybody really cared one way or t'other. We loved Billie Jo and we all loved Little Trey. We just all took care of each other." He continued staring at the guitar, so I couldn't judge his eyes. The story confirmed other things I'd read or surmised. Besides, both Billie Jo and Trey were dead now. Linc had no legitimate reason to lie.

"What happened the night Trey died?" I asked.

He took a long drag on the cigarette and looked straight at me for the first time since we had sat down. He seemed to be judging whether he'd answer me or not. He knew I was helping Harris, and that was why I had come. Something made up his mind for him; what had done so wasn't obvious to me.

"We had a gig at the fronton that night. We played 'til late. Trey was pretty drunk. When they got home, Trey and Billie Jo got to fightin'. He hit her all the time, 'tho she denied it, if you asked her. She'd show up sometimes with bruises on her or wearing a long skirt with long sleeves to hide 'em." He took another, longer swig of the beer, while mine remained untasted.

Linc was back in time now, reminiscing quietly to himself. "That night, Billie Jo took the boy and left. She just drove for a while, and then went to Johnny's to wait it out. That's what she usually did. Waited at Johnny's 'til she figured Trey had calmed down. Or passed out." He stopped there and stared off into the distant past. "When Johnny took her and Little Trey home, they found him. Dead. She ran over and hugged Trey. She got blood all over her. She saw the knife. She must a touched it or somethin'. I never knowed what all the evidence was."

Linc stood up and put his dirty foot on the chair, resting the guitar on his knee and turning his head back down toward his fiddling fingers. He played a little, neither of us saying anything for a while. When I set my beer bottle down, its contents still untasted, he continued. "Anyway, they arrested Billie Jo. The other Bills all supported her, but she was convicted anyway. Little Trey was sent to live with Trey Steam's mama and daddy." He finished his story and his beer at the same time, holding another cigarette in his mouth and strumming the guitar. He eyed the bottle I'd been holding and I handed it over to him.

I wondered how many Lincs there were in this country today, old hippies who never quite made it, and who never let it go. Woodstock was the high point of their lives, whether they had gone there or not. While many of these Woodstock baby boomers had turned into card-carrying conservatives with stock portfolios and real estate, some had fallen through society's cracks and floated on the edge of commerce—not quite homeless, but not firmly ensconced in the everyday world, either.

Linc played a little tune for me on his guitar and sang a bit, too. He wasn't half bad. From the way he lived, it appeared that no one had paid him much to play and sing in quite a long while. But Linc was a bundle of contradictions. Like his bad grammar and heavy accent, maybe he chose to live modestly for personal reasons. After our first meeting, I liked Linc, but I was only too aware that I didn't know him.

By the time I got home, the day had already gone to bed. The sunset was over, but the dusky pink sky remained. Quite a few cars filled the parking lot at Minaret, telling me George's dinner crowd was in full swing. As I'd been doing often of late, I avoided the lobby by taking the back stairs. I was barely able to push open the back door when I reached the top—because the welcoming committee blocked it.

Once inside, Harry and Bess "told me" they'd been cooped up for too many hours. I let them run out without me, knowing they'd be down in the bay until I called them back. I went into my den and glanced at the blinking answering machine but ignored it. I poured myself a Sapphire and tonic, lit a Partagas, flipped through the mail, and called the dogs back for a quiet half hour on the veranda. As I sat there, staring at the now dark water, George came out with his Glenfiddich.

"I thought I'd have to join you here, I see you so seldom these days," he said as he bent down to kiss me. He settled himself into the other chaise lounge.

"It's been a long week already," I told him, fully aware that today was just Tuesday.

"Care to share?" he asked.

Grateful for the opportunity, I related the entire story to him. Or what I knew of it, so far, ending with my visit to Linc tonight. When I finished, George considered for a while. He's a fabulous strategist. I was expecting a brilliant suggestion.

"You sort of stepped in the middle of this one, didn't you?" he finally said, which was not what I was looking for. Seeing I was anticipating something more helpful, he continued gently. "It's a no-win situation, Willa. You know that. Billie Jo and her husband are both dead. Regardless of who killed them, they will always be dead."

Although he echoed my own thoughts about the futility of the Stanley Madison case currently in my courtroom, I didn't take what he said well. George tried again. "What I mean is, Harris has had a lot of tragedy in his short life. Whatever you might feel you owe him, or whatever you can do for him, you can't erase that tragedy as if it never happened."

"I know that. But the cycle has to stop somewhere. Harris doesn't belong in prison. His children don't need to spend their lives the same way he spent his," I told George.

"They won't. They have their mother. She'll be with them," he pointed out, reasonably.

"They'll have their father, too, dammit! I know he didn't kill Billie Jo." I pounded the table and said this with a great deal of vehemence for a person with no evidence.

"Then why say he did?" Again, a reasonable question.

But I was in no mood to be reasonable. "That's one of the things I intend to find out."

George rose, taking the last sip of his single malt scotch as he did so. "I have to get back to work. Why don't you come down and have dinner with me? Take your mind off all this."

"I can't face it tonight. Send me something up, okay?"

He bent down to kiss me again. "Sure, Mighty Mouse," he said, with the affection he always uses when he calls me that, no matter how pissed off it makes me. "I'll send you up some gourmet cheese." I threw a pillow at his retreating back, and missed.

Hours later, I woke up in a cold sweat. I had had the dream again. This time, Mom and I were not in her sickroom. We were in Harris Steam's jail cell. But her bed was there. The acrid, hopeless pine scent from the jail replaced the gentle, fragrant lilacs. Instead of dying peacefully while my back was turned, Mom was thrashing on the bed, crying out, trying to say something. I couldn't make out her words. Then she died, and in my dream, I began to sob.

As before, the dream-contained sobs were the jerking that awakened me. It was five o'clock. I got up, leaving George and both Labradors snoring.

The quiet morning was still mostly night. Out here on Plant Key, we had no traffic and no neighbors. Little noise came to me in the predawn, except the bay washing gently against the beach. The air was warm enough to take my Cuban coffee outside to spend an hour with my journal. I reread everything I'd written last night about Harris and Linc and my plans for the next few days.

Today would be a reprise of yesterday, for the most part. I felt like a hamster on a wheel. I had delayed the *Madison* trial as much as I could during the Billie Jo parole work. I had no choice but to continue to slog through the trial until they finished, or their two-week trial limit expired, whichever came first. But I could end the court day at four o'clock. Then I'd make further progress on my investigation.

After my coffee, I dressed and called quietly to the dogs, letting George sleep. He hadn't come upstairs until well after midnight. I could see no point in waking him, too. Harry and Bess inhaled their breakfast and bounded down the stairs, dashed out into the bay, and then passed me by as I made my way slowly into my morning run.

One foot pounding in front of the other, I talked to myself about my nightmare. Mostly, I tried to tell my thirty-nine-year-old self to let my sixteen-year-old self go in peace. Mother's Day was over. I must now return to the present and the living.

About halfway around Plant Key, running west now, my view toward Ballast Point and the Tampa Yacht Club, I changed direction mentally and physically. I reviewed what I knew about Trey Steam's murder, Billie Jo's murder, and Six Bills. I went over in my head what I planned to do after court today.

I returned to the house, washed off the dogs, and put them in their kennel. Then I showered, dressed, and left for work. The plan still made sense to me. In any event, I couldn't come up with a better one.

Chapter Twenty-Three

Eva Steam's office was in the professional building near Memorial Hospital, at the corner of Swann and Habana. I got there a little after four-thirty. Parking the car in the open lot, I walked through the small courtyard to the back entrance of the three-story building.

Eva's office was on the first floor in the back, at the end of a long, narrow corridor, with doctors' offices on both sides. "Eva Raines, M.D., Neurologist," read the sign on her door. She had no partners.

I gave my name to the receptionist. She told me Eva was with her last appointment of the day and would be free in a few minutes, if I wanted to wait. The waiting area was typical of a prosperous solo practitioner's medical practice. In the corner were children's magazines and a small table with crayons and coloring books. I assumed these were for visitors and not for patients, since Eva wasn't a pediatric neurologist.

I sat in one of the chairs farthest from the blaring big-screen television and picked up this week's copy of *Time*, preparing myself to wait "a few minutes."

In law, we estimate how much time something should take and then multiply by four to get the amount of life it will actually devour. Medical waiting was the same, I thought, as I checked my watch. An hour had passed. The receptionist seemed to have forgotten about me. I was just about to remind her when the door separating the waiting room from the examination rooms opened and Walter Westfield walked out, straightening his tie, with his suit coat over his arm.

"Walter," I called to him, getting up to chat.

He looked my way and jerked his head quickly, shocked to see me. "Willa," he answered, rapidly gathering his composure

and coming over. "What brings you here?" He put on his coat, losing his balance a little, with both arms in the air simultaneously.

"The same thing that brought you, I suppose. I wanted to
chat with Eva for a few minutes, but you beat me to it. I thought
your wife was the journalist," I teased him by suggesting he was
here to interview Eva because of Billie Jo's death.

"Well, I offered to do Ursula a favor," he said as he raised a
shaky hand to looked at his watch.

"The senatorial candidate is not here for medical reasons,
then?" I asked.

"Of course not. Fit as a horse." He thumped himself on the
chest with his fist. "I need to run, though. I've got another
appointment. My perpetual calendar seems never to have an
empty slot." We said our goodbyes and he let himself out.

The receptionist beckoned me toward the inner office,
escorting me to Eva's private office in the back where she now
sat. There, Eva had a clear view of the courtyard. If she'd been
looking out the window as I came in, Eva would have seen me
enter the building. Not that she had any reason to avoid me. But
I just noticed that she could have, if she'd decided to. I watched
through Eva's window now as Walter Westfield hurried to the
parking lot. Again, he seemed unsteady on his feet.

Behind her desk, Eva wore her white lab coat and her reading glasses. They made her look older than I'd thought her to be
and more scientific, somehow. Her hair was held firmly in place
by a severe French twist. Very professional. She had a couple of
pills in her hand and swallowed them with a glass of water.

"Sorry. I've got a bit of a headache. Been burning the candle
at both ends lately," she apologized. Eva looked as frazzled as I
felt. Her eyes had deep circles under them and her complexion
was sallow. Blush stood out on her cheeks like two pink circles on
the face of a clown. She'd chewed off her lipstick long ago.

After the preliminaries, I said, "I saw Walter Westfield in
your waiting room . . . " and just sort of left it there for her to fill

in the blank. No way was his wife letting Walter do her fieldwork. Nor would he have agreed to do so, even before Billie Jo was murdered, and certainly not now. That Walter had lied to me as to why he was here meant he had something to lie about.

Eva shook her head sadly as her mouth formed a tense line. "I can't discuss my patients with you without their consent," she said, rubbing her temples with both hands, inadvertently confirming my suspicions. Something was wrong with Walter. It could be a minor problem, but neurologists don't often treat patients with minor problems, either, if yesterday's expert witness in the *Madison* trial was to be believed.

Walter's medical condition was none of my business, except that he was married to my friend and I wished him good health. I also wondered whether Ursula knew Walter was consulting a neurologist. If she knew, she'd never mentioned it to me. Ursula was a woman with secrets.

"Will it interfere with his being a senator, assuming he's elected?" I asked, attempting to suggest I knew exactly what Walter's condition was.

She didn't answer me. Instead, she replied, "Not to be rude, Willa, but I do have quite a few things to do here before I can go home to my girls. They really need me now. Is there something I can help you with?"

"You know I don't believe Harris killed Billie Jo . . . " I started as I sat down in one of the chairs across the desk from her. She needn't think that I was going to make this quick. There were things I needed to know.

"That's because you weren't there. If you'd been there, you'd believe it," she said, without venom, but with resignation and conviction.

I shook my head. "No. I'm sure I wouldn't."

"You don't know him. He has a violent temper. He's broken things, hurt himself. He used to get into bar fights when he was younger. That's how he got that broken nose and the scar over his eye that the groupies think is so charming." She said the word "charming" as if a scar over Harris's left eye was the least attractive thing on the planet.

"There's a difference between the types of behavior you're describing and murder," I told her with a conviction of my own. But was there, really? Didn't violence escalate? I'd heard tales of it hundreds of times in my courtroom. One thing leads to another, mixed with drugs and alcohol to lower inhibitions, and tragedy often resulted. Even without knowing the common character traits of a murderer that I'd heard from the expert yesterday in court, I saw enough examples to know such things happened.

"You weren't there," she said again.

"No, I wasn't. Which is why I wanted to talk to you. When did you get to the party?"

"I don't know. Sometime around seven, I guess." She appeared impatient, as if her time was being imposed upon, which it was. She continued straightening her desk, moving the pens into the pen cup, flipping through a few medical charts, making some notes here and there, and just generally fidgeting.

"Tell me what happened. I need someone with some objectivity," I said, giving her credit that probably wasn't really deserved.

"It was a party. Everything seemed to be fine. Then, Harris and Billie Jo had some sort of disagreement. I think it happened when she told him something he didn't want to hear. The argument escalated into a shouting match. Harris stomped off into his room, like a child." Eva had closed her eyes while she told me this. A grimace of either distaste or pain crossed her face.

"What happened after Harris went to his room?"

"Everyone started to leave. They were embarrassed and it's a little hard to party when your host has deserted the crowd. I tried to smooth things over, convince people to stay and have a good time. I didn't want my girls to be any more upset than they already were, and I felt like, in a way, I was still the hostess. Still responsible for him." She sighed as if she'd tired of being responsible for Harris years ago.

"How so? You and Harris are divorced, aren't you?"

"We are. But neither of us has remarried and we try to remain cordial because of the girls. We had a pretty acrimonious divorce, as I'm sure you know," she said, in a tone acknowledging that everyone in Tampa knew how bitter their divorce had been, which was true. No one keeps secrets in Tampa for long and their divorce had been front-page news for several weeks. Between Harris's celebrity and Eva's being a Raines, the papers couldn't leave it alone. In the headlines, she'd accused Harris of being a spoiled child. Apparently she still felt that way.

"So you felt you should at least see everyone out that night. Does that mean you were the last to leave?" I prodded, trying to get a feel for the party and Eva's role in it.

She shook her head in the negative. "I tried to go when Ricky and Janet did. Billie Jo was still there. She had convinced Johnny to let Linc drive him home. She'd had no luck talking Harris into coming out and speaking with her. She didn't want to leave with that bitterness still between them. Billie Jo said she'd sleep at Harris's and talk to Johnny in the morning."

"Not much of a wedding night," I observed.

Eva continued to work at updating her charts, closing the folders one at a time and piling them neatly on the corner of her desk, as if I was interrupting her. "No. But they'd been apart for a long time until now. Billie Jo figured another night wouldn't matter. And Johnny was pretty drunk, himself. He was probably going to pass out somewhere, anyway." She pressed at her forehead, at some pain that wouldn't disappear.

I could picture the scene: Everyone quietly breaking up the party, embarrassed because the host had behaved badly. Going their separate ways. Now, they all wished they had stayed around.

"When did you leave?" I asked her, after a while.

"I don't know. About two or three in the morning, I guess. We'd made some coffee and sat around talking. Harris never did come out of his room and nobody was especially tired at first." She shrugged as she finished the last chart. "When Billie Jo seemed to nod off, Ricky and I laid her down on the couch. Then Ricky and Janet helped me put the girls in the car just before they left. The girls had gone to sleep in one of the bedrooms quite a while earlier. I should have left when they got tired, of course, but I didn't. Don't ask me why." She said this with the hindsight of the Monday morning quarterback.

"Then I drove the girls back home. When I got up in the morning, I heard the same news you heard," she finished her narrative.

"The party wasn't fun?"

"Sure it was. Everyone had been having a wonderful time. We were all celebrating Billie Jo and Johnny finally getting married. Everybody living happily ever after. It was great." Under those circumstances, who would want to leave when a couple of kids got sleepy? "Until Harris spoiled it," she added, sourly.

"And then what happened?" I asked her, when she'd allowed herself to lapse into reverie.

"When Harris went to his room, Billie Jo was really upset. She and I talked for a while. She told me about Harris as a little boy. What she knew, anyway." Eva stood up and walked over to the coat hook on the back of her office door. She took off her white lab coat and hung it there. Then she turned around, plainly suggesting it was time for me to go.

Eva then told me what I was already aware of, that Harris had only been two years old when his mother was sent to prison. Since Billie Jo's parents were deceased, she'd had no choice but to leave Harris with Trey Steam's parents. They disliked Billie Jo, even before they thought she'd killed their son. So Billie Jo didn't see Harris much until he was old enough to drive himself to visit her. Then, she asked me to let her go home to her kids as she showed me the door.

I walked thoughtfully to my car. Even a blind man, or a vindictive ex-wife, could see the tragedy in Harris's situation—a boy deprived of both parents because the justice system had failed. When the system finally did the right thing and let the mother go, thirty years later, the damaged boy just couldn't lose the mother to marriage and the father's memory to a different man. It was an explanation for an otherwise inexplicable reaction. I just didn't believe it.

Chapter Twenty-Four

Billie Jo's funeral was held at Hyde Park Presbyterian Church on Thursday afternoon. George and I went. When we drove up to the front door, there were so many cameras and microphones on the scene that a private security firm had been hired to keep the walkway to the church open.

The throng of reporters and photographers reminded me of television coverage I've seen of the Academy Awards. The red crowd-control ropes you see in airports or at movie theaters held spectators back. Security guards were posted at intervals of about six to eight feet, to be sure that only funeral attendees used the walkway. Ben Hathaway had asked the judge to release Harris from jail to attend the funeral. Strictly speaking, killers aren't allowed to attend the funerals of their victims. Ben had made an exception for Harris because he felt it was something he could do for Billie Jo.

The parking lot was full and we couldn't avoid using the valet. We'd come in George's Bentley, which he rarely allows anyone else to drive. But we had no choice. He handed the keys to one of the valets and hoped for the best.

We made our way slowly into the church, walking past cameras, microphones, and mourners. At the door, we were handed a printed program. When we made it into the church itself, the pews were full. The closed white casket was at the front of the aisle. We sat down in the back and maintained a respectful silence until the program began.

I say program because that's exactly what it was. The pastor of the church came out and explained that Billie Jo, like many religious southerners, had prepared her funeral program herself because she had terminal cancer. A collective gasp went up through the mourners when he said that, so Billie Jo's illness must not have been printed in the papers.

Because she knew she didn't have long to live, Billie Jo had made meticulous plans for her funeral.

According to the small booklet we'd been handed at the church entrance, the service would begin with the organ and the choir, but, shortly after, the program would segue into rock music from the Six Bills, or at least the four of them who remained alive.

A song from Billie Jo's son Harris was listed, and I wondered whether he would sing it or not. The service would close with "Just a Closer Walk with Thee," sung by Harris and the Six Bills together with the choir.

As the organ and the choir began, I looked around at the crowded church. People were standing in the back. Most of the mourners were unknown to me, but I recognized some of them from the victory party Harris had hosted at Minaret when his mother was first released from prison. More likely than not, Billie Jo Steam's murderer was here. Not only because murderers often visit the funerals of their victims, but also because over seventy percent of homicides are committed by someone known to the deceased. Everyone Billie Jo had ever known who wasn't in prison had to be here, judging from the size of the crowd.

I wished I'd had the temerity to bring a camera with me. I hadn't. My original plan was to get a copy of Ursula's news video of the mourners as they entered and exited the building. Fortunately, too, the program was professionally videotaped. I also noticed a guest book at the front of the church. I made a mental note to ask Harris for a copy of its pages along with the professional video.

The program continued, much as any Christian funeral, the familiar scripture and hymns comforting the mourners. The pastor delivered his portion of the eulogy. Then a few of Billie Jo's former prison inmates, whom she had helped long before, stood to tell of her good works while she was incarcerated. Finally, Six Bills played its three big songs, the ones that had actually made it to the charts back in the early 1970s. I had also heard them at the victory party. The melodies were familiar to the crowd so that the mourners were humming along.

Harris got up to sing his father's love song to Billie Jo. Today, Harris's voice was gravelly and tender, just as his father's had been, according to Linc. The song brought tears to every pair of eyes I could see, as Harris sang to the closed white casket. He seemed unable to carry on at several points in the melody, but the band continued to play and Harris the performer understood that he owed his mother the funeral she had wanted.

Finally, I heard the familiar strains of "Just a Closer Walk with Thee," while the remaining members of Six Bills and Harris Steam lifted the casket and carried it down the aisle to the waiting hearse as they sang. The pastor encouraged the congregation to join in the mournful but consoling tune.

Because we were at the back of the church, George and I were among the last to follow the casket. Everyone in the front pews filed by us on the way outside. Eva, Billie Jo's two grand-daughters, and Eva's parents were the first to walk by. Trey Steam's parents filed past us then, followed closely by Prescott Roberts, who gave me another of his steely glares. If I'd thought he'd forgotten about my part in this, his glare told me that was pure wishful thinking. Men like Prescott Roberts had long memories. The wives and children of the remaining Bills came next.

Everyone we knew acknowledged us as they went outside and filled the waiting limousines to travel to the graveside service.

By the time George and I made it out of the church, the media and the public had dispersed, filing into their cars so they could follow this photo opportunity all the way to Billie Jo's grave. We had considered not going to the graveside, but George's Bentley was parked first behind the limousines and now it would be too awkward not to go. We sat in the car, waiting in silence for the procession to begin.

The long, slow funeral ride took us to the cemetery and the

Steam family plot, where Billie Jo would be buried, next to Trey Steam. "It's odd that she'd be buried here, don't you think?" George asked.

"Johnny Tyson was much more like a devoted husband to Billie Jo than Trey Steam ever was," I told him. Why she chose to be buried here was another of Billie Jo's mysteries. Perhaps she'd made the decision thinking her death would finally allow Johnny to find another woman to marry.

After the short graveside service, I found little chance to mill around and talk to people, even if investigating murder at the victim's funeral were not in exceedingly poor taste. George and I walked hand-in-hand back toward the Bentley. Without intending to do so, we caught up with Mary Steam, flanked at either elbow by her husband and Prescott Roberts, her brother. Both of the Steams appeared ten years older than when I'd seen them a brief while before at Billie Jo's parole hearing. Prescott Roberts seemed to look right through to my soul and I turned away.

George arrived at the parking area first and opened the car door for the Steams, assisting the older couple into their vehicle. After Mary Steam was seated, her husband turned to me and said, "I hope you're satisfied now, young lady. I can't imagine how you could make our lives any worse, but I'd appreciate it if you didn't try."

I stepped back as if he'd assaulted me. For good measure, Prescott Roberts added, "I'm sure Judge Carson has learned her lesson," in a menacing tone of voice.

Both of them entered the car and George closed the door. "Forgive him, Willa," Eva Steam said, as she came up behind us with her parents and her daughters. "He wouldn't normally be so rude. Bill's very upset today. He's lost his son and now his grand-son and he's not coping with it well."

"It's been a great tragedy for your entire family." I looked down at Willie and Billie. "I'm so sorry," I said to their tear-streaked, freckled faces.

Instantly, Eva's complexion flushed bright red, her eyes widened, and her nostrils flared. She was enraged. At what? I was merely trying to be kind to her daughters.

Eva quickly ushered her children into the waiting limo. Her parents followed the girls, leaving Eva with George and me for just a few moments. She controlled her anger at me, but it cost her.

"Don't get me wrong, Willa. I'm not happy with you, or with Ursula Westfield, either, for that matter. But circumstances killed Billie Jo Steam. Circumstances that were put in place long before you ever met her. Don't start thinking you're some kind of martyr. Your part in the drama was just in the final act." With that, she stepped into the car and slammed the door behind her, leaving me as nonplussed as Prescott Roberts had.

"What did she mean by that?" George asked, more than a little annoyed, himself.

"I don't know," I told him, bewildered.

Chapter Twenty-Five

That evening, I was tired, emotionally and physically. I hadn't been sleeping well. The Steam murders were constantly on my mind. My workload was piling up while I spent what should have been my evening work hours investigating homicide. And on top of everything else, Paul Robbins had informed me that Harris would no longer see me.

I changed into comfortable clothes, and took the newspapers out to the veranda when we got home. George went off to his restaurant, while I tried to catch up on what was going on in the world, as well as locally.

The news stories began to run together while I squinted to read them, even with my reading glasses on. Another innocent man had been executed in Texas because a pathologist had lied about evidence that convicted the accused. A Russian diplomat was assassinated. The school millage proposal was rejected again. The Chiselers had released a new cookbook, with proceeds to support the Henry Plant Museum at the University of Tampa. Scientists had studied a family of centenarians and found a potential genetic link to longevity. *Corgi* cartoons continued on the feature pages. The Ann Landers column discussed couples that paired older women with younger men. Another man on death row, in a bid for clemency, claimed his lawyer was drunk at his trial.

At some point, the news was so gripping that I dozed off. George woke me when he came upstairs after midnight and I stumbled into bed, too tired for nightmares.

The next morning, all I could think of was "Thank God it's Friday." This would be my last day this week with the *Madison* trial. We were moving right along, though. We would finish by next Friday. Only one more week, I encouraged myself, as I parked

Greta and waited for the elevator.

I dragged through the workday. Sitting down to my lunch of crab salad, sparkling water, and a chocolate brownie didn't even provoke a smile. By the time we recessed the trial for the week at four-thirty, I sorely needed a nap. Augustus had packed my briefcase with matters I needed to review over the weekend. I grabbed it up and trudged home to bed.

I got up around eight o'clock, ate dinner from a tray, watched a few mindless sitcoms on television, and went back to sleep at eleven. You would have thought I was eighty-nine, not thirty-nine.

Saturday morning found me well rested and full of the energy I'd need to get through my list of jobs for the day. The first thing on my agenda involved a short drive. I didn't know Enrique "Ricky" Gutierrez or his wife, Janet, but Ricky had played guitar for Six Bills. Now, he and Janet owned a cigar factory in Tampa, one of the longest continuously operated family-owned businesses in the city.

Janet was a stay-at-home mother who seemed to have little involvement with law, politics, golf, or charity, so no opportunity to meet her had presented itself. Ricky was a political conservative, as most of the Tampa Cuban community is, so George knew him, although not well. When we'd met briefly at Billie Jo's party at Minaret, Ricky and his wife had seemed nice enough, but not particularly outgoing or personally remarkable. Janet was a flashy dresser, but, otherwise, quiet.

Again, they had been there at Billie Jo's funeral. I'd nodded to Ricky at the graveside. I'd decided to interview him Saturday morning. His name was at the top of the alphabet of characters still on my list. And people say I'm not methodical.

The Gutierrez Cigar Company was located on Seventeenth Street and Eighth Avenue in Ybor City. The old brick building had no need to be restored, unlike many of its sister structures in this area. The Gutierrez family had kept the factory and warehouse in excellent condition for the past one hundred years. The yellow brick, three-story facade faced Seventeenth Street, majestically inviting customers within. I climbed the steps to the covered entrance and twisted the metal doorknob at the top of the stairs.

The lead-paned door took only a small push to open. When I crossed over the threshold, I entered another era, almost like time travel.

The lobby was furnished in Spanish antiques—dark wood, ornately carved, with velvet cushions on the chairs and heavy gold brocade everywhere. The dark wood floors were worn with age, but highly polished. On the walls, sconces that once burned with gaslights were now equipped with electricity. The dim light they provided cast a museum-like shadow over the entire room.

A Cuban-looking matron occupied a heavy, dark wood desk off to the side. She smiled warmly and asked me to be seated while she told "Mr. Ricky" that I was waiting. She was old enough to be his mother, but on the phone she treated him with the respect due the boss, in an old-world way that added to the antiquarian feel of the place.

Ricky Gutierrez came out into the lobby to greet me, both hands extended in a gracious reception. "Judge Carson," he all but exclaimed. "It's good to see you. Welcome to the Gutierrez Cigar Company. Welcome. Please come into my office." He spoke in the formal way of one whose first language is not English. He was dressed in a business suit, complete with coat and tie. On a Saturday.

Ricky took both my hands in his, beamed at me, and I actually thought for a minute that he was going to kiss both my cheeks. Which was interesting since Ricky Gutierrez had been born in the same U.S. of A. that I had.

After I declined his offer of refreshments, we settled in a cozy corner of his office at a small round table, in two tiny and uncomfortable chairs. Ricky Gutierrez waited for me to state my business, but beginning was awkward.

Although I'd thought this out for days and rehearsed on the way over, I wasn't prepared for the reality of Ricky Gutierrez. I looked around his office, searching for safe conversational gambits, to give myself a little more time to compose my approach. I saw pictures of what must have been Ricky's father and grandfather, his wife and their five children. Five children? I don't meet that many large families anymore. It's kind of refreshing, actually. "Are these your kids? They're beautiful." And they were. All five were small, dark, and handsome, like their parents.

He fairly beamed in response. "Yes. Thank you for saying so. Although, my sons wouldn't be happy to hear you call them beautiful. They think they're so manly, you know."

"How old are they?" I smiled at the proud papa.

"The youngest is ten and the oldest is twenty," he was more than happy to say. "But I'm sure you didn't come here to talk about my children," he prompted gently.

Mentally, at least, I squared my shoulders. "No. No, that's not why I came. I wanted to talk to you about Six Bills."

He didn't seem surprised in the least. "What would you like to know?" he asked.

"Actually, I'd like to know everything you know, but I'll settle for anything you'd care to tell me."

He considered my request for a short while, then bent down to a humidor on his small table and opened it. "Try one of our finest cigars, Willa. These are the special reserves. We import the tobacco from the Dominican Republic now. It's impossible to get it from Cuba, of course. But this is the same tobacco my family has used for over two hundred years to make cigars." Whether he was being polite or had heard of my habit, I didn't know.

I told myself I didn't want to offend him before the interview, but really, I loved the smell of the cigars when he opened the humidor. I'd never tried a Gutierrez special reserve. If I liked them, I might consider it patriotic to switch. Support the local economy and all. Besides, I rationalized, a refusal would be impolite. I selected one of the cigars. "Take another. For later," he urged. So I did.

Smoking a cigar is a delight to all my senses. At first, I tested the feel of the unlit cigar. This one was well rolled, firm, yet soft and pliable. Touching it, rolling it in my hand and between my fingers, my expectations built. Next, I savored the aroma of the rich and spicy tobacco, fresh and inviting as it yearned for fire. Then, I allowed Ricky to snip the end for me and offer me a light from his gold lighter.

As I drew the flame to the cigar, the fine tobacco was immediately apparent in its full-bodied taste and the aromatic smoke that filled the room.

Once lit, the cigar's taste and smoke lingered to keep me company, like a good friend. In the aura of a good cigar come true relaxation and a sense of well-being. The journey taken to reach the moment of enjoyment adds to the fine cigar's mystery. Or maybe I just remember sitting on my grandfather's knee while he puffed on a cigar. The aroma returns my childhood to me in a way that makes me feel happy and young, safe and secure.

Ricky and I puffed in sociable appreciation for a while, without any concern for the passing time. He'd poured two small brandies to go with the cigars, and we enjoyed the interlude before we returned to discuss the sordid business of murder.

"I was the first person in my family to attend college in this country. My parents came here from Cuba and, although my father was well educated, my mother was not. My father insisted that all of his children get an American education. Our mother was frantic at the thought that we might move away from home. Now that I'm a parent myself, I understand this perhaps a little better than I did at eighteen," he laughed, heartily.

"I'm sure," I laughed with him. What a charming man, I thought. And, yes, I would have thought so even if I didn't like the cigar. I hadn't touched the brandy, but Ricky had taken a few sips while smoking. I'm not fond of brandy and drinking it this early in the morning was more than I could face.

He continued. "So, I enrolled at the University of Tampa to study business administration. My plan, and my father's plan for me, was always to remain in Tampa and run the family business. This was 1968, and I was as red-blooded as any other American teenager of the time. But I was more conservative than most and my family was much, much more conservative than my new friends at UT." He smiled again. I could imagine what that "free love" time must have been like on a college campus for a sheltered, studious young man such as Ricky.

"Well, my parents allowed me to live on campus, but only because freshmen were required to do so then," he continued. "Shortly after I arrived, I found myself in a dorm with four other young men, all with the same name as me. 'William.'" He gave a mirthful chuckle. "The coincidence, you see, amused us and pulled us together. It made us feel special, like we belonged in this new environment. Soon, we were walking around campus calling each other 'Bill,' even though I had never before in my life been called 'Bill'."

Before long, their classmates started to call them 'the five Bills.' Once Trey Steam met Billie Jo, of course, they became 'the six Bills,' and they loved it. They were a clique, a group of friends, something that met a need for the six teenagers away from home in a strange and frivolous time. That tie bound them together. "See?" Ricky asked me.

I did see. I found the typical story of American teens in college familiar and reassuring. "How did you get started as a band?" He smiled again, then took another sip of his brandy and more puffs of his cigar. I wasn't talking much, so I could enjoy the cigar without interruption. "Trey, Wally, and Linc had known each other in high school and they had a garage band already put together," Ricky explained. "All kids wanted to play in a rock band in those days, if they weren't jocks, and none of the Bills were."

"Wally?" I laughed. "You mean Walter Westfield was called Wally? That's hysterical!"

Ricky laughed, too. "Yes, it is now. We were all a lot different then, of course. Free. Fun. Just enjoying life." He stopped again, remembering that happy time. He described it so vividly that I felt happy, too. "Anyway, they already had a band and Johnny and I joined it. We couldn't think of a good name at first, but about that time Trey began dating Billie Jo and kids started calling us the six Bills, so we settled on Six Bills as the name for the group."

Part of this story I'd already heard from Linc, but getting more than one version was a good idea. Besides, the cigar was wonderful and I had nowhere special to go just now. God knows I'd had plenty of sleep.

"So, you became a band," I prompted.

"So, we became a band," he repeated. "We were friends. We loved each other, life, and everything in it."

"For a while," I reminded him.

His face darkened then, and he put down the brandy. "Yes, for a while. Until Trey began to drink too much, and take drugs. He attracted groupies. Oh, he wasn't as popular as Harris is now, of course. But he was getting to be well known. The combination of the drinking and the fans caused Trey to get pretty full of himself. He'd started being nasty to Billie Jo and to everyone else whenever we were around. Even before we went to Woodstock, things were starting to get out of hand." Ricky was troubled, the happy memories giving way to darker ones.

"Tell me about that. The trip to Woodstock. Who's idea was it? How'd you get there?"

He wrinkled his brow in concentration. He told me that he hadn't thought about those days in a long time, but that the idea of going might have been Linc's. Linc had been the most serious musician in the group. The rest realized they'd never make a living with music, but Linc had always believed he would make it big. He idolized the great rock guitarists, Ricky said. Santana,

Hendrix, and a few others were Linc's idols. A number of them were supposed to play at Woodstock.

"Linc felt he just had to go. Really, what else would six college kids in a band do for a summer vacation?" Ricky laughed out loud.

"Anyway, we all started to get excited about it. I can tell you, my mother nearly had a stroke!" He shook his head, either at the foolishness of their behavior or the pleasant memory. Maybe both. "We were kids," Ricky said. "We had no idea what we were getting into or what it would take to get there and back, but we went."

Wally had a van and they all had some money, since the band was starting to get paid for little gigs around town. "Before that, Trey and Billie Jo had gotten married. You knew that, right?" Ricky asked me, looking to be sure I was following along.

"I also heard that Trey Steam was already knocking Billie Jo around by that time," I told him, "that he was sleeping with other girls and just generally treating Billie Jo like a piece of property he didn't care about too much." I wanted to let him know I wasn't interested in a snow job.

Ricky nodded solemnly and his tone changed to one of seriousness. "By the time we got in Wally's van to go to Woodstock, the relationship between Trey and Billie Jo was icy, to say the least. Trey smoked himself into oblivion and the rest of us were actually relieved." Ricky raised his eyebrows to let me know he meant Trey was high on marijuana—and who knew what else.

Ricky told me then about the three days they spent at Woodstock. The weather had been mostly miserably cold and wet, and the grounds had offered very little in the way of bath or shower facilities. All six of them took turns sleeping in the van. They'd brought sleeping bags to camp outside, but the rain made that impossible. Yet they were luckier than one attendee they met who slept in the trunk of his car, using his belt to tie down the lid against the elements. When Trey stomped off to a tent with some girls he'd found and slept there, Billie Jo was heartbroken. Johnny consoled her.

One night, they all sat around with marijuana, and Ricky thought maybe LSD, but he couldn't say for sure. Alcohol flowed freely. Someone had a gallon jug of "Purple Jesus," which was wine mixed with vodka, and other unknown ingredients. In a relatively short time, they were all high or drunk or both. And Billie Jo was sad or lonely, or both.

"The next day, Trey came back and we all drove home." Ricky shrugged. "I'm embarrassed about it, now, thirty years later. Certainly, I wouldn't want my own children to do something like that. But even with the tawdriness of the whole experience, somehow, it brought us all closer together, too. It changed us. Forever."

"How so?" My cigar was gone; he'd finished his brandy and his story.

Ricky had dropped the old-world Cuban facade somewhere in the telling. "It's hard to describe, really. The Bills were close before, but now we were inseparable. We just loved each other. Deeply. We felt our trip was probably the single most significant thing six college students had ever done together. We all knew Woodstock would never be over for us."

He leaned forward in his chair, closer, looking at me intently, as if he could infuse me with understanding. "Until Billie Jo killed Trey. That blew us all to smithereens. We drifted for a while. Johnny went to Vietnam. Wally went off to Europe and then on to law school. I went to graduate school for an MBA and stayed lucky in the lottery system until Nixon brought the boys home. Linc went to Canada and only came back when President Ford declared amnesty for draft dodgers. The world changed. And we all changed, too, I guess." His eyes were mournful.

We sat together for a while, thinking quietly. Ricky was the most candid source of information about Six Bills I'd found so far. Maybe I could try to push him a little further. "Tell me what happened the night Trey Steam died."

Ricky considered the question for a long time. Then he shook his head back and forth, denying my request. "That's ancient history now, isn't it? We should let Trey and Billie Jo rest in peace."

"I can't do that, Ricky. Harris is in jail. He'll not only go to prison, he may well get the death penalty." I didn't say how desperate I was to prevent just that result.

Ricky remained unpersuaded. He continued to shake his head back and forth. "So sad. Such a sad story."

I took the plunge. "Harris didn't kill Billie Jo. Just like Billie Jo didn't kill Trey Steam." Ricky drew in his breath quickly, as if I'd frightened him. I pressed on. "The real killer is still out there. You've got to help me find out who killed Billie Jo, so that we can both help Harris."

Ricky regained his composure, but kept shaking his head, saying a silent "no." He'd put down his brandy snifter and returned his cigar butt to the ashtray he'd set out. The formal Ricky returned. He looked at his watch and changed the tone of our meeting completely. "You must forgive me, Willa. I have another appointment I've already kept waiting for half an hour. I can't discuss any more of this today." He rose, and gestured me to the door, indicating that I should stand and leave.

I tried one last time. "You can help Harris, Ricky. Do it. For your old friends," I urged him.

"I'm sorry, Willa. I really have another engagement. Please excuse me." He walked me to the door of his inner office. "My secretary will show you out, and give you a box of cigars. I hope you enjoy them, with my compliments." He smiled his friendly smile, but not as broadly as he had when I arrived.

I'd been given the bum's rush. Politely. But my dismissal was still final. I found myself out on the street, holding a box of Gutierrez special reserves and a head full of information. I looked down at my own watch now and realized why my stomach was growling. It was lunchtime and I was in Ybor City. I knew plenty of places to eat in Ybor on a Saturday.

I drove Greta to the parking garage they'd built for Centro Ybor, the new shopping and entertainment complex over on Fifteenth Street. I collected my briefcase and hoofed it over to a new brew-pub I'd heard about. I planned a thinking lunch. My journal, my thoughts, and me.

The short walk north on Fifteenth Street, across Seventh Avenue, and a quick sprint up the stairs placed me right in front of Barley Hopper's at a little after one o'clock. The place was busy, with both tourists and locals enjoying the sports bar atmosphere and the variety of microbrewed beer the upscale pub served. I guessed that the new movie theaters here at Centro Ybor would provide a respite from the heat after lunch for many of the other diners. Judging from the size of the crowd, a slew of films must be starting at about two o'clock.

I asked the hostess to seat me at a table in the back, away from the plasma screen televisions. I could understand the sports channels, but the other half of the screens were tuned to the Victoria's Secret channel. "What's up with that?" I asked the raven-haired waitress when she came over to take my order. She shrugged her answer.

After I'd requested a sinful cheeseburger with fries and a salad, and rejected the server's offer of beer in favor of iced tea, I opened my briefcase. I'd tossed my journal inside before I'd left home for my meeting with Ricky Gutierrez.

Now, examining the contents for the first time since I'd left the office yesterday, I saw that Augustus had enclosed a memo saying he'd ordered the court file on the trial for *State of Florida v. Willetta Johnson Steam*. The file had been returned from archives and was waiting for me in the clerk's office for pickup. Alternatively, the clerk would copy the file, at my expense, and I could keep the duplicate. The trial had been short and the file was only two volumes. It would probably be faster just to run over there and look at it. The courthouse was closed for the weekend, so I made a note to go over on Monday at lunchtime.

The waitress came back with my tea in a frosty mug and I took a long, cool, thirst-quenching sip. I could smell the heavenly aroma of grilling burgers. My mouth was watering just thinking about mine. Nothing better than a cheeseburger in paradise.

I spent a few minutes recording the high points of my talk with Ricky in my journal, and then reviewing my action plan. His description of the trip taken by Six Bills was more information than I'd gotten from Linc. Neither Walter Westfield nor Billie Jo had ever mentioned going to the famous music festival. I could understand why Walter wouldn't want to flaunt his participation in what was, perhaps, the most notorious "love-in" of the hippie era. Everybody at Woodstock had inhaled secondhand smoke, if nothing else. Walter could probably still get elected, but a history of drug use, even in youthful indiscretion, would limit many of his aspirations to higher office.

But why wouldn't Billie Jo have told me? People who attended Woodstock were a rather exclusive club. There weren't that many of them in the whole country. Here, all six of the Bills had gone to the festival. When I had first started working on this project, five of the six were still alive. The omission might be insignificant, in the long run, but it bothered me that the bond they'd forged there seemed so strong to Ricky, yet not something Billie Jo or Walter ever mentioned.

I was unsettled, too, because Ricky wouldn't talk about the night of Trey Steam's murder. Again, his refusal seemed incongruous with the rest of our conversation. What did Ricky know about the murder? Or maybe, what did he suspect?

Ricky Gutierrez is a well-respected businessman. He wouldn't be thrilled to have the community know that he'd been involved in drugs, sex, and rock 'n roll, even if he had been just a kid at the time. If nothing else, he had five children to shelter from that knowledge. It was curious that he would tell me about going to Woodstock, something so personally explosive, but would not talk about Trey Steam's murder, to which he hadn't even been a witness.

When the waitress brought my hamburger and fries, I set the journal aside. I put lettuce, tomato, a big slice of raw onion, and a load of dill pickles on the burger, along with a big splash of mustard. I'd have added mayonnaise, but that would be too fattening. I dabbed my fries in mustard and ate them with my fingers one at a time. Heaven.

When I finished up my lunch, I wiped the grease off my chin, repacked my briefcase, and took a quick look at my watch. I had time for one more stop before I headed home.

Chapter Twenty-Six

Johnny Tyson lived in a small Florida ranch house in Carrollwood Village, a suburb built out on North Dale Mabry Highway in the fifties and sixties. Johnny's yard was seriously undercared for, something the Village undoubtedly frowned upon. Precious little grass dotted the lawn and what grass remained in the front was yellow from lack of rainfall. Florida has been going through a cyclical drought for several years and local restrictions would have prevented Johnny from watering the lawn often enough to keep the grass green. But I saw no sign of a sprinkling system or a garden hose. Johnny's house didn't look as if a gardener lived there.

The front door was closed. The storm windows were in place. Some Floridians just turned on the air conditioning and never turned it off, no matter what the temperature. Johnny Tyson fell into that set.

I rang the bell, stood and waited. After a while, I rang the bell again. I could hear a chime noise inside the house, even with the door and windows closed up tighter than a magnet hugged steel. One more try, then I'd have to come back another time. I pushed the button and held it for a few seconds. Before I moved my hand off the button, the door opened. "What? What?" he ranted, angry at the noise, or me, or maybe the world.

The man standing behind the screen looked nothing like the Johnny Tyson I'd met before. If I hadn't known Johnny lived alone, I'd have thought I had the wrong address. Johnny wore boxer shorts and a tank type T-shirt, neither of which had been washed in several days. He was barefoot, unshaven, unwashed, and, from the smell of him, pickled in alcohol. It was enough to make me swear off drinking.

"Johnny, it's Willa Carson. We had an appointment.

215

Remember? Can I come in?" At this point, I wasn't sure I wanted to enter. If he looked this bad, what would the interior of the house be like?

He turned around and walked further inside, leaving me to open the screen and follow behind. "Sure, sure, sure," he said, as he walked away.

I let myself into a small, sparsely furnished living room where the floor and every available surface, including chair seats, were stacked with newspapers, books, and writing tablets. A computer sat on a small desk in the corner, the monitor turned on, the screen-saver's flying windows making a mesmerizing pattern. The desk chair was the only unoccupied seat in the room. Johnny must have been sitting there, ignoring the noise, when I rang the bell.

The desk itself was cluttered with papers. A large, green ashtray, resting in the middle of a five-inch high tepee of cigarette butts and ashes, was barely visible. The odor of stale cigarettes was overwhelming, but it camouflaged the other disgusting odors here. A tumbler, half-full of brown liquid that was likely bourbon and not iced tea, sat next to the green ash tepee.

Johnny walked over to the desk, picked up his glass, and his smoldering cigarette. He stood in the middle of the room, looking around, presumably for a place to sit. Finding none, he then walked into the kitchen. I followed him from a safe distance, breathing through my mouth, trying to avoid the garbage dump smells.

In the kitchen, more piles of paper were stacked on the table and all six of the dinette chairs. Johnny put the tumbler on a small patch of brown surface that peeked through the piles, lifted a stack of papers from one chair, and gestured for me to sit. Then, he took the tumbler and went over to stand in front of the sink. Looking vaguely in my direction, holding the cigarette in one hand and the drink in the other, he waited. He didn't offer me any-thing. In fact, he didn't say anything at all.

"Johnny," I started. "I wanted to talk to you about the night Billie Jo died." He still said nothing, just took another drag and another sip. The contrast from the Johnny I'd met at the victory party was so complete I'd almost believe this man was Johnny's evil twin. If I believed in evil twins. Which I don't.

"Is that okay? Can we talk about that?" He nodded imperceptibly, I thought, which gave me the boldness to continue. "You were at Harris's house that night for a party, right?" He nodded again. "When did you get there?"

He cleared his throat and took a sip from the tumbler and a drag from the cigarette. He tried his voice, but no sound emerged. He cleared his throat again. Then, he rasped, "'Bout eight."

"Where had you been before that?"

Johnny's eyes started to water as he considered where he and Billie Jo had been before they went to Harris Steam's party. He hung his head. I didn't try to prod him again, feeling maybe this was just going to be impossible. Maybe I'd come too soon after Billie Jo's death, too soon after he'd buried the love of his life. Maybe he just couldn't talk about it now.

Johnny cleared his throat again and raised his head, glancing at me and then darting away his gaze. "Billie Jo and I went to the county clerk's office last week. Sunday, we got a friend to marry us. She wanted you to do it." He looked at me as if I had let Billie Jo down.

"She never asked me to marry the two of you. I'd have been pleased to," I said. Officiating at a wedding was one of the few happy things a judge gets to do. Usually. I'd have enjoyed doing so for Billie Jo and Johnny.

He ignored my protest. "Then we went to dinner at Bern's," he went on. He meant Bern's Steak House, a standard for big celebrations in Tampa. "She was so happy. Finally. Billie Jo didn't have many happy times in her life. But we were both happy that day." He'd started to talk now, and he didn't stop. He was telling me the story of Billie Jo's death. I turned on the tape recorder I'd taken out of my pocket and placed it on the kitchen table.

"Billie Jo wore a blue dress, the color of her eyes. Had her hair styled. Makeup done. She looked so beautiful. We toasted ourselves with champagne. We wanted to spend whatever time she had left together."

He drank more, smoked more, thought a while. Then he continued. "After dinner, we took a taxi over to Harris's house. We were both too high to drive. We got there about eight o'clock. Harris has a studio in the back. He'd set up for the Bills to play a few tunes for the guests. You know, the wives and the kids. Couple of friends."

He shook his head back and forth. "It was just a real nice day. A wonderful day for Billie Jo. She shouldn't have told him. She'd be alive if she hadn't told him. He didn't know all these years. Why'd she have to tell him now that I was his daddy?"

At that point, Johnny stopped again, closed his eyes, and pinched the bridge of his nose to keep himself from crying. And then, he could hold it back no longer. He began the crying jag of a drunken man who has suffered a terrible loss. I reached down and turned off the tape recorder.

I got up, went to him, and attempted to comfort him, but nothing I did made him feel any better. He was drunk and Billie Jo was dead. I could change neither circumstance.

Once I had held him for a while, I no longer noticed his unwashed stench of booze and cigarettes. I helped him back to the bedroom of the small house. I moved several mounds of paper off the dirty linens on the bed and helped him lie down. He was snoring loudly before I left the room.

I put Greta's top down so that I could stand to be inside the car with myself. Johnny's noxious garbage dump perfume stayed with me the whole trip home.

In the shower, after I'd put my clothes in the washing machine on the way through the laundry room, I thought about what Johnny had said. Harris Steam was Johnny's child. Linc had suggested the possibility. But how could they know for sure? Florida law presumes that a child born in wedlock was fathered by the husband. The only way to prove Johnny was Harris's biological father was through a DNA paternity test. As far as I knew, such a test had never been done, couldn't be done without

Harris's knowledge. And even then, Trey Steam would still be Harris's legal father.

Trey and Billie Jo were, from all accounts, constant lovers until his death. How could Billie Jo really know that Johnny was Harris's father? And, if she didn't know for sure, why tell Harris something so upsetting? Maybe Billie Jo wished Johnny was Harris's father. And maybe Johnny actually was Harris's father. Even so, why would that matter to Harris now?

Trey Steam came from a prominent Tampa family. As hard and rigid as Bill and Mary Steam were, they had raised Harris in the same privileged background they'd given their son. Harris's identity was the only thing he had that he could call his own. Also, Harris was well known, partly because of his father's tragic death.

The romance of the dead singer's son being a successful singer himself had served Harris's career very well. Harris had just recorded the duet CD of his dad's old tunes, which he hoped to sell into double or triple gold numbers. Would his fans care if Harris wasn't Trey Steam's child? It wasn't as if Trey Steam was a rock and roll icon. Six Bills had barely gotten started when Trey died. Trey Steam wasn't Ricky Nelson or Jim Morrison, or someone else of that stature.

I supposed there would be some embarrassment if Harris turned out to be Johnny's child, but surely not enough for Harris to kill Billie Jo. It would have made more sense for Harris to kill *Johnny*, if Harris was a killer. Which he wasn't. I'd already made up my mind about that.

As I finished my shower, I was no closer to forcing these recent pieces to fit my predesigned puzzle. I continued to wiggle the facts around in my mind, moving the pieces from one side of the puzzle to the other, as I got dressed and put on Saturday afternoon's minimal makeup. While I was giving my hair a quick blow-dry, the telephone rang.

"Hello, darling," George said. "Busy tonight?"

"What did you have in mind?"

"I thought you might want to join your brother Jason and

me for dinner downstairs. Around seven o'clock." I looked quickly at the clock. It was just four o'clock now. That would give me three hours to finish my work for today and then get dressed.

"Jason's in town?"

Jason Austin is the closest thing to a big brother I've ever had or will ever have. His mother, Kate, took me in when my stepfather couldn't face life without Mom. I had only been sixteen then. It's true that I don't see Jason often, and I do enjoy his company, but he is just so much work because he's so brilliant. An intellectual. It's exhausting.

Jason also happens to be the chief counsel to the Senate Judiciary Committee. So he thinks he knows everything.

"If you're planning to strategize and discuss politics, I'll pass, thanks. Do you think we can avoid the upcoming Senate race as a topic of conversation over dinner?" Jason works for Senator Sheldon Warwick, Tampa's Democratic senator. The rumor was that Warwick was planning to retire. Jason expected to be Warwick's handpicked successor. This was the senatorial seat Walter Westfield was already campaigning for, so Jason was really here to discuss politics with George.

"For you, anything," he said. I pictured George's grin.

"Really. You won't hurt my feelings. I just don't have the energy to deal with Jason's ambitions tonight."

"Well, I thought you might want to talk to Jason about Leo Colombo, actually. If you don't, that's okay. I can send something up for you."

"You know, I'd almost forgotten about Leo. Yes. I would like that. I'll meet you at seven." I looked at the clock to be sure there was still time for my last appointment before dinner.

"Come a little early and we'll have a quiet half hour before he arrives, if you like," George invited me. "And, don't forget our date tomorrow night. I've hardly seen you lately, Mighty Mouse."

Chapter Twenty-Seven

Since she was both a doctor and a single mother, I hoped Eva would be at home on that Saturday afternoon instead of working or out with her kids. Harris had insisted that I leave Eva alone, but he wasn't the one calling the shots. I was doing this investigation for my own peace of mind. I hoped to prove that I hadn't gotten Billie Jo killed and ruined Harris's life by helping Billie Jo get out of prison. So far, I was making little progress.

Since the divorce, Eva and the girls had moved back home with Eva's parents, Alex and Cindy Raines. I knew of the family, of course. Everyone did. They had lived in Tampa forever and owned one of Tampa's favorite clothing stores. They both worked in the store, which had moved from its original downtown Florida Avenue location into Old Hyde Park Village about ten years ago.

Raines's carried typical Tampa-wear, which is to say, fairly conservative clothes for both men and women that were of good quality, if a little higher priced. Trendier shops now offered the designer labels like Tommy Bahama, Lauren, and Nautica that many Tampans were wearing. But Raines's had been selling clothes for Tampa's semi-tropical climate for over fifty years.

The faithful patrons who shopped there wanted replacements that were identical—or nearly identical—to their favorites when their old clothes were worn out. The tag line under the Raines's label said it all: "Traditional clothing for men and women."

Alex and Cindy Raines lived on Golf View, aptly named because of its panoramic view of the Great Oaks golf course. The course was one of the prettiest views in South Tampa, if you didn't feel the need to see the water. I checked the street address again and found the house easily. The Raines house was modest by today's standards for a family with their means. It was a ranch-style, red brick, about three thousand square feet and, like the Raines's themselves, traditional.

I could hear children in the yard when I pulled up in the driveway. On Saturday, Alex and Cindy would have been at the store until noon. They kept traditional retail hours, too. Now, I was fairly late, so they were probably home with Eva and the girls.

The front door was covered by a screen that let the breezes through the house. I could see Eva inside at the kitchen sink. I called her name rather than ringing the bell. She picked up a towel and wiped her hands on it as she came toward the door.

"Come in, Willa. What a surprise to see you," she said. I noticed she didn't say the surprise was a pleasant one.

Eva looked the way she always did, traditional. She had on a sleeveless white cotton shirt that hugged her slender form and was tucked into green khaki shorts. On her feet she wore loafers. Her curly hair was pulled back into a scrunchee and she wore no makeup.

I opened the screen door and let myself into the house. She had already turned and walked away from me, saying, "Please come back to the kitchen where I can keep an eye on the girls in the pool."

I followed her through to the large, sunny kitchen, where I could see several children, not just Eva's girls, having the time of their lives in the backyard pool. Was I ever that carefree? I must have been, at the age of seven, surely. I saw Cindy Raines, bent over, working in her rose garden at the back of the lot. Alex was sitting in a lounge chair on the lanai with his newspaper and a glass of iced tea. Eva and I engaged in strained small talk about the girls, the garden, and the weather. A few minutes of awkward silence followed.

"Coffee?" Eva eventually asked me, as she got out the mugs, more for something to do with me than because either of us wanted the beverage. "Sure," I said, letting her busy herself with the small task. Eva set about the project without conversation and I let her avoid me a while longer. As she was pouring the water into the coffeemaker, she spilled water on the tile and it ran onto the floor. I watched in fascination as Eva slammed the carafe down onto the counter. It shattered into a thousand pieces, splattering water everywhere. She shouted, "Dammit! I hate this coffee pot! I've told mother to buy another one! Do I have to do everything in this house myself?"

Eva stormed out of the room, went to the back of the house, and slammed a distant door so hard it shook the floor underneath my chair. The violence she displayed was so disproportionate to the event that I sat there in frozen silence. No one out in the backyard had heard Eva's outburst, or seemed to know I was here. Now what?

After a few minutes, not knowing what else to do, I cleaned up the glass and the water Eva had spilled. I found another carafe and made the coffee. I'd just turned the coffeemaker on, the aroma filling the air, when Cindy Raines came into the kitchen.

"Oh!" she said, startled to see me. "I'm sorry. I didn't know Eva had company." Cindy Raines was about sixty-five, I guessed, and built like her daughter. She was tall, slender, and well cared for, in an upper-middle-class sort of way. Her skin was smooth, her hair stylish, and her pearl stud earrings were in place, even for a Saturday afternoon in the garden.

"Hello, Mrs. Raines," I said.

"Call me Cindy, dear. Have we met?" She had taken off her gardening gloves and was washing her hands at the sink. One of the realities of moving to an old town like Tampa was that if you'd been here less than twenty years, you were still a newcomer. I'd met Cindy Raines several times, but she honestly had no idea who I was.

"Yes, ma'am. In your store. I'm Willa Carson." I didn't want to mention Billie Jo's funeral, too.

If she recognized my name, she gave no outward sign of it.

Cindy kept looking at me as if she couldn't quite place me, but her training did not desert her. "Well, it's so nice to see you again, dear. I see Eva's got the coffee brewing. Would you like a cup?" I accepted and she took up the task Eva had begun before she'd had her tantrum. After Cindy poured the coffee, she joined me at the table, taking a seat to the side of me that allowed her to see the children outside, where Eva had been sitting before I arrived. I had to turn to face her.

We sipped our coffee together quietly for a few minutes, saying nothing, both lost in our own thoughts and letting the joyous cackles of the kids in the pool drown all despondency.

"It's a birthday party. Willie is ten today," Cindy said, while I finished my unwanted caffeine fix. "Eva will be taking the cake out soon, I'm sure. Won't you stay for a slice?"

"No, ma'am, I really can't do that, I'm afraid. I'm going to have to be leaving shortly."

"Oh. Well, I can't imagine where Eva has gone. Surely, she'll be back in a minute. She's forgetful sometimes, you know? Since her car accident, she's never been quite the same. One minute, she's just fine and the next, she's upset herself terribly." Cindy seemed to have guessed why I was here alone in her kitchen.

"Well, yes, ma'am, that's what happened. Eva spilled the water when she was making the coffee and it upset her. I think she went back to her room."

Cindy frowned. "I was afraid of that. When she's under stress, like today with the party, it's harder for her." Cindy shook her head slowly. "The doctors said she damaged her brain when her head hit the windshield. Most of the time, she can control herself with her medication. But sometimes, she just can't. She doesn't do it on purpose. Usually, she doesn't even remember being rude. I'm very sorry. Maybe you'd better come back to visit her another time."

Cindy Raines saw me to the front door. As I left, she said, "It might be best to call first. We have so many things going on around here. With the children and all . . . ." She let her voice drift away.

George was waiting for me at the door to the Sunset Bar when I arrived at six-thirty, as planned, for dinner with him and my brother. He had on his Saturday night summer work uniform, playing the role of gentleman restaurateur brilliantly. Tonight, he wore a pair of charcoal grey linen trousers. His long-sleeved grey linen shirt was buttoned at the collar, but he wore no tie or jacket. I noticed he wore no socks with his black Gucci loafers, either. He looked elegant, but casual. Exactly the way his clientele expected him to dress. Which wasn't the reason he dressed this way. George actually liked his conservative but elegant style. He'd dressed in the same basic clothes when I'd first met him in college.

He kissed me, then led us over to our favorite table. He'd already placed our order for white wine, and we sat in comfortable, long-married silence while we enjoyed the cool, crisp taste of my favorite chardonnay. "So, what were you up to today?" he asked me. I shared my conversations with Ricky Gutierrez and Johnny Tyson.

"You're saying Harris killed Billie Jo because he didn't like the idea of Johnny being his father?" George asked me, skepticism plain on his face.

"I'm not saying that. I don't believe Harris killed Billie Jo at all. I'm just telling you what Johnny Tyson said," I explained, feeling again my impatience over the story.

"I suppose it would be unsettling, at least, to find out the man you thought was your father wasn't your father," George said, following my earlier train of thought. "Especially if your father was from a prominent Tampa family. I guess Harris's whole identity would be in question then, wouldn't it?"

"Yes," I agreed. "But that doesn't mean he'd kill his mother over it. That makes no sense."

"Yet Eva told you that Harris was enraged over the news didn't she, although she didn't say just what that news was? Maybe he just flew off the handle in a fit of passion?" George suggested.

I shook my head. "No. That won't work. Billie Jo wasn't killed until hours after Harris had his temper tantrum. You'd have to believe that he waited until everyone left his party, came out, and shot Billie Jo in cold blood. I just don't believe that."

"You don't believe it? Or, you won't believe it?" George challenged gently.

"Okay, then. I won't believe it. Not until I see some proof that it happened that way."

"What kind of proof do you need? The police have enough independent evidence to convict Harris, even if he hadn't confessed. Harris was the only one in the house when Billie Jo was killed. Now Johnny has supplied you with a motive, too. What more will it take to convince you?" The reasonableness of the question burst my bubble completely.

"I don't know. But I just won't believe Harris did this, George. I can't."

He reached over and took my hand, holding it on the table between us. "Billie Jo's murder isn't your fault, you know. You're not responsible for how these adults behave. They're all responsible for their own choices. You were just in the wrong place at the wrong time."

I was miserable. "I'd like to believe that. It would make forgiving myself somewhat easier. But you know I took an active part in all this, on Harris's behalf. I put the pieces in play that resulted in Billie Jo's death. The only way I can even try to get past this is if I can find her real killer and prove that the murder had nothing to do with Harris Steam."

The man who has been like an older brother to me, Jason Austin, walked up just then. "Well, I thought I might find you two in here." George got up to shake his hand, and Jason sat down beside me on the bench, giving me a kiss hello. George waved over another glass of white wine for Jason, along with a small bowl of smoked almonds. We watched the end of the sunset, nibbled the nuts, and caught up with each other since Jason's last visit.

After we'd moved to the dining room, our initial social chatter lagged. I asked Jason, "What brings you here this weekend?"

He allowed a troubled frown to settle on his face. "I finally had to bring Sheldon home," he said, referring to his boss, shaking his head in sorrow.

Senator Sheldon Warwick and I are not friends. He is a ruthless politician who would sell out his own mother if it suited him. I hadn't seen him in quite a while, by my own choice. I avoid Sheldon whenever possible. Still, basic compassion demanded that I ask, "Is Sheldon sick?"

"How bad is he?" George asked at the same time.

Jason looked at me strangely. "You didn't know? I thought George would have told you. Or, perhaps, the news would have leaked out somehow. I figured it was why that jackass Walter Westfield had the nerve to declare his candidacy for Sheldon's Senate seat."

Now it was my turn to be completely confused. "What are you talking about?" I asked sourly. "The last time I saw Sheldon, he was as strong as a horse." What I didn't say was that the last time I'd seen Sheldon, he'd made a complete fool of me. Not an experience I'd planned to give him the opportunity to repeat.

"Sheldon has Alzheimer's disease. It will eventually be fatal in a few months. He was diagnosed a couple of years ago. He's been carrying on as best he can, but he never planned to run for reelection," Jason said.

George asked, "The disease has progressed much faster than expected, then?"

"Yes, but I think that's because they took so long figuring out what he had. At first, he had symptoms similar to

Huntington's disease—his speech was slurred, he was clumsy and dropped things, he was having trouble with his balance. But when they did the testing, the doctors ruled HD out."

"He must have been glad about that," George said.

"Well, HD is a terrible disease, and it's fatal, but at least it progresses slowly, and the doctors understand how to treat it. Sheldon's condition has progressed very quickly. Now, it looks like he'll be bedridden for the final stages over the next few months," Jason said. "He and Victoria are dealing with it as well as they can. But it's a tragedy. Thank God, they only had one child."

"Why? Wouldn't children help to comfort them now?" I asked.

"Maybe. But Alzheimer's is often hereditary. Sheldon could have passed it on to his children."

"What will this mean for your career?" I asked him.

"For me, the worst of it is that people will think I've stayed with him, watched him die, and then tried to fill his shoes. All for avarice. Which is absolutely not true," Jason vowed.

"No one who knows you will think that, Jason," George said. "Most of us have known about Sheldon's condition for quite a while. He's made it known that he wants you to fill his seat. If he dies before the election, the Senate will likely give you the position for the rest of his term, as the House did for Mary Bono, Sonny Bono's widow, and a few others." George's typical support for Jason touched me and reminded me why I love them both.

Jason was visibly affected, too. "Thanks. I appreciate the vote of confidence. I know being the incumbent will help me in the election against Westfield. Sheldon and I have talked about it quite a bit. I think he intends to ask Westfield to drop out of the race. But Prescott Roberts won't let Walter do that, even as a personal favor to Sheldon," Jason finished.

"Well," George said, "I promised Willa we wouldn't talk politics all through dinner. Let's wait until after our dessert. Then you

and I can talk about it privately." This was George's code for saying that he would help Jason achieve the Senate seat.

In the world of trading political favors, this was probably
somehow related to the favor I had asked from the governor on
Billie Jo's behalf. I supposed the governor didn't want Walter
Westfield in the Senate. The governor had pledged to help me and
now George would pay back the favor by helping the governor
keep Westfield out of the Senate. Or maybe, family was simply
more important to George than politics. Whatever his reasons, I
appreciated not being involved in the process.

One of George's most experienced waiters had been hover-
ing in the background for a few minutes. When George lifted his
eyes, the man came to take our orders, giving us an opportunity
to segue to a new conversational topic afterward.

"So, what's up with Leo Colombo?" I asked Jason.

He laughed. "Same old Willa. Never beat around the bush
when a nosy question will do the trick."

I shrugged in the face of his mockery. "I prefer to think of
myself as forthright."

He and George burst out laughing. "I'm sure you do. I'm sure
you do," said my brother.

After they'd had their fun, I repeated my question.
"Seriously, Jason. What do you know about your mother's new
husband?"

"Ah, the dashing, mysterious Leo Colombo," he mocked.

Chapter Twenty-Eight

"Saved by the food," Jason said, when the waiter had brought our appetizers. I ordered the Venison Carpaccio, George had the Hot and Cold Foie Gras and Jason was looking at his plate as if he hadn't eaten in weeks. As soon as he could politely do so, meaning right after the waiter removed his hand from the plate to avoid being pierced by a fork, Jason consumed the small portion of assorted mushrooms, fava beans, and summer truffles with morel sauce and watercress coulis, in three bites. George attacked his foie gras with equal gusto.

I addressed my venison with much more restraint. The green beans, celery root, pickled red onions and Gala apples were served with thinly sliced raw venison, whole grain mustard and rosemary-parmesan croutons. I only knew the ingredients because they were printed on George's daily menu.

The combination, something I would never have dreamed up myself, was great. I tried not to think of Bambi while I ate it, and instead concentrated on how destructive deer are to the gardens of my friends in Traverse City, Michigan. Deer cut down flowers and plants with the devouring power of a high-speed lawn mower. Not to mention that they are more plentiful than cows in some states and twice as tasty.

"So, what's up with Leo?" I asked again. The waiter would not return to remove Jason's plate or serve our second dishes until I finished my venison. I ate slowly.

"You never give up, do you?" Jason remarked, with affection, I think. He took a deep breath and recited the facts in a rush. "Okay. Leo Colombo is exactly what he and Mom say he is. He is thirty-five years old. His father is Leonardo Colombo Senior, who was an old boyfriend of Mom's, back in her salad days. Leo was working as a male model in Florence when Mom went to visit

Leo's father in a small village nearby. She and Leo met, fell in love, and married. Then, they moved back here." He looked at me with an expression that said he had nothing more to report and would I please hurry up with the damn venison.

I slowly put my fork on the side of the plate and took an appreciative sip of the Les Forts De Latour 1997 George had selected. The red bordeaux table wine felt smooth and dry on my tongue, as if I hadn't yet sipped it after it had already left my mouth. "And?"

"And, what?" Jason was truculent.

"And what is it that Leo has you investigating about these children?" Not eating the venison would have been much more difficult if I hadn't had that fabulous cheeseburger for lunch. As it was, I felt as if I could hold out for quite a while longer. Jason, on the other hand, must have skipped breakfast and lunch, expecting one of George's sumptuous dining experiences.

"How do you live with her?" he asked George in mock exasperation.

George smiled and said, "Mostly, I just try to stay out of the way." He was enjoying the play of wills between Jason and me, but George bets on the winner.

Jason turned an exasperated glare toward me. "If you eat that last bite of venison so we can get on with this meal, I'll tell you." Ah, the bribe. I put the last of the venison in my mouth and smiled with victory as the smooth, cool feel of it slid down to my stomach and lodged there to my complete joy.

Almost instantaneously, the waiter appeared and removed the plates. I sipped my wine and waited. "Okay. Leo was never married before Mom," Jason said, again reciting as if I held a gun to his head. "However, he did have at least one long-term affair that produced two children. The woman left Leo and took the children with her. She moved to Rome and he lost track of her. He wants me to help him find the mother, prove the children are his, and arrange for him to have visitation rights."

I wasn't sure whether Leo having no ex-wife was better or worse than his having one. "What's this about bringing the kids here to live with him and Kate?" I asked.

Jason turned to George and said, "Can't you keep anything to yourself?"

"You've tried it," George said in mock seriousness. "How well did that work?"

The waiter appeared again, this time with our salads. Jason and I had ordered the Asparagus and Vidalia Onion Salad while George had opted for the other one, something the chef called Composed Salad. To me, it just looked like a tossed salad, but at these prices, he had to name the food something that didn't sound like you could get it at a fast food restaurant.

Once he makes a deal, Jason will stick by it. I didn't have to prompt him to continue. "Mom insists that the children's mother is not fit to raise the boys. Some evidence exists to support that theory. And you know Mom, she's wanted grandchildren for ages and my brother is the only one who's come up with any. Mom's ready to have youngsters around again." He smiled his indulgence of his mother's idiosyncrasies.

He'd slowed down now, taking his time to enjoy the food and my discomfort. "If you want to prevent Mom from helping Leo, the best way to do it would be to have a couple of kids and give them to her," Jason teased me.

I shuddered. "So Leo is using Kate then. Just as I thought."

"Well, I'd say it's more of a case of 'you scratch my back and I'll scratch yours.' I've talked to Mom about it quite a bit. I don't think she's agreed to help without full knowledge of the facts. If your idea is that Leo is making a fool out of her, I have to honestly say that I don't see any evidence of any such thing," Jason made his report with all the objectivity I hadn't been able to muster.

"How can this possibly be in Kate's best interest? Once Leo gets what he wants, he's just going to leave her for someone closer to his own age," I protested, expressing my deepest fears for Kate. She deserved unfettered happiness. I didn't want her heart broken by Leo Colombo. The INS files were filled with foreign nationals who married American citizens just to get a life in this country. I wanted to shield Kate from the heartbreak.

"I won't tell you the thought hasn't crossed my mind. Or hers. But I think you should discuss your concerns with her, Willa. Mom is a lot savvier about the ways of the world than you give her credit for. She's a senior citizen, but she's not senile," Jason said. "Far from it, in fact. Mom knows what she's doing, even if she doesn't fully realize the implications of it all."

The waiter had removed our salad plates and now approached with what he called our Principal Dishes. All three of us had ordered the Roasted Colorado Lamb Loin, served with Spring Peas, Chanterelles, and Pearl Onions with Dijon Sauce. The food was too good to fuss through so we spent our time giving it due appreciation, while drinking a second bottle of the dry, red wine.

There was no more talk about Kate and Leo as we finished our delightful repast and elected to defer the cheese course. As the dishes were cleared, I left Jason and George to discuss politics while I went back to our flat to have an after-dinner espresso in my sweats, keeping company with my thoughts.

Sunday morning dawned clear and sunny with the temperatures already in the high seventies. George was in the kitchen with his coffee, *The Washington Post*, and the two Tampa papers when I awoke. Harry and Bess were lying on the floor at his feet. I patted all three heads, gathered my own coffee, and returned to the veranda for my journal hour. I don't run on Sunday. Even God rested one day a week.

Since we had several hours before our Sunday night date, George had scheduled a few personal errands. I found myself with time on my hands that I should have spent working. But I had no desire to work today. I idled a while with the newspapers, passed an hour exercising the dogs in the water, and got ready to face the day. After that, I could come up with no further excuses. I had to go talk with Kate.

Jason's story last night about Leo was meant to reassure me. And it did. Somewhat. But Kate is a loving woman, charitable in the extreme, and somewhat naive about the ways of the world. She is easily used and Leo is a user. All I cared about was that Kate would end up none the worse for the experience, when Leo got what he'd come for and then moved on to a younger woman. Talking with Kate about that was a difficult matter. I'd been trying to decide on the best approach since I'd left Jason last night. I hadn't come up with anything yet.

In response to my stomach, I decided to get a sandwich before I started out. I picked up my minuscule purse and the key to Greta, closed the door, and bounced down the stairs to the Sunset Bar. I'd have made a tuna sandwich for lunch if we'd had any groceries in the flat. Which we never do. My pantry is filled with wine, microwave popcorn, and coffee. The gin and cigars are always plentiful, but supply little nourishment.

I hurried into the Sunset Bar, intending to order my sandwich there, saving the lone bartender the energy to serve me at a table. When I walked in the door, however, Ursula Westfield was sitting in my favorite booth, facing the entrance, as if she'd been waiting for me to appear.

Ursula had a tall, cold drink in front of her that looked like a strawberry margarita on the rocks with salt. I looked at my watch. Sure enough, the time was after noon. Sweeps were over now that it was June and Ursula had taken the time to come home for a while. At her position in the hierarchy, she could take several weeks off at a time, as long as they weren't during the television ratings season.

I joined her when she beckoned me over to the table, but skipped the booze. "What's up with that?" I gestured to the margarita.

"It's Sunday. Join me. You're way too stodgy to be the 'free-wheeling young judge' the papers describe."

"Don't believe everything you read," I told her, smiling, too. I've always liked Ursula. She's a likable person. Which is what all of America enjoys about her as well. Back when her husband, Walter, was ruling his firm with an iron hand and he and I were butting heads on a regular basis, Ursula would "take me to lunch," the euphemism for a conference in which intelligent, argumentative people of goodwill try to work out their differences in a public setting where neither would risk an act of violence.

In those days, Ursula was Kissinger to Walter's Nixon. He'd tick people off; she'd smooth the ruffled feathers. She was taking partners to lunch two or three times a week. I'd long suspected that she was the glue behind the throne, even before she became so blindingly famous and well respected by millions of viewers. No wonder Walter wanted to run for the Senate. Being eclipsed by his beautiful wife was something a limelight-hound like Walter could never tolerate.

"Walter wants me to give up this story, you know," Ursula told me.

"Sounds like a good idea, don't you think?" She was shaking her head even before I finished the sentence. "Aren't you just a little too close to this to be able to cover it now, anyway?"

She laughed again. "Look who's talking. Like you're not playing Nancy Drew because you feel responsible?"

Okay. She had a point. "But I am responsible, Ursula. Billie Jo would still be in prison if it weren't for me. And she'd be alive."

"Yes. And I can say the same. What gives you a corner on the guilt market?"

We were at a standoff here, and we both knew it. "So, what are you going to do?" I asked.

"Credibility with viewers is my only asset. I have to see this thing through. Or give up my career." She looked straight at me, then. "I'm not prepared to retire."

"No matter where this story leads?"

"No matter where it leads."

I took a deep breath. I'd done a lot of journaling since Billie Jo died. I had quite a few questions I needed answered. Ursula knew more than she'd shared with me, or with the public. Now was the time to find out how deep her commitment to helping Harris went. And how much guilt she actually felt for Billie Jo's death.

"Tell me why you were at Harris's house the night Billie Jo died," I asked her, starting right out with the important things. Someone else could clear up the details, later.

Now it was Ursula's turn to take a deep breath. "It was the Six Bills reunion party."

"I didn't know Six Bills had reunions. How long have they been doing that?" I gave her a quizzical look.

"Well, I can't say for sure, but quite a while. As long as Walter and I have been married, they've been getting together. Maybe fifteen years or more." She sipped at her drink.

"All of the Bills come to these reunions? Harris, too?"

"Well, except Billie Jo and Trey Steam, of course."

This information shocked me because I'd thought the Bills were no longer in touch with each other. "When was the last reunion?"

"Last June. The get-togethers are always in June because that was when the Bills played its last gig. The reunion memorializes the last time they were all together and happy. The night Trey Steam died."

I didn't have my notes, so perhaps I was mistaken. Or maybe no one ever actually told me the Bills had been out of touch all these years. Maybe I just assumed as much, making an ass out of me, for sure. I have more and more "senior moments," but I usually remember the big stuff.

"So, that Sunday night was the anniversary of Trey Steam's

murder and the Six Bills reunion? Sounds a little morbid, don't you think?" My sandwich arrived and I tried not to wolf it down as if I hadn't eaten in a week. For some reason, I was starving.

"Perhaps at first," replied Ursula thoughtfully, playing with the straw in her drink. "You know, Trey Steam's been dead a long time. I think the Bills just wanted to reminisce about the 'good old days,' maybe play together a little. Woodstock was a sort of annealing experience for them, you know. It's not something any of them have ever taken lightly or wanted to forget."

When Trey died, she pointed out, the message delivered to the surviving Bills was that opportunities to form lifelong friend-ships like the ones they had were finite. "They were smart enough to figure out they wanted to keep their special feelings for each other alive," she told me.

I chewed my tuna sandwich thoughtfully, sipping iced tea between the bites. "What do you know about the night Trey Steam was murdered?"

"Not a lot," answered Ursula. "I've read the court files. I talked to Billie Jo and Johnny while we were working on the *News This Week* story. The facts are old and cold now. Walter won't talk about it," she said.

Insight, when it hits me, slaps me silly. "Did you start all of this to find out your husband's deep dark secrets, Ursula? Is that why we're here?" This made me more than mildly annoyed. I'm not in the domestic bliss business.

Ursula had the grace to recognize my irritation and accept its cause. "Partly. The rest is that I'm worried about Walter's run for the Senate."

"Why? How is Trey Steam's murder related to Walter's ambi-tion?" If I still sounded annoyed, it's because I was.

"Calm down, Willa. I'm sorry. I never actually lied to you, you know. Billie Jo was innocent. I was doing the *News This Week* story. Harris did need and want your help." She was trying to pla-cate me.

"But you didn't tell me the whole truth, did you? You had a private agenda here and you suckered me into helping you with it. The least you can do now that we're in this mess is to tell me why. You owe me that much, Ursula," I scolded.

She had the decency to look apologetic. She shrugged. "A political campaign is a vicious thing. You and Prescott Roberts know that a good deal better than Walter does. He's never run for office before. George and the entire Republican Party will oppose him. That much he thinks he understands. But Jason, Sheldon Warwick, and a large number of Democrats will oppose him, too. Politics is a dirty game. I didn't want Walter to get hurt. He's not as strong as people think." She was pleading with me now.

Again, the flash of insight. "You thought something in the Trey Steam story might hurt Walter and you wanted to prove otherwise before his political enemies killed him with innuendo?" I tried to keep the anger out of my voice, but with difficulty. If there's one thing I hate, it's being used. Especially by people I consider to be my friends, and most especially for political reasons. That she attempted to use me against my own family, without my knowledge, boiled my anger to the surface.

Ursula nodded. "And I knew you'd never help me do that. I know you hate politics. You're not Walter's biggest fan, either. Nor would you oppose George or Jason. So I got Harris to ask Leo to persuade you."

My anger exploded, like a white-hot, volcanic eruption. "You used me, Ursula. You deliberately set out to use me to do something you knew I would never do voluntarily. How could you be so calculating? How could you?" I stood up now, threw down my napkin, gathered my purse, and turned toward the door. But I wanted to jolt her. "One last thing you should know, Ursula. Walter's not out of the woods on this. Billie Jo didn't kill Trey Steam. And that leaves Walter as one of the prime suspects."

Then Ursula delivered her coup de grace. "What you don't know is that Walter left right after the gig that night for a flight to

Europe. He was backpacking for weeks. He told you he didn't even know Trey had been murdered until he got back. Walter's not involved in Trey Steam's death. I made sure of that before we even started." Obviously, she was a smart woman.

"You'd better pray you're right, Ursula," I seethed before I left her holding her empty glass.

I stomped my way out to Greta, quickly lowered the convertible top, and sped out of the parking lot, taking out my anger on Greta's German engineering. I felt the need for speed, so I turned left from our drive onto the Bayshore and made a quick right, taking Gandy. I kept Greta within the thirty-five mile an hour speed limit with difficulty, until I passed Westshore and opened her up on the Gandy Bridge. Halfway across, I looked down at the speedometer, which registered one hundred miles an hour. Greta wasn't even breathing hard. But I still was.

I backed off the accelerator slightly as we came to the end of the bridge. The wind that blew through my hair had not blown away my anger. Even now, I realized I was mostly furious with myself.

Ursula hadn't forced me to help Billie Jo. I had stepped into it with my usual spontaneity because I'd decided what the facts were before I investigated. I had cast Billie Jo in the role of victim and Harris in the role of devoted son long before I knew whether those descriptions fit. I alone had put myself in a compromised position and I was pissed off at myself for doing so.

My desire to outrun my own stupidity hadn't abated by the time I got to the tollbooth at the Sunshine Skyway Bridge. I paid the toll and drove on toward Sarasota. My thoughts were a tumble; my mind wasn't on the driving. Several times, I caught myself passing every other vehicle on the road, and slowed my speed back to eighty. When I once again became conscious of my surroundings, I was almost to Naples, normally more than a three-hour trip. I'd been driving a little more than two hours. I needed a break.

Realizing I was getting farther from home, but not farther from my troubles, I dropped Greta at the valet parking entrance to the Naples Ritz Carlton, where I walked through the hotel and onto the beach. I knew I'd be alone here, with nothing but nature to confront me. I continued to stroll with my thoughts until I realized I'd actually gone quite a distance.

Finally, my emotional energy would propel me no farther, and I turned with a heavy tread to make my way back to the hotel that had been made in the image of the larger, world-renowned Breakers Hotel in Palm Beach. Then I sat in one of the lounge chairs on the sand, allowing an attendant to bring me a lemonade and an umbrella, and stared out toward Mexico.

Eventually, I found some forgiveness for myself in the sparkling water of the Gulf of Mexico. My biggest mistake here was the one I make over and over: not trusting my instincts.

There are two things I know for sure. The first is that you can't make anyone do something he doesn't want to do. I know that because I've spent my career trying to make people do things they don't want to do. It never works. Oh, we can take their money, threaten, convict people, put them in prison, and even kill them, but, in the end, all humans do just what they choose. All of us, me, Harris, Ursula, even Billie Jo, had done exactly what we wanted to do, whether we were willing to admit that or not.

The second thing I know is that nothing in the world is ever certain. What seemed true yesterday is often proved false tomorrow. And that assumes everyone believed in the truth of it yesterday. Plentiful are those who lie and distort the facts at the outset. Honesty is as old-fashioned and scarce as gold coins. Even in my friends.

What rankled the most was that I had been duped. I'd allowed myself to be used because I hadn't thought this thing through. I'd liked the idea of helping Harris and his mother. I'd have been better off just dealing with my own issues. Like, why do I always need to be the hero? Maybe I wanted to blame Ursula for sucking me into this mess, but there was really no one to blame but me.

Now, I had to find Trey Steam's murderer and figure out who'd killed Billie Jo. I had no choice. I steeled my resolve to prove my own infallibility. To myself. For today, I'd have to be satisfied with that. I trudged back to the valet, collected Greta and made my way home.

Chapter Twenty-Nine

George and I love to watch movies. We rarely watch television. But movies are another matter. We belong to the Tampa Theater Film Society and I sit on the board there. We see new films at least once a week, when we can. Art films, comedies, dramas, even cartoons interest us both.

We've always talked about going to the Cannes Film Festival, or at least to Sundance, but, somehow, such a trip had never made it into our schedule. So, spending our Sunday night date at Channelside Cinemas was perfect for both of us. We would watch the film and dissect it later. Maybe, this one would provide us with enough conversation to last several days.

As luck would have it, Ricky and Janet Gutierrez were in line ahead of us at the box office when we arrived. Channelside is an "open-air entertainment, shopping, and dining destination." It was built as part of the waterfront development that has been revitalizing downtown Tampa. We liked Channelside because of its waterfront dining and its theaters show the independent films we enjoy.

George approached Janet and Ricky, chatting for a few minutes, while I stood in line for the movie tickets. They were going to the same small art film we'd chosen, a Sundance Film Festival winner. The theater was already crowded. We walked in together, but they were meeting friends and they left us just inside the darkened auditorium.

During the previews, I ducked out to the ladies' room. I hate missing even part of a movie when nature calls. My early childhood training was to go whenever the opportunity presented itself because you never know when you'd have another chance.

While I was washing my hands, Janet Gutierrez exited one of the stalls behind me. She gave a nervous "fancy meeting you here" laugh as she joined me at the sink. Janet, a petite woman, was dressed in a bright red designer pantsuit that reminded me of a flashy sports car.

Her look was right out of a 1980's issue of *Cosmopolitan* magazine. She sported a football helmet of shaggy dark hair and her face was sharply defined by dramatic makeup. She wore large, obviously expensive jewelry, and carried a thousand dollar Prada handbag. Her red shoes were of the pointed toe, stiletto heel variety. I felt like a giant, sloppy poor relation standing next to her, looking at our side-by-side reflections.

"I thought we might have seen you at the Six Bills reunion," she said, fluffing the wispy football-helmet hair with her long, manicured red nails. As soon as the statement was out of her mouth, she looked as if she wished she could take it back. I often felt that way, myself.

Billie Jo had been killed the night of the reunion, but Janet wasn't a vicious gossip. Janet Gutierrez was harmless. She was a very nice wife and mother who was just trying to be friendly to a woman she didn't know at all, in the bathroom at the movies.

I skipped over the unpleasantness and attempted to put her at ease. "How was the party? I understand everyone had a good time early in the evening."

She seemed relieved that I had let her off the hook. "Oh, yes. The Bills' reunions are always fun. They play in Harris's studio, just like their last gig. Then, they get together around the kitchen table and tell tales about how they used to celebrate at Billie Jo and Trey's after every performance. The children love to see Ricky happy, playing his guitar and acting like a kid again. And Harris has such a wonderful voice."

"You never knew his father, then?"

"Oh, no! I met Ricky when he came home from graduate school and his rock and roll days were already over. But Ricky's always been devoted to the Bills. He treats Harris just like our own children." She applied a fresh coat of Chanel red lipstick to her already bright red mouth.

"Really? I had the impression Ricky rarely saw Harris or the other Bills," I said.

"Not at all! Harris comes to the house every week. His girls and our youngest kids are great friends. Harris and Eva are like part of the family," she gushed. "Why, Eva's our doctor, too. I mean, she's a neurologist, but she just does the general stuff for us. You know, colds, shots for the kids, stuff like that."

This was new information. When I'd seen Walter Westfield in Eva's office, I'd assumed he was ill. Maybe Eva treated all of the Bills and Walter's was just a wellness visit. I had been thinking about Eva treating Walter and the more I'd thought about it, the less sense it made. But if she was the doctor for all the Bills, then maybe Walter's condition wasn't as serious as I'd feared.

"Harris and Eva still come over together, even since the divorce?"

"Sometimes," she looked troubled again. "You know, Eva just hasn't been the same since her accident."

"In what way?" I already knew Eva had suffered a head injury, but I didn't know how she'd behaved before her accident.

"Well, she's irritable. She flies off the handle at the smallest thing." Janet realized she was giving me the wrong impression. "Oh, I don't mean she's mean or anything. And she's just as good a doctor as she ever was. Some of her patients deserted her, after she got hurt, but none of the Bills did. We all still see her, like always." Unwittingly, she confirmed my earlier thoughts.

Janet finished her primping and said to me, "Eva blamed Harris and Billie Jo for a lot of the problems in her marriage, but it takes two, you know? Harris was so heartbroken when they divorced. I think they might be getting back together," she finished, hopefully.

"Were you still at the party when Billie Jo and Johnny announced their marriage?" I asked as we made our way back to the theater.

She nodded enthusiastically. "It was so romantic, don't you think? Him waiting for her all those years? They were so in love." She said this like a woman who reads romances regularly. In her world, love conquered all. Harris and Eva, Billie Jo and Johnny. Janet would be disappointed in the movie tonight, which was the story of a tragic love, a modern day version of Romeo and Juliet.

Four more days, I promised myself silently, as I walked quickly over to the Hillsborough County Clerk's office at lunchtime on Monday. Only four more days and I'd be finished with what I'd come to call "the case from hell," a.k.a. *Madison v. Cardio Medical.*

I'd arrived at the office early, taken care of as much of my real workload as possible, and then returned to the den of inequity that had become the defense case. At the lunch recess, I had reminded all parties that we would be sending the case to the jury on Friday morning. I tried, unsuccessfully, to hide my relief at the prospect.

Hillsborough County Circuit Court is located on Pierce Street. Like everything else in downtown Tampa, it was just a few short blocks from my courtroom. This courthouse was much newer than mine, but had very little character. The building is three stories of plain vanilla construction that look even worse on the inside. The county renovated the structure a few years ago, but it was only marginally improved. The Hillsborough County Courthouse is one of the least impressive in the state. A new courthouse is under construction and should be finished soon, thankfully.

The staff in the clerk's office was at lunch when I arrived, but Augustus had called ahead and the file was waiting for me. I took both volumes over to yet another government-issue metal table and chair, and sat there to eat my tuna sandwich and look through the file.

There wasn't much to look at that I hadn't already seen. Most of what the pleadings in the case reflected was contained in the summaries Harris had given me initially. One of the things I was looking for wasn't there: I found no order entered for the destruction of the trial evidence.

Routinely, at some point after trial, an administrative order would be entered requiring the destruction of evidence. Until that order is entered, the evidence is stored in the court clerk's office. I saw no such order here. I flipped through each page of both volumes, one at a time, just to be sure the order wasn't misfiled. It wasn't. For once, someone's failure to follow up on the details of their job might benefit me.

Without an order requiring the destruction of the trial evidence, that evidence should still be available somewhere. I hadn't really pushed Ben Hathaway when he came up with Trey Steam's old clothes and the murder weapon. I'd been happy to have the evidence found and tested for DNA. But now, I saw a real chance of all that old evidence still being around—both what was admitted at trial and what wasn't admitted. The admitted evidence should be somewhere here in the clerk's office.

Forensic techniques today are significantly advanced over what they were in 1972. If I could find the physical evidence from the crime scene and have it reexamined, it could tell me things the witnesses could not, things the scientists might not have known when Trey Steam was killed. Maybe even identify his killer. It was a long shot, but at the moment, the only shot I had.

I found the list of evidence admitted at the trial and put a post-it note on that page. For good measure, I selected the witness and exhibit lists for copying, too. More than just the three witnesses who had actually testified at the trial were listed. Some of the names I recognized, some I didn't.

I asked the desk attendant to make me a copy of the tagged pleadings, paid her the one-dollar fee per page, and slid the pages into my file folder when she handed them to me. Then, I quickly made my way back to my courtroom, just in time to retake the bench for more unexciting testimony in the *Madison* case.

Again, when I recessed at four-thirty, I quickly left the bench, grabbed up my briefcase and my small purse, and exited the building. I had to rush to make my next appointment, but I arrived promptly at four-forty-five.

The next interview on my list was with Walter Westfield, or "Wally," as they called him back then. I smiled to myself as I repeated the childish nickname out loud. What a hoot! William Walter Westfield III being called Wally.

Walter's office was in one of the "A" buildings in downtown Tampa—200 North Tampa, the same one that housed Southern Bank. The Jameson firm had been in one of the older buildings, but had moved to Southern several years ago. A big firm jumping from one large office building to another was seldom seen here. The move had made news in all the business pages for several months before it actually happened, shaking up the real estate business in town.

Managers of the big buildings believe they have a captive tenant once they've leased several floors of space. But Walter Westfield didn't think like that. Walter looked at the old building and concluded it didn't project the image he wanted for Jameson as its new leader. He'd leased the first large chunk of space available at the recently constructed 200 North Tampa address and sold the idea to his partners later on.

Walter is not a detail man; he's a concept thinker. Walter couldn't be bothered with how such a move would be accomplished. He was more interested in making things happen.

Driving around and around and around the circular driveway to the fourteenth floor of Southern's parking garage for a space made me dizzy. I took two elevator rides, one from the parking garage and then, dodging the exercisers on their way to the gym in the basement, a second elevator to the office suites. I spent almost as much time reaching Walter's office as I had parking the car.

The second elevator opened onto a spacious lobby with

views to the southwest and southeast of Tampa. Farther from the water than the Tampa Club, and several stories higher, this view was more panoramic and less obstructed. Walter's offices were on the forty-ninth floor of the tallest building in town. His firm might not be the largest or the oldest, he wanted the offices to say, but it was the best. The decor delivered the message.

Walter's personal office was in the southwest corner, next to the boardroom and taking up the rest of the south side of the office space on the top floor. The furnishings were classic Walter, but not classic law firm.

Elegant, expensive, and extravagant were the descriptions most often employed by magazines such as *Florida Today, Architectural Digest,* and *Fortune* when they photographed stories here about Walter and his firm. When Walter was profiled in *The American Lawyer* as "the most influential lawyer in Florida" last year, the prestigious newspaper for the legal industry devoted a full two columns to a description of his offices and the art objects he displayed.

While I waited for Walter to finish a telephone conversation with the president of his largest client company, I spent the time appreciating the new painting that adorned the north wall of his personal office. The canvas was six feet high and ten feet wide. Beyond that, I had no idea what it was supposed to represent. The colors were vibrant blues, reds, and yellows. I recognized the name of the artist as one of the latest darlings of the New York art crowd.

"Like it?" Walter asked me when he'd hung up the phone.

"I don't know. Am I supposed to like it?"

He laughed. "That's how I feel, but Ursula says it's the latest thing. So, of course, she had to buy it. Sometimes I think my life would be easier if I'd married the quiet debutante my parents wanted me to, don't you?"

But he was kidding. One thing Walter loved at least as much as being the managing partner of the best law firm in Florida, was being the husband of Ursula Westfield. The circles they traveled in were far wider than Florida alone. Ursula's popularity and celebrity might just make it possible for Walter to win the next senatorial election.

Like Ricky Gutierrez, Walter had several sitting areas in his office. The one we moved to was set up like a small, formal living room. Walter sat on one end of the sofa and I took a seat in the adjacent antique chair. He'd had iced tea delivered to the small cocktail table and he sat back with his legs crossed and his hands folded. His fingers tapped on his knee and his foot swung from front to back.

While I feared Walter wouldn't be willing to talk to me at all after my recent argument with his wife, he adopted a look of earnest interest as he posed to listen to my queries and chat. Walter carefully arranged his handsome face, with its classic features, in sincere repose. He must have practiced this position in front of a mirror. I found it hard not to laugh.

"I'm trying to figure out what happened at Harris Steam's house the night Billie Jo Steam was killed. You were there. I was hoping you'd tell me." I got right to the point.

"Why do you want to know, Willa? Isn't it time you got out of this whole mess? It isn't doing you or your reputation any good to keep going with this. I know you became involved because Ursula asked you to help Billie Jo, but we're way beyond that now, aren't we?" This was the Walter I remembered trying to deal with when I was a practicing lawyer. The Walter who was used to getting what he wanted and to having his suggestions obeyed like the not-so-subtle orders they were.

"I appreciate your concern for me, Walter, truly I do. But, just tell me what happened at the party, okay?"

"I already told Ben Hathaway all about it," he said as his face twitched a little on the left side. I hadn't noticed that twitch before, and thought at first I imagined it, until he raised his left hand to his eye to make it stop.

"Humor me. Please," I requested.

He relented. "Well, I guess you're asking about later in the evening, after the Six Bills performed a few musical numbers for the crowd. Alas, no one was inviting us to make a new CD," he said in his self-deprecating way, meant to convey that he thought he was pretty damn good, in fact.

"I've heard you play," I said, "twice," referring to Billie Jo's victory party and her funeral.

He cleared his throat and went on. "Yes. Well, anyway, we played a few tunes and then just had the usual party food and drink and conversation. Ursula and I left about ten o'clock. It's not the kind of crowd we travel in these days, except for Ricky and Janet Gutierrez, of course. When we left, everyone was still there and Billie Jo was very much alive. That's it."

"What about Johnny's and Billie Jo's marriage? Were you there when they announced that?"

Walter looked a little discomfited by this question. His fingers tap, tap, tapped on his crossed knee. "We all toasted the bride and groom. It was high time they married, actually. They'd been in love for years. Everyone was very happy for them both." Each time he finished a sentence, he acted as if he were saying "And that's all, folks." But it most assuredly wasn't all, so I pressed him.

"And were you there when Billie Jo told Harris that Johnny was really Harris's father?"

Now, Walter narrowed his eyes at me, flattening out the tic again with his left hand. His patience was evaporating. "Where are you going with this, Willa? The woman is dead, killed by her own son. What possible good can it do to bring down Johnny Tyson as well?"

"Were you there when Billie Jo said Johnny was Harris's father or not?"

"Yes. I was there," he said, exasperated with me.

"How did everybody take it?"

"Actually, I don't think most of us were surprised. As I said, Billie Jo and Johnny had been lovers for a long time."

"What about Harris? How did he take it?"

"Not well."

"What do you mean?"

Walter sighed. "You're going to make me spell it out for you? Harris blew up. He raged. In front of everyone. Calling Billie Jo and Johnny names I won't repeat. He said Johnny would 'screw his best friend's wife when he wasn't looking.'"

Well, I'd wanted to hear it. "Is that all?" I asked, hoping that the answer would be an emphatic affirmative.

"No. That's not all. He threw things, a glass I believe, that broke and cut Janet Gutierrez's hand; a guitar; and a few other things that I don't really remember."

Weakly, I pressed on. "Anything else?"

"Yes, Willa. One more thing. But you're not going to like it. Harris hit Billie Jo across the face and knocked her to the ground. Then he stomped out of the room and went somewhere else in the house. We left. Ricky and Janet left at the same time. I can't tell you what happened after that. I don't know."

"Why didn't Ursula tell me all of this?" I wondered, shaken.

"You'll have to ask her that." He rose. He'd served his own agenda and now, he was finished with me. "Now, if you'll excuse me, I have another meeting." He walked to the door and held it open for me. "Give this up, Willa. Stop before you hurt someone else. Maybe even yourself."

Chapter Thirty

When I got home, I called Ben Hathaway. Miraculously, he was still in his office and his secretary put me straight through. "Hey, Ben," I said in greeting.

He sighed hugely, feigning to be terribly put out at having to answer yet another of my telephone calls. "I figured I might be hearing from you today."

Truly puzzled, I said "Why?"

"The autopsy report came in on Billie Jo Steam. Isn't that why you're calling?" He sounded wary now.

I improvised quickly, "Partly. When can I pick it up?"

"Tonight, if you want to come by. I've already given a copy to Harris and his lawyer, and they left one here for you. Or I can drop it off on my way home. I wouldn't mind dinner at George's," he hinted strongly.

"I have some work to do, but if you want to come by around nine, we can have a late sandwich," I told him. Making my request in person would be better, anyway. If I bought him a hamburger, he'd be more likely to help. The way to Ben Hathaway's heart is definitely through his exceptionally large stomach. He agreed and we rung off.

I pulled out my journal, my Sapphire, and my thoughts, planning to review what I knew and add what Janet had inadvertently told me. I found the notes I'd made when I first got involved with Billie Jo and reread my interview with Walter.

I think better with music, usually piano nocturnes or something quiet. I found the disk Harris had given me, the early release of his new CD that contained the remastered duets with his father. I turned on the player and slid in the disk, carrying the plastic CD case back to my chair.

The printed insert listed the new songs as well as the duets

Harris and his father sang together. I pulled out the booklet included in the case and thumbed through it. The pictures of Trey and Six Bills were reprints of photos taken back in the early 1970s. The photographer had mimicked the Six Bills poses with the members of Harris's band and printed the pictures of the two bands, side by side, on the same page.

All the members of the Six Bills looked very young and happy. Linc was a handsome man then, from what I could see of his face under the shoulder-length hair, huge moustache, and chin-length sideburns that almost touched in the front to form a full beard. Walter looked comical as a hippie and Ricky was cute in a smallish way. Johnny sat behind the drums with a spacey expression on his face.

When I compared the father and son, I found Trey and Harris were much alike, although Harris was and appeared older than the ancient photographs of his father. Trey would remain forever young in his pictures and our memories. A paradox of early death was that one's visage remained eternally youthful and attractive.

Billie Jo, though, was spectacular, in a Joni Mitchell/Mary Traverse kind of way. Her hair was long and blonde, albeit not smooth. She'd not ironed it in those days, as so many young girls did. She had a thin braid pulled back on each side of her center part, anchored in the back, in the style of the time.

Billie Jo's dress was shapeless, her bare feet long and narrow. Bird-thin arms poked out of the sleeves of her shift. Still, she was lumihous, despite the old, grainy quality of the pictures. Even without movement and speech, it was easy to see how the Bills could all have loved her. She looked like a sweet child, with a hint of sexuality just beneath the surface.

Harris's band was almost the same configuration, but with no female member. I'd seen both bands perform at Billie Jo's victory party, but the crowd was thick and I'd paid no attention to the individuals in the band. I held the booklet up to the light to be sure.

Pictured on the far right of Harris's band, with an acoustic guitar, was the Linc of today. He had the same long hair, now streaked with grey, and the same long, lanky build. The face was worn, but still sporting that moustache. Unmistakably, Linc.

If Linc played in Harris's band, the two men must have been in regular contact for years. Maybe they'd even seen each other every day. The Bills had given me the impression that they'd lost touch, had no contact for three decades. Even when I learned about the annual reunions, Harris's relationship with Janet and Ricky and Eva's medical treatment, I still believed the Bills had been leading essentially separate lives.

Yet now I knew that Johnny and Billie Jo had maintained regular contact all the time she was in prison. Linc and Harris worked together. Why had Walter lied to me about this? What difference could it possibly have made to know that they'd all stayed in touch? What other lies had they told me? And why?

I took a quick look at my watch. It was only seven o'clock. Not too late. I grabbed up my things and hurried down to Greta. We drove quickly over to the small trailer park.

Linc was home when I got there, sitting on the same white plastic chair, again fooling around with his guitar in the twilight. He had a cigarette in his mouth and the identical overflowing ashtray on the table that probably hadn't been emptied since long before the last time I was here.

"Hey, Linc," I said as I approached.

"Hey, Willa," he replied, as if he'd seen me every day of his life, forever. He made no effort to stop futzing with the guitar, or whatever musicians called the mindless strumming. I sat down in the same chair I'd occupied before.

"Linc," I said, to get his attention.

He said, "Hmmm?" and continued to play.

"Can I talk to you?"

"Sure," he said, still fiddling with and looking down at his guitar. His braided, grey-streaked hair was gathered in a leather thong at the base of his neck, making it possible for me to see his face. He seemed sober and focused on his guitar. He wasn't rude, but he wasn't particularly interested in me, either.

"How long have you been playing guitar with Harris?"

"Always."

"What does that mean?"

"Since Harris was born, I've been jamming with him. I played my guitar for him when he was in his crib. I thought we'd have to stop when Trey's parents took Harris, but they let us spend time with him. By the time he was four, he was singing along. About six, he started to play, too. We've been jamming together forever." He smiled with memory.

"Why?" I asked. Linc looked truly puzzled at my question, as he kept his face turned down toward the guitar, still picking the strings, still focused. He made no effort to answer. "Why did you keep in touch with Harris all these years?"

Now, Linc looked up at me, continuing to strum, adjust his strings, pick a small melody I recognized from the CD. "Well," he finally said, "nobody ever asked me that question before. But I guess that's because everybody else who'd be interested already knows the reason." He shrugged.

"Which is what?"

"How old were you in '69?" I could see no relevance to the question, but I answered him anyway and he looked at me through narrowed eyes. "Too young, then, to know or understand us. Or Woodstock."

"Tell me what I need to know to understand it, then."

He shook his head and gave a small chuckle. "Not sure I can. Oh, we were all so smart. We were gonna change the world. We knew world peace was possible and we could make that happen."

"Peace, love, and understanding, you mean? 'Give peace a chance?'" I said, quoting a John Lennon lyric from the era.

"Kinda," he agreed, nodding. "Kinda. We were kids. We lived away from home. We found a bond in our music. We were a family. It was just the thing to do. At Woodstock, we had this incredible experience of love and peace and kindness. It stayed with us. All our lives."

I struggled to understand his meaning. "So, you're saying that you've kept in touch with Harris and the other Bills all these years because of the bonding experience you had at Woodstock?"

"Partly."

"But there's something else, too, isn't there?" I asked him, running on instinct.

He looked at me again, measuring me, coming to his own conclusions about whether he could trust me or whether he wanted to. Finally, he made some decision. "Harris could be my own boy."

He couldn't have shocked me more if he'd said he was an alien from another planet. Indeed, I might have believed that sooner than this. Billie Jo and Linc? "What do you mean?"

A beat passed. Two. "We sorta had what we called in those days a 'love fest.' But, then, Billie Jo turned up pregnant shortly after Woodstock. Little Trey became a part of our family. We all felt responsible for him. Maybe we weren't. Legally, we weren't. But we felt we were."

"No one ever told Trey Steam about this?" I asked him, incredulous. "He thought he was Harris's father all that time and no one ever said otherwise?"

"Well," Linc seemed more than a bit chagrined now, "you see, we never knew for sure. Trey coulda been Harris's daddy. He for certain looked like Trey, much more than he looked like Billie Jo or any of the rest of us. And we all loved him and took care of him."

"But, it's possible that Trey Steam wasn't Harris's father?" I persisted.

"After Trey was killed, we never wanted to find out for sure. It seemed better for Little Trey to have four daddies. So, that's how we left it. While Billie Jo was in prison, Little Trey needed us to be his family. We've all kept in touch with him. He's our boy. The only boy I'm ever likely to have." Linc turned back to his tune, changing the melody a little, playing a riff here and there.

I pressed him. "Are you sure Trey never knew about your 'love fest'? Or about Harris's questionable paternity?" I couldn't reasonably believe that Trey Steam had been so oblivious to his own family.

"None of us ever told him, far as I know," Linc said.

Mindful of the time, I switched gears. "Tell me what happened the night Trey died."

He continued to play while he smoked one cigarette after another. "Why don't you get us a beer. Bring me two. This is a thirsty story." He gestured with his head toward the inside of the trailer.

I walked up the two metal steps and entered the low, dark space. With no lights on inside and not enough daylight left, I could just make out the kitchen sink and figured the refrigerator had to be nearby. After groping a bit, I found the small, round appliance that had probably been running since 1950 or so, which appeared to be the vintage of the trailer's furnishings—what I could see of them, anyway.

The small light inside the refrigerator illuminated the same type of green, long-neck bottles of Rolling Rock we'd shared the last time I was here, and little else. I pulled out three and stood there letting my eyes adjust to the dimness again after I closed the refrigerator.

I fumbled my way back to the door, took the bottles outside, handed two to Linc, and kept the other for myself. He stopped long enough to twist off the top and take a healthy swig of the beer. I sipped mine more slowly, while he returned to the melody and I waited.

"It was Sunday. We'd been hired to play out at the fronton, like I told you before. It was a big gig for us. We were gettin' paid pretty regular by this time. We'd had a couple of records—the college kids knew us, even the high school kids came around whenever we played weekends." Linc strummed and talked, with a break now and then to light a new cigarette when the one in his mouth burned down to his lips, or swig the beer.

"So, we all started out at Billie Jo's and Trey's place. We went to the Fronton together in Wally's van, like we always did. Little Trey was with us, like usual. We set up, played our sets, and were having a good time." He stopped there to finish the first bottle, and threw it off to the ground under the trailer.

I heard the bottle hit a piece of glass and figured he must have quite a collection down there. He lit another cigarette and stuck it back into the corner of his mouth. After he had it going, he returned to the playing and the telling.

"Trey had been flirting with some girls in the audience. He was high, like always. They were screaming his name, about to faint over him. At the end of the set, they came backstage. Trey was fooling around with them and Billie Jo saw him. She'd sure seen this sort of thing before. But this time, it made her mad. So she went right up to Johnny and started kissing him, in front of Trey and everybody." Linc shook his head, played a while, letting me use my imagination to reconstruct the scene.

I did see it all clearly in my mind: the noise, the heat. A Sunday night in June, outside at the jai alai fronton. Loud music, added to drugs and alcohol, and Trey Steam's explosive personality. The spontaneous combustion was waiting to happen, even if Billie Jo hadn't lit the spark by kissing Johnny.

"Trey just exploded. He hit Johnny and Johnny punched Trey in the face. Broke Trey's nose. Trey was bleeding like a stuck pig. The three of 'em got into a big screaming match. Wally tried to calm everybody down. Wally had known Trey the longest and he usually had more luck getting Trey to be reasonable than the rest of us did. But this time Trey pushed Wally back and Wally fell off the platform and cut up his leg pretty bad. That pissed Wally off, too, so he quit trying to deal with Trey." Linc finished the second beer and threw the bottle down with the first one.

At that point, Linc told me, Trey took off with the girls, who must have had a car, leaving the others there. Wally got a ride from someone, Linc didn't know who it was, to the hospital for stitches in his bleeding leg. The rest of the band went on for their final numbers. "I don't know if you know how it works, but if we didn't play 'til the end, we didn't get paid?" Linc looked at me to see if I understood his point. I nodded.

"What happened after you finished the final set?" I asked him.

"We picked up our equipment, got our check, and drove Wally's van back to Billie Jo's place," Linc answered. "Billie Jo was still crying and upset. Johnny was trying to calm her down."

"Was Trey there when you arrived?"

"Nope. The place was empty. Ricky and I left, but Johnny helped Billie Jo and Little Trey get inside and get to bed before he went home."

"So, Trey never came back?"

Linc shook his head back and forth. "I never saw him alive again. Next thing I knew, Trey was dead, Billie Jo in jail, and every-thing all—" he looked at me for a second, checking his language, "fowled up. Ain't never been right since." Linc ended his story with a sorrowful look and a blues chord or two to emphasize his point. Then he got up and went inside.

While he was gone, I planned our last set of questions. He brought out two more long-necks, and offered me one. When I told him I had another appointment tonight, he shrugged, chugged half the first beer, and went back to his guitar.

"Linc, what did you think about Billie Jo being in prison?"

"She'd be alive today if you'd left her there, now wouldn't she?" he said.

By the time I returned to Minaret, Ben Hathaway's unmarked car was already there. I sat with Greta and jotted down the main points of Linc's story for later reflection. Something about it didn't fit with the other facts I had learned, but I hadn't brought my tape recorder and I didn't have my journal.

The sense of something being out of place niggled me, floating around in my brain in one of those "TOTs," or "tip of the tongue" memory losses, the experts say we all have every day. The secret to remembering is to stop trying. I recorded the main points of what Linc had told me, counting on my notes to jog my memory when I got back to my journal.

George's hostess told me George and Ben Hathaway were in the Sunset Bar, so I went directly there. Ben must have arrived first, because they weren't sitting at my favorite table. Instead, they were at a booth in the back.

"Hello, darling," George greeted me. "I'm glad you're here. I have a large party I need to check on, if I can leave you two alone?"

"See you later, George," Ben said as I nodded my consent.

"Here," Ben told me, sliding a thin envelope toward me with the Tampa Police Department logo on it. "It's a copy of Billie Jo's autopsy report. When can we eat? I'm starving."

I laughed out loud. Ben always gets right to the point. He's even more forthright than I am. Maybe that's why we're often at loggerheads even though we like and respect each other. Too much honesty does that sometimes.

"How's Harris doing?" I asked him, picking up the envelope and putting it in my pocket.

"I haven't seen him. The state attorney's office told me Harris still planned to plead guilty. Of course, there's no bail, so he's still sitting over in the Orient Road jail right now," Ben answered me, while quaffing beer from a frosty mug. Under Florida law, granting a defendant charged with a capital crime pretrial release was unusual. Because Harris had confessed and seemed determined to plead guilty, no reason to make an exception to normal procedure existed.

"Do you know why Harris won't see me?" I asked.

Ben gave me his best "nunnuvyerbiznez" stare. "Like I said, I haven't seen Harris. My guess is that he doesn't want you pestering him to prove he didn't kill his mother. The man wants to plead guilty, Willa. I know that's unusual. Nobody wants to take responsibility for his own actions anymore. But that's between him and his maker. You should stay out of it."

I said nothing. I wasn't going to argue the merits of my behavior with Ben Hathaway. When his burger was delivered, the hungry bear across the table began his feeding. "Thanks for the report, Ben. But that wasn't why I called earlier," I started.

"No kidding," he mumbled around the food in his mouth, some of which fell out when he talked. I didn't feel quite so hungry, after all. Watching mastication isn't particularly appetizing. Maybe I could write a best-selling diet book on the subject.

"Right. I want to have all of the forensic evidence from the Trey Steam murder reevaluated," I told him.

Now his full mouth literally gaped open. I looked away from the sight. After he closed it again, chewed some more, and swallowed, he said, "What on earth do you want to do that for?"

"It's just a hunch I have. Come on, Ben. You've already found DNA evidence we didn't know existed. What if there's something else? Shouldn't we look? We know Billie Jo didn't kill Trey Steam. Maybe we can find out who did," I coaxed.

"What you're thinking is that whoever killed Trey Steam also killed his wife, is that it?" Ben stated, more than a little snidely. *And maybe threateningly, too,* I thought.

"It's a theory worth exploring, isn't it?" I said, so defensively that I insulted him.

"Do you honestly think we're a bunch of idiots, Willa? Of course, it's worth looking at. We've been looking at the idea. Our job is to solve murders, you know. We try to do it every once in a while, whether you high and mighty judges think so or not." Ben, apparently, was more than a little put out. It was the situation that had him so frustrated. He chomped on his hamburger and ate every one of his french fries before I said anything else, on the theory that he'd be better on a full stomach.

"Dessert?" I asked him. He glared at me, but ordered a hot fudge sundae, made with the chef's golden vanilla ice cream and smothered in the Sander's milk chocolate topping George imports from Michigan.

"No coffee," he growled, raising his beer mug for a refill instead. My stomach recoiled at the idea of beer and ice cream, but, hey, I wasn't eating it.

"Why not review the physical evidence, too, Ben? Mistakes could have been made. You weren't running the department then. Or maybe, you just have better forensic tools now. What can it hurt?"

"What makes you think there is any physical evidence left to look at?" he asked me, belligerent still.

I eyed him. "I didn't find a court order scheduling the trial evidence for destruction. And other evidence was collected at the scene and not admitted at the trial. You found the murder weapon and Trey Steam's clothes. I never asked you where they were." He started to protest and I held up my hand. "I'm not saying anything about that. I don't care where you found them. But there's more evidence. Why not let your guys look it all over? Or send it to the crime lab? A man's life hangs in the balance here," I reminded him.

I don't know if the ice cream sweetened him up or if he still felt guilty, just like I did. In any event, this time giving me a view of melting ice cream mixed liberally with chocolate and beer, he asked me, "What is it you're looking for, exactly?"

"I'm not sure," I told him trying not to heave. "Anything that would help prove Harris didn't kill Billie Jo." He eyed me again as I sipped my water and tried to breathe through my mouth at the same time. "And if we could find out who did kill Trey Steam, that would be a bonus, too."

As Ben finished up his desert, I made up my mind. "Have you considered Linc as a suspect?"

Appeased by a full stomach of food he didn't have to pay for, Ben was a little friendlier. "As far as I'm concerned, they're all suspects."

Chapter Thirty-One

I saw Ben to the door, retrieved my briefcase, and preoccupied with the murders, trudged up the stairs. Lost in the past, I opened the door to let myself into the flat, intending to relax for a short half hour and then call it a night.

"Hello, Willa."

I dropped my briefcase on the floor and jumped almost completely out of my skin.

Without thinking, I snapped, "You just took ten years off my life." I glared at Harry and Bess, both sitting quietly at Kate's feet. "Fine watchdogs. If someone breaks in, you just lick them to death, is that the idea?" I collapsed onto the sofa.

"I'm sorry. I didn't mean to startle you. I saw you downstairs with Ben Hathaway, so I asked George if I could come up and wait. I thought he told you I was here," Kate apologized.

"No," I said, still trying to slow my pounding heart. "No, I didn't see him before I came up. It's okay. I'm sorry. I'm just tired and preoccupied."

"I fixed us a cup of tea," she said, leaning over the teapot on the highly polished mahogany butler's table. "Let me pour you a cup." Hot tea is Kate's cure for all that ails you. She had taken out my mother's Royal Albert tea service, the one I use when I need a calming ritual.

"It's late for you to be here, isn't it?" I asked her, after I'd taken a few sips of the heavily sweetened tea with cream and felt a little fortified.

"Yes. It's late, dear. I should have been here weeks ago." She deliberately twisted my meaning. "I should have come when I first returned from Italy with Leo. But I thought you'd make the time to talk to me about it when you were ready. I've finally figured out that Mohammed must come to the mountain."

"Leo told you about our argument," I accused.

"Of course, he didn't tell me." She shook her head with a smile.

"Jason, then."

"No. Not Jason, either. Actually, it was Augustus, and he meant well."

"Augustus? How do you know Augustus? Are you just accumulating good-looking, younger men like charms for your bracelet, now?" I asked her, regretting my hostility the instant it slipped out of my mouth. I wasn't angry with Kate. I was scared for her, and my concern made me harsher than I intended.

Kate was unperturbed. "Why not?" she smiled. "They're fun to have around, don't you think? Young men are good for us old dames. They keep the juices flowing."

"Okay. I get it. You're teasing me. But, really. What is up with you and Leo?" I sincerely wanted to know how a woman as self-assured and collected as Kate could have such a serious lapse in judgment. I have always looked to her for guidance. Now, our roles were inexplicably reversed.

"Is it so hard for you to believe I've found love with Leo?" She looked at me straight on, her body language relaxed and easy. Apparently, she felt she had no reason to be defensive.

"He's thirty-five years old! He's not much older than Carly! Younger than me!" I mentioned Kate's notoriously flighty, wayward younger daughter, whom we hadn't seen in months.

Kate set her teacup down on the silver tray holding the tea service. "Do you think I did this to hurt Carly? Or any of my children? Do you think I would see my children any more often if I hadn't married Leo? I rarely saw my children before I married him. Carly's off, God knows where. Jason is too busy in Washington to bother with his mother and both you and Mark live right here in town, but I rarely see you. Do you want me to be lonely all my days, Willa? Do you think that's fair?" Her tone was gentle.

I was properly chagrined. "I thought you were busy with your life. Happy."

She reached over and took my hand and patted it. "I am happy. I was happy before Leo and I'm happier now. We have fun, Willa. Do you know how important it is to have fun at my age? And how rare it is when someone comes along who shares my interests?" Kate sounded like an elderly woman, instead of the sexy sixty-something she was.

"Like square dancing?" I asked, remembering the cowhand outfits she and Leo had worn to the victory party. "I've never known you to square dance in my life before Leo!"

"Well, it's time I started to do some things like that. I won't always be young, you know. A time will come when I can't go dancing. Until then, I plan to spend as much of my life with Leo as he's interested in spending with me." She looked at me with the stern countenance that meant she would brook no further argument.

"And raise his children, too?" Without my consent, my voice expressed disapproval.

"If we can. Yes. I think that would put the spring back in my step, don't you?" Her blue eyes sparkled and her lips smiled in the outward manifestation of the joy she felt inside. One didn't need a Ouija board to divine how happy Kate truly felt.

I shrugged. I couldn't bring myself to say what I was thinking. What if Leo left her for a younger woman, someone more his own age? She'd be heartbroken. And even more so if she'd brought his children into her home and he took them with him when he left. I wasn't just jealous and distrustful of Leo, although that was part of it. I was genuinely concerned for Kate's long-term happiness.

Kate might be a mystic. She is telepathic often enough. "The biggest obstacle to my long term happiness is the judgmental opinions of my friends and family," she said, reading my thoughts verbatim. "The way medical science is going, I may live to be a hundred. I've found a man who wants to be with me. We have a wonderful time when we're together. We like talking, walking, going to the movies. We laugh a lot. Leo makes me laugh every day. We watch football, go to hockey games. Can you imagine?"

She smiled and went on. "I'm enjoying my life, Willa. When I'm with Leo, I feel like *I'm* thirty-five again, right along with him. You don't want to take care of me. You have your own life to live. You should be grateful that I've found Leo to make me happy."

I mentally braced myself and attempted to raise my most serious concern. "Okay. But, what if . . . "

"Relationships don't come with guarantees, dear. I could marry a man my own age and be divorced or widowed in six months or less. Similar ages don't necessarily mean happiness."

She left me alone to wrestle with my thoughts, while she took the tea things into the kitchen to wash up. When she came back, she had on her jacket and was carrying her handbag. I stood, still concerned, and she gave me a kiss and a small hug.

"You've worn me down, Kate. I wish you and Leo the best. Go and be happy, that's all I want for you," I told her with all the grace I could muster, hiding my fear behind a mask of support.

"Thank you, dear. Don't be a stranger," she said on her way out.

I still didn't trust Leo. And I didn't like him. But I would try to keep my feelings on the subject to myself. And he'd better never give Kate a moment's reason to be sorry she asked me to bless this relationship, or he'd have me to answer to, I promised myself silently. Kate was already out the door before I remembered that she hadn't told me why she'd been discussing me with Augustus.

"It's only Tuesday," my brain groaned as I dragged myself out of bed at five o'clock. Dawn had not yet even approached the horizon. George was snoring softly and both dogs were snoring, too. None of them even wiggled an eyebrow as I extracted myself from under all three and pulled my body out of bed.

In the kitchen, I put an extra scoop into the Italian espresso maker I use for my Cuban coffee. While it brewed, the cream heating in the microwave, I dressed for my run. Once the coffee smells drifted into the bedroom, Harry and Bess decided to join me for their two-second breakfast. We were out the door and into our run in less than fifteen minutes.

Pounding the sand, one foot in front of the other and breathing heavy, I felt my mind slowly begin to clear. By the end of the first mile, I was back to thinking about the Six Bills.

So many loose ends remained because I hadn't been able to write my thoughts down in my journal for a couple of days now. I have a good memory, but I've learned not to rely on it. The details of a case, the little things that can slip past recall, have solved more crimes than the easily retained big picture. One of the reasons I had gotten up so early today was to put my thinking cap on and try to see what was in plain sight around me.

I saw gaping holes in the facts I had accumulated. The timeline wasn't clear. Possible motives for killing Trey abounded, jealousy and anger being at the top of the list for all of the remaining Bills. Why someone would kill Billie Jo still escaped me. Each of the Bills had both the opportunity and the means to kill both Billie Jo and Trey Steam. And that assumed that the killer was one of the Bills, which wasn't necessarily the case, just the most likely answer.

Regardless of what George had to say on the subject, random violence had always existed in Tampa. Granted, homicides are usually committed by someone who knows the victim. Still, that didn't rule out a killer who only knew the victim tangentially—say, a gas station attendant, a cashier at the grocery store, or a fan. The possibilities were endless. But a random act of violence was beyond my ability to resolve. I could only consider the people who were closest to the victims as potential suspects.

I listed them out loud, repeating the names into my small recorder between ragged breaths as I ran. Visualizing the pages in my journal where I'd written their names, I reported everything I could remember about the potential alibis of all five of the other Bills at the time Trey Steam was murdered.

Harris couldn't have been his father's killer, of course. But I listed him for completeness. I also listed his grandparents, Bill and Mary Steam, for the same reason. There was no real chance that either of them had killed their son. Only frustration insisted on my including them, too.

Trey Steam was murdered sometime between two o'clock and five o'clock in the morning. According to the story Linc told me, the last time he saw Trey alive was about midnight, at Jai Alai Fronton on Dale Mabry, when Trey left with the two female fans.

While blaming the fans would be helpful and easy, I had found no information about them in any of the file materials I'd received. If they hadn't been identified and interviewed at the time of Trey's death, I had no chance of ever finding them now.

Ricky, too, had left Trey's house long before Trey was killed. Walter was at the hospital, having stitches put in his thigh, so he wasn't at Trey's after the gig. According to Ursula, Walter left for a trip to Europe, a trip that lasted the whole summer. He said he hadn't known that Trey died until the fall, after Billie Jo had already been tried, convicted, and sentenced to prison.

But both Johnny and Billie Jo were at the house when Linc and Ricky left. They both could have still been there when Trey came home. They could have killed him together.

Still, would Johnny have let Billie Jo take full responsibility for killing Trey? It seemed unlikely. Johnny was protective of Billie Jo. He loved her. He had stuck with her through thirty years of prison time. When I saw him on Saturday, he was literally prostrate with grief.

The idea that he and Billie Jo had agreed to keep Johnny's involvement in Trey's murder a secret made no sense. If Johnny had been the one tried and convicted, I'd believe they killed Trey together and Johnny was protecting her. But that's not what had happened.

So, maybe Billie Jo did kill Trey, herself. She was home alone, with Harris, after Johnny left. Maybe when Trey came home, they continued their argument. Maybe the fight turned physical, as the argument between Trey, Johnny, and Walter had turned physical earlier. Maybe Billie Jo did kill Trey, in self-defense, or out of fear or rage.

But if that was so, what about the new DNA evidence that I used to free Billie Jo in the first place? If Billie Jo had killed Trey, with his defensive wounds and all the blood on him, surely some of Billie Jo's blood would have been on either the murder weapon or Trey's clothes. And none was found.

Simultaneously, I returned to the house and back to the idea that maybe one of the Bills hadn't killed Trey at all. Maybe the perpetrator was someone else altogether. I needed more facts. As soon as I could breathe again, I'd make an effort to obtain them.

After I'd showered and dressed for court, I still had an hour before having to be back on the bench for the *Madison* trial. I sat down at my home computer and quickly transcribed my dictation and the taped interviews. I printed out the transcripts and tossed them in my briefcase, along with my journal and Billie Jo's autopsy report, and zipped over to the courthouse.

Once again, I entered my chambers, picked up my robe, and walked immediately out to the bench. All the members of the Greek chorus that had become this trial were in place. Phillip Sloat had only two more days to finish up his proofs on behalf of Cardio Medical, I reminded everyone else and myself. No one objected to the reminder.

Everyone in the room now knew what I had realized from the outset. The end of the trial would not mean a satisfactory resolution to this case. All we were doing at this point was making a good appellate record so that the parties could live on to fight another day in another forum. We brought in the jury and I gave the floor over to Sloat.

Sloat recalled his expert witness to the stand, the one who had been testifying when we had recessed yesterday. The large, ruddy-complexioned man looked uncomfortable in his suit and tie. He was a surgeon by training, and a medical school professor at Johns Hopkins. He spent his days in surgical scrubs and his nights in blue jeans, I imagined. He had been hired by the defense to blame Stanley Madison's surgeon for his death.

The man's testimony was long on self-congratulation for the length of his résumé and short on explanations as to why Stanley Madison had died. Without such testimony in the record, I would have no choice but to grant Marilyn Madison's motion for directed verdict once Sloat finished his proofs. Every lawyer in the room understood the significance of the expert's testimony. But the jury was clueless as to the drama going on.

The action here was akin to a soccer match in which one team was constantly trying to kick the ball into the net, while the other team kept attempting to block the effort. Every time Sloat would ask the multimillion dollar question, either Lehman or Royal would object. Each objection was a good one, and I had no choice but to sustain them all. Sloat was blocked at every question from getting in his vital proofs. His frustration was showing in his face, his body language, and, finally, the way he was handling his witness.

Of course, the expert had been thoroughly prepared before he took the stand, and Sloat had thought he knew the testimony in advance. A trial lawyer's nightmare is the rogue witness—the one who doesn't testify as he is expected to.

Frustrated, Sloat requested a recess to confer with his witness. Lehman and Royal objected to any conversations with the witness during the recess. I denied the objection, creating yet another appealable issue. If Sloat got his witness to testify against the doctor, the case would go to the jury. The decision would be out of my hands. If the witness wouldn't testify against the doctor, who had already settled the claims against him and paid a million dollars, then I'd have no choice but to grant the plaintiff's motion for directed verdict. Either way, blessedly, the case would be over when Sloat rested on Thursday or after the jury returned on Friday afternoon.

During the recess, I had no time to do anything but flip through my pink telephone message slips. Today, the stack was so tall that Augustus had placed a paperweight on it to keep it from toppling over. I moved the brass Labrador to one side and picked up all of the slips. I found mostly business calls from colleagues, a few social invitations to professional functions, two calls yesterday and two more today from the C.J., and, at the bottom of the stack, a call from Ben Hathaway and one from Johnny Tyson.

I tried Hathaway first. He answered his own phone on the second ring. "Ben, Willa Carson here. Returning your call."

"I'm a little rushed right now, Willa. Just wanted to let you know that we're looking for the rest of the evidence. We have most of it and I've sent it all to the lab. We should have the results in a few days." Now that Ben had agreed with my desire to review the physical evidence, he'd adopted the plan as his own. It was nice of him to keep me up to speed and I appreciated it.

"A few days? For an open investigation?" I protested.

"This investigation isn't urgent, Willa. We have a confessed inmate for one killing and the other case is thirty years old. A few days is the best I can do."

I tried Johnny Tyson next. He never picked up the phone, but his answering machine kicked on after about six rings. "Johnny, this is Willa Carson, returning your call. I'm in court today, but I'll be through around four-thirty. I'll come by to see you then." I had no idea whether Johnny was requesting I visit him again, but that was what I intended to do, anyway.

Augustus came in with a glass of passion-fruit tea as I was disconnecting. "Do you know who Benedict Arnold was,

Augustus?" I asked him, without looking up from my task.

"The brilliant Revolutionary War general who saved Washington's butt more than once and might have single-handedly defeated the British?" he replied, sweetly.

"I was thinking more of later in history, when he was convicted of treason," I countered in a stern voice.

"But he had good motives, even then," Augustus countered. Apparently, he was a better student of American History than most Jamaicans, too. "For example, he tried to warn Washington several times, but Washington wouldn't listen. Arnold sent Washington several letters, which Washington ignored."

Tired of the game, I said, "So it was you, then? You left the note on my car and the e-mail on my desk warning me against freeing Billie Jo Steam from prison?"

Augustus didn't look at all chagrinned. "It was wise advice, wasn't it?"

Since he was right, I ignored him. "No matter what your motives are, conversations that you and I have in these chambers are private. They are not to be disclosed. Not to anyone. That includes Kate Austin and it most definitely means Leo Colombo."

Augustus looked like he wanted to argue the point, then thought the better of it. "Yes, Judge," he said, instead. "But, Leo and Kate were worried about you. They thought . . . "

I interrupted him. "I don't care what they thought, or what you thought, or what anybody thinks. Our conversations are confidential. Always. That's all."

"Yes, Judge," he said again, letting himself out of my chambers and closing the door softly behind him. Augustus seemed to have my best interests at heart and loyalty is a quality I prize over almost everything else. Still, I mulled over the connection between Augustus and Leo. I didn't understand it and I liked it even less.

Back in the courtroom, we called in the jury and Sloat had the expert on the stand again. Three or four more times, Sloat asked him whether the operating surgeon was grossly negligent and had acted below the standard of care during Stanley Madison's surgery. The expert refused to give Sloat the answer he was looking for, even after I overruled Lehman's appropriate objections to the leading questions Sloat eventually resorted to asking.

Finally, defeated, Sloat passed the witness and returned to counsel table. Unless he could pull a rabbit out of his hat with his final witnesses tomorrow and Thursday, I'd be forced to enter judgment for Marilyn Madison on Friday morning.

Sometimes, our decisions are inevitable, no matter how improbable they seem at the outset. I dismissed the jury, picked up my robe, my briefcase, and went to the car. Greta and I were on our way to Johnny Tyson's before anyone else had even left the courtroom.

Johnny's house didn't look any better today than it had on Saturday. The grass was the same dry brown, the windows were still closed up tight, and no one answered the doorbell when I rang it. An older model Honda sat in the driveway. Since nothing else had changed here since Saturday, that probably meant Johnny was still inside, too.

I leaned on the doorbell again, this time holding it down, as I had before. In a while, Johnny opened the door. He had on the same clothes he'd worn on Saturday. He looked and smelled worse. How long could a man survive on bourbon alone?

He said nothing to me, just turned and walked back into the house. I opened the screen and followed him directly to the kitchen. I avoided gagging on the garbage smell only by sheer willpower. "Why did you call me, Johnny?" I asked him.

"Just wanted to thank you for helping me on Saturday. And for helping Billie Jo. If it wasn't for you, we wouldn't ever have been married. I just wanted to put my affairs in order. That's all." As before, he looked everywhere but at me, mumbling down into his filthy undershirt for most of the speech.

"You're very welcome, Johnny. Now, you can do something for me. To repay me for helping you and Billie Jo," I said. I knew he wouldn't do anything unless he felt he owed it to Billie Jo. Johnny wasn't capable of much besides pouring the rest of the bourbon down his throat.

He thought about it for a while, but, finally, he said, "What is it you want?"

I pulled my recorder out of my pocket and put it on the table in plain sight. I turned it on. "Tell me what happened the night Trey Steam was murdered. After Linc and Ricky left you and Billie Jo at her house that night. What happened?"

Johnny looked at a point above my head and saw into his past, decades ago. He began to talk as if repeating a rote memory, one he'd repeated to himself many times over the years. "Linc and Ricky left. Billie Jo and I took Little Trey in the house and put him to bed. Big Trey wasn't there. We sat around for a while, thinking he might come home, but he didn't. Billie Jo was just tired and wrung out. She went to bed, too. I waited a while longer. Then, I closed the door and went outside to walk home."

"Walk home?"

He nodded. "None of us had a car, except Trey had the one his daddy gave him for college graduation, and Wally had his van. Wally's van was still there in the yard, but I didn't live far away. Besides, I needed the air."

"So Wally must have gotten to and from the hospital some other way, then?"

"I guess so."

"Why didn't one of you drive the van to pick Wally up?"

He sighed. "I don't know anymore. It was a long time ago. I'm sure there was some reason for it."

"Then what happened?"

"I walked home. Went inside. Went to bed."

There had to be more to this story, I knew. Walter had said Johnny was with Billie Jo when they found Trey Steam's body. If

Trey wasn't dead inside the house when Linc and Ricky left, Johnny had to have gone back to the house later on. "And then what?"

"I guess I slept a couple of hours, until Billie Jo came in and woke me up. None of us locked our doors in those days." He gave a wheezy laugh. "We didn't have anything worth stealing. Anyway, she said Trey had come home, still drunk, or high, or both. She heard him banging around in the kitchen, cussing away, slamming stuff all over. She was afraid of him, you understand?"

I nodded. "So she picked up Little Trey and snuck away in Trey's car. She drove around a while and stopped at a park to sleep in the car. Then she came to get me, to see if I'd go home with her, in case Trey was still awake when we got there. We both thought he'd have passed out and then he'd be better in the morning."

"Is that how it normally worked? Would Trey be better the next day?" I asked.

Johnny moved his head up and down, slowly. "Usually. Trey did this sort of thing once in a while. He'd be better the next day. Apologize. You know."

I did know. I heard the same story from every battered woman I'd ever talked to. He'd be fine, he drank, he was violent, then he'd sleep it off. The next day, he was apologetic. The pattern was predictable.

Johnny refilled his glass and offered me the bottle. I declined. "What happened when you got back to Billie Jo's house?" Some of this I knew from the court testimony, the summaries I had read, and what I'd already heard. But Johnny hadn't testified at the trial. And he had been there, at least for some of it.

"Trey was on the floor, blood all over his clothes, all over him. He wasn't moving. I thought he was just passed out at first. So did Billie Jo. Little Trey ran over to Trey, in the darkness, and started saying 'Daddy, wake up.' Trey didn't move. When Little Trey turned back to us, he had blood all over him, too." Johnny shuddered a little bit, took a big gulp of the bourbon, and continued. "I was pretty shaken up. I couldn't really do anything. Billie Jo ran over to both of them, picked up Little Trey and gave him to me. She told me to take him outside. I took Little Trey and put him in the car and then I spent about ten minutes puking my guts out." Johnny was living it over, now. He was there. He held his stomach with his free arm, the way he must have then.

"In a little while, the cops came. They arrested Billie Jo. I took Little Trey to his grandparents." He looked at me straight on for the first time. "The rest, you know."

"Did you ever believe that Billie Jo killed Trey?" I summoned the nerve to ask him.

"No. But he deserved it. Always knocking her around, disrespecting her and Little Trey. If she'd killed him, it wouldn't have mattered to me. I loved Billie Jo. She should have been my wife in the first place. Little Trey was my son," he said as he thumped himself on the chest. "All Trey Steam did was to ruin my family. He acted like Billie Jo wasn't good enough for him. His parents hated her. I don't know why he married her in the first place. Trey never loved Billie Jo like I did. Never!" He glared his conviction directly at me. "And now, I don't even have Harris any more. He hates me now. Trey won in the end, didn't he?" Then, Johnny began to cry.

Chapter Thirty-Two

I had so many facts churning around in my memory that I needed to bring some order to the chaos. I went straight home, let the dogs out, and made a large pot of very strong coffee. When it finished brewing, I collected my briefcase and settled in my den with a cup.

I turned on the computer and transcribed tonight's interview with Johnny, first. I printed out the pages and added them to my stack of transcription from the morning. Then, I settled in my favorite chair with my journal and recorded everything I'd learned since my last opportunity to write things down.

I reviewed Billie Jo's autopsy report. The cause of death was listed as two gunshot wounds to the brain, but the secondary diagnosis was advanced colon cancer. So Billie Jo's intuition and self-diagnosis had been right, after all. She did have terminal cancer and would likely have died within six months.

So again, why kill her now? And why shoot her twice? One of the gunshot wounds to the head would have killed her instantly. The second one was unnecessary.

I took more than two hours just recording what I knew. Even so, I wrote my notes cryptically and quickly. The penmanship was much worse than my sixth grade teacher would have allowed, but I thought I'd be able to decipher it when the time came. I refilled my coffee cup three times before I finished writing. After hours of working, my neck was cramped, my back hurt, and my head was a jumbled mess of jitters. I had to take a break.

I stood up, stretching each of my aching limbs in turn. When I twisted my trunk to the right, I noticed the clock. It was already nine o'clock. My stomach had been growling for a while, but I'd ignored it, wanting to finish my project first. Now, I wandered into the kitchen, looking for something I could munch on.

As usual, the cupboard was bare of everything except microwave popcorn. I took out a bag, stripped off the cellophane with my teeth, and stuck the bag in the microwave, pushing the popcorn button. As it popped, I opened a bottle of cabernet and poured it into the balloon wine glass I was willing to carry all over the house. When the popcorn finished, I poured it into a small bowl and took the bowl, the wine, and my thoughts back to the den.

There, I flipped the journal pages to the plan I'd originally made for investigating Trey Steam's murder. Looking at my list, which had been put together long before I knew anything at all about his murder, I saw that I had failed to follow through on my intention to talk to Billie Jo about the night Trey died.

Billie Jo was the one with the most information about the time immediately before Trey's murder. But I'd never been able to discuss that with her. After chastising myself for failing to have such a basic conversation, I thumped my brain for an acceptable substitute. After a few tries, a thought came to me.

I rifled through my files and folders to find the transcript of the interview done by the investigating officer when the police were called to the scene. I had read the summary of the officer's statements while working on Billie Jo's parole hearing, but never the full testimony. I didn't have a copy of his tape recorded interview with Billie Jo, if one existed. Hearing the story from her point of view might have given me some additional insight. But all I had was the initial interview transcript and Officer Benson's trial testimony, which was better than nothing. I took the pages over to the chair along with my popcorn and wine, put my feet up and began to read.

Officer Benson's testimony was succinct, the way police officers are taught to testify to "just the facts." He said he had been sent to Trey Steam's home after the dispatcher received a call from Billie Jo reporting an accident. When he arrived, he saw a man and a young boy standing near a 1970 Ford Mustang in the driveway. That would have been Johnny and Little Trey.

Officer Benson entered the house and found Billie Jo hold-ing a large knife, her clothes covered with blood. The officer saw a man on the floor, also covered in bloody clothes. When he examined the man, Benson found he was not breathing.

The victim had sustained several stab wounds and appeared to be dead. Officer Benson called an ambulance and then requested back up. When he asked her what had happened, Billie Jo said, "Trey is dead. I can't believe Trey is dead." She said nothing else.

Officer Benson placed Billie Jo under arrest and took her from the scene to the police department, where she was ques-tioned, charged, and placed in a jail cell. Other police department personnel took over the crime scene.

Although the testimony went on for several more pages, lit-tle additional information was revealed about Billie Jo's activities that night after Johnny left the house. So I pulled out the original trial transcript of Billie Jo's testimony now, too. As with all of the trial documents, I'd only reviewed the summary earlier.

Billie Jo testified that Johnny had helped her to get Little Trey into bed and then went home. She said she waited for Trey for a while, but when he didn't return, she went to bed, too. Sometime later, Billie Jo heard Trey. As he was coming into the house, she heard him in an argument with someone else, outside. Another man. She didn't recognize the voice, which wasn't as loud as Trey's. Then Trey came inside, still drunk and cursing.

The testimony was flat and uninspired on the page. Billie Jo had testified with so little enthusiasm, it's no wonder she was convicted. The jury wouldn't have believed her story. Too many holes seemed to be left. Billie Jo offered no theories as to how Trey might have died. Not that she was required to, but a jury likes to hear the accused explain the death.

After I read the rest of her description, I closed my eyes and imagined the scene. *She wasn't quite sleeping when she heard him arguing with someone outside. He slammed the front door and came into the small rented house they'd lived in since their child was born. He was drunk. And angry . . .*

When I'd gotten to the end of Billie Jo's story, I shook myself out of my self-induced trance and returned to the cold transcript. I was surprised to feel myself alive with adrenaline. How must she have felt?

Billie Jo said she took Little Trey out to the car and sped away. She testified that she and Little Trey slept in the car until morning, when they went to Johnny's house. Johnny rode back to Billie Jo's home with her in Trey's car, where she and Johnny discovered Trey dead in the living room.

Billie Jo's defense was solely that the state hadn't proved its case. Sometimes that approach works. But where the young son of a prominent citizen is killed in his home, Tampa jurors of the time would have wanted to put the matter firmly behind them. Convicting the wife, who was from a questionable background and offered no excuse for herself, was the easy way out.

My eyes were feeling heavy and scratchy. I stood up, flexed again, and refilled my wine glass. I found the Gutierrez Special Reserve cigars Ricky had given me and lit one. Pacing the floor, waving the cigar, sipping the wine, I tried to weave a narrative from the disjointed facts I'd learned about Trey Steam's murder. The pieces just wouldn't fit cohesively.

All six of the Bills had been together from about seven o'clock that evening until the end of the penultimate set at the Fronton. Then, all hell broke loose between the members of the group. The storm had begun years before but built just like a tropical storm builds from a small squall into a ferocious hurricane. When Trey saw Billie Jo and Johnny kissing that last night at the gig, Trey lost control and started a fistfight.

Like many philanderers, Trey was intensely jealous and possessive. Yet Billie Jo had to know Trey was capable of such a reaction. Did she kiss Johnny on purpose? Was she trying to get Trey to fight with the others?

Some of these battered spouse situations are a morass of complicated psychology. She knew Trey was insecure. Maybe on some level, Billie Jo thought Trey's violent reaction would prove he loved her. Or, maybe, she just didn't care about him anymore and wanted to push him over the edge in public to make sure the rest of the Bills would be on her side in the divorce. Or to exact revenge.

Whatever her motives, and I doubted I'd ever learn what they were at this point, Billie Jo's behavior lit the fuse that had blown the group into smithereens. Except that it hadn't. What happened was that the remaining five Bills stayed together after Trey's death. They kept in touch. They took care of each other. It was as if they were truly related by blood instead of Woodstock. Was their loyalty due solely to their shared secret about Little Trey's paternity?

And what about that? I asked myself, as I poured the last of the wine into my glass. I continued to wander in a big circle through the halls of our flat, talking this through out loud. Harris Steam could have been fathered by any one of the five Bills. Although the likelihood that his father was someone other than Trey Steam was remote, it was still possible.

Paternity can be determined definitively now with DNA evidence. The law hasn't caught up with the science, though, and still presumes a child born in wedlock is fathered by the husband. Yet the Bills could have settled Harris's paternity with relative certainty years ago by the testing methods then available. They hadn't done so out of some sense of loyalty to Trey, to Billie Jo, to Woodstock, and to their own lost youth, it seemed. It was a decision that still affected them all.

Which left me with the question: Did it matter? For a little boy whose parents were taken from him by death and the state, having four remaining dads must have been preferable to living his life solely with the dour and unforgiving grandparents I'd met at Billie Jo's funeral. Still, did Harris ever know prior to the last Six

Bills reunion that his paternity was in question? Did Eva? And how did they feel about it?

"And what about Billie Jo?" the wine asked me, in my voice. *What if Billie Jo knew who killed Trey? Why would she keep quiet about it, serve all those years in prison? Billie Jo didn't kill her husband, but she'd had a long time to think about who had. Did she think Johnny had killed Trey? Is that why she never pursued the real killer? Was she as protective of Johnny as he was of her?*

By the time I'd finished the wine and the cigar, my mind was going around in circles. I was tired, sleepy, and fresh out of ideas. I let the dogs upstairs and called it a night. Maybe my subconscious could sort out this tangle.

Chapter Thirty-Three

Eva agreed to meet me for a quick late lunch at Café BT, my favorite French Vietnamese bistro, located on Gandy Boulevard. I'd recessed the *Madison* trial for an hour and a half. Knowing we'd be finished in one more day, I pushed my workload aside yet again to follow my thoughts about Trey Steam's murder.

I arrived a few minutes after one o'clock and was rewarded with a small table in the back, where I sat facing the door so I could see when Eva arrived. She soon made her way through the narrow aisle, stopping to talk to a couple of women I didn't know.

After our Vietnamese tea had been served and we'd ordered fresh rolls, hot and sour soup, and warm noodle salads, Eva and I shared a few moments of companionship while we waited. She was a truly beautiful woman, in a fresh-scrubbed way. Devoid of makeup, her dark lashes framed her eyes and her dark brows accented them. The unruly curls were again tied back, leaving delicate earlobes exposed to display two tiny diamond studs in each. Her physical resemblance to the young Billie Jo was probably what had attracted Harris to her initially.

The plain white shirt fitted her slender form, flaring slightly over a denim skirt that stopped midcalf. Her feet were shod in Birkenstocks, her toenails buffed but unpolished. The entire outfit probably came from her parents' store. All in all, she looked like an Ivy League back-to-school college catalog. Eva acted as if her outburst of temper the last time I saw her had never happened, and so did I.

Women share their secrets with other women. Of all the possibilities, I figured that Billie Jo would have confided in Eva, if she had confided in anyone. "Eva, I'm hoping you'll tell me about your relationship with Billie Jo Steam," I opened when our lunches had been served.

"What relationship?" she asked, bitterly, her easy, casual manner disappearing faster than a speeding bullet.

"Well, she was your mother-in-law. Surely you had some contact with her." I spoke softly, without accusation or much intensity. Eva seemed too fragile.

"Contact with her? She was in prison when I met and married Harris. She was still there when we divorced. I didn't visit her there, if that's what you're suggesting." Eva's ire escalated.

I tried again. "You didn't know her at all? I had the impression she was close to you, close to Harris and your children."

"She was close to them. Not that I was happy about it." The level of hostility Eva demonstrated approached hot hatred. She contained herself with difficulty. "Look, Willa. Billie Jo was a problem in our marriage from the beginning. Harris worshiped her. He visited her every chance he got. He loved her beyond all reason."

She bit her lip, exhaled heavily, but continued. "When the girls were born, he insisted on taking them to see Billie Jo whenever he could. He spent every spare dime and extra minute he had trying to get Billie Jo out of prison. It was probably the biggest single factor in our divorce."

"How so?"

"Harris had no time for me or his daughters. He spent all his time on her. How could we be a family?" Ah. Eva was jealous. Of Harris's mother, a woman destined to spend all her days in prison. And Eva, an only child, had probably married Harris thinking she would be a woman who never had to deal with an interfering mother-in-law. She wasn't interested in sharing him at all.

Eva's temper was still hot. "Don't look at me with that judgmental expression on your face. You may think mine were petty grievances, but you didn't have to live with the two of them. Do you know he actually wanted to get married in that place, just so she could attend our wedding?"

"Did you? Get married there, I mean?" I schooled my features into a flat appearance.

She scowled. "Of course not. We had a normal wedding. It might have been the only normal thing we ever did."

"Was Harris okay with that?"

"Harris was never 'okay' with anything related to Billie Jo. Never. You want to know the truth? It doesn't surprise me that he killed her. His attachment to that woman was unnatural."

She shocked me with that one. "You're a mother, Eva. Wouldn't you want your children to be as devoted to you?"

"I didn't kill their father. That should count for something," she snapped back at me, her nostrils flaring as the hot color rose in her face and a vein pulsed in the middle of her forehead.

Well, of course it mattered that Eva hadn't killed Willie and Billie's father. But I didn't point out that Billie Jo hadn't killed Trey Steam, either. Instead, I deemed it prudent to change the subject slightly.

"Janet Gutierrez told me that you're the general practice physician for all the Bills and their families. You must have quite a few opportunities to talk to them all." Janet said the Bills had remained loyal to Eva, being treated by her despite the frontal lobe damage that caused her to have such poor impulse control and memory lapses. Nor was her judgment what it should have been. Of course, the car accident wouldn't have necessarily affected her skill as a physician, if the frontal lobe damage was mild.

Most people want to be treated by a doctor whom they know and respect, someone they like, and someone who makes that treatment easy. Eva probably fit all those requirements for her husband's friends. "Janet said they come to you for all their routine care," I said.

She accepted the change of topic easily. "Right. Colds, flu, hypertension, high cholesterol, infections, routine things like that," she told me, disclosing nothing confidential about their health care. "They're a pretty healthy bunch," she said. That much was a little hard for me to believe, given all the heavy drinking I'd seen Linc and Johnny engage in, but I now knew better than to challenge her.

She was talking normally again, sure of herself on the ground of her profession and her medical expertise. Her color had returned to normal and she'd taken a few more bites of her lunch.

"Were you surprised when Billie Jo told Harris that Johnny was his father? That seemed to be the catalyst that set Harris off on his rampage the night of the Six Bills' reunion." Again, I tried to set my query before her in a tempered tone.

Eva considered the question for just a second before she answered. "I guess I was surprised to hear her say that at the time. Especially since it was just wishful thinking on Billie Jo's part."

"What do you mean?"

She looked at me carefully, weighing her decisions while she ate her lunch. "I'd like to discuss this with you, Willa, but I can't."

"Why not?"

"Because it concerns my patients. You'll need to get their consent, first."

"Consent to what?"

"To any discussion about their medical treatment," she looked at me as if she felt particularly clever, "or lack thereof."

"Are you saying that no paternity test was done before Billie Jo told Harris that Johnny was his father?" I asked her.

"I'm not saying, one way or the other," she replied. While I was thinking this through, Eva continued. "I'll tell you this much, though. It would kill Harris to know that Trey Steam wasn't his father."

"Why?" Here was a point I'd had trouble understanding.

"Harris idolized the man. Harris has built his whole life around replacing his father. In the abstract, the Oedipus complex doesn't make a lot of sense to me. But until Billie Jo died, I was living it first hand," she said, with obvious distaste.

Eva went on to suggest that she might have expected Harris to kill Johnny, instead of his mother. She said Harris's desire to replace Trey in his mother's life was motive enough for Harris to kill Johnny—simply because Billie Jo had married him. Besides that, she said Harris always thought Johnny had killed Trey.

"Really? Why would Harris think that?" I asked her.

"Because Billie Jo was in love with Johnny. She wouldn't ever allow anyone to say anything against him. Harris always figured that Billie Jo was protecting Johnny. Harris thought that was why Billie Jo would never say who she believed had been her husband's killer." Eva explained this as if Harris's views were the most logical explanation for Billie Jo's behavior. And perhaps she was right. Then, adding to the bonfire was Billie Jo's claim that Johnny was Harris's father. Eva saw a disaster waiting to happen.

"You'd think she would have found out for sure before she destroyed everything her son believed in. That was Billie Jo. Always thinking about herself." The raging fire of jealousy returned to Eva's eyes as she inadvertently disclosed to me what she had earlier refused to say. She knew that Johnny wasn't Harris's father. But how?

A definitive paternity test would have required blood work. When would that have been done? Trying to puzzle it all out, I asked, "Were you Billie Jo's doctor, too?" As soon as the question was out of my mouth, I wished I could take it back.

Instantly, Eva glared at me and her face flushed again, redder this time. She slammed down her fork against the plate, clanging loud enough to startle nearby diners. "I told you, I had nothing to do with the woman. She was dead to me a long time ago. I'm only sorry she wasn't dead to Harris, too. We might have had a life together."

The venom against a woman who had died violently just a few short days ago was vicious. Eva threw down her napkin, pushed back her chair, and stormed out of the restaurant. *Well*, I thought to myself, *please let me get the check.*

Sloat was more demoralized every time we reconvened his case. This afternoon, he was putting the last of his batting order on the witness stand. As each witness testified, I perceived with greater clarity that Sloat wasn't going to be able to introduce the necessary proofs to get the case to the jury. Lehman and Royal, smelling blood in the water, approached me at the afternoon recess.

Sid Lehman was the first to speak. "Judge, I think, under the circumstances, another settlement conference on this case might be productive. I wonder if the court would give us the afternoon to discuss the possibility among ourselves."

"I don't intend to extend this trial beyond Thursday at four-thirty, gentlemen." I turned to Phillip Sloat. "Counsel, do you wish to devote some of your time this afternoon to discussing settlement with Mrs. Madison and her lawyers?" Sloat looked like one of those actors on an Alka-Seltzer commercial after he's taken the antacid: positively relieved. His face all but said, *I thought you'd never ask.*

What Sloat actually said was, "Judge, Mr. Lehman approached me with this suggestion during the lunch recess. My clients are interested in discussing the matter this afternoon. We know that will mean less time to put on the remainder of our evidence if we don't settle. But we think we should take this one last chance to reach some accord here."

I looked at the Cardio Medical representatives. "Is that what you want?"

"Yes, Your Honor," they said, as if I'd just removed their heads from the guillotine.

I turned to the insurance adjuster, who looked even more relieved than Sloat. "Yes, Judge," he replied, too weak in the knees to say more.

"All right. Let's recess today for the rest of the afternoon. We'll reconvene in the morning for the last of your proofs, Mr. Sloat. If you reach a settlement before then, please advise my office."

I restrained myself from dancing a little jig on my way back to my chambers. I felt like a freed slave, a pardoned death row inmate, a woman released from indenture, a—well, a very lucky person.

The possibility that this case could be over today and I could return to the more meritorious cases assigned to me was just about the best present I could think of. Better than a cruise around the world, or winning the lotto, or—well, I felt really, really, good.

Chapter Thirty-Four

"Your brother called," Augustus told me, holding out one of the hated pink message slips when I returned to my chambers. "He left a number. He said it was important."

Jason greeted me on the second ring. "Thanks for calling me back so quickly," he said. "I've got a thousand things to do here, but I wanted to let you know that Sheldon Warwick died a few hours ago. The media will have it in the next few minutes. He had a heart attack."

"Oh, Jason! I'm sorry to hear that," I replied. Sheldon had been a jerk and I didn't care for him, but Jason was genuinely fond of his boss.

"Such a sad death, too," Jason said. "The senator had been sick for quite a while, but we didn't realize he might die so quickly." Jason sounded honestly distraught, something he would hide from everyone but me.

"He was being treated here by Eva Raines. When she told him he had a more serious form of Alzheimer's disease, we were all pretty upset. Eva said the disease usually doesn't progress so quickly. His symptoms had increased and he was seriously depressed," Jason finished.

We discussed the senator's declining health over the past couple of years. Jason told me that the senator had become almost reckless since his diagnosis. He'd become convinced he had only a limited time to live and he needed to accomplish everything he wanted to do quickly. Then, Jason said, "This information isn't being released to the press, Willa. The cause of death we've reported is heart attack. There's no reason to get into the rest of it, now that he's dead."

"Of course. The cause of his death is of no concern to anyone but his family," I agreed. "Will you want to stay with us for a few days while this sorts itself out?"

"Actually, I'll need to stay over at the Warwicks. His wife isn't taking Sheldon's death very well. Her alcoholism has gotten worse since his diagnosis and she shouldn't be alone. But I hope to see you after the funeral tomorrow." We rung off with expressions of affection.

Death certainly does have a way of reminding us of our mortality, and I'd been getting that message loud and clear for several weeks now. Kate was right. We should all grab whatever happiness we could wherever we can get it.

I sat at my desk, thinking about the relatively mild symptoms Senator Warwick started out with and how they had eventually killed him. Problems with his balance, a short temper, Jason had said. Later, he'd developed memory lapses, a few tremors and some erratic conversational patterns that they'd thought was Huntington's disease at first. Then, after his diagnosis of Alzheimer's he'd become convinced he should follow his dreams until he inevitably declined into full dementia. In a way, he was lucky that his heart attack had gotten him first.

Only a few symptoms. A couple of tics, mental instability, lack of balance. Why all of us have that kind of thing some of the time. How could we know whether we were on the verge of some terrible calamity, and just not yet diagnosed?

Take me, for example. I have more and more senior moments, times when I can't remember things at the tip of my tongue. That's why I've come to rely on my journals. Or consider Kate. Until she talked to me about her reasons, I thought Kate had lost her mind by marrying Leo. Even after we spoke, I wasn't so sure she was entirely stable. And Walter Westfield had that tic on his face, those shaking hands, that trouble with his balance and his temper.

I sat bolt upright in my chair. I remembered my last few encounters with him. I played the video over in my head. My hypothesis had to be true.

Walter Westfield had Huntington's disease. That's why he was being treated by Eva Raines, a neurologist. And Ursula had to know. That had to be it. After my trip to Naples, I wasn't going to make the same mistakes I'd made before. This time, I would trust my instincts.

My first thoughts were about how tragic the situation was, if it was true. Huntington's disease is a fatal neurological disorder, which can be diagnosed, but not cured. One of the big questions that would have surfaced if they'd had children was whether or not to have those children tested. If an incurable disease was in my future, would I want to know?

Poor Walter. And poor Ursula. My friend was in for a rough time over the next few years. Walter's health would steadily decline until he would need twenty-four hour care. How long would his deterioration take? In Senator Warwick's case, not that long, but he didn't have Huntington's.

Which caused another light bulb to go off in my head. How could Walter think of running for senator without disclosing his illness? How could Ursula think of letting him do so? This amounted to a fraud on the voters.

It was one thing not to disclose Senator Warwick's cause of death, but quite another to run for public office knowing one had a fatal neurological disease that would impair one's judgment as well as one's physical ability to do the job. And that brought my thoughts to Prescott Roberts. Did Walter's desire not to disappoint Prescott run all the way to fraud? Wouldn't Prescott understand that Walter couldn't hold public office for very long, even if he got elected?

Now that I had this piece of information, what was I going to do with it? I wanted to give back my observations and conjecture, tuck my deduction under the edge of my brain and leave it there to gather dust. I wanted my surmise to be untrue, and if it had to be true, I wanted not to know what I knew.

If Walter's diagnosis was confirmed and I told George, would his dedication to the political process lead him to disclose Walter's private medical history? Jason would disclose it, although Jason's motives would be less altruistic. I played with my pencil, thumping its eraser on the desk as I considered my options. What should I do? I made an interim decision.

I picked up the telephone and dialed Ursula's cell phone number. She didn't answer. I left her a message to meet me at Minaret at five-thirty this afternoon. I told her it was an urgent matter, extremely important to her and to Walter.

By then, I would have figured out what to do. Senator Warwick's death would be announced soon, if it hadn't been already. Walter would be making his candidacy more and more obvious in the next few hours. I had to stop him from campaigning until we could talk.

As soon as I hung up, Augustus called me on the intercom. "The C.J. is on the phone, Judge. What shall I tell him?"

I picked up my briefcase, my purse, and stood up quickly. I hoofed it out to Augustus's desk and opened the door, smiling at the bewildered look on his face. "Tell him you're sorry, but I just left." And I hurried through the exit, down the stairs, and out to Greta before the C.J. could get over here to stop me.

I didn't know what to do with myself, once Greta and I were out of the garage. I'd had no time to consider my next steps. I found myself with an unexpected few free hours. I thought it likely that the *Madison v. Cardio Medical* case would be over soon. But even if the case continued tomorrow, I couldn't work on those motions now. My mind wouldn't concentrate on *Madison* when I had more important issues to consider.

I sat literally at the crossroads, until a car came up behind me and blew its horn. I needed to move. Almost of her own accord, Greta turned toward Great Oaks Country Club. I hadn't played golf in weeks. Hitting a couple of buckets of balls was a great meditative relaxer. Maybe sending a few dozen balls into the stratosphere would give me some badly needed answers to my questions, or, at least, a constructive vent for my frustrations.

The easiest way to get anywhere in South Tampa is to travel on Bayshore Boulevard and then turn onto the South Tampa streets. Greta and I were traveling across Cass to South Boulevard, and then to the Bayshore. As we crossed Swann, an address on the left side of Boulevard caught my eye. My odd memory for numbers kicked in again. Sometimes, numbers just stick in my subconscious when other forms of information can be easily forgotten. Where did I know this address from? Who lived there?

Greta continued to the Bayshore and turned right, when I decided to go back for another pass in front of the house. I turned right again on Willow, another right on Swann, and then right again onto Boulevard. I drove by the house a second time and went around the block again. This time, I parked on the street, directly across from the curbside house numbers.

Like many of the homes in Hyde Park, this one was a turn of the century Victorian. Painted yellow with white trim, the two-story structure had black shingles, a wrap around porch, and a modern driveway ending at a two-car garage.

The home was well kept, with strict flowerbeds in neat rows on either side of the walk, the driveway, and around the house. The front door was teal green with highly polished brass trim. Everything was neat and orderly. I'd never been here before, but felt I knew the place.

I got out of the car and walked up the steps to the entrance, where I rang the bell, although I could plainly see through the glass on the top half of the door that no one was inside. The window in the door gave a clear view of the entire interior of the first floor. The open living and dining area was tidily arranged and traditionally furnished. Who lived here?

No one answered the bell, so I walked down the driveway, around to the back of the house. The backyard was as neatly kept and well manicured as the front, with a white picket fence that separated the driveway from the flower garden, and a brick walkway to the back door. I opened the gate and walked along the bricks to the back door, where I rang the doorbell as I had in the front. Again, no one answered.

I turned around to leave and that's when I saw it. Parked on a cement pad near the back of the garage—a 1968 Volkswagen bus. The bus had been beige on the top and orange on the bottom at one time, although now it was faded a sickly cooked-carrot color. The artwork on the van's sides was faint now, too, after spending years in the sunlight with no protection from the elements. An ancient peace symbol was still visible on the cargo door. Could it be?

This was the van that Wally had owned. The one Six Bills had taken to Woodstock. I'd seen it in the pictures reproduced inside Harris's new CD. Only, back in 1968, when Wally got the van for his high school graduation, and, later, when the Bills used it for transportation to Woodstock and to their gigs, it had been in much better condition. I couldn't believe I'd found Wally's van. How could something so patently ridiculous be true?

I poked around the van for a while, checking all the doors, which were locked up tight. Except the door in the rear over the 1972 Florida license plate. The lock was broken. I gripped the handle and tried to open it. The old van was rusted almost into powder and the doors were firmly shut. I couldn't budge the handle.

I looked in the back windows, which were covered with gauzy curtains. Enough natural light dimly illuminated the interior, however, and I could see inside the van. All over everything in the front seats was something brown, as if someone had spilled chocolate syrup, the kind you use to make a chocolate sundae. In the cargo area, the old seats were bursting at the seams. Boxes and other debris lay on the floor.

I tried again to open each of the doors. Not one would budge. I had no doubt in my mind that this was Walter Westfield's van, but why was it here? When I'd seen all I could, I went back to the driveway and walked toward the street. Just as I got to the front of the house, a car pulled into the driveway. I stepped aside and let Mary Steam, Harris's grandmother, park her small Cadillac in the garage.

"Hello," she said, tentatively, walking toward me. "Can I help you?"

"Mrs. Steam, I'm Willa Carson. We met at Billie Jo's funeral," I reminded her. I didn't offer to shake hands. Southern ladies of a certain age don't shake hands. If they know you well, they'll give you a hug. Otherwise, a gentle smile is thought to be the best well-bred greeting.

"Of course, Mrs. Carson. So nice to see you again. Did you need something?"

"I was just looking at Walter Westfield's van out back," I said, letting my voice trail off.

She seemed a little flustered. "Really? Why would you be interested in that old thing?"

"I guess I just didn't realize it still existed."

"Well, Bill and I just didn't have the heart to get rid of it. It's been back there for so many years, I forget about it, sometimes. Trey had so many happy days in that van." Her voice drifted downward in reverie.

"Where did you get it?"

"Oh, I think Wally brought it over here before he went to Europe. Then he just never came back for it. So much was going on then . . . " She let her voice trail away, then shook herself back to the present. "Afterward, we kept it because of Trey. Prescott offered to destroy it, but I couldn't bear to lose any more of my son."

"Do you have the keys?" She looked at me blankly. "To open the doors. The doors are locked," I explained.

"Oh, goodness, no. I don't know where those might be. You could ask my husband. He'll be home soon if you'd like to come in and wait for him," she invited. I could think of nothing I'd like less. I'd already talked with Bill Steam more than I'd ever have freely chosen to.

"I could show you Trey's room while you wait," she offered hopefully, as if showing Trey's room was one of her great joys in life.

"Trey's room?"

"Yes. It's just the way he left it when he went off to college," she said, as if college were where Trey had gone last week. "Come. Let me show you."

She turned and took me into the house, up the stairs I had seen through the front window, and into a bedroom on the front. She talked the whole time about her son. "Trey was such a good boy. Smart, too. He was a baseball player. Did you know that?"

"No, ma'am."

"Oh, yes. All-state in high school."

Like many parents who had lost a child, Mary Steam had created a shrine to Trey in his former room. The furnishings here included a twin bed, a small desk and chair for schoolwork, and a couple of bookcases. A shelf ran the full circumference of the room, about sixteen inches from the ceiling. Memorabilia Trey had collected when he lived here decorated the ledge.

The walls were covered with pictures of Trey playing baseball, in the Plant High School band, collecting his high school diploma, and many others. Almost every picture, from the time he was about eight years old, showed Trey Steam standing next to Wally Westfield, their arms around each other's shoulders, big grins on their faces. A number of the pictures showed Trey and Wally in front of Wally's van.

"So Trey and Walter were good friends, then?" I asked her, more for something to say than any other reason.

"Oh, yes. Wally lived next door. They were best buddies since childhood. Why, those two were inseparable." She began to reminisce about the adventures of Trey and Wally, telling me one tale after another of boyhood pranks. Mary Steam was making me uncomfortable now. She didn't seem quite normal, mentally. And

I was getting a tingling feeling across my scalp.

"Mrs. Steam, Trey's room is just lovely. I do need to get going, though," I said, gently.

"Of course, dear." We turned to retreat down the stairs. "Harris spent hours in Trey's room as a boy. Just looking at everything. Talking to his father. I was so sad to see it," she told me as we reached the first floor.

The tingling hadn't stopped since it began up in Trey's room. I felt as if I was in the presence of madness. The poor woman had certainly gone through hell in her life. Who could blame her if she was just a little out of touch? And who could blame the men in her life, her brother, Prescott Roberts, and her husband, Bill Steam, for trying to protect her?

I was already walking back toward my car. "It was nice to see you again," I said, by way of a social parting remark.

"Come and visit soon, dear. Bring your husband next time," she called to me as I got into Greta and started her engine. Mary Steam waved to me as I pulled away. I waved back, while I punched Ben Hathaway's number into my cell phone.

"Just tell him Wilhelmina Carson called, and ask him to call me at home," I told the secretary, giving her my telephone number. Why is it you can never find a cop when you need one?

So Walter had dropped his van at the home of Trey Steam's parents before he left for Europe, the night their son was killed. When did he pick up the van at Trey's house? Why leave it here?

That Mary Steam's madness caused her to keep the van all these years was a great stroke of luck for me. If the van hadn't been used since the night of the Bills' last gig, it might be hiding forensic evidence. All thoughts of the golf course vanished as I began again to think through the Trey and Billie Jo Steam murders.

As soon as I got home, I let the dogs out and checked the answering machine for a return call from Ben Hathaway. I had four messages: one was from Ursula, saying she'd be here at five-thirty. But I had gotten no call from Ben. I mixed myself a Sapphire and tonic with lemon, even if it was a mite early to begin the cock-tail hour. I wouldn't be driving anywhere else tonight, I rational-ized, and I do think better on a relaxed brain.

An hour on the veranda with the gin and a cigar brought me no good answers. I would simply have to tell Ursula what I knew. Then she and Walter could decide what to do. George had gone to Miami overnight, so the two of them had a reprieve until tomorrow. When George returned, I intended to tell him what I suspected about Walter's illness. George would know how to han-dle it. Politics was his arena, not mine. And I knew I could count on his discretion until we made a joint decision as to how to han-dle the situation.

While I waited for Ursula, I gathered my journal and my wits about me and sat down in my den. I started by recording my last conversation with Eva and what I had learned about Walter Westfield. Something was nagging at me, still, but the more I chased the little gremlin, the more it hid behind the corners in my brain. To coax whatever it was out into the daylight, I turned to a new project. I began to review and update my notes and inter-views on the Steam murders.

Several holes in parts of the story I had woven didn't fit any of my theories. The night Trey Steam was killed, I'd originally been told that Billie Jo and Trey left Jai Alai Fronton together with Little Trey after the gig at about two o'clock in the morning. At the trial, the testimony was that Billie Jo and Trey fought, Billie Jo left with Little Trey, and, when she returned with Johnny Tyson, Trey was dead.

Now I knew both of these versions of the facts were fan-tasies that had never happened. Yet, the Six Bills allowed this ver-sion to be put before the world and an innocent woman to go to prison. Why? What would make four southern gentlemen—or at least four young hippies—in love with Billie Jo, let her go to prison on facts they knew were false?

Trey and Billie Jo had argued, but that was before they left the Fronton. Trey took off with the fans, Walter went alone to the hospital, and the other Bills, along with Little Trey, all returned to the Steam home together in the van owned by Walter.

Trey came home sometime later, after the group left. Billie Jo heard him arguing with a man outside. Then Trey came into the house, still cursing and angry. Who was he talking to?

Billie Jo soon left the house with Little Trey and had several hours unaccounted for before she went to Johnny's. What had happened in those hours? She didn't kill Trey, because the DNA suggested her innocence. But someone did. In those crucial hours.

Where was everyone else? Ricky and Linc had left together. Linc told me he never saw Trey again. I hadn't asked Ricky that question, and I made a note to do so. Walter had gone to the hospital and later that night his van was dropped off at Bill and Mary Steam's garage. When did that happen? Walter said he didn't know Trey had been killed until he returned from the planned trip to Europe. So, did he move the van before Trey came home?

The DNA and circumstantial evidence Ben had uncovered proved that Billie Jo, although she certainly had motive in Trey's physical and emotional abuse, as well as opportunity, hadn't killed him. Someone else had killed Trey. The odds were that that someone was a person known to Trey. It seemed likely to me the killer was one of the five remaining Bills. Which one?

I thumbed through all the papers I'd accumulated thus far: the police file, the old appeals files, the trial transcript. Everything was now a complete jumble of documents, having been sorted and put away haphazardly so many times. I couldn't find my copy of the DNA file as I shuffled through, until I looked down and saw it under my desk with a group of files I'd set there the last time I'd done this exercise.

As I got on my knees to retrieve the file, my subconscious slapped me silly. Or maybe that was how I felt with my head hitting the underside of the desk when I shot upright in amazement. In any event, the DNA file was staring me right in the face. As was the obvious solution.

Chapter Thirty-Five

Billie Jo Steam didn't kill her husband, but she knew or thought she knew who had. And she'd kept it quiet all these years. The killer must have worried about her silence. Enduring years of imprisonment for something she hadn't done would be hard. But Billie Jo had been loyal and true. She'd never disclosed the identity of her husband's real killer. Maybe she'd be alive now if she had, I thought sourly. Why kill her now?

Billie Jo had believed that one of the Bills killed Trey. She also knew that one of the five, Trey or one of the others, was Harris Steam's father. At the time, did she think Harris's father was Johnny? Walter? Linc? Ricky? Billie Jo was young and naive. She must have believed the judicial system would work the way it was supposed to and she would be set free, because she knew she didn't kill Trey. Yet even as she realized she would be convicted, she wouldn't disclose the ambiguity of Harris's paternity. Nor would she name the real killer, if she knew it. Her guilty conscience had led her to accept a far harsher punishment than she deserved.

Worse, though, at least one of the Bills had reached the same conclusions. They all suspected that one of them fathered Harris. Did all four of the remaining Bills believe Billie Jo had killed Trey? Or did they know who had killed him? Billie Jo was convicted and all five of them had lived with the guilty knowledge of Harris's paternity for thirty years. What could possibly have made any one of them feel he needed to kill Billie Jo after everything they had all been through? I could imagine nothing of sufficient magnitude to do so. But my imagination was firmly grounded in logic. Maybe the killer's was not.

Ben Hathaway could get DNA from the other four Bills. The DNA reports that had freed Billy Jo would prove my theory conclusively. The other blood on the murder weapon and Trey Steam's clothes belonged to one of the other Bills. The one who had really killed Trey Steam.

But as for who killed Billie Jo, that was another issue altogether. While I believed one of the Bills killed Trey, it seemed unlikely to me now that one of them had killed Billie Jo. None of them had a reason to kill her over the old news of Trey's death. If Billie Jo was going to name Trey's killer, she would have done it long ago. No, it made no logical sense to me that one of the Bills had killed Billie Jo.

Which left Harris, his confession, and his gun. He had gunshot residue on his hands. He'd fired the gun. Yet I still would not accept Harris as his mother's killer. The little boy who spent hours in his father's room, worshiping his parents, spending every spare minute and every spare dollar to free his mother, would not have killed his dream. Such a conclusion made no sense. There had to be another answer.

I looked at my watch. Ten minutes before Ursula arrived. I straightened myself up, combed my hair with my fingers, and headed downstairs. Before I got to the door, the telephone rang. I picked it up. "Willa Carson here."

"Ben Hathaway here," he mimicked. "Your personal public servant. What can I do for you now?"

I was so focused on Ursula and Walter at that moment, remembering why I called him took me a couple of seconds. I was tired and in no mood to argue. "Ben, I found out today that Walter Westfield's van, the one the Bills used the night Trey Steam was murdered, still exists. Mary Steam said no one has touched it since the night Trey died."

My serious tone penetrated his teasing. "You're kidding."

"No."

"Where is it?"

"It's parked in back of Bill Steam's garage. You'd better get a warrant. I think you'll find evidence inside."

"What kind of evidence?"

"I'm not sure, but I think there's blood on both of the front bucket seats." I told him about the brown stains that looked like dried chocolate syrup. The stain could have been anything, even the remains of an actual hot fudge sundae. But I didn't think so. I thought the van was the murder scene.

Ben was in a hurry to hang up now, and get over to the judge for his warrant. "One more thing, Ben," I said before we signed off. "While you're getting warrants, you should get one for DNA samples from Walter Westfield, Johnny Tyson, William Lincoln, and Ricky Gutierrez."

"Why?" he asked me.

"Unless I miss my guess, I think you'll find a match with one of them for the DNA on the murder weapon and Trey Steam's clothes and the van." I believed I already knew whose blood would be there. But I didn't want to falsely accuse him. I could wait for Ben. I was pretty sure that what he found would confirm my hunch.

"Ursula, I know about Walter's illness," I told her, without preamble, when she'd settled across from me in my favorite booth. She sucked in her breath, her eyes widened, and her lips pursed to let the air out slowly.

"What illness?" She tried to bluff me.

"I saw him in Eva Raines's office. Eva wouldn't tell me why he was there, but he wasn't in for a checkup. He has Huntington's disease, doesn't he?"

She instantly seemed to age by ten years. Her already weak smile faded completely and she slumped lower in the booth, folding in on herself like a deflated balloon. "Have you told anyone?"

"Not yet. But I'm going to have to tell George." I was unequivocal.

"He'll ruin Walter's chances of getting elected with that knowledge, Willa. Prescott will be furious. You can't tell George."

I was already shaking my head. "I can't not tell him. You know that. And Walter can't run for public office without disclosing his health history to the people before they vote for him."

"He might as well withdraw. He'll never do that. Prescott wouldn't allow it," she said.

"They might vote for him anyway. Give the voters a little credit. It's happened before." But I doubted the truth of what I'd just said, given the Huntington's diagnosis. Janet Reno ran for governor with Parkinson's disease and voters had reelected politicians after a diagnosis of cancer, but Huntington's was different. Eventually, it would affect Walter's mental capacity and shorten his life. The likelihood of his election was slim.

Ursula hung her head, refusing to consider the possibility. Knowing Walter, he'd probably already submitted the question to more than one focus group. He probably understood for sure that his illness would deny him the victory he badly wanted. Or maybe just Prescott Roberts wanted victory and Walter was unable, once again, to thwart him. Either way, Walter must have known his election was a long shot if his illness was made public.

"I'm so sorry, Ursula, but Walter must either disclose his condition or withdraw from the race. I can't keep this knowledge to myself." Prescott Roberts wouldn't like it, but there was nothing else I could do. I'd already made an enemy of the man and at every turn I seemed to be digging myself in deeper.

She sighed, and raised herself slowly from the booth. "Let me discuss it with him. The decision should be his, Willa, not yours or mine. Give me twenty-four hours to let him think it over and make up his mind."

George wouldn't be home until tomorrow, anyway. It wouldn't hurt to give them both a little time to think. "Call me by this time tomorrow," I conceded. "If I don't hear from you, I'll discuss it with George and we'll decide our next step."

"Will you tell me what you've decided?" She begged.

"I'm hoping I won't have to. I'm hoping that you and Walter

will do the right thing," I told her. And I was hoping Prescott Roberts would never find out that I'd played any role in Walter's decision.

I spent the next hour wrestling with my conscience, marveling at the power of denial. Walter and Ursula were intelligent people. They had to know that Walter's condition would surface when his symptoms became worse. Why put him through the public humiliation? After I thought about it, the answer became obvious.

Of course they knew. And Walter wanted to withdraw from the race, but Prescott Roberts wouldn't allow it. As she'd done on the Billie Jo parole hearing, Ursula used me to get the evidence needed to persuade Prescott Roberts to let Walter withdraw.

Ursula knew me. She knew I'd figure everything out and that she could count on my discretion once I'd discovered the truth, as long as the right thing was done. In other words, she knew I wouldn't publicly humiliate her husband unnecessarily, for my sake as well as his. This time, I couldn't dredge up the energy to be angry with her.

I fully expected Walter to withdraw from the Senate race, but my issues were all about what I'd do if my guess was wrong. Lawyers are always hoping for the best, while planning for the worst. It's impossible to avoid that aspect of my training. Believe me, I've tried.

I was still sitting in the Sunset Bar an hour later when the bartender told me I had a telephone call. He brought over the cordless. It was Walter Westfield. He asked me to meet him at the Tampa Country Club in thirty minutes for dinner. It hadn't taken Ursula long to apprise him of the situation, apparently. I made another phone call. After that I trudged upstairs to change clothes, then I took a cab over there.

One of the safest places to confront a killer is in a federal courthouse. Since the Oklahoma City bombing, federal courthouses were about the safest location on the planet, although no building in America is truly safe these days. But killers usually won't accept an informal invitation to my office, so the next best place is a public location with witnesses, should something go awry.

I found Walter at the Tampa Club, where he'd asked me to meet him. This time, he was already seated before I walked into the main dining room and over to his table. "Don't get up, Walter," I said to him, my hand resting lightly on his shoulder.

I saw Ben Hathaway seated a few tables behind Walter, which was the way I'd planned it. After I'd talked with Walter, I intended to tell Ben everything I knew or had surmised. That was why I'd asked him to meet me here in another hour, knowing Ben would feel the need to come early and eat on my tab beforehand.

"That's one of the things that surprised me at first," I said to Walter after I'd sat down. "You've always seemed to me to be such a chivalrous man. That you would let a woman take the blame for something you had done didn't really occur to me."

"What are you talking about? I thought you were here about my Huntington's. Believe me, if I could get someone else to take it from me, even a woman, I'd let her have it," he joked weakly, as he stroked his thigh as if he was in pain.

"I'm very sorry about your disease, Walter. Truly I am. But I'm talking about murder. Specifically, that you killed Trey Steam and let Billie Jo take the blame for it. How could you do that?"

"Come on, Willa. You think I would kill my best friend and then hide behind his wife? I didn't realize you had such a low opinion of me." Walter's indignation seemed genuine. He picked up his glass, raised a trembling hand to his mouth, and knocked back a shot of scotch, neat. It was one of the few times I'd seen him drink alcohol over the past few weeks.

"I didn't."

"What?"

"Have such a low opinion of you. That's why it took me so long to figure it out. I gave you more credit than you deserved." I had promised myself to trust my instincts and I wasn't going to be put off by Walter's tactics any longer.

"Ursula said you were holding me hostage over my Huntington's. That's a pretty low blow, even for you. Now you want to accuse me of murder of my best friend, too?" He kept his voice down, but his face demonstrated his anger.

Was I wrong? No. It had to have been Walter. But I'd known him and Ursula for years. Did I think he was so cold-blooded?

"I don't think you murdered Trey. No. I'm pretty sure you didn't mean to kill him." I waited a beat or two, and then allowed him to see me wave to Chief Hathaway to imply that I was going to take my guesses to the police. "But that's what happened, wasn't it?"

I thought he would keep up his denials. Maybe he considered it. But the scotch or the years seemed to have loosened him up. He appeared less controlled. Having a terminal illness coupled with the lifetime of lies he'd told about Trey Steam's death had finally overcome him, I imagined. As a younger, healthier man, he had been stronger. He would have bluffed his way out of this confrontation. Now, he appeared resigned to his fate at the hands of the karma he'd created with his own acts. It was as if he felt the fight was over and he didn't have the energy for it anymore. He looked down at the table, not meeting my steady gaze.

"I didn't want Billie Jo to be convicted. I didn't even know she'd been arrested until I got back from Europe, months later. Oh, I'll admit I was scared and I didn't want to go to jail. And I was maybe a little too anxious to get out of the entire mess." *No kidding,* I thought as he continued. "I've gotten older and wiser. I probably could have avoided being convicted, if I'd just told the truth about what had happened. It was self-defense, you know," he said, finally admitting what I'd guessed as the truth.

I waited. Walter frowned and met my eyes, searching for the words that could describe what had occurred that night. "Trey was high and drunk and pissed off at me. He was the one who came to the hospital to pick me up. He drove over in my van." Walter shook his head, as if he still had trouble believing what came next, as if a different ride home from the hospital would have changed his life.

"Trey was so pissed off at me for sleeping with Billie Jo. He screamed at me and called me every imaginable name. The more he yelled, the more his anger escalated. He was driving crazy, swerving all over the road." Walter stopped for another swig of his drink. He took a deep breath and made one last stab at convincing me that he had been the victim. "And then he just lunged at me with that knife."

Sure, I thought. I'd heard stories like this a thousand times in my courtroom. The instigator rarely took responsibility for starting a fight. "What did you say to him to set him off again?"

Walter snorted, like he'd been the stupidest jerk on earth. "I said Billie Jo was a good lay and every one of the Bills agreed with me."

"And then what happened?" I asked him, when it looked like he wouldn't continue.

"We just kept arguing. He cut my leg open again, the one I'd just had stitched up at the hospital. I was bleeding like a stuck pig and he was, too. We struggled. The van nearly went over the median at one point. It was so late, there weren't many cars on the road, or we'd probably have hit someone." Walter shuddered then, perhaps realizing how much more damage could have been done.

"How did you ever make it back to Trey's home?"

Walter seemed bewildered and his eyes were glassy, as if he was far away, back in the moment. His tone softened. "I don't know. It wasn't far to the little house on Packwood from Tampa General Hospital. Somehow, we just made it back there."

"How did you get the knife away from him?"

Walter pursed his lips, thinking. Was he trying to remember? Or trying to make up a story for me? I couldn't tell.

"I guess, as we struggled inside the van, since he was driving, he'd had to pay some attention to the road. I managed to get the knife away from him then. At some point, I must have stabbed him. Then when we got to the house," Walter stopped again and took another swallow of the scotch. "When we got to the house, I was panting, out of breath. I was bleeding, scared. He was, too. Trey just reached over and grabbed at the knife again. He lunged at me with it one last time, but I opened the door and got out. He chased me, but I was able to evade him and make it over to the driver's side. I jumped in and just got the hell out of there. He was screaming at me as I got in the van and drove away. It's all pretty hazy now." He looked my way. "Surely you realize I've tried to forget."

I didn't for a second believe he'd forgotten any of the details of their fight. He had killed his best friend and been cut up pretty badly himself. There was no way he'd been able to simply let those memories go. He must have been pretty angry at the time. Or maybe, he was just scared and hurt himself.

Trey's death wasn't quick, but the autopsy was clear that an earlier puncture to his lung was what finally did him in. He'd drowned in his own blood. Billie Jo didn't kill him in their brief struggle in the little house before she ran out that night. Trey had already been weakened by his fight with Walter and his loss of blood. The bad luck had been when Trey knocked off the room's only lamp, breaking the bulb and reducing the light in that room to the point that Billie Jo couldn't see how badly he'd been hurt. If she'd known, she would have taken him to the hospital and he might have lived. All that followed might have been avoided.

"What about Billie Jo? How'd she get stuck for your crime?"

"By the time I figured out that I had a valid claim of self-defense, it was too late to help Billie Jo by telling the truth. Even if she would have let me, which she refused to do." Walter's version of this part of the story was so sanitized, I didn't believe it for an instant.

"You mean she was willing to give up her own son just to help you?" Billie Jo would give up her own life, that I believed. But from what I'd seen, she loved Harris too deeply to abandon him.

"She knew she couldn't take care of Harris. She knew Trey's parents would never have allowed that, even if Billie Jo had wanted to try. Billie Jo thought of herself as a nobody from nowhere. She believed it was best for Harris that he have the background he'd become comfortable with," Walter explained.

"How nice for you." If I live to be a hundred, I thought, I'll never understand what motivates some people.

"She was as strong-willed and gallant a woman as I've ever met," he said, as if he was delivering his own mother's eulogy.

Trey had made it into the house and stumbled around a while before Billie Jo tussled with him. Maybe she felt guilty when she was first arrested, thinking she had injured Trey when he fell with the knife. Maybe that's why she didn't put up much of a defense to the murder charge in the beginning. But Walter must have known that wasn't true, even then. Walter had capitalized on Billie Jo's innocence. He was despicable, whether he realized it or not.

Walter shook his head with that little smile he wore which always got him whatever he wanted, the one I now recognized he had passed on to Harris, his son. The smile didn't work this time. Billie Jo was dead and Harris was in jail. This had gone on long enough.

I changed my tack. "When did you take the van over to the Steam's house?" I asked him. I'd surprised him.

He started, and the tick over his left eye got going. He took a few moments to calm it with a shaky hand. "That same night, after I dropped Trey off at home. I didn't realize how badly he was hurt."

"Come on, Walter. Trey had multiple stab wounds to his torso. He bled to death, for God's sake. How could that happen without you realizing it?" Although Trey's wounds were not instantly fatal, he must have been bleeding enough for Walter to realize he was badly hurt. If Walter had cared.

"You didn't know him, Willa. He was a mean son-of-a-bitch. We used to fight when we were kids and he wouldn't quit until he had me bloody on the ground. I was already hurt, my leg bleeding all over the place, and he just kept coming at me." Walter shuddered. "I had to make him stop. And somehow, he ended up worse off than me, I guess," he finished weakly. Walter raised the Scotch glass to his mouth again, signaling to the waiter for another round when he realized it was empty.

"Dropping the van at Trey's parents' doesn't seem like the act of an innocent man to me, Walter."

"I really was on my way to Europe. And I never wanted to have anything to do with the damn van again. The night Trey and I fought over my sleeping with Billie Jo was the worst of my life. I really thought Trey's dad would burn the van. But then his mother got so attached to anything related to Trey that Prescott couldn't bear to take the van away from her."

"Did he know you'd killed his nephew in that van?" Prescott wasn't the kind of man who would allow such incriminating evidence to linger for emotional reasons.

"Of course not. Do you think all of this was some grand conspiracy or something?" The waiter brought the scotch and Walter ordered an immediate refill as he took another big gulp.

That was exactly what I thought. Prescott Roberts wanted to give his sister back a substitute child to replace her dead son. Walter wanted his success and not to face the possibility of prison. Billie Jo was easy to stow away and forget about, since she had no clout, just as she'd told me that long ago afternoon when I visited her in prison. And the rest of the Bills didn't really know what happened, but made no real effort to find out, either. Oh, yes, it was a conspiracy, even if all the players didn't know all the facts.

"I couldn't tell Prescott at first and then later, I tried to forget it all. Trey was already dead. There was nothing I could do to bring him back. I never wanted to even *think* about that night. I can't believe that damn van has been there all these years." He drained the glass again.

"You never see the bullet that gets you," I told him.

He looked at me crookedly. "Is that how you figured it out? If I'd just had the thing crushed, you'd never have known?"

I didn't answer him. On some level, I believed that Walter wanted to be caught, that he had what the psychiatrists call survivor guilt. Otherwise, such a smart man would have taken care of so obvious a "smoking gun" long before now, despite his rather weak protests to the contrary.

"You know I have to tell Ben Hathaway about this, don't you?" I asked quietly, nodding in Ben's direction.

"It's not always a good thing to right old wrongs, Willa," Walter objected as his gaze followed mine to Chief Hathaway's table. Walter said that Billie Jo had made the choice not to blame him after she was convicted and he'd eventually confessed to her because she wanted him to watch over Harris, to the extent he could, given the careful scrutiny of the Steams. Walter told me that Billie Jo knew Walter and Trey had been close friends and that Trey's parents would welcome Walter into her son's life in a way they would never have allowed Billie Jo, herself.

"She felt guilty for sleeping with all of us and for setting Trey off that night. She felt she should pay for that. And she thought she'd be released someday," he said.

"Did she know you were Harris's biological father?"

He shook his head. "She thought Johnny was. But she knew Johnny couldn't take care of Harris." He took a deep breath and exhaled slowly. "I didn't know I was Harris's biological father for sure, myself, until recently. Like the other Bills, and because of my promise to Billie Jo, I tried to be a good role model for Harris. Once I found out I was his biological father, I thought it was best to just keep that information to myself. I never told Harris or Billie Jo. I was a hell of a lot better role model for him than Trey would have been." But telling Harris all this now wouldn't be the right thing to do, Walter said, because Harris idolized Trey.

Harris had thought his father was a god. He wanted to grow up just like Trey. The tragedy was that he accomplished that dream, smiled Walter. "Harris knew Billie Jo was his mother and he still killed her. I'm concerned about what he would do to me or to himself if we sprung it on him now that I was his real father." He shook his head in regret and confusion as he finished the scotch and signaled for yet another round. He'd be drunk before long, if he wasn't already.

As much as I understood the skunk was just trying to save his own skin once again, I had to agree that he could be right. He was not going to live more than a few years, and those years would be hellish ones as his disease progressed. Maybe it was better for Harris to be left with some illusions than to have knowledge that would destroy him further. In any case, it wasn't my decision to make.

"Besides that, I'm going to die soon," Walter continued, echoing my own thoughts. "Why give Harris another father to mourn? Why send me to prison now? Billie Jo already paid for this crime. Does the state need another sacrificial lamb?"

What he didn't say was how Prescott Roberts would view his role in Trey Steam's murder. Prescott had been Walter's protector and mentor for all of Walter's adult life. Letting Prescott down was something Walter never intended to do and being on the wrong side of Prescott's wrath would be far from pleasant. Prescott was planning on putting Walter in the Senate. Now that would never happen. Walter needed some time to figure out how he wanted to handle it. What I wanted was to keep my name out of the discussions. Prescott Roberts was a man used to exacting revenge and I'd already given him enough reason to add me to his list.

"I'll think about it, Walter. And I expect to see you announce on the morning news, if not before, that you're withdrawing from the Senate race," I stood and excused myself from the table.

I could see that Walter had suffered over his role in what I'd come to think of as the Six Bills *mess*. But he hadn't suffered as much as Billie Jo or Harris or even Trey's parents. Walter had lived a pretty good life, with a wife who loved him and a great deal of material success. He didn't deserve to be let totally off the hook just because Billie Jo had already served her sentence.

"I don't believe Harris killed Billie Jo, either. That's something you should think about," I said in parting before I joined Chief Hathaway. I let Walter see who my companion was and allowed him to squirm. But Ben and I only discussed how his case against Harris was shaping up. The rest could wait until tomorrow.

When I stepped out of the shower in the morning, I caught Walter's picture inset into the screen above the newscaster's talking head. The volume was turned low so I couldn't hear the voice-over. I breathed a sigh of relief.

Walter's withdrawing from the Senate race on the day of the incumbent's funeral would be big news on all the local stations. He'd cite "family commitment," and say that he'd decided to "face the challenges presented to the manager of the State's Best Law Firm" as his reason. I figured I'd listen to the story once right now and then I could ignore it the rest of the day. I reached over and pressed the volume button.

"Again, senatorial candidate William Walter Westfield, the Third has been killed. Westfield was found by a neighbor on the street near his Palma Ceia home early this morning. Westfield had been hit by a car during his routine morning jog and died instantly. Evidence of the impact found at the scene includes paint from a white vehicle. Police found pieces of a headlight assembly at the scene. Police are looking for a late-model Lexus SUV. At this time, neither the driver nor the car has been found. We'll have more details for you on this story as the day progresses."

"Idiot!" I screamed at myself, as the gremlin I couldn't find now jumped out to bite me. "How could you be so stupid?" But all my screaming made no difference. Walter was still dead.

Chapter Thirty-Six

Eva's parents were not home when I pulled up in front of their house. This time, the front door was closed, the better to keep that precious air conditioning from flowing out. The garage door was open and Eva's Lexus SUV was running. I rang the bell and waited. Eva answered the door, dressed in travel clothes.

"What's up, Willa? I'm just on my way out. The girls are already in the car and it's stifling hot." She wasn't rude, exactly, but not warm and welcoming, either.

"I need to talk to you and I'm afraid it can't wait."

"What do you want to talk to me about? I'm really late already and we have a long way to drive today."

I needed to go right to the point to get her to let me inside. "Walter Westfield has Huntington's disease. But you already knew that, didn't you? That's what you've been treating him for, all this time."

"That's really between Walter and me. He's my patient. I can't discuss his condition with you."

"Maybe not. But when did you figure out that Walter was Harris's real father, Eva? When did you know that Harris and your girls might carry the HD gene?" I was pushing her now.

She had killed Walter Westfield, I was sure of it. It wasn't just a coincidence that the elementary school her daughters attended was on the same street where Walter was jogging and he was killed about the time Eva would have been taking the girls to school. I thought I knew why she'd done it. She was going to confess to me and then to Ben Hathaway. I'd seen enough killing among the members of this messed up Woodstock family. They were all so enmeshed with each other, they had no idea where one of them ended and the other began.

"I don't know what you're talking about," she tried.

319

"That won't work, Eva. You do know. You were the only one who had access to Walter's DNA. You tested his blood all the time, to monitor the progress of his disease. When you did the paternity test on Johnny Tyson and Harris, you recognized Walter's DNA patterns were similar to Harris's. You figured out Walter was Harris's father, didn't you?"

"That's insane! Really!" She was beginning to get the wild look on her face that I'd seen twice before, once in the kitchen of this house when she had spilled water on the floor. The other time was at Café BT when we had lunched. Eva might well be incapable of controlling her impulses.

I backed off the pressure, changed my tone. "Why don't you go get the kids out of the car and I'll wait in the living room, Eva. We need to talk. You can't go anywhere right now," I told her, because she could so easily take off with the children.

She looked uncertain, but apparently decided I wasn't going to leave without talking this through. "All right. Come on in." She unlatched and opened the screen door, waved me into the living room, and closing both the screen and the door, followed after me.

"Sit down and I'll go get the girls. It'll take a minute because they're all set up with their coloring books and games and have their seat belts on." She was already walking toward the kitchen as she gave me these instructions. I should have followed her, but I didn't want to upset the children and I'd seen how volatile Eva could be.

I was too anxious to sit, so I wandered around the room looking at the family photographs I hadn't paid attention to before. Eva as a child, a young lady, a graduate from high school, college, medical school. Portraits of Eva and Harris on their wedding day. Larger versions of the studio shots of Willie and Billie that Harris carried in his wallet. Not one picture of Billie Jo or Trey adorned the walls.

I didn't realize what I heard until it was too late. I looked out the large front window and saw the back of Eva's white Lexus SUV headed south toward the Bayshore, while, at the same time, I heard the garage door closing. I ran to the door and attempted to turn the doorknob to let myself out. But Eva had locked the door behind me and thrown the deadbolt.

I spent a few seconds figuring that out, turning the deadbolt back, and yanking the door open. As soon as I did that, the house alarm began to sound. Eva must have turned it on remotely as she was leaving in the car. The noise was deafening, but I had no time to try to turn it off. The alarm would bring the police as well, which I counted as a good thing at the moment.

I reached for the screen door and hit the lever handle to open it with the palm of my hand while my body's momentum was already moving forward. Only the door didn't open. I ran right into the screen, bumping my head on the wire mesh. Eva had thrown the small latch on it as well, after she let me inside.

As hard as I banged into the screen, amazingly, the door held fast. Again, I fumbled with the small latch, which had stuck hard when I hit the handle. Precious seconds were lost, but I finally was able to open the lever and swing the door wide. I loped down the small stoop and ran the short distance to my car.

Out of habit, I'd locked Greta, too. I had to rummage around in my pockets for the key, press the keyless entry button, and finally let myself in. My car was facing north, so I pulled into the driveway and turned around. By the time I headed toward the Bayshore, Eva had about a three to four minute head start.

If I could guess which way they'd gone, Greta's powerful engine could overtake Eva's SUV quickly. When I reached the intersection at Bayshore, I looked toward Howard, thinking it was the quickest route to the interstate. But I didn't see Eva's SUV. Surely, she hadn't had time to make it to Howard and turn north.

Indecision gripped me. Should I take Howard, betting that Eva had taken the fastest route? I turned my head in the opposite direction, toward Gandy Boulevard, and saw Eva's SUV, speeding and weaving through traffic.

Greta and I raced down Bayshore Boulevard, following Eva as closely as the heavy traffic would allow. We were gaining ground, Greta and I, when the traffic started to back up at the signal. Eva was ahead of the traffic light, and speeding up, getting away from me. Pounding my palm impatiently on Greta's steering wheel, I said, "Come on, come on," willing the light to change to green. Just as the light changed, I heard a loud horn blowing. Then a crash. The sound of metal striking metal at high velocity. Smoke billowed out ahead.

With a sinking feeling, I sped toward the smoke as quickly as I could maneuver in the traffic. When I reached the intersection, I could see the two vehicles that had collided. A rental moving truck had been knocked across the intersection and two lanes of traffic. It rested facing the opposite direction from oncoming traffic, on the other side of the boulevard.

Eva's SUV had rolled over, onto its roof, the driver's side door open, pedestrians already running toward the car. The SUV was turned sideways, giving me a clear view of the smashed right front headlight and crumpled fender that had killed Walter Westcott.

I pulled Greta up onto the grassy median, opened the door and sprinted to the crash site. Willie and Billie, crying, were hanging from their seat belts, their heads parallel to the ground. The SUV's roof held the bottom of the vehicle up in the air.

Passersby were already opening the doors to get the girls out of the car. I looked around for Eva. She had been thrown from the car and lay in the traveled portion of the roadway on the eastbound side.

I reached Eva shortly after a couple of joggers did. They were giving her first aid, while another stood nearby with a cell phone, talking to the police. I knelt down beside her. "Take care of my girls," the young mother said, just before she stopped breathing.

I bent down to administer CPR. I kept breathing for Eva as long as I could, until I was exhausted. Then one of the other pedestrians took over. I sat back on my heels on the ground, watching him try to make Eva breathe again.

Emergency vehicles arrived shortly after that. Two paramedics jumped out and took over. They worked frantically at first, but then seemed to slow down their efforts. They put Eva on a gurney and loaded her into the ambulance as the rest of us stood around, helpless. The ambulance took off for Tampa General Hospital, but it wasn't moving very fast and didn't use its siren.

Chapter Thirty-Seven

Augustus came into my chambers holding a motion as if it were a python with fangs. "Emergency motion, Judge," he said, as he set it down on my desk.

I picked up the offending pages. The caption read *Estate of Stanley Madison v. Cardio Medical Corporation*. I groaned. "It gets worse," Augustus said to me. "Look what they want." I glanced further down the first page.

We have a procedural rule here in the United States District Court for the Middle District of Florida. Whatever a formal court document concerns must be plainly stated in its title. I could not mistake the nature of this motion. The title was: *Cardio Medical Corporation's Motion to Set Aside Settlement Procured by Fraud and for New Trial*. I put my head down on the desk, tempted to cry or pound the table in frustration. I had been so happy when they settled. Now this. Would the damn case never leave me alone?

But before I could shed a tear, Augustus buzzed me on the intercom. "Ursula Westfield is here to see you," he said quietly. I got up from my desk, went to the door, and motioned her inside. She hugged me tight, and I returned her hug. The stress, the fatigue, and the awful outcome of Walter's murder and Eva's death threatened to overwhelm us both.

Ursula pulled back from me and went over to sit in one of my ugly green client chairs. I poured us a cup of strong black coffee and sat in the other horrid seat. "Thanks for seeing me, Willa," she started, quietly.

"Ursula, thank you for coming. I thought you might never speak to me again," I told her truthfully. "If it weren't for me—well . . ."

She started to laugh. "Don't let's start that again. It wasn't your fault, Willa, really. It was mine. I used you, just as you accused me of doing. I used Leo, too. And Harris, for that matter. This is totally my doing and I take full responsibility."

"Why? How can it be your fault?"

She sighed, a long, exhausted sound. She shook her head, ruefully. "I had the best of intentions. Truly, I did. All I wanted was to get an innocent woman out of jail without sending my husband to prison. I figured out that Walter had killed Trey, and I knew what it had cost him to keep that secret to himself all those years. Walter was dying, Willa. I thought I could do this for him and ease the last years of his life." As a motive, it was better than most.

"What I didn't count on," she said, "was the intensity of Eva's reaction. I never thought she would kill Billie Jo. Or Walter. But I probably should have known it. The road to hell is paved with good intentions"

Harris had known Eva killed Billie Jo. He'd found Eva with the gun still in her hand that night, after Billie Jo had died. He took the gun and fired the second shot into his mother's head. To cover up the crime. To prove his loyalty to Eva. That's why he confessed, why he told me to leave Eva alone, and why he wasn't talking to me now. Harris blamed me for killing Eva, as unfair as that was. I shuddered to think how Prescott Roberts would look at my involvement in Eva's death. To a man like Prescott, blood was thicker than water. I only hoped learning that Harris wasn't his grandnephew would distract him from exacting any type of revenge on me. I pushed those thoughts aside as unproductive at the moment.

"How could you possibly have predicted Eva's behavior? She was irrational. She couldn't control herself. It's foolish to think someone else could have controlled her," I soothed, although I, too, felt someone should have watched Eva more closely that night. They all knew that she was unreliable, at best. And Harris had created quite a scene. They should never have left Eva alone with Billie Jo. It was more likely than not that something terrible would happen.

Yet, I couldn't blame them for not believing Eva would kill Billie Jo. The murder was, in the eyes of the law, premeditated. But I wasn't willing to hold the other Bills and their wives responsible for Eva's intentional acts.

"Well, I knew about Eva's car accident. We all did. She had pretty severe frontal lobe damage and developed all the usual symptoms of that. She was alright, cognitively. But she developed poor impulse control, poor memory. I'd seen her acting out under stress and I knew she had epilepsy. I just didn't understand the extent of her jealousy. If I'd thought it through, I might have realized the impact all of this would have had on her." Ursula shook her head in defeat. "I didn't count on Eva figuring out that Walter was Harris's father. And I didn't realize what that knowledge would do to her."

I shook my head. There had been enough denial here. Even I was willing to go only so far. "No. Eva was a neurologist, Ursula. She knew that Huntington's disease was hereditary. She had the ability to test Harris and her children for the gene. Did you think she wouldn't do that? Just considering the possibility that her children carried a time bomb in their genes would have severely stressed her—you had to know that. Normally, patients who undergo those gene tests have psychological counseling for months, both before and after and Eva didn't have so much as someone she could discuss her children's potential condition with. How could Eva ever have expected to handle that? And why would you think she could?" I felt sorry for all of us, but I wasn't going to let us pretend that we had no control over our actions and judgments. I believe we create our own lives. I have to believe that. Otherwise, I couldn't do the job I do. I'd go crazy.

Slow tears escaped Ursula's eyes then. "Willie and Billie don't carry the gene. That we know. Neither does Harris. If Eva had just waited for the test results before she killed Billie Jo, she would have known that, too. This could all have been avoided," she said. "She let her fear lead her to murder."

"With her frontal lobe damage, Eva couldn't handle the pressure, that's all. Her mother told me that even small stresses would send Eva into fits of rage that she completely forgot after she recovered from them." I imagined the fury Eva must have felt toward Billie Jo. Billie Jo had had a frivolous affair with Walter. That affair had put Eva's husband and her children at risk for a fatal and terrible hereditary disease. Had Eva been in possession of all of her faculties, she might have been able to reason a solution to her fear.

I could also picture the anger Eva had at Harris for getting Billie Jo out of prison, where Eva must have felt Billie Jo belonged. Killing Billie Jo and blaming Harris for it probably resolved all of her moral outrage. And Harris felt she was entitled to that outrage. His guilt, and a desire to spare his children his own motherless childhood, convinced him to help Eva and to confess to killing his mother. Until Eva died and there was no longer any point in doing so. Had the other Bills known Eva had killed Billie Jo? I didn't think so. Surely their loyalty to Harris would have made the other Bills disclose Eva as the killer, if they'd known. But maybe not. The Six Bills had been keeping secrets from the rest of the world for a long time. Killing secrets.

Ursula and I sat with that knowledge for a while without speaking before Ursula had the strength to continue. "Have you seen Harris since they let him out of jail? He's got the girls with him. They miss their mother." Tears leaked from the corners of her eyes again.

I shook my head. "No. I don't expect I will see him, either. I don't think he's very happy with me right now. The entire foundation of his life has been shaken. I'm just a reminder of that."

She nodded. "Me, too." We sipped our coffee for a while, then Ursula gathered her giant-sized carryall that she used for a purse and prepared to leave. "Walter was going to withdraw from the Senate race," she said before rising. "We had planned to retire, leave the country. We were thinking about Tuscany. We loved it there. I might still go." She stood and I walked her to the door.

"Be careful," I laughed. "When Kate went to Tuscany, she came home with a young hottie."

Ursula laughed with me. "I think it's a little too early for me to be interested in hotties. But you should forgive Kate for her choice. Leo may leave Kate someday. But until then, let her enjoy him. She can't do that if you keep resisting Leo." She put her hand on my arm. "Kate needs you to be on her side. She's always been on your side. Jealousy destroys love, Willa. Look at the chain reaction Billie Jo's jealousy started with the Six Bills. Kate deserves your loyalty."

My intercom buzzed. Augustus said, "Chief Judge Richardson is on the phone. He says he knows you're in there and if you don't talk to him, he'll be right over."

"Put him through," I responded as Ursula let herself out the door. I picked up the phone and braced myself for the news that Prescott Roberts had filed a complaint against me with the Justice Department. I still hadn't figured out who slashed Greta's tires that day. It didn't seem like Prescott Roberts' style and Augustus had denied any involvement. Although I couldn't actually imagine him doing such a thing, it seemed that only Walter would have stooped so low.

Trying to keep the weariness out of my voice, I said, "Willa Carson here."

"I thought maybe you could use some good news today, Willa," C.J. said. "I've finally been able to get enough money to move you over to the new courthouse. We've got you scheduled for mid-July. Will that give you enough time?"

I was dumfounded. What had made him give in? There had to be a catch. Maybe he was tired of not being able to keep better tabs on me and thought that this way I'd be more controllable. Whatever his reasons, I accepted immediately. "Mid-July will be perfect, Oz. We'll get everything ready to go before then." Never mind that mid-July was the absolute pinnacle of Tampa's hellish heat and the workmen would sweat enough to water a small village while relocating us.

"Great. I'll put you down," he said, ringing off.

"What was that about?" Augustus asked me.

"We're finally getting to move. We'll get a new courtroom. Yes!" I jumped up, giving Augustus a high five.

He smiled at me, shaking his head as he walked back into his office. "I heard they'd condemned this building last month. I guessed they'd move us out before they closed it. Asbestos, don't you know? Probably been poisoning you for years."

Sunday, George surprised me with a trip to Key West. He woke me up early, saying, "Get dressed, Willa. I have a big surprise." We drove over to Peter O'Knight Airport on Davis Islands where we met a friend of ours with a private plane. A short, one-hour flight to Key West in the early morning sunshine was more picturesque than a travel video. We flew over the Dry Tortugas and were low enough to see Fort Williams under the clear morning sky. By ten-thirty, we were breakfasting at The Reach, sitting outside, enjoying the sun, the surf, and, most especially, the solitude.

"What a perfect Sunday date," I told him, as we sipped our morning orange juice. We ate sinful pastries and read the morning papers. I had on the big straw hat I'd worn to Kate's on Mother's Day and dark sunglasses to keep out the ocean's glare.

George reached over and kissed the jam off my mouth. "Glad you like it. I thought we needed a getaway."

"Umm," was my total, contented reply.

Someone came up behind me and put his hands over my eyes. "Guess who?" said a voice I recalled only too clearly. Restraining a groan, I said, "Leo Colombo."

When he removed his hands, I saw Kate sitting across from me at the table. "Right!" she exclaimed. "Isn't this a fabulous place?"

Leo kissed me on the cheek and sat across from George. I

had been ambushed. "And a great surprise?" Leo said, sounding like the child he was. His beautiful smile stretched across his face from one ear to the other.

Before I could answer, Kate said, "We're staying here for a couple of weeks. Leo's kids are joining us tomorrow. Leo called Augustus and told him to get George to bring you down. I'm so glad you could come! Isn't life wonderful?"

So, another mystery solved. This was the surprise Augustus had been working on with Leo. "If there's anything I detest, it's a conspiracy," I told her, smiling with all the genuine affection and loyalty I felt.

"How do you know Augustus, anyway?" I asked Leo.

"Oh, I met him years ago on a trip to Jamaica," he said. "Did you know he's Prescott Roberts's nephew?" I nearly choked on my orange juice and George had to slap me on the back to get my breath going again.

Later, as we dressed for the sunset festivities on Mallory Square, I thought about all I had been involved in during the past few weeks, all the death and needless suffering I'd witnessed, the foolishness going on in my courtroom between people who should have known better.

Nothing that had happened to the Steam family or to Walter had been my fault. The Six Bills story was put in motion long ago by actions that were still rippling out from the center of a rock band at Woodstock. Was I the catalyst for the conclusion? Maybe. But if she hadn't died, Eva would have been in prison for the murders of Billie Jo Steam and Walter Westfield. Her girls would have been visiting her there all their lives. The cycle would have begun again. Living in prison would have been better than dying, I had thought bitterly for a long time. But maybe not.

Maybe all that life should be is sun, surf, pastries, tropical memories, and young hotties. George had better be careful. I laughed at the thought.